Maria Edgeworth

The life and letters of Maria Edgeworth

Maria Edgeworth

The life and letters of Maria Edgeworth

ISBN/EAN: 9783337136529

Printed in Europe, USA, Canada, Australia, Japan

Cover: Foto ©Raphael Reischuk / pixelio.de

More available books at **www.hansebooks.com**

THE LIFE AND LETTERS

OF

MARIA EDGEWORTH

EDITED BY

AUGUSTUS J. C. HARE

AUTHOR OF "MEMORIALS OF A QUIET LIFE,"
"THE STORY OF TWO NOBLE LIVES"

IN TWO VOLUMES

VOLUME I.

BOSTON AND NEW YORK
HOUGHTON, MIFFLIN AND COMPANY
The Riverside Press, Cambridge
1895

The Riverside Press, Cambridge, Mass., U. S. A.
Electrotyped and Printed by H. O. Houghton and Company.

PREFACE

In her later years Miss Edgeworth was often asked to write a biographical preface to her novels. She refused. "As a woman," she said, "my life, wholly domestic, can offer nothing of interest to the public." Incidents indeed, in that quiet happy home existence, there were none to narrate, nothing but the ordinary joys and sorrows which attend every human life. Yet the letters of one so clear - sighted and sagacious — one whom Macaulay considered to be the second woman of her age — are valuable, not only as a record of her times, and of many who were prominent figures in them, but from the picture they naturally give of a simple, honest, generous, high-minded character, filled from youth to age with love and goodwill to her fellow-creatures, and a desire for their highest good.

An admirable collection of Miss Edgeworth's letters was printed after her death by her stepmother and life-long friend, but only for private circulation. As all her generation has long since passed away, her family now permit that these letters should be read beyond the limits of their own circle. An editor has had little more to do than to make a selection, and to write such a thread of biography as might unite the links of the chain.

Augustus J. C. Hare.

CONTENTS

VOLUME I.

1767–1787.

Childhood of Maria Edgeworth — Death of her mother, and marriage of her father to Miss Honora Sneyd — Death of Mrs. Honora Edgeworth, and marriage of Mr. Edgeworth to Miss Elizabeth Sneyd — Life at Edgeworthstown . . . . pp. 5–14

1787–1793.

Letters from Maria Edgeworth, from Edgeworthstown, Clifton, and London, to Miss Charlotte Sneyd, Mr. and Mrs. Ruxton, and Miss Sophy Ruxton.

Journey to Clifton — Dr. Darwin, Mrs. Yearsly, and Hannah More — Visit to Mrs. Charles Hoare — Dr. Beddoes — Return to Ireland 14–33

1793–1795.

Letters from Edgeworthstown to Miss Sophy Ruxton, Mrs. Ruxton, Mrs. Elizabeth Edgeworth.

Literary occupations of Maria Edgeworth : " Letters for Literary Ladies," " Practical Education " — Disturbances in Ireland : Lord Granard, The White Tooths, General Crosby's Adventure . 33–42

1795–1798.

Letters from Edgeworthstown to Mrs. Ruxton, Miss Sophy Ruxton, Miss Beaufort.

Publication of " Letters for Literary Ladies " and " The Parent's Assistant " — Mr. Edgeworth's election to the Irish Parliament —

Literary work and study: "Moral Tales," " Irish Bulls " — Madame Roland's Memoirs — Death of Mrs. Edgeworth, and marriage of Mr. Edgeworth to Miss Beaufort   43–55

1798–1799.

Letters from Edgeworthstown, Longford, and Dublin to Miss Sophy Ruxton, Mrs. Ruxton, Miss Charlotte Sneyd.

The Irish Rebellion: Lord Cornwallis, Lady Anne Fox — Flight from Edgeworthstown to Longford — Return to Edgeworthstown — Publication of "Practical Education" — Theatricals: " Whim for Whim " — At Dublin   55–68

1799–1802.

Letters from Clifton, Edgeworthstown, and Loughborough to Mrs. Ruxton, Miss Ruxton.

At Clifton: Sir Humphry Davy, Dr. Beddoes, Mrs. Barbauld — Death of Dr. Darwin — Literary work at Edgeworthstown: "Castle Rackrent," " Belinda," " Early Lessons," " Moral Tales," " Essay on Irish Bulls " — Visits of Mr. Chenevix and Professor Pictet — Journey to London   68–84

1802–1803.

Letters from London, Brussels, Chantilly, Paris, Calais, Edinburgh, to Miss Sneyd, Miss Sophy Ruxton, Miss Mary Sneyd, Mrs. Ruxton, C. S. Edgeworth.

A visit to Miss Watts at Leicester — Journey to Paris: Calais, Dunkirk, Bruges, Ghent — Madame Talma in "Andromaque" at Brussels — Palace of Chantilly — Paris: Madame Delessert, Madame Gautier. Madame de Pastoret, M. Dumont, Abbé Morellet, M. Suard, Marquis of Lansdowne, M. Degerando, M. Camille Jordan, Madame Campan, Madame Récamier, Baron de Prouy, Rogers, M. Pictet, Kosciusko — Monsieur Edelcrantz proposes to Maria Edgeworth; her feelings towards him — Buonaparte — Madame d'Oudinot and Rousseau — Rumors of war — The Edgeworths return to England — Account of a visit to Madame de Genlis . . .   84–142

1803–1809.

Letters from Edinburgh, Glasgow, Black Castle, Edgeworthstown, Rosstrevor, Allenstown, Pakenham Hall, to Mrs. Ruxton, Miss

CONTENTS vii

Honora Edgeworth, Miss Charlotte Sneyd, Miss Ruxton, Henry Edgeworth, C. Sneyd Edgeworth, Miss Margaret Ruxton, Mrs. Edgeworth.

Visit to Lindley Murray at Newcastle — Dugald Stewart at Edinburgh — Return to Edgeworthstown — Literary work: "Popular Tales," "Leonora," "Griselda" — Marriage of Miss Pakenham to Sir Arthur Wellesley (Duke of Wellington) — Death of Dr. Beddoes 142–173

1809–1813.

Letters from Edgeworthstown, Black Castle, Bangor Ferry, Liverpool, Derby, Cambridge, London, to Miss Ruxton, Miss Honora Edgeworth, Mrs. Ruxton, C. Sneyd Edgeworth, Miss Sneyd. Miss Margaret Ruxton, Mrs. Edgeworth.

Publication of "Tales of Fashionable Life": Madame de Staël, Lord Dudley, Lord Jeffrey, upon — Life at Edgeworthstown: Mr. Chenevix, Miss Lydia White, Sir Henry Holland, Mrs. Inchbald, Mrs. Barbauld, Hannah More. Lady Wellington — Marriage of Sir Humphry Davy — Literary pursuits: Byron's "English Bards," Scott's "Lady of the Lake" and "Rokeby," Campbell; "Patronage," "Tales of Fashionable Life" (second series), "The Absentee" — Balloon ascent of Sadler — Journey to London: Roscoe, Dr. Ferrier, Sir Henry Holland — Visit to Cambridge and to Dr. Clarke at Trumpington 173–218

1813–1817.

Letters from London, Malvern Links, Ross, Edgeworthstown. Dublin, Black Castle, to Miss Ruxton, Mrs. Ruxton, Miss Sneyd, Sir Walter Scott, C. S. Edgeworth.

Visit to London: Madame de Staël, Davy, Byron, Miss Berry's, Lord Lansdowne, Lady Wellington, Mrs. Siddons, The Prince Regent, Lady Elizabeth Monk, Dukes of Kent and Sussex, Sir James Mackintosh, Dumont, Sir Samuel Romilly, Dr. Parr, Malthus, Madame d'Arblay, Rogers — Return to and life at Edgeworthstown: "Early Lessons," "Popular Plays," "Harrington," "Ormond" — "Waverley" — Illness and death of Mr. Edgeworth . . 218–238

1817–1820.

Letters from Edgeworthstown, Mount Kennedy, Bowood, Epping, Hampstead, Byrkely Lodge, Tetsworth, London, Dublin, Heathfield. Canterbury, to Mrs. Ruxton, Mrs. Stark, Mrs. Edgeworth, Miss Ruxton, Miss Waller, Miss Lucy Edgeworth, Miss Honora Edgeworth.

Literary pursuits at Edgeworthstown: Miss Austen — Visits to Bowood: Lord Lansdowne, Dumont, Lord Grenville, Mr. Hare, Dugald Stewart — Death of Sir Samuel Romilly — Joanna Baillie, Watt, Campbell — London: Mill, Wilberforce, Duke and Duchess of Wellington, Lord Palmerston — Visit to Ireland — Journey to Paris 258–291

1820.

Letters from Paris, La Celle, Passy, Geneva, Pregny, Berne, to Mrs. Edgeworth, Misses Mary and Charlotte Sneyd, Mrs. Ruxton, Miss Ruxton, Miss Lucy Edgeworth, Miss Honora Edgeworth.

Paris: Duchesse de Broglie, Madame Récamier, Camille Jordan, Cuvier — Prony's anecdotes of Buonaparte — Visit to M. de Vindé's country house — A visit to the Duke of Orleans at Neuilly — Duchesse d'Angoulême, Casimir Perrier, Duchesse d'Uzès, Humboldt, Malthus — Journey through Switzerland: Dumont, M. de Staël 292–339

LIFE AND LETTERS

OF

MARIA EDGEWORTH

In the flats of the featureless county of Longford stands the large and handsome but unpretentious house of Edgeworthstown. The scenery here has few natural attractions, but the loving care of several generations has gradually beautified the surroundings of the house, and few homes have been more valued or more the centre round which a large family circle has gathered in unusual sympathy and love. In his "Memoirs," Mr. Edgeworth tells us how his family, which had given a name to Edgeworth, now Edgeware, near London, came to settle in Ireland more than three hundred years ago. Roger Edgeworth, a monk, having taken advantage of the religious changes under Henry VIII., had married and left two sons, who, about 1583, established themselves in Ireland. Of these, Edward, the elder, became Bishop of Down and Connor, and died without children; but the younger, Francis, became the founder of the family of Edgeworthstown. Always intensely Protestant, often intensely extravagant, each generation of the Edgeworth family afterwards had its own picturesque story, till Richard Edgeworth repaired the broken fortunes of his house, partly by success as a lawyer, partly by his marriage, in 1732, with Jane Lovell, daughter of a Welsh judge.

Their eldest son, Richard Lovell Edgeworth, was born in 1744, and educated in his boyhood at Drogheda School and Dublin University. Strong, handsome, clever, ingenious, and devoted to sports of every kind, he was a general favorite. But his high spirits often led him into scrapes; the most serious of these occurred during the festivities attendant on his eldest sister's marriage with Mr. Fox of Fox Hall, at which he played at being married to a young lady who was present, by one of the guests dressed up in a white cloak, with a door-key for a ring. This foolish escapade would not deserve the faintest notice, if it had not been seriously treated as an actual marriage by a writer in the "Quarterly Review."

In 1761 Richard Edgeworth was removed from Dublin to Corpus Christi College at Oxford. There he arrived, regretting the gayeties of Dublin, and anxious to make the most of any little excitements which his new life could offer. Amongst the introductions he brought with him was one to Mr. Paul Elers, who, himself of German extraction, had made a romantic marriage with Miss Hungerford, the heiress of Black Bourton in Oxfordshire. Mr. Elers honorably warned Mr. Edgeworth, who was an old friend of his, that he had four daughters who were very pretty, and that his friend had better be careful, as their small fortunes would scarcely fit one of them to be the wife of his son. But the elder Mr. Edgeworth took no notice — Richard was constantly at Black Bourton; and in 1763, being then only nineteen, he fled with Miss Anna Maria Elers to Gretna Green, where they were married. Great as was Mr. Edgeworth's displeasure, he wisely afterwards had the young couple remarried by license.

The union turned out unhappily. "I soon felt the inconveniences of an early and hasty marriage," wrote the bridegroom; "but, though I heartily repented my folly, I determined to bear with firmness and temper the evil which I had brought on myself." His eldest child, Richard, was born before he was twenty; his second, Maria, when he was twenty-four. Though he became master of Edgeworthstown by the death of his father in 1769, he lived for some years chiefly at Hare Hatch, near Maidenhead, where he already began to distract his attention from an ungenial home, by the endless plans for progress in agriculture and industry, and the disinterested schemes for the good of Ireland, which always continued to be the chief occupation of his life. It was his inventive genius which led to his paying a long visit to Lichfield to see Dr. Darwin. There he lingered long in pleasant intimacy with the doctor and his wife, with Mr. Wedgwood, Miss Anna Seward, — "the Swan of Lichfield," — and, still more, with the eccentric Thomas Day, author of "Sandford and Merton," who became his most intimate friend, and who wished to marry his favorite sister Margaret, though she could not make up her mind to accept him, and eventually became the wife of Mr. Ruxton of Black Castle. With Mrs. Seward and her daughters lived at that time — partly for educational purposes — Honora Sneyd, a beautiful and gifted girl, who had rejected the addresses of the afterwards famous Major André, and who now also refused those of Mr. Day. "In her, Honora Sneyd," wrote Mr. Edgeworth, "I saw for the first time in my life a woman that equaled the picture of perfection existing in my imagination. And then

my not being happy at home exposed me to the danger
of being too happy elsewhere." When he began to feel
as if the sunshine of his life emanated from his friendship with Miss Sneyd, he was certain flight was the
only safety. So leaving Mrs. Edgeworth and her little
girls with her mother, he made his escape to France,
taking with him only his boy, whom he determined to
educate according to the system of Rousseau. Then,
for two years, he remained at Lyons, employing his
inventive and mechanical powers in building bridges.

Meantime, the early childhood of Maria Edgeworth,
who was born 1st January, 1767, in the house of her
grandfather, Mr. Elers, at Black Bourton, was spent
almost entirely with relations in Oxfordshire, or with
her maternal great-aunts, the Misses Blake, in Great
Russell Street in London. It was in their house that
her neglected and unloved mother — always a kind and
excellent, though a very sad woman — died after her
confinement of a third daughter (Anna) in 1773. On
hearing of what he considered to be his release, Mr.
Edgeworth hurried back at once to England, and, before
four months were over, he was married to Miss Honora Sneyd, whose assent to so hasty a marriage would
scarcely prepare those who were unacquainted with her
for the noble, simple, and faithful way in which she
ever fulfilled the duties of a wife and stepmother. The
son of the first marriage, Richard Edgeworth, went, by
his own choice, to sea; but the three little girls, Maria,
Emmeline, and Anna, returned with their father and
stepmother to Edgeworthstown, where they had a childhood of unclouded happiness.

In 1775 Maria Edgeworth, being then eight years

old, was sent to a school at Derby, kept by Mrs. Lataffiere, to whom she always felt much indebted, though her stepmother, then in very failing health, continued to take part in her education by letter.

MRS. HONORA EDGEWORTH TO MARIA.

BEIGHTERTON, NEAR SHIFFNALL,
October 10, 1779.

I have received your letter, and I thank you for it, though I assure you I did not expect it. I am particularly desirous you should be convinced of this, as I *told* you I would write first. It is in vain to attempt to please a person who will not tell us what they *do* and what they do *not* desire; but as I tell you very fully what I think may be expected from a girl of your age, abilities, and education, I assure you, my dear Maria, you may entirely depend upon me, that as long as I have the use of my understanding,'I shall not be displeased with you for omitting anything which I had before told you I did not expect. Perhaps you may not quite understand what I mean, for I have not expressed myself clearly. If you do not, I will explain myself to you when we meet; for it is very agreeable to me to think of conversing with you as my equal in every respect but age, and of my making that inequality of use to you by giving you the advantage of the experience I have had, and the observations I have been able to make, as these are parts of knowledge which nothing but time can bestow.

In the spring of 1780 Mrs. Honora Edgeworth died of consumption, leaving an only son, Lovell, and a

daughter, Honora. Mr. Edgeworth announced this —
which to her was a most real sorrow — to his daughter
Maria in a very touching letter, in which he urges her
to follow her lost stepmother's example, especially in
endeavoring to be "amiable, prudent, and *of use ; "* but
within eight months he married again. Mrs. Honora
Edgeworth, when dying, had been certain that he would
do so, and had herself indicated her own sister Elizabeth
as the person whose character was most likely to secure
a happy home to him and his children. So, with his
usual singularity, though he liked her less than any of
her other sisters, and though he believed her utterly
unsuited to himself, he followed the advice which had
been given; and in spite of law and public opinion,
Elizabeth Sneyd became the third Mrs. Edgeworth
within eight months of her sister's death.

"Nothing," wrote Mr. Edgeworth, "is more erroneous
than the common belief that a man who has lived in
the greatest happiness with one wife will be the most
averse to take another. On the contrary, the loss of
happiness which he feels when he loses her necessarily
urges him to endeavor to be again placed in the situation which constituted his former felicity.

"I felt that Honora had judged wisely and from a
thorough knowledge of my character, when she advised
me to marry again as soon as I could meet with a woman
who would make a good mother to my children, and an
agreeable companion to me. She had formed an idea
that her sister Elizabeth was better suited to me than
any other woman, and thought I was equally suited to
her. But, of all Honora's sisters, I had seen the least
of Elizabeth."

Mrs. Elizabeth Edgeworth proved herself worthy of her sister's confidence. She was soon adored by her stepchildren, and her conduct to them was in all respects maternal. Maria at this time was removed from Bath to the school of Mrs. Davis, in Upper Wimpole Street, London, where she had excellent masters. Here her talent as an improvisatrice was first manifested in the tales she used to tell to her companions in their bedroom at night. She also, by his desire, frequently wrote stories and sent them for her father's criticism and approval. During holidays, which she often spent with his old friend Mr. Day at Anningsly, she benefited by an admirable library and by Mr. Day's advice as to her reading.

In 1782 Mr. and Mrs. Edgeworth returned to Ireland, taking the whole family with them. Maria was now fifteen, and was old enough to be interested in all the peculiarities of the Irish as contrasted with the English character, soon showing such natural aptitude for dealing with those around her, that her father intrusted her with all his accounts, and practically employed her as his agent for many years. Thus she obtained an insight into the lives and characters of her humbler neighbors, which was of inestimable value to her when afterwards writing her sketches of Irish life. She already began to plan many stories, most of which were never finished. But Mr. Edgeworth discouraged this. In the last year of her life Miss Edgeworth wrote: "I remember a number of literary projects, if I may so call them, or *aperçus* of things which I might have written if I had time or capacity so to do. The word *aperçu* my father used to object to. 'Let us have none of your *aperçus*, Maria: either follow a thing out clearly to a conclusion, or do not begin it: begin nothing without finishing it.' "

Building and planning alterations and improvements of every kind at Edgeworthstown were at once begun by Mr. Edgeworth, but always within his income. He also made two rules: he employed no middlemen, and he always left a year's rent in his tenants' hands. "Go before Mr. Edgeworth, and you will surely get justice," became a saying in the neighborhood.

"Some men live with their families without letting them know their affairs," wrote Miss Edgeworth, "and, however great may be their affection and esteem for their wives and children, think that they have nothing to do with business. This was not my father's way of thinking. On the contrary, not only his wife, but his children, knew all his affairs. Whatever business he had to do was done in the midst of his family, usually in the common sitting-room; so that we were intimately acquainted, not only with his general principles of conduct, but with the minute details of their every-day application. I further enjoyed some peculiar advantages: he kindly wished to give me habits of business, and for this purpose allowed me, during many years, to assist him in copying his letters of business, and in receiving his rents."

With the younger children Mr. Edgeworth's educational system was of the most cheerful kind; they were connected with all that was going on, made sharers in all the occupations of their elders, and not so much taught as shown how best to teach themselves. "I do not think one tear per month is shed in this house, nor the voice of reproof heard, nor the hand of restraint felt," wrote Mr. Edgeworth to Dr. Darwin. In both precept and practice he was the first to recommend what is described by Bacon as the experimental mode of education. "Surely," says Miss Edgeworth, "it would be doing good service to bring into a popular form all that metaphysicians have discovered which can be applied to practice in education. This was early and long my father's object. The art of teaching to invent — I dare not say, but of awakening and assisting the inventive power by daily exercise and excitement, and by the application of philosophic principles to trivial occurrences — he believed might be pursued with infinite advantage to the rising generation."

Maria Edgeworth found very congenial society in the family of her relation, Lord Longford, at Pakenham, which was twelve miles from Edgeworthstown, and in that of Lord Granard, at Castle Forbes, nine miles distant. Lady Granard's mother, Lady Moira, full of wit and wisdom, and with great nobility of character, would pour out her rich stores of reminiscence for the young girl with ceaseless kindness. But more than any other was her life influenced, helped, cheered, and animated by the love of her father's sister Margaret, Mrs. Ruxton, the intimate friend and correspondent of forty-two years, whose home, Black Castle, was within a long drive of Edgeworthstown. Mrs. Ruxton's three children — Richard, Sophy, and Margaret — were Maria Edgeworth's dearest companions and friends.

The great love which Miss Edgeworth always felt for children was tried and developed out to its fullest extent in the ever-increasing family circle. Mrs. Eliza-

beth Edgeworth added nine more brothers and sisters
to the group of six which already existed; the eldest of
them, Henry, born in 1782, was intrusted to Maria's
especial care.

MARIA TO MISS CHARLOTTE SNEYD.

EDGEWORTHSTOWN, December 9, 1787.

I think, my dear Aunt Charlotte, I did not know till
Henry returned to us after his six weeks' absence, how
very agreeable even a child of his age can make himself,
but I am sure that his journey has been productive of
so much pleasure to me from the kindness and approbation you have shown, and has left on my mind so full
a conviction of your skill in the art of education, that I
should part with Henry again to-morrow with infinitely
more security and satisfaction than I did two months
ago. I was really surprised to see with what ease and
alacrity little Henry returned to all his former habits
and occupations, and the very slight change that appeared in his manner or mind; nothing seemed strange
to him in anything, or anybody about him. When he
spoke of you to us he seemed to think that we were all
necessarily connected in all our commands and wishes,
that we were all one *whole* — one great polypus soul.
I hope my father will tell you himself how much he
liked your letter, "the overflowings of a full mind, not
the froth of an empty one."

In 1790 the family group was first broken by the
death from consumption, at fifteen, of Honora, the
beautiful only daughter of Mrs. Honora Edgeworth.

TO MRS. RUXTON.

EDGEWORTHSTOWN, February 11, 1790.

Your friendship, my dear Aunt Ruxton, has, I am sure, considerably alleviated the anguish of mind my father has had to feel, and your letter and well-deserved praise of my dear mother's fortitude and exertion were a real pleasure to her. She has indeed had a great deal to bear, and I think her health has suffered, but I hope not materially. In my father's absence, she ordered everything, did everything, felt everything herself. Unless, my dear aunt, you had been present during the last week of dear Honora's sufferings, I think you could not form an idea of anything so terrible or so touching. Such extreme fortitude, such affection, such attention to the smallest feelings of others, as she showed on her deathbed!

My father has carefully kept his mind occupied ever since his return, but we cannot help seeing his feelings at intervals. He has not slept for two or three nights, and is, I think, far from well to-day.

He said the other day, speaking of Honora, "My dear daughters, I promise you one thing, I never will reproach any of you with Honora. I will never re-proach you with any of her virtues." There could not be a kinder or more generous promise, but I could not help fearing that my father should refrain from speaking of her too much, and that it would hurt his mind. He used to say it was a great relief to him to talk of my mother Honora.

In the summer of 1791 Mr. and Mrs. Edgeworth went to England, leaving Maria in sole charge of the large family at home. She used to amuse her young sisters at this time by stories, which she would write on a slate during the leisure moments which her many occupations permitted, and which she would read aloud to them in the evening. By their interest or questions she estimated the stories, which became the foundation of "The Parent's Assistant." When her father was with her she always wrote a sketch of an intended story, and submitted it to his approval, being invariably guided by his advice. In October Maria was desired to follow her parents to Clifton, bringing nearly all the children with her, a formidable undertaking for a young girl in those days of difficult traveling.

TO MRS. RUXTON.[1]

EDGEWORTHSTOWN, October, 1791.

My dear mother is safe and well, and a fine new sister, I suppose you have heard. My very dear aunt, since the moment I came home till this instant my hands have trembled, and my head whirled with business; but the delightful hope of seeing my dear father and mother at Bristol is in fine perspective at the end. My father has just written the kindest letter possible, and Emmeline is transcribing his directions about our journey. We are to set off as soon as we can — on Tuesday morning next, I believe, for my father is extremely impatient for us to come over. I write by this night's post to Mr. Hanna, to take lodgings for us in Dublin, and we are, as you will see, to go by Holyhead.

---

[1] After returning from a visit to Black Castle.

As to coming round by Black Castle, it is out of the question. For everybody's sake but my own, I regret this: for my own I do not, the few hours I should have to spend in your company would not, my dearest aunt, balance the pain of parting with you all again, which I did feel thoroughly, and if I had not had the kindest friends and the fullest occupation the moment I came home, I should have been in the lamentables a long time. Tell my dear uncle I never shall forget the kindness of his manner towards me during the whole of my stay at Black Castle, and the belief that he thinks well of his little niece adds much to her happiness, perhaps to her vanity, which he will say there was no occasion to increase. And now, dear Sophy, for your *roaring blade*, Thomas Day, Esq.,[1] he is in readiness to wait upon you whenever you can; will you have the charity to receive him? Name the day, my dear aunt, which will be the least inconvenient if you can, and Molly or John Langan shall bring him in the old or new chaise to your door, where I hope he will not salute you with a cry, but if he does, do not be surprised.

You see, my dear aunt, that I am in a great hurry by my writing, but no hurry, believe me, can drive out of my mind the remembrance of all the kindness I received at Black Castle. Oh, continue to love your niece; you cannot imagine the pleasure she felt when you kissed her, and said you loved her a thousand times better than ever you did before.

---

[1] This little brother was born the day before the Edgeworth family received the news of the sudden death of their old friend Mr. Day, in 1789.

MR. SMITH'S, HOLYHEAD, Friday Morning.

We are this instant arrived, my dear aunt, after a thirty-three hours' passage; all the children safe and well, but desperately sick; poor little Sneyd especially. The packet is just returning, and my head is so giddy that I scarcely know what I write, but you will only expect a few shabby lines to say we are not drowned. Mr. Ussher Edgeworth [1] and my Aunt Fox's servant saw us on board, and Mr. E. was so very good to come in the wherry with us and see us into the ship. We had the whole cabin to ourselves; no passenger, except one gentleman, son-in-law to Mr. Dawson, of Ardee; he was very civil to us, and assisted us much in landing, etc. I felt, besides, very glad to see one who knew anything even of the name of Ruxton. Adieu, my dear aunt; all the sick pale figures around me with faint voices send their love to you and my uncle.

TO MR. RUXTON.

PRINCE'S BUILDINGS, CLIFTON,
December 29, 1791.

MY DEAR UNCLE, — If you are going to the canal put this letter in your pocket, and do not be troubled in your conscience about reading it, but keep it till you are perfectly at leisure: for I have nothing strange or new to tell you. We live just the same kind of life that we used to do at Edgeworthstown; and, though we move amongst numbers, are not moved by them, but feel independent of them for our daily amusement. All the *phantasmas* I had conjured up to frighten myself van-

---

[1] Brother to the Abbé Edgeworth, who resided in Dublin.

ished after I had been here a week, for I found that
they were but phantoms of my imagination, as you very
truly told me. We live very near the Downs, where
we have almost every day charming walks, and all the
children go bounding about over hill and dale along
with us. My aunt told me that once when you were at
Clifton, when full dressed to go to a ball at Bath, you
suddenly changed your mind, and undressed again, to
go out a walking with her, and now that I see the
walks, I am not surprised, even if you were not to have
had the pleasure of my aunt's company. My father has
got a *transfer* of a ticket for the Bristol library, which
is an extremely fine one; and what makes it appear ten
times finer is, that it is very difficult for strangers to get
into. From thence he can get almost any book for us
he pleases, except a few of the most scarce, which are
by the laws of the library immovable. No ladies go
to the library, but Mr. Johns, the librarian, is very
civil, and my mother went to his rooms and saw the
beautiful prints in Boydell's Shakespeare. Lavater is
to come home in a coach to-day. My father seems to
think much the same of him that you did when you saw
him abroad, that to some genius he adds a good deal of
the mountebank. My father is going soon to Bath.
Madame de Genlis is there, and he means to present the
translation of "Adele and Theodore" to her;[1] he had
intended to have had me introduced to her, but upon
inquiry he was informed that she is not visited by
demoiselles in England.

---

[1] Maria Edgeworth, by her father's advice, had made a translation
of *Adèle et Théodore* in 1782, but the appearance of Holcroft's translation prevented its publication.

For some time I kept a Bristol journal, which I intended to send to Black Castle in form of a newspaper, but I found that though every day's conversation and occurrences appeared of prodigious importance just at the moment they were passing, yet afterwards they seemed so flat and stale as not to be worth sending. I must however tell you that I had materials for one brilliant paragraph about the Duchess of York. Mr. Lloyd had seen the wondrous sight. "When she was to be presented to the Queen, H. R. H. kept Her Majesty waiting nearly an hour, till at last the Queen, fearing that some accident had happened, sent to let the Duchess know that she was waiting for her. When the Duchess at length arrived, she was so frightened — for a Royal Duchess can be frightened as well as another — that she trembled and tottered in crossing the presence chamber so that she was obliged to be supported. She is very timid, and never once raised her eyes, so that our correspondent cannot speak decidedly as to the expression of her countenance, but if we may be allowed to say so, she is not a beauty, and is very low. She was dressed in white and gold," etc., etc.

The children all desire their love; they were playing the other day at going to Black Castle, and begged me to *be* Aunt Ruxton, which I assured them I would if I could! but they insisted on my *being* Sophy, Letty, and Margaret at the same time, and were not quite contented at my pleading this to be out of my power.

TO MISS SOPHY RUXTON.

CLIFTON, March 9, 1792.

I wish, my dear Sophy, that you could know how often I think of you and wish for you, whenever we see or hear anything that I imagine you would like. How does your ward go on? My mother desires me to say the kindest things to you, and assure yourself, my dear Sophy, that when my mother says the kindest, they are always at the same time the truest. She is not a person ever to forget a favor, and the care and trouble you are now bestowing on little Thomas Day will be remembered probably after you have forgotten it. But my father interrupts me at this moment, to say that if I am writing to Sophy I must give him some room at the end, so I shall leave off my fine speeches. We spend our time very agreeably here, and have in particular great choice of books. I don't think the children are quite as happy here as they used to be at home; it is impossible they should be, for they have neither the same occupations or liberty. It is however "restraint that sweetens liberty," and the joy they show when they run upon the Downs, hunting fossils, and clambering, is indeed very great. Henry flatters himself that he shall some time or other have the pleasure of exhibiting his collection to Cousin Sophy, and rehearses frequently in the character of showman. Dr. Darwin has been so good as to send him several fossils, etc., with their names written upon them, and he is every day adding to his little stock of *larning*. There is a very sensible man here who has also made him presents of little things which he values much, and he begins to *mess* a great deal with gums, camphor, etc.   He will at least never come under Dr. Darwin's definition of a fool.   "A fool, Mr. Edgeworth, you know, is a man who never tried an experiment in his life."   My father tells me that Henry has acquired a taste for improving himself, and that all he has now to fear is my taste for improving him.

We went the other day to see a collection of natural curiosities at a Mr. Broderip's, of Bristol, which entertained us very much.   My father observed he had but very few butterflies, and he said, "No, sir, a circumstance which happened to me some time ago determined me never to collect any more butterflies.   I caught a most beautiful butterfly, thought I had killed it, and ran a pin through its body to fasten it to a cork: a *fortnight* afterward I happened to look in the box where I had left it, and I saw it writhing in agony: since that time I have never destroyed another."

My father has just returned from Dr. Darwin's, where he has been nearly three weeks; they were extremely kind, and pressed him very much to take a house in or near Derby for the summer.   He has been, as Dr. Darwin expressed it, "breathing the breath of life into the brazen lungs of a clock" which he had made at Edgeworthstown as a present for him.   He saw the first part of Dr. Darwin's "Botanic Garden;" £900 was what his bookseller gave him for the whole!   On his return from Derby, my father spent a day with Mr. Keir, the great chemist, at Birmingham: he was speaking to him of the late discovery of fulminating silver, with which I suppose your ladyship is well acquainted, though it be new to Henry and me.   A lady and gentleman went into a laboratory where a few grains of fulminating silver were lying in a mortar: the gentleman, as he was talking, happened to stir it with the end of his cane, which was tipped with iron, — the fulminating silver exploded instantly, and blew the lady, the gentleman, and the whole laboratory to pieces! Take care how you go into laboratories with gentlemen, unless they are, like Sir Plume, skilled in the "nice conduct" of their canes.

Have you seen any of the things that have been lately published about the negroes? We have just read a very small pamphlet of about ten pages, merely an account of the facts stated to the House of Commons. Twenty-five thousand people in England have absolutely left off eating West India sugar, from the hope that when there is no longer any demand for sugar the slaves will not be so cruelly treated. Children in several schools have given up sweet things, which is surely very benevolent; though whether it will at all conduce to the end proposed is perhaps wholly uncertain, and in the mean time we go on eating apple pies sweetened with sugar instead of with honey. At Mr. Keir's, however, my father avers that he ate excellent custards sweetened with honey. Will it not be rather hard upon the poor bees in the end?

Mrs. Yearsly, the milkwoman, whose poems I dare say my aunt has seen, lives very near us at Clifton: we have never seen her, and probably never shall, for my father is so indignant against her for her ingratitude to her benefactress, Miss Hannah More, that he thinks she deserves to be treated with *neglect*. She was dying, absolutely expiring with hunger, when Miss More found her. Her mother was a washerwoman, and washed for Miss More's family; by accident, in a tablecloth which was sent to her was left a silver spoon, which Mrs. Yearsly returned. Struck with this instance of honesty, which was repeated to her by the servants, Miss More sent for her, discovered her distress and her genius, and though she was extremely eager in preparing some of her own works for the press, she threw them all aside to correct Mrs. Yearsly's poems, and obtained for her a subscription of £600. In return, Mrs. Yearsly accused her of having defrauded her, of having been actuated only by vanity in bringing her abilities to light — a new species of vanity from one authoress to another — in short, abused her in the basest and most virulent manner. Would you go to see Mrs. Yearsly?

Lo! I have almost filled the Bristol Chronicle, and have yet much that I wish to say to you, dear Sophy, and that I could tell you in one half hour, talking at my usual rate of nine miles an hour; when that will be, it is impossible to tell. My mother is now getting better. All the children are perfectly well; Bessy's eyes are not inflamed; Charlotte *est faite à peindre et plus encore à aimer*, if that were French.

Little Thomas Day Edgeworth died at the age of three, whilst he was in the care of the Ruxtons, and about the same time Maria Edgeworth's own brother Richard, who had paid a long visit to his family at Clifton, returned to North Carolina, where he had married and was already a father.

TO MISS SOPHY RUXTON.

ASHTON BOWER, CLIFTON, August 14, 1792.

Last Saturday my poor brother Richard took leave of us to return to America. He has gone up to London with my father and mother, and is to sail from thence. We could not part with him without great pain and regret, for he made us all extremely fond of him. I wish my dear aunt could have seen him; he was very sensible of her kindness, and longed to have a letter from her. He is to come over in '95. Emmeline is still with Lady Holt and Mrs. Bracebridge, at Atherstone, in Warwickshire. Miss Bracebridge, granddaughter to Lady Holt, is a very agreeable companion to my sister, though some years younger, and she enjoys the society at Atherstone very much. They are most unwilling to part with her; but now she has been absent two months, and we all begin to *growl* for her return, especially now that my brother is gone, who was "in himself a host."

I am engaged to go in October to pay a visit to Mrs. Charles Hoare. I believe you may remember my talking to you of this lady, and my telling you that she was my friend at school,[1] and had corresponded with me since. She was at Lisbon when we first came to England, and I thought I had little prospect of seeing her, but the moment she returned to England she wrote to me in the kindest and most pressing manner to beg I would come to her. Immediately after this, I dare not add that she is a most amiable and sensible woman, lest

1 Miss Robinson.

Sophy should exclaim, "Ah! vanity! because she likes you, Mademoiselle Marie!"

My uncle, William Sneyd, whom I believe you saw at Edgeworthstown, has just been with us for three weeks, and in that time filled five quires of paper with dried plants from the neighboring rocks. He says there is at Clifton the richest harvest for botanists. How I wish you were here to reap it. Henry and I will collect anything that we are informed is worthy of your Serene Highness's collection. There is a species of cistus which grows on S. Vincent's rock, which is not, I am told, to be found in any other part of England. Helpless as I am and scoffed at in these matters, I will contrive to get some of it for you. A shoemaker showed us a tortoise shell which he had for sale. I wished to have bought it for La Sophie, but upon inquiry I found it could not be had for less than a guinea; now I thought at the utmost it would not give Sophy above half a crown's worth of pleasure, so I left the shoemaker in quiet possession of his African tortoise. He had better fortune with two shells, admirals, which he sold to Lady Valentia for three guineas.

We begin to be hungry for letters. The children all desire their love to you; Charlotte is very engaging, and promises to be handsome; Sneyd *is* and promises everything; Henry will, I think, through life always do more than he promises; little Honora is a sprightly, blue-eyed child, at nurse with a woman who is the picture of health and simplicity, in a beautiful romantic cottage, just such a cottage as you would imagine for the residence of health and simplicity. Lovell is perfectly well, and desires his kind love to you. Dr.

Darwin has paid him very handsome compliments in his lines on the Barbarini vase, in the first part of the "Botanic Garden," which my father has just got.

Has my aunt seen the "Romance of the Forest"? It has been the fashionable novel here, everybody read and talked of it; we were much interested in some parts of it. It is something in the style of the "Castle of Otranto," and the horrible parts are, we thought, well worked up, but it is very difficult to keep Horror breathless with his mouth wide open through three volumes.

Adieu, my dear Sophy: do not let my aunt forget me, for I love her very much; and as for yourself, take care not to think too highly of Cousin Maria, but see her faults with indulgence, and you will, I think, find her a steady and affectionate friend.

TO MISS SOPHY RUXTON.

FLEET STREET, LONDON, October 17, 1792.

I have been with Mrs. Charles Hoare a week, and before I left Clifton had a budget in my head for a letter to you, which I really had not a moment's time to write. I left them all very well, just going to leave Ashton Bower, which I am not sorry for, though it has such a pretty, romantic name; it is not a fit Bower to live in in winter, it is so cold and damp. They are going to Prince's Place again, and I dare say will fix there for the winter, though my father has talked of Bath and Plymouth.

I find in half-rubbed-out notes in my pocket-book, "Sophy — Slave-ship: Sophy — Rope-walk: Sophy — Marine acid: Sophy — Earthquake: Sophy — Glass-house," etc.: and I intended to tell you *au longue* of these.

We went on board a slave-ship with my brother, and saw the dreadfully small hole in which the poor slaves are stowed together, so that they cannot stir. But probably you know all this.

Mrs. Hoare was at Lisbon during two slight shocks of an earthquake; she says the night was remarkably fine, there was no unwholesome feeling that she can remember in the air, immediately preceding the shock: but they were sitting with the windows open down to the ground, looking at the clearness of the sky, when they felt the shock. The doors and windows, and all the furniture in the room, shook for a few instants; they looked at one another in silent terror. But in another instant everything was still, and they came to the use of their voices. Numbers of exaggerated accounts were put into the public papers, and she received vast numbers of terrified letters from her friends in England. So much for the earthquake. The marine acid I must leave till I have my father at my elbow, lest in my great wisdom I should set you wrong.

About the glasshouse: there is one Stephens, an Englishman, who has set up a splendid glasshouse at Lisbon, and the government have granted him a pine wood sixteen miles in extent to supply his glasshouse with fuel. He has erected a theatre for his workmen, supplied them with scenes, dresses, etc.; and they have acquired such a taste for theatrical amusements that it has conquered their violent passion for drinking, which formerly made them incapable of work three days in the week; now they work as hard as possible, and amuse themselves for one day in the week.

Of the beauty of the Tagus, and its golden sands,

and the wolves which Mrs. Hoare had the satisfaction of seeing hunted, I must speak when I see you. Mrs Hoare is as kind as possible to me, and I spend my time at Roehampton as I like; in London that is not entirely possible. We have only come up to town for a few days. Mr. Hoare's house at Roehampton is an excellent one indeed — a library with nice books, small tables upon casters, low sofas, and all the other things which make rooms comfortable. Lady Hoare, his mother, is said to be a very amiable, sensible woman: I have seen her only once, but I was much entertained at her house at Barnelms, looking at the pictures. I saw Zeluco's figure in Le Brun's "Massacre of the Innocents." My aunt will laugh, and think that I am giving myself great airs when I talk of being entertained looking at pictures; but assure her that I remember what she used to say about taste, and that without affectation I have endeavored to look at everything worth seeing.

TO MRS. RUXTON.

STANHOPE STREET, LONDON,
November 6, 1792.

I left Roehampton yesterday, and took leave of my friend Mrs. Charles Hoare, with a high opinion of her abilities, and a still higher opinion of her goodness. She was exceedingly kind to me, and I spent most of my time with her as I liked; I say most, because a good deal of it was spent in company where I heard of nothing but chariots and horses, and curricles and tandems. Oh, to what contempt I exposed myself in a luckless hour by asking what a tandem was! I am

going in a few days to meet Mrs. Powys at Bath.
Since I have been away from home I have missed the
society and fondness of my father, mother, and sisters
more than I can express, and more than beforehand I
should have thought possible; I long to see them all
again.   Even when I am most amused I feel a void,
and now I understand what an aching void is perfectly
well.   You know they are going back to Prince's Buildings to the nice house we had last winter; and Emmeline writes me word that the great red puddle which we
used to call the Red Sea, and which we were forced to
wade through before we could get to the Downs, will
not this winter be so terrible, for my father has made
a footpath for his "host."

Clifton, December 13, 1792.
(The day we received yours.)

The day of retribution is at hand, my dear aunt: the
month of May will soon come, and then, when we meet
face to face, and voucher to voucher, it shall be truly
seen whose letter-writing account stands fullest and
fairest in the world.   Till then, "we 'll leave it all to
your honor's honor."   But why does my dear aunt
write, "I can have but little more time to spend with
my brother in my life?"[1] as if she was an old woman
of one hundred and ninety-nine and upwards!   I remember, the day I left Black Castle, you told me, if
you recollect, that you "had one foot in the grave;"
and though I saw you standing before me in perfect
health, sound wind and limb, I had the weakness to
feel frightened, and never to think of examining where
your feet really were.   But in the month of May we

---

[1] Mrs. Ruxton lived thirty-nine years after this letter was written.

hope to find them safe in your shoes, and I hope that the sun will then shine out, and that all the black clouds in the political horizon will be dispersed, and that "freemen" will by that time eat their puddings and hold their tongues. Anna and I stayed one week with Mrs. Powys[1] at Bath, and were very thoroughly occupied all the time with seeing and — I won't say with being seen; for though we were at three balls, I do not believe any one saw us. The Upper Rooms we thought very splendid, and the playhouse pretty, but not so good as the theatre at Bristol. We walked all over Bath with my father, and liked it extremely: he showed us the house where he was born.

GLOUCESTER ROW, CLIFTON,
July 21, 1793.

My father is just returned to us from Mr. Keir's. . . . Come over to us, since we cannot go to you. "Ah, Maria, you know I would come if I could." But can't you, who are a great woman, trample upon impossibilities? It is two years since we saw you, and we are tired of *recollecting* how kind and agreeable you were. Are you the same Aunt Ruxton? Come and see whether we are the same, and whether there are any people in the world out of your own house who know your value better.

During the hot weather the thermometer was often 80, and once 88. Mr. Neville, a banker, has taken a house here, and was to have been my father's traveling companion, but left him at Birmingham: he has a fishing-stool and a wife. We like the fishing-stool and the

----

[1] The most intimate friend of Mrs. Honora Edgeworth.

wife, but have not yet seen the family. My father last night wrote a letter of recommendation to you for a Mr. Jimbernat, a Spanish gentleman, son to the King of Spain's surgeon, who is employed by his Court to travel for scientific purposes: he drank tea with us, and seems very intelligent. Till I saw him I thought a Spaniard must be tall and stately: one may be mistaken.

Adieu, for there are matters of high import coming, fit only for the pen of pens.

R. L. EDGEWORTH, *in continuation.*

The matters of high importance, my dear sister, have been already communicated to you in brief, and indeed cannot be detailed by any but the parties. Dr. Beddoes, the object of Anna's vows,[1] is a man of abilities, and of great name in the scientific world as a naturalist and chemist — good-humored, good-natured, a man of honor and virtue, enthusiastic and sanguine, and very fond of Anna.

MARIA TO MRS. RUXTON.

EDGEWORTHSTOWN, November 18, 1793.

This evening my father has been reading out Gay's "Trivia" to our great entertainment. I wished very much, my dear aunt, that you and Sophy had been sitting round the fire with us. If you have "Trivia," and if you have time, will you humor your niece so far as to look at it? I think there are many things in it which will please you, especially the "Patten and the Shoeblack," and the old woman hovering over her little

---

[1] Dr. Thomas Beddoes, the celebrated physician and chemist, followed the Edgeworth family to Ireland, where he was married to Anna Edgeworth, Maria's youngest *own* sister.

fire in a hard winter. Pray tell me if you like it. I
had much rather make a bargain with any one I loved
to read the same book with them at the same hour, than
to look at the moon like Rousseau's famous lovers.
"Ah! that is because my dear niece has no taste and no
eyes." But I assure you I am learning the use of my
eyes main fast, and make no doubt, please Heaven I
live to be sixty, to see as well as my neighbors.

I am scratching away very hard at the Freeman
Family.[1]

In November, 1793, the Edgeworth family returned to
Ireland, where Mr. Edgeworth's inventive genius became
occupied with a system of telegraphy on which he expended much time and money. It was offered to the
government, but declined. Maria Edgeworth was occupied at this time with her "Letters for Literary Ladies,"
as well as with "Toys and Tasks," which formed one of
her chapters on "Practical Education."

TO MISS SOPHY RUXTON.

Edgeworthstown, February 23, 1794.

Thank my aunt and thank yourself for kind inquiries
after "Letters for Literary Ladies."[2] I am sorry to
say they are not as well as can be expected, nor are they
likely to mend at present: when they are fit to be seen
— if that happy time ever arrives — their first visit
shall be to Black Castle. They are now disfigured by
all manner of crooked marks of papa's critical indigna-

---

1 *Patronage*, which, however, was laid aside, and not published till
1813.

2 Published in 1795 — an early plea in favor of female education.

tion, besides various abusive marginal notes, which I would not have you see for half a crown sterling, nor my aunt for a whole crown as pure as King Hiero's; with which crown I am sure you are acquainted, and know how to weigh it as Honora did at eight years old, though Mr. Day would not believe it. I think my mother is better this evening, but she is so very cheerful when she has a moment's respite that it deceives us. She calls Lovell the Minute Philosopher at this instant, because he is drawing with the assistance of a magnifying glass with a universal joint in his mouth; so that one eye can see through it while he draws a beautifully small drawing of the new front of the house. I have just excited his envy even to clasping his hands in distraction, by telling him of a man I met with in the middle of Grainger's "Worthies of England," who drew a mill, a miller, a bridge, a man and horse going over the bridge with a sack of corn, all visible, upon a surface that would just cover a sixpence.

TO MRS. RUXTON.

EDGEWORTHSTOWN, May 8, 1794.

My father is perfectly well, and very busy out of doors and indoors. He brought back certain books from Black Castle, amongst which I was glad to see the "Fairy Tales;" and he has related, with various embellishments suited to the occasion, the story of Fortunatus, to the great delight of young and old, especially of Sneyd, whose eyes and cheeks expressed strong approbation, and who repeated it afterwards in a style of dramatic oratory which you would have known how to admire.

We are reading a new book for children, "Evenings at Home," which we admire extremely. Has Sophy seen them? And has she seen the fine Aurora Borealis which was to be seen last week, and which my father and Lovell saw with ecstasies? The candles were all put out in the library, and a wonderful bustle made, before I rightly comprehended what was going on.

EDGEWORTHSTOWN, 1794.

I will look for the volume of the "Tableau de Paris" which you think I have; and if it is in the land of the living, it shall be coming forth at your call. Do you remember our reading in it of the *garçon perruquier* who dresses in black on a Sunday, and leaves his every-day clothes, white and heavy with powder, in the middle of the room, which he dares not peep into after his metamorphosis? I like to read as well as to talk with you, my dear aunt, because you mix the grave and gay together, and put your long finger upon the very passages which my short, stumpy one was just starting forward to point out, if it could point.

You are very good indeed to wish for "Toys and Tasks," but I think it would be most unreasonable to send them to you now. We are a very small party, now that my father, Anna, and Lovell are gone; but I hope we shall be better when you come.

TO MRS. ELIZABETH EDGEWORTH.

EDGEWORTHSTOWN, 1794.

All 's well at home; the chickens are all good and thriving, and there is plenty of provender, and of every-thing that we can want or wish for: therefore we all hope that you will fully enjoy the pleasures of Black Castle without being anxious for your bairns.

Pray tell my dear aunt that I am not ungrateful for all the kindness she showed to me while I was with her: it rejoiced my heart to hear her say, when she took leave of me, that she did not love me less for knowing me better.

Kitty wakened me this morning saying, "Dear, ma'am, how charming you smell of coals! quite charming!" and she snuffed the ambient air.[1]

TO MISS SOPHY RUXTON.

> EDGEWORTHSTOWN, July 2, 1794, having the honor to be the fair day of Edgeworthstown, as is well proclaimed to the neighborhood by the noise of pigs squeaking, men bawling, women brawling, and children squealing, etc.

I will tell you what is going on, that you may see whether you like your daily bill of fare.

There are, an't please you, ma'am, a great many good things here. There is a balloon hanging up, and another going to be put on the stocks; there is soap made, and making from a receipt in Nicholson's "Chemistry;" there is excellent ink made, and to be made by the same book; there is a cake of roses just squeezed in a vise, by my father, according to the advice of Madame De Lagaraye, the woman in the black cloak and ruffles, who weighs with unwearied scales, in the frontispiece of a book, which perhaps my aunt remembers, entitled

---

[1] The coals burned at Black Castle were naturally more agreeable to Mrs. Billamore (a faithful servant) than the bog turf used at Edgeworthstown.

"Chemie de Goût et de l'Odorat." There are a set of accurate weights, just completed by the ingenious Messrs. Lovell and Henry Edgeworth, partners: for Henry is now a junior partner, and grown an inch and a half upon the strength of it in two months. The use and ingenuity of these weights I do, or did, understand; it is great, but I am afraid of puzzling you and disgracing myself attempting to explain it; especially as, my mother says, I once sent you a receipt for purifying water with charcoal, which she avers to have been above, or below, the comprehension of any rational being.

My father bought a great many books at Mr. Dean's sale. Six volumes of "Machines Approuvés," full of prints of paper mills, gunpowder mills, *machines pour ramonter les batteaux, machines pour* — a great many things which you would like to see, I am sure, over my father's shoulder. And my aunt would like to see the new staircase, and to see a kitcat view of a robin redbreast sitting on her nest in a sawpit, discovered by Lovell; and you would both like to pick Emmeline's fine strawberries round the crowded oval table after dinner, and to see my mother look so much better in the midst of us.

> If these delights thy soul can move,
> Come live with us and be our love.

TO MRS. RUXTON.

EDGEWORTHSTOWN, August 11, 1794.

Nothing wonderful or interesting, nothing which touches our hopes or fears, which either moves us to laugh or to be doleful, can happen without the idea of Aunt Ruxton immediately arising. This, you will think, is the preface to at least either death or marriage; but it is *only* the preface to a history of Defenders.

There have been lately several flying reports of Defenders, but we never thought the danger *near* till to-day. Last night a party of forty attacked the house of one Hoxey, about half a mile from us, and took, as usual, the arms. They have also been at Ringowny, where there was only one servant left to take care of the house; they took the arms and broke all the windows. To-day Mr. Bond, our high sheriff, paid us a *pale* visit, thought it was proper something should be done for the internal defense of the town of Edgeworthstown and the county of Longford, and wished my father would apply to him for a meeting of the county. My father first rode over to the scene of action, to inquire into the truth of the reports; found them true, and on his return to dinner found Mr. Thompson, of Clonfin, and Captain Doyle, nephew to the general and the wounded colonel, who is now at Granard. Captain Doyle will send a sergeant and twelve to-morrow; to-night a watch is to sit up, but it is supposed that the sight of two redcoats riding across the country together will keep the evil sprites from appearing to mortal eyes "this watch." My father has spoken to many of the householders, and he imagines they will come here to a meeting to-morrow, to consider how best they can defend their lands and tenements; they bring their arms to my father to take care of. You will be surprised at our making such a mighty matter of a visit from the Defenders, you who have had soldiers sitting up in your kitchen for weeks; but you will consider that this is our first visit.

[illegible] [illegible] of [illegible] [illegible] [illegible] in [illegible]. The [illegible] [illegible] is [illegible] back, and the [illegible] is [illegible] [illegible] [illegible] [illegible] [illegible] to [illegible] [illegible] [illegible] [illegible] and love I.

[illegible] [illegible] [illegible]

[illegible]. [illegible]

I will [illegible] [illegible], my [illegible] [illegible], [illegible] a [illegible] for [illegible], and [illegible] to [illegible] [illegible] [illegible] [illegible] [illegible], because you [illegible] [illegible] [illegible]; if you should be [illegible] before you [illegible] [illegible], I shall [illegible] of the [illegible] of my [illegible]. I believe it was you — at any [illegible], the [illegible] of all [illegible] — who [illegible] me of a [illegible] who [illegible] a [illegible] [illegible] to see her sister, who she [illegible] was very ill, but [illegible], the sister was well before she got to her [illegible]; and she was so [illegible] that she [illegible] with her well sister, and would never have [illegible] [illegible] more to do with her.

You will [illegible] very [illegible] when you come back from the sea and [illegible] what [illegible] [illegible] have been at [illegible] Castle in your absence. [illegible] was [illegible] sorry that she would not see you again before she left [illegible]; but you will [illegible] be in the same [illegible] again, and there is one great [illegible] [illegible], as Mr. [illegible], a [illegible] [illegible] [illegible], who [illegible] her [illegible] about it a [illegible], said it. "[illegible]," said he to my [illegible], "when you look at a [illegible], do you know that the east is always on your right hand, and the west on your left?" "Yes," [illegible] my [illegible], with a very [illegible] look, "I believe I do." "Well," said the [illegible] of [illegible], "then 's a [illegible] [illegible] [illegible]."

TO MRS. RUXTON.

EDGEWORTHSTOWN, 1795.

My father returned late on Friday night, bringing with him a very bad and a very good thing; the bad thing was a bad cold, the good is Aunt Mary Sneyd. Emmeline was delayed some days at Lichfield by the broken bridges and bad roads, floods and snows, which have stopped man, and beast, and mail coaches. Mr. Cox, the man who sells camomile drops under the title of Oriental Pearls, wrote an apology to my Aunt Mary for neglecting to send the Pearls, in the following elegant phrase: "That the mistake she mentioned he could no ways account for but by presuming that it must have arisen from impediments occasioned by the inclemencies of the season!"

When my father went to see Lord Charlemont, he came to meet him, saying, "I must claim relationship with you, Mr. Edgeworth. I am related to the Abbé Edgeworth, who is, I think, an honor to the kingdom — I should say to human nature."

TO THE SAME.

EDGEWORTHSTOWN, April 11, 1795.

My father and Lovell have been out almost every day, when there are no robbers to be committed to jail, at the Logograph.[1] This is the new name instead of the Telegraph, because of its allusion to the logographic printing press, which prints words instead of letters. Phænologue was thought of, but Logograph sounds better. My father will allow me to manufacture an

___
[1] A name invented to suit the anti-Gallican prejudices of the day.

essay on the Logograph, he furnishing the solid materials and I spinning them.   I am now looking over, for this purpose, Wilkins's "Real Character, or an Essay towards a Universal Philosophical Language."   It is a scarce and very ingenious book; some of the phraseology is so much out of the present fashion that it would make you smile: such as the synonym for a little man, a Dandiprat.   Likewise two prints — one of them a long sheet of men with their throats cut, so as to show the windpipe whilst working out the different letters of the alphabet; the other print of all the birds and beasts packed ready to go into the ark.

Sir Walter James has written a very kind and sensible letter to my father, promising all his influence with his Viceregal brother-in-law about the telegraph.   My father means to get a letter from him to Lord Camden, and present it himself, though he rather doubts whether, all things taken together, it is prudent to tie himself to government.   The raising the militia has occasioned disturbances in this county.   Lord Granard's carriage was pelted at Athlone.   The poor people here are robbed every night.   Last night a poor old woman was considerably roasted: the man, who called himself Captain Roast, is committed to jail; he was positively sworn to here this morning.   Do you know what they mean by the White Tooths?   Men who stick two pieces of broken tobacco pipes at each corner of the mouth, to disguise the face and voice.

April 20.

Here is a whirlwind in our county, and no angel to direct it, though many booted and spurred desire no

better than to ride *in* it. There is indeed an old
woman in Ballymahon, who has been the guardian angel
of General Crosby; she has averted a terrible storm,
which was just ready to burst over his head. The
General, by mistake, went into the town of Ballymahon,
before his troops came up; and while he was in the inn,
a mob of five hundred people gathered in the street.
The landlady of the inn called General Crosby aside,
and told him that if the people found him they would
certainly tear him to pieces. The General hesitated,
but the abler general, the landlady, sallied forth and
called aloud in a distinct voice, "Bring round the
chaise-and-four for the gentleman *from* Lanesborough,
who is going *to* Athlone." The General got into the
chaise incog., and returning towards Athlone met his
troops, and thus effected a most admirable retreat.

Monday Night.

Richard [1] and Lovell are at the Bracket Gate. I
hope you know the Bracket Gate: it is near Mr. Whit-
ney's, and so called, as tradition informs me, from being
painted red and white like a bracket cow. I am not
clear what sort of an animal a bracket cow is, but I
suppose it is something not unlike a dun cow and a gate
joined together. Richard and Lovell have a nice tent,
and a clock, and white lights, and are trying nocturnal
telegraphs, which are now brought to satisfactory perfection.

I am finishing "Toys and Tasks;" I wish I might
insert your letter to Sneyd,[2] with the receipt for the

[1] His last visit to Ireland. He returned to America, and died there,
in 1796.

[2] Mrs. Elizabeth Edgeworth's second boy.

dye, as a specimen of experiments for children. Sneyd with sparkling eyes returns you his sincere thanks, and my mother with her love sends you the following lines, which she composed to-day for him: —

> "To give me all that art can give,
> My aunt and mother try :
> One teaches me the way to live,
> The other how to *dye*."

But though she makes epigrams, my mother is far from well.

This year "Letters for Literary Ladies," Miss Edgeworth's first published work, was produced by Johnson. In 1796 she published the collection of stories known as "The Parent's Assistant." In these, in the simplest language, and with wonderful understanding of children and what would come home to their hearts, she continued to illustrate the maxims of her father. The "Purple Jar" and "Lazy Lawrence" are perhaps the best known stories of the first edition. To another was added "Simple Susan," of which Sir Walter Scott said, "that when the boy brings back the lamb to the little girl, there is nothing for it but to put down the book and cry." Most of these stories were written in the excitement of very troubled times in Ireland.

TO MRS. RUXTON.

EDGEWORTHSTOWN,
Saturday Night, January, 1796.

My father is gone to a Longford committee, where he will, I suppose, hear many dreadful Defender stories: he came home yesterday fully persuaded that a poor man in this neighborhood, a Mr. Houlton, had been murdered; but he found he was only *kilt*, and "as well as could be expected," after being twice robbed and twice cut with a bayonet. You, my dear aunt, who were so brave when the county of Meath was the seat of war, must know that we emulate your courage; and I assure you in your own words, "that whilst our terrified neighbors see nightly visions of massacres, we sleep with our doors and windows unbarred."

I must observe, though, that it is only those doors and windows which have neither bolts nor bars that we leave unbarred, and these are more at present than we wish, even for the reputation of our valor. All that I crave for my own part is, that if I am to have my throat cut, it may not be by a man with his face blackened with charcoal. I shall look at every person that comes here very closely, to see if there be any marks of charcoal upon their visages. Old wrinkled offenders I should suppose would never be able to wash out their stains; but in others a *very* clean face will in my mind be a strong symptom of guilt, clean hands proof positive, and clean nails ought to hang a man.

TO MISS SOPHY RUXTON.

EDGEWORTHSTOWN, February 27, 1796.

Long may you feel impatient to hear from your friends, my dear Sophy, and long may you express your impatience as agreeably. I have a great deal bottled, or rather bundled up for you. Though I most earnestly wish that my father was in that situation [1] which Sir T. Fetherstone now graces, and though my father had done

---

[1] M. P. for the County of Longford.

me the honor to let me copy his election letters for him, I am not the least infected with the electioneering rage. Whilst the election lasted we saw him only a few minutes in the course of the day; then indeed he entertained us to our heart's content; now his mind seems relieved from a disagreeable load, and we have more of his company.

You do not mention Madame Roland, therefore I am not sure whether you have read her; if you have only read her in the translation which talks of her Uncle Bimont's dying of a "fit of the gout *translated* to his chest," you have done her injustice. We think some of her memoirs beautifully written, and like Rousseau: she was a great woman and died heroically, but I don't think she became more amiable, and certainly not more happy by meddling with politics; *for* — her head is cut off, and her husband has shot himself. I think if I had been Mons. Roland I should not have shot myself for her sake, and I question whether he would not have left undrawn the trigger if he could have seen all she intended to say of him to posterity: she has painted him as a harsh, stiff, pedantic man, to whom she devoted herself from a sense of duty; her own superiority, and his infinite obligations to her, she has taken sufficient pains to blazon forth to the world. I do not like all this, and her duty work, and her full-length portrait *of* herself *by* herself. The foolish and haughty Madame De Boismorrel, who sat upon the sofa, and asked her if she ever wore feathers, was probably one of the remote causes of the French Revolution: for Madame Roland's republican spirit seems to have retained a long and lively remembrance of this aristocratic visit.

As soon as the blind bookseller[1] can find them for us, we shall read Miss Williams's "Letters." I am glad we both prefer the same parts in Dr. Aikin's "Letters:" I liked that on the choice of a wife, but I beg to except the word *helper*, which is used so often and is associated with a helper in the stables. Lovell dined with Mr. Aikin at Mr. Stewart's, at Edinburgh, and has seen the Count d'Artois, who he says has rather a silly face, especially when it smiles. Sneyd is delighted with the four volumes of "Evenings at Home," which we have just got, and has pitched upon the best stories, which he does not, like M. Dalambert, spoil in the reading — "Perseverance against Fortune," "The Price of a Victory," and "Capriole." We were reading an account of the pinna the other day, and very much regretted that your pinna's brown silk tuft had been eaten by the mice — what will they not eat? — they have eaten my thimble case! I am sorry to say that, from these last accounts of the pinna and his cancer friend, Dr. Darwin's beautiful description is more poetic than accurate. The cancer is neither watchman nor market-woman to the pinna, nor yet his friend: he has free ingress to his house, it is true, and is often found there, but he does not visit on equal terms or on a friendly footing, for the moment the pinna gets him in he shuts the door and eats him; or, if he is not hungry, kills the poor shrimp and keeps him in the house till the next day's dinner. I am sorry Dr. Darwin's story is not true.

[1] A peddler who travelled through the country, and sometimes picked up at sales curious books new and old.

Saturday Night.

I do not know whether you ever heard of a Mr. Pallas, who lives at Grouse Hall. He lately received information that a certain Defender was to be found in a lone house, which was described to him; he took a party of men with him in the night, and got to the house very early in the morning: it was scarcely light. The soldiers searched the house, but no man was to be found. Mr. Pallas ordered them to search again, for that he was certain the man was there; they searched again, in vain. They gave up the point, and were preparing to mount their horses, when one man, who had stayed a little behind his companions, saw something moving at the end of the garden behind the house; he looked again, and beheld a man's arm come out of the ground. He ran towards the spot and called his companions, but the arm had disappeared; they searched, but nothing was to be seen, and though the soldier persisted in his story he was not believed. "Come," said one of the party, "don't waste your time here looking for an apparition among these cabbage-stalks; come back once more to the house." They went to the house, and there stood the man they were in search of, in the middle of the kitchen.

Upon examination, it was found that a secret passage had been practiced from the kitchen to the garden, opening under an old meal chest with a false bottom, which he could push up and down at pleasure. He had returned one moment too soon.

I beg, dear Sophy, that you will not call my little stories by the sublime title of "my works;" I shall else be ashamed when the little mouse comes forth. The stories are printed and bound the same size as "Evenings at Home," but I am afraid you will dislike the title; my father had sent "The Parent's Friend,"[1] but Mr. Johnson has degraded it into "The Parent's Assistant," which I dislike particularly, from association with an old book of arithmetic called "The Tutor's Assistant."

This was the first appearance of "The Parent's Assistant," in one small volume, with the "Purple Jar," which afterwards formed part of "Rosamond."

TO MRS. RUXTON.

1796.

We heard from Lovell[2] last post. He had reached London, and waited immediately on Colonel Brownrigg, who was extremely civil, and said he would present him any day he pleased to the Duke of York. He was delighted with the telegraphic prospect in his journey: from Nettlebed to Long Compton, a distance of fifty miles, he saw plainly. He was afraid that the motion of the stage would have been too violent to agree with his model telegraph — "his pretty, delicate little telly," as Lovell calls it. He therefore indulged her all the way with a seat in a post-chaise, "which I bestowed upon her with pleasure, because I am convinced that, when she comes to stand in the world upon ground of her own, she will be an honor to her guardian, her parents, and her country."

---

[1] Mr. Edgeworth had wished the book to bear this title.
[2] Gone to London with Mr. Edgeworth's telegraphic invention.

Miss Edgeworth now began to write some of the stories which were afterwards published under the title of "Moral Tales," but which she at first intended as a sequel to "The Parent's Assistant;" and she began to think of writing "Irish Bulls."

TO MISS SOPHY RUXTON.

Edgeworthstown, October, 1797.

I do not like to pour out the gratitude I feel for your unremitting kindness to me, my dear Sophy, in vain thanks; but I may as well pour it out in words, as I shall probably never be able to return the many good turns you have done me. I am not nearly ready yet for "Irish Bulls." I am going directly to "Parent's Assistant." Any good anecdotes from the age of five to fifteen, good latitude and longitude, will suit me; and if you can tell me any pleasing misfortunes of emigrants, so much the better. I have a great desire to draw a picture of an anti-Mademoiselle Panache, a well-informed, well-bred French governess, an emigrant.

By the blind bookseller my father will send you some books, and I hope that we shall soon have finished Godwin, that he may set out for Black Castle. There are some parts of his book[1] that I think you will like much — "On Frankness" and "Self-taught Genius;" but you will find much to blame in his style, and you will be surprised that he should have written a dissertation upon English style. I think his essay on Avarice and Profusion will please you, even after Smith; he has gone a step farther. I am going to write a story for boys,[2] which will, I believe, make a volume to fol-

----

[1] *Essays*, by the author of *Caleb Williams*.　　　[2] *The Good Aunt.*

low the "Good French Governess." My father thinks a volume of trials and a volume of plays would be good for children. He met the other day with two men who were ready to go to law about a horse which one had bought from the other, because he had one little fault. "What is the fault?" said my father. "Sir, the horse was standing with us all the other day in our cabin at the fire, and plump he fell down upon the middle of the fire and put it out; and it was a mercy he did n't kill my wife and children, as he fell into the midst of them all. But this is not all, sir; he strayed into a neighbor's field of oats, and fell down in the midst of the oats, and spoiled as much as he could have eaten honestly in a week. But that 's not all, sir; one day, please your honor, I rode him out in a hurry to a fair, and he lay down with me in the ford, and I lost my fair."

Mrs. Edgeworth died in November, 1797.

For the last few years Mrs. Elizabeth Edgeworth's sisters, Charlotte and Mary Sneyd, had lived entirely at Edgeworthstown, not only beloved and honored by the children of their two sisters, but tenderly welcomed and cherished by the children of their predecessors, especially by Maria, to whom no real aunts could have been more dear. During the seventeen years through which her married life lasted, Mrs. Elizabeth Edgeworth had become increasingly the centre of the family circle, to which she had herself added five sons and four daughters. In every relation of life she was admirable. Through the summer of 1797 her health rapidly declined, and in November she died.

Mr. Edgeworth, then past fifty, had truly valued his

third wife, of whom he said that he had "never seen her out of temper, and never received from her an unkind word or an angry look." Yet, when he lost her, after his peculiar fashion he immediately began to think of marrying again.

Dr. Beaufort, Vicar of Collon, was an agreeable and cultivated man, and had long been a welcome guest at Mrs. Ruxton's house of Black Castle. His eldest daughter, who was a clever artist, had designed and drawn some illustrations for Maria Edgeworth's stories. With these Mr. Edgeworth found fault, and the good-humor and sense with which his criticisms were received charmed him, and led to an intimacy. Six months after his wife's death he married Miss Beaufort.

It may sound strange, but it is nevertheless true, that in Miss Beaufort, even more than in her predecessors, he gave to his children a wise and kind mother, and a most entirely devoted friend.

TO MISS BEAUFORT.

EDGEWORTHSTOWN, May 16, 1798.

Whilst you, my dear Miss Beaufort, have been toiling in Dublin, my father has been delighting himself in preparations for June. The little boudoir looks as if it intends to be pretty. This is the only room in the house which my father will allow to be finished, as he wishes that your taste should finish the rest. Like the man who begged to have the eclipse put off, we have been here praying to have the spring put off, as this place never looks so pretty as when the lilacs and laburnums are in full flower. I fear, notwithstanding all our prayers, that their purple and yellow honors will be

gone before your arrival. There is one other flower
which I am sure will not be in blow for you, "a little
western flower called love in idleness." Amongst the
many kindnesses my father has shown me, the greatest,
I think, has been his permitting me to see his heart *à
découverte ;* and I have seen, by your kind sincerity
and his, that, in good and cultivated minds, love is no
idle passion, but one that inspires useful and generous
energy. I have been convinced by your example of
what I was always inclined to believe, that the power
of feeling affection is increased by the cultivation of the
understanding. The wife of an Indian yogii (if a yogii
be permitted to have a wife) might be a very affectionate woman, but her sympathy with her husband could
not have a very extensive sphere. As his eyes are to
be continually fixed upon the point of his nose, hers
in duteous sympathy must squint in like manner; and
if the perfection of his virtue be to sit so still that the
birds (*vide* Sacontala) may unmolested build nests in
his hair, his wife cannot better show her affection than
by yielding her tresses to them with similar patient stupidity. Are there not European yogiis, or men whose
ideas do not go much further than *le bout du nez?*
And how delightful it must be to be chained for better
for worse to one of this species! I should guess — for
I know nothing of the matter — that the courtship of
an ignorant lover must be almost as insipid as a marriage
with him; for "my jewel" continually repeated, without new setting, must surely fatigue a little.

You call yourself, dear Miss Beaufort, my friend and
companion; I hope you will never have reason to repent
beginning in this style towards me. I think you will

not find me encroach upon you. The overflowings of your kindness, if I know anything of my own heart, will fertilize the land, but will not destroy the land-marks. I do not know whether I most hate or despise the temper which will take an ell where an inch is given. A well-bred person never forgets that species of respect which is due to situation and rank: though his superiors in rank treat him with the utmost conde-scension, he never is "Hail fellow well met" with them; he never calls them Jack or Tom by way of increasing his own consequence.

I flatter myself that you will find me gratefully exact *en belle fille.* I think there is a great deal of difference between that species of ceremony which exists with acquaintance, and that which should always exist with the best of friends: the one prevents the growth of affection, the other preserves it in youth and age. Many foolish people make fine plantations, and forget to fence them; so the young trees are destroyed by the young cattle, and the bark of the forest trees is sometimes injured. You need not, dear Miss Beaufort, fence yourself round with very strong palings in this family, where all have been early accustomed to mind their boundaries. As for me, you see my intentions, or at least my theories, are good enough; if my practice be but half as good, you will be content, will you not? But Theory was born in Brobdignag, and Practice in Lilliput. So much the better for *me.* I have often considered, since my return home, as I have seen all this family pursuing their several occupations and amusements, how much you will have it in your power to add to their happiness. In a stupid or indolent family, your knowledge and talents would be thrown away; here, if it may be said without vanity, they will be the certain source of your daily happiness. You will come into a new family, but you will not come as a stranger, dear Miss Beaufort: you will not lead a new life, but only continue to lead the life you have been used to in your own happy, cultivated family.

Mr. Edgeworth and Miss Beaufort were married 31st May, 1798, at St. Anne's Church in Dublin. Mrs. Edgeworth writes: —

We set off from the church door for Edgeworthstown, and the rebellion had broken out in many parts of Ireland.

Soon after we had passed the second stage from Dublin, one of the carriage wheels broke down. Mr. Edgeworth went back to the inn, then called the Nineteen-mile House,[1] to get assistance. Very few people were to be found, and a woman who was alone in the kitchen came up to him and whispered, "The boys [the rebels] are hid in the potato furrows beyond." He was rather startled at this intelligence, but took no notice. He found an ostler who lent him a wheel, which they managed to put on, and we drove off without being stopped by any of *the boys*. A little farther on I saw something very odd on the side of the road before us. "What is that?" "Look to the other side — don't look at it!" cried Mr. Edgeworth; and when we had passed he said it was a car turned up, between the shafts of which a man was hung — murdered by the rebels.

[1] Now Enfield; a railway station.

We reached Edgeworthstown late in the evening. The family at that time consisted of the two Miss Sneyds, Maria, Emmeline, Bessy, Charlotte (Lovell was then at Edinburgh), Henry, Sneyd, Honora, and William. Sneyd was not twelve years old, and the other two were much younger. All agreed in making me feel at once at home, and part of the family; all received me with the most unaffected cordiality, but from Maria it was something more. She more than fulfilled the promise of her letter; she made me at once her most intimate friend; and in all the serious concerns of life, and in every trifle of the day, treated me with the most generous confidence.

MARIA TO MISS SOPHY RUXTON IN NORTH WALES.

EDGEWORTHSTOWN, June 20, 1798.

Hitherto all has been quiet in our county, and we know nothing of the dreadful disturbances in other parts of the country but what we see in the newspapers. I am sorry my uncle and Richard were obliged to leave you and my dear aunt, as I know the continual state of suspense and anxiety in which you must live while they are away. I fear that we may soon know by experience what you feel, for my father sees in to-night's paper that Lord Cornwallis is coming over here as Lord-Lieutenant; and he thinks it will be his duty to offer his services in any manner in which they can be advantageous. Why cannot we be left in peace to enjoy our happiness? that is all we have the conscience to ask! We are indeed happy: the more I see of my friend and mother, the more I love and esteem her, and the more I feel the truth of all that I have heard you say in her

praise. I do not think I am *much* prejudiced by her
partiality for me, though I do feel most grateful for
her kindness. I never saw my father at any period of
his life appear so happy as he does, and has done for
this month past; and you know that he *tastes* happiness
as much as any human being can. He is not of the
number of those *qui avalent leurs plaisirs, il sait les
gouter.* So little change has been made in the way of
living, that you would feel as if you were going on with
your usual occupations and conversation amongst us.
We laugh and talk, and enjoy the good of every day,
which is more than sufficient. How long this may last
we cannot tell. I am going on in the old way, writing
stories. I cannot be a captain of dragoons, and sitting
with my hands before me would not make any of us
one degree safer. I know nothing more of "Practical
Education;" it is advertised to be published. I have
finished a volume of wee-wee stories, about the size of
the "Purple Jar," all about Rosamond. "Simple
Susan" went to Foxhall a few days ago, for Lady Anne
to carry to England.

My father has made our little rooms so nice for us;
they are all fresh painted and papered. Oh, rebels!
oh, French! spare them! We have never injured you,
and all we wish is to see everybody as happy as ourselves.

EDGEWORTHSTOWN, August 29, 1798.

We have this moment learned from the sheriff of this
county, Mr. Wilder, who has been at Athlone, that the
French have got to Castlebar. They changed clothes
with some peasants, and so deceived our troops. They

have almost entirely cut off the carbineers, the Longford
militia, and a large body of yeomanry who opposed
them. The Lord-Lieutenant is now at Athlone, and it
is supposed that it will be their next object of attack.
My father's corps of yeomanry are extremely attached
to him, and seem fully in earnest; but, alas! by some
strange negligence their arms have not yet arrived from
Dublin. My father this morning sent a letter by an
officer going to Athlone, to Lord Cornwallis, offering
his services to convey intelligence or reconnoitre, as he
feels himself in a most terrible situation, without arms
for his men, and no power of being serviceable to his
country. We who are so near the scene of action cannot by any means discover what *number* of the French
actually landed; some say 800, some 1800, some 18,000,
some 4000. The troops march and countermarch, as
they say themselves, without knowing where they are
going, or for what.

Poor Lady Anne Fox![1] she is in a dreadful situation;
so near her confinement she is unable to move from
Foxhall to any place of greater safety, and exposed
every moment to hear the most alarming reports. She
shows admirable calmness and strength of mind. Francis and Barry[2] set out to-morrow morning for England; as they do not go near Conway, my father ad-
vises me not to send by them "Simple Susan" and
sundry other little volumes which I wish were in your
kind hands.

God send the French may soon go, and that you may
soon come.

[1] Wife of Mrs. Edgeworth's nephew.
[2] Brothers of the fourth Mrs. Edgeworth.

TO MRS. RUXTON.

Mrs. FALLON'S INN, LONGFORD,
September 5, 1798.

We are all safe and well, my dearest aunt, and have had two most fortunate escapes from rebels and from the explosion of an ammunition cart. Yesterday we heard, about ten o'clock in the morning, that a large body of rebels, armed with pikes, were within a few miles of Edgeworthstown. My father's yeomanry were at this moment gone to Longford for their arms, which Government had delayed sending. We were ordered to decamp, each with a small bundle; the two chaises full, and my mother and Aunt Charlotte on horseback. We were all ready to move, when the report was contradicted: only twenty or thirty men were now, it was said, in arms, and my father hoped we might still hold fast to our dear home.

Two officers and six dragoons happened at this moment to be on their way through Edgeworthstown, escorting an ammunition cart from Mullingar to Longford; they promised to take us under their protection, and the officer came up to the door to say he was ready. My father most fortunately detained us; they set out without us. Half an hour afterwards, as we were quietly sitting in the portico, we heard — as we thought close to us — a clap of thunder which shook the house. The officer soon afterwards returned, almost speechless; he could hardly explain what had happened. The ammunition cart, containing nearly three barrels of gunpowder, packed in tin cases, took fire and burst, halfway on the road to Longford. The man who drove the cart was blown to atoms — nothing of him could be found; two of the horses were killed, others were blown to pieces and their limbs scattered to a distance; the head and body of a man were found a hundred and twenty yards from the spot. Mr. Murray was the name of the officer I am speaking of: he had with him a Mr. Rochfort and a Mr. Nugent. Mr. Rochfort was thrown from his horse, one side of his face terribly burnt, and stuck over with gunpowder. He was carried into a cabin; they thought he would die, but they now say he will recover. The carriage has been sent to take him to Longford. I have not time or room, my dear aunt, to dilate or tell you half I have to say. If we had gone with this ammunition, we must have been killed.

An hour or two afterwards, however, we were obliged to fly from Edgeworthstown. The pikemen, three hundred in number, actually were within a mile of the town. My mother, Aunt Charlotte, and I rode; passed the trunk of the dead man, bloody limbs of horses, and two dead horses, by the help of men who pulled on our steeds: we are all safely lodged now in Mrs. Fallon's inn.

Mrs. Edgeworth narrates: —

Before we had reached the place where the cart had been blown up, Mr. Edgeworth suddenly recollected that he had left on the table in his study a list of the yeomanry corps, which he feared might endanger the poor fellows and their families if it fell into the hands of the rebels. He galloped back for it — it was at the hazard of his life — but the rebels had not yet appeared. He burned the paper, and rejoined us safely.

The landlady of the inn at Longford did all she could to make us comfortable, and we were squeezed into the already crowded house. Mrs. Billamore, our excellent housekeeper, we had left behind for the return of the carriage which had taken Mr. Rochfort to Longford; but it was detained, and she did not reach us till the next morning, when we learned from her that the rebels had not come up to the house. They had halted at the gate, but were prevented from entering by a man whom she did not remember to have ever seen; but he was grateful to her for having lent money to his wife when she was in great distress, and we now, at our utmost need, owed our safety and that of the house to his gratitude. We were surprised to find that this was thought by some to be a suspicious circumstance, and that it showed Mr. Edgeworth to be a favorer of the rebels! An express arrived at night to say the French were close to Longford: Mr. Edgeworth undertook to defend the jail, which commanded the road by which the enemy must pass, where they could be detained till the King's troops came up. He was supplied with men and ammunition, and watched all night; but in the morning news came that the French had turned in a different direction, and gone to Granard, about seven miles off; but this seemed so unlikely, that Mr. Edgeworth rode out to reconnoitre, and Henry went to the top of the Court House to look out with a telescope. We were all at the windows of a room in the inn looking into the street, when we saw people running, throwing up their hats and huzzaing. A dragoon had just arrived with the news that General Lake's army had come up with the French and the rebels, and completely defeated them at a place called Ballinamuck, near Granard.　But we soon saw a man in a sergeant's uniform haranguing the mob, not in honor of General Lake's victory, but against Mr. Edgeworth; we distinctly heard the words, "that young Edgeworth ought to be dragged down from the Court House."　The landlady was terrified; she said Mr. Edgeworth was accused of having made signals to the French from the jail, and she thought the mob would pull down her house; but they ran on to the end of the town, where they expected to meet Mr. Edgeworth.　We sent a messenger in one direction to warn him, while Maria and I drove to meet him on the other road.　We heard that he had passed some time before with Major Eustace; the mob seeing an officer in uniform with him went back to the town, and on our return we found them safe at the inn.　We saw the French prisoners brought in in the evening, when Mr. Edgeworth went after dinner with Major Eustace to the barrack.　Some time after, dreadful yells were heard in the street: the mob had attacked them on their return from the barrack — Major Eustace being now in colored clothes, they did not recognize him as an officer.　They had struck Mr. Edgeworth with a brickbat in the neck, and as they were now, just in front of the inn, collaring the major, Mr. Edgeworth cried out in a loud voice, "Major Eustace is in danger."　Several officers who were at dinner in the inn, hearing the words through the open window, rushed out sword in hand, dispersed the crowd in a moment, and all the danger was over.　The military patrolled the streets, and the sergeant who had made all this disturbance was put under arrest.　He was a poor, half-crazed fanatic.

The next day, the 9th of September, we returned home, where everything was exactly as we had left it, all serene and happy, five days before — only five days, which seemed almost a lifetime, from the dangers and anxiety we had gone through.

MARIA TO MISS SOPHY RUXTON.

EDGEWORTHSTOWN, September 9, 1798.

You will rejoice, I am sure, my dear Sophy, to see by the date of this letter that we are safe back at Edgeworthstown. The scenes we have gone through for some days past have succeeded one another like the pictures in a magic-lantern, and have scarcely left the impression of reality upon the mind. It all seems like a dream, a mixture of the ridiculous and the horrid. "Oh ho!" says my aunt, "things cannot be very bad with my brother, if Maria begins her letters with magic-lantern and reflections on dreams."

When we got into the town this morning we saw the picture of a deserted, or rather a shattered village — many joyful faces greeted us at the doors of the houses — none of the windows of the new houses in Charlotte Row were broken: the mob declared they would not meddle with them because they were built by the two good ladies, meaning my aunts.

Last night my father was alarmed at finding that both Samuel and John,[1] who had stood by him with the utmost fidelity through the Longford business, were at length panic-struck; they wished now to leave him. Samuel said: "Sir, I would stay with you to the last

[1] John Jenkins, a Welsh lad; both he and Samuel thought better of it and remained in the service.

gasp, if you were not so foolhardy," and here he cried bitterly; "but, sir, indeed you have not heard all I have heard. I have heard about two hundred men in Longford swear they would have your life." All the town were during the whole of last night under a similar panic, they were certain the violent Longford yeomen would come and cut them to pieces. Last night was not pleasant, but this morning was pleasant — and why it was a pleasant morning I will tell you in my next.

September 19.

I forgot to tell you of a remarkable event in the history of our return; all the cats, even those who properly belong to the stable, and who had never been admitted to the honors of the sitting in the kitchen, all crowded round Kitty with congratulatory faces, crawling up her gown, insisting upon caressing and being caressed when she reappeared in the lower regions. Mr. Gilpin's slander against cats as selfish, unfeeling animals is thus refuted by stubborn facts.

When Colonel Handfield told the whole story of the Longford mob to Lord Cornwallis, he said he never saw a man so much astonished. Lord Longford, Mr. Pakenham, and Major Edward Pakenham have shown much warmth of friendship upon this occasion.

Inclosed I send you a little sketch, which I traced from one my mother drew for her father, of the situation of the field of battle at Ballinamuck. It is about four miles from The Hills. My father, mother, and I rode to look at the camp; perhaps you recollect a pretty turn in the road, where there is a little stream with a three-arched bridge: in the fields which rise in a gentle slope, on the right-hand side of this stream, about sixty bell tents were pitched, the arms all ranged on the grass; before the tents, poles with little streamers flying here and there; groups of men leading their horses to water, others filling kettles and back pots, some cooking under the hedges; the various uniforms looked pretty; Highlanders gathering blackberries. My father took us to the tent of Lord Henry Seymour, who is an old friend of his; he breakfasted here to-day, and his plain English civility, and quiet good sense, was a fine contrast to the mob, etc. Dapple,[1] your old acquaintance, did not like all the sights at the camp as well as I did.

October 3, 1798.

My father went to Dublin the day before yesterday, to see Lord Cornwallis about the Court of Inquiry on the sergeant who harangued the mob. About one o'clock to-day Lovell returned from the Assizes at Longford with the news, met on the road, that expresses had come an hour before from Granard to Longford, for the Reay Fencibles, and all the troops; that there was another *rising* and an attack upon Granard: four thousand men the first report said, seven hundred the second. What the truth may be it is impossible to tell; it is certain that the troops are gone to Granard, and it is yet more certain that all the windows in this house are built halfway up, guns and bayonets dispersed by Captain Lovell in every room. The yeomanry corps paraded to-day, all steady: guard sitting up in house and in the town to-night.

1 Maria Edgeworth's horse.

Thursday Morning.

All alive and well. A letter from my father: he stays to see Lord Cornwallis on Friday. Deficient arms for the corps are given by Lord Castlereagh.

Mrs. Edgeworth writes: —

The sergeant was to have been tried at the next sessions, but he was by this time ashamed and penitent, and Mr. Edgeworth did not press the trial, but knowing the man was, among his other weaknesses, very much afraid of ghosts, he said to him as he came out of the Court House, "I believe, after all, you had rather see me alive than have my ghost haunting you!"

In 1798 "Practical Education" was published in two large octavo volumes, bearing the joint names of Richard and Maria Edgeworth upon their title-page. This was the first work of that literary partnership of father and daughter which Maria Edgeworth describes as "the joy and pride of my life."

MARIA TO MISS SOPHY RUXTON.

EDGEWORTHSTOWN, November 19, 1798.

You have, I suppose, or are conscious that you ought to have, whitlows upon your thumb and all your four fingers for not writing to me! Tell me what you are saying and doing, and above all where you are going. My father has taken me into a new partnership — we are writing a comedy; will you come and see it acted? He is making a charming theatre in the room over his study: it will be twice as large as old Poz's little theatre in the dining-room. My aunt's woolen wig for old Poz is in high estimation in the memory of man, woman, and child here. I give you the play-bill: —

Mrs. Fangle (a rich and whimsical widow) .	Emmeline.
Caroline (a sprightly heiress)	Charlotte.
Jemima (Mrs. Fangle's waiting-maid) . .	Bessy.
Sir Mordant Idem (in love with Mrs. Fangle, and elderly, and hating anything *new*)	Henry.
Opal (nephew to Sir Mordant, and hating everything *old*, in love with Caroline, and wild for illuminatism)	Sneyd.
Count Babelhausen (a German illuminatus, trying to marry either Mrs. Fangle or Caroline)	Lovell.
Heliodorus and Christina (Mrs. Fangle's children, on whom she tries strange experiments)	William and Honora.

To explain illuminatism I refer you to Robinson's book called "Proofs of a Conspiracy." It was from this book, which gives a history of the cheats of Free-masonry and Illuminatism, that we took the idea of Count Babelhausen. The book is tiresome, and no sufficient proofs given of the facts, but parts of it will probably interest you.

Lovell has bought a fine apparatus and materials for a course of chemical lectures which he is going to give us. The study is to be the laboratory; I wish you were *in it*.

In the "Monthly Review" for October there is this anecdote. After the King of Denmark, who was somewhat silly, had left Paris, a Frenchman, who was in company with the Danish Ambassador, but did not know him, began to ridicule the King. "Ma foi! il a une tête! une tête —"   "Couronnée," replied the Ambassador, with presence of mind and politeness.   My father, who was much delighted with this answer, asked Lovell, Henry, and Sneyd, without telling the right answer, what they would have said.

> Lovell: "A head — and a heart, sir."
> Henry: "A head — upon his shoulders."
> Sneyd: "A head — of a King."

Tell me which answer you like best.   Richard will take your "Practical Education" to you.

The play mentioned in the foregoing letter was twice acted in January, 1799, with great applause, under the title of "Whim for Whim."   Mr. Edgeworth's mechanism for the scenery, and for the experiments tried on the children, were most ingenious.   Mrs. Edgeworth painted the scenery and arranged the dresses.

The day after the last performance of "Whim for Whim," the family went to Dublin for Mr. Edgeworth to attend Parliament, the last Irish Parliament, he having been returned for the borough of St. John's Town, in the County of Longford, and in the spring Mrs. Edgeworth and Maria accompanied him to England.

TO MISS CHARLOTTE SNEYD.

DUBLIN, April 2, 1799.

In the paper of to-night you will see my father's farewell speech on the Education Bill.

Some time ago, amongst some hints to the Chairman of the Committee of Education, you sent one which I have pursued: you said that the early lessons for the poor should speak with detestation of the spirit of revenge: I have just finished a little story called "Forgive and Forget," upon this idea. I am now writing one on a subject recommended to me by Dr. Beaufort, on the evils of procrastination; the title of it is "By and Bye." [1] I am very much obliged to Bessy and Charlotte for copying the Errata of "Practical Education" for me, and should be *extremely* obliged to the whole Committee of Education and Criticism at Edgeworthstown, if they would send corrections to me from their own brains; the same eye (if I may judge by my own) can only see the same things in looking over the book twenty times. Tell Sneyd that there is a political print just come out, of a woman, meant for Hibernia, dressed in orange and green, and holding a pistol in her hand to oppose the Union.

MRS. EDGEWORTH TO MRS. RUXTON.

RICHMOND PLACE, CLIFTON, May 26, 1799.

We are very well settled here, and this house is quite retired and quite quiet. The prospects are very beautiful, and we have charming green fields in which we walk, and in which dear Sophy could botanize at her ease.

A young man, a Mr. Davy,[2] at Dr. Beddoes', who has applied himself much to chemistry, has made some discoveries of importance, and enthusiastically expects wonders will be performed by the use of certain gases, which inebriate in the most delightful manner, having

---

[1] The title was afterwards changed to "To-morrow."

[2] Sir Humphry Davy, the distinguished chemist and philosopher, born 1778, died 1829.

the oblivious effects of Lethe, and at the same time giving the rapturous sensations of the Nectar of the Gods! Pleasure even to madness is the consequence of this draught. But faith, great faith, is I believe necessary to produce any effect upon the drinkers, and I have seen some of the adventurous philosophers who sought in vain for satisfaction in the bag of *Gaseous Oxyd*, and found nothing but a sick stomach and a giddy head.

"Our stay at Clifton was made very agreeable," writes Mrs. Edgeworth, "by the charm of Dr. and Mrs. Beddoes' society;[1] her grace, genius, vivacity, and kindness, and his great abilities, knowledge, and benevolence, rendered their house extremely pleasant. We met at Clifton Mr. and Mrs. Barbauld. He was an amiable and benevolent man, so eager against the slave-trade that, when he drank tea with us, he always brought some East India sugar, that he might not share our wickedness in eating that made by the negro slave. Mrs. Barbauld, whose ' Evenings at Home ' had so much delighted Maria and her father, was very pretty, and conversed with great ability in admirable language."

MARIA TO MRS. RUXTON.

CLIFTON, June 5, 1799.

Good news, my dearest aunt, my mother is fast asleep: she has a fine little daughter, who has just fin-

---

[1] Dr. Beddoes, described by Sir Humphry Davy as "short and fat, with nothing *externally* of genius or science," was very peculiar. One of his hobbies was to convey cows into invalids' bedrooms, that they might "inhale the breath of the animals," a prescription which naturally gave umbrage to the Clifton lodging-house-keepers, who protested that they had not built or furnished their rooms for the troops of cattle. Mrs. Beddoes had a wonderful charm of wit and cheerfulness.

ished eating a hearty supper. At nine minutes before six this evening, to my great joy, my little sister Fanny came into the world.

We are impatient for dear Sophy's arrival. My father sends his kindest love to his dear sister, who has been always the sharer of his pains and pleasures. I said my mother was asleep, and though my father and I talk in our sleep, all people do not; if she did, I am sure she would say, "Love to my Sister Ruxton, and my friend Letty."

During this summer the Edgeworths visited Dr. Darwin, whom Maria Edgeworth considered not only a first-rate genius, but one of the most benevolent, as well as wittiest of men. He stuttered, but far from this lessening the charm of his conversation, Miss Edgeworth used to say that the hesitation and slowness with which his words came forth added to the effect of his humor and shrewd good sense. Dr. Darwin's sudden death, 17th April, 1802, whilst he was writing to Mr. Edgeworth, was a great sorrow to his Irish friends.

The family returned home in September, 1799.

MARIA TO MISS RUXTON, LIVING AT ARUNDEL IN SUSSEX.

EDGEWORTHSTOWN, January 29, 1800.

More precious to us than Arundelian marbles are letters from Arundel, and after an interval of almost three months dear Sophy's letter was most welcome. I have no complaints to make of you — *sorrow* bit of right have I to complain of you. Some time ago we took a walk to see the old castle of Cranalagh, from which in

the last Rebellion (but one) Lady Edgeworth was turned
out; part of it, just enough to swear by, remains to this
day, and with a venerable wig of ivy at top cuts a very
respectable figure; and, moreover, there are some of the
finest laurels and hollies there that I ever saw, and as
fine a smell of a pigsty as ever I smelt, and an arbor-
vitæ tree, of which I gathered a leaf, and thought that
I and my gloves should never for the remainder of our
lives get rid of the smell of bad apples, of which this
same tree of life smells.   But I have not yet come to
the thing I was going to say about the castle of Cranalagh, viz. — for I love old-fashioned viz. — when we
got near the ruined castle, out comes a barking dog, just
such another as assailed us at the old castle near Black
Castle, to which we walked full fifteen years ago; the
first walk I ever took with Sophy, and how she got
home without her shoe, to this hour I cannot compre-
hend.   It was this barking dog which brought you
immediately to my mind, and if I have given you too
much of it you must forgive me.   Now we are upon
the subject of old castles, do you remember my retailing
to you, at second hand, a description of my father's
visit to the Marquis de la Poype's old chateau in Dauphiny, with the cavern of bats and stalactites?   A little
while ago my father received a letter in a strange hand,
which I copy for my aunt and you, as I think it will
please you as it did us, to see that this old friend of my
father's remembers him with so much kindness through
all the changes and chances that have happened in
France.   The letter is from the Marquis de la Poype,
who addressed it to the Abbé Edgeworth, in hopes that
the Abbé could transmit it to my father — the lines at

the end are in the Abbé's own hand — the handwriting of so great and good a man is a curiosity.

Before this reaches you my father will be in Dublin: he goes on Saturday next to the call of the House for the grand Union business. Tell my aunt that he means to speak on the subject on Monday. His sentiments are unchanged: that the Union would be advantageous to all the parties concerned, but that England has not any right to do to Ireland *good against her will.*

Will you tell me what means you have of getting parcels from London to Arundel? because I wish to send to my aunt a few "Popular Tales," which I have finished, as they cannot be wanted for some months by Mr. Johnson. We have begged Johnson to send "Castle Rackrent:"[1] I hope it has reached you: do not mention to any one that it is ours. Have you seen "Moral Morals," by Mrs. Smith? There is in it a beautiful little botanical poem called the "Calendar of Flora."

"Castle Rackrent," the story of an Irish estate, as told by Thady, the old steward, was first published anonymously in 1800. Its combination of Irish humour and pathos, and its illustration of the national character, first led Walter Scott to try his own skill in depicting Scotch character in the same way. "If I could," he said to James Ballantyne, "but hit Miss Edgeworth's wonderful power of vivifying all her persons, and making them live as *beings* in your mind, I should not be afraid." With the publication of "Castle Rackrent," which was intended to depict the follies of fashionable

[1] Published without the author's name in 1800.

life, and was speedily followed by "Belinda,"[1] the Edgeworths immediately became famous, and the books were at once translated into French and German.

TO MISS SOPHY RUXTON.

EDGEWORTHSTOWN, October 20, 1800.

This morning dear Henry[2] took leave of home, and set out for Edinburgh. "God prosper him," as I in the language of a fond old nurse keep continually saying to myself.

Mr. Chenevix, a famous chemist, was so good as to come here lately to see my father upon the faith of Mr. Kirwan's assurance that he would "like Mr. Edgeworth." I often wished for you, my dear Sophy, whilst this gentleman was here, because you would have been so much entertained with his conversation about bogs, and mines, and airs, and acids, etc., etc. His history of his imprisonment during the French Revolution in Paris I found more to my taste. When he was thrown into prison he studied Chaptal and Lavoisier's "Chemistry" with all his might, and then represented himself as an English gentleman come over to study chemistry in France, and M. Chaptal got him released, and employed him, and he got acquainted with all the chemists and scientific men in France. Mr. Chenevix has taken a house in Brook Street, London, and turned the cellar into a laboratory; the people were much afraid to let it to him, they expected he would blow it up.

1 There is no doubt that *Belinda* was much marred by the alterations made by Mr. Edgeworth, in whose wisdom and skill his far cleverer daughter had unlimited and touching confidence.

2 Eldest son of Mrs. Elizabeth Edgeworth.

EDGEWORTHSTOWN, December 2, 1800.

My mother has had a sore throat, and Aunt Charlotte
and Honora have had feverish attacks, and John Jenkins has had fever, so that my father was obliged to
remove him to his own house in the village.   There
has been and is a fever in the lanes of Edgeworthstown,
and so quickly does ill news fly, that this got before us
to Collon, to the Speaker's, where we were invited, and
had actually set out last week to spend a few days there.
When we got to Allenstown, we were told that a servant from the Speaker's had arrived with a letter, and
had gone on to Edgeworthstown with it; we waited for
his return with the letter, which was to forbid our going
to Collon, as Mrs. Foster, widow of the Bishop, was
there with her daughters, and was afraid of our bringing
infection!   We performed quarantine very pleasantly
for a week at Allenstown.   Mrs. Waller's inexhaustible
fund of kindness and generosity is like Aboulcasin's
treasure, it is not only inexhaustible, but take what you
will from it it cannot be perceptibly diminished.   Harriet Beaufort[1] is indeed a charming excellent girl; I
love and esteem her more and more as I know her better; she has been at different times between three and
four months in the house with us, and I have had full
opportunities of seeing down to the kitchen, and up to
the garret of her mind.

You are so near Johnson,[2] that you must of course
know more of Maria's sublime works than Maria knows
of them herself; and besides Lovell, who thinks of
them ten times more than Johnson, has not let you
burst in ignorance.   An octavo edition of "Practical

---

[1] Sister of Mrs. Edgeworth.   [2] The bookseller.

Education" is to come out at Christmas; we have seen a volume, which looks as well as can be expected. The two first parts of "Early Lessons," containing Harry and Lucy, two wee-wee volumes, have just come over to us. Frank and Rosamond will, I suppose, come after with all convenient speed. How "Moral Tales" are arranged, or in what size they are to appear, I do not know, but I guess they will soon be published, because some weeks ago we received four engravings for frontispieces; they are beautifully engraved by Neagle, and do justice to the designs, two of which are by my mother, and two by Charlotte. I hope you will like them. There are three stories which will be new to you, "The Knapsack," "The Prussian Vase," and "Angelina."

Now, my dear friend, you cannot say that I do not tell you what I am doing. My father is employed making out Charts of History and Chronology, such as are mentioned in "Practical Education." He has just finished a little volume containing Explanations of Poetry for children: it explains the "Elegy in a Country Churchyard," "L'Allegro," "Il Penseroso," and the "Ode to Fear." It will be a very useful schoolbook. It goes over to-night to Johnson, but how long it will remain with him before you see it in print I cannot divine.

Mrs. Edgeworth narrates: —

"Belinda" was published in 1801. Maria was at Black Castle when the first copy reached her; she contrived, before her aunt saw it, to tear out the title-pages of the three volumes, and her aunt read it without the least suspicion of who was the author, and excessively entertained and delighted, she insisted on Maria's listening to passage after passage as she went on. Maria affected to be deeply interested in some book she held in her hand, and when Mrs. Ruxton exclaimed, "Is not that admirably written?" Maria coldly replied, "Admirably read, I think." And then her aunt, as if she had said too much, added, "It may not be so very good, but it shows just the sort of knowledge of high life which people have who live in the world." Then again and again she called upon Maria for her sympathy, till quite provoked at her faint acquiescence, she at last accused her of being envious: "I am sorry to see my little Maria unable to bear the praises of a rival author."

At this Maria burst into tears, and showing her aunt the title-page she declared herself the author. But Mrs. Ruxton was not pleased — she never liked "Belinda" afterwards, and Maria had always a painful recollection of her aunt's suspecting her of the meanness of envy.

In 1801 a second edition of "Castle Rackrent" was published, by Maria Edgeworth, as its success was so triumphant that some one — I heard his name at the time but do not now remember it, and it is better forgotten — not only asserted that he was the author, but actually took the trouble to copy out several pages with corrections and erasures, as if it was his original MS.!

The "Essay on Irish Bulls" was published in 1802, by R. L. Edgeworth and Maria Edgeworth, author of "Castle Rackrent." A gentleman, much interested in improving the breed of Irish cattle, sent, on seeing the advertisement, for this work on Irish Bulls; he was rather confounded by the appearance of the classical bull at the top of the first page, which I had designed from a gem, and when he began to read the book he threw it away in disgust; he had purchased it as Secretary to the Irish Agricultural Society.

Of the partnership in this book, Miss Edgeworth writes long afterwards: —

The first design of the essay was my father's; under the semblance of attack, he wished to show the English public the eloquence, wit, and talents of the lower classes of people in Ireland. Working zealously upon the ideas which he suggested, sometimes what was spoken by him was afterwards written by me; or when I wrote my first thoughts, they were corrected and improved by him; so that no book was ever written more completely in partnership. On this, as on most subjects, whether light or serious, when we wrote together, it would now be difficult, almost impossible, to recollect which thoughts were originally his and which were mine.

The notes on the Dublin shoeblacks' metaphorical language are chiefly his. I have heard him tell that story with all the natural, indescribable Irish tones and gestures of which written language can give but a faint idea. He excelled in imitating the Irish, because he never overstepped the modesty or the assurance of nature. He marked exquisitely the happy confidence, the shrewd wit of the people, without condescending to produce effect by caricature. He knew not only their comic talents, but their powers of pathos; and often when he had just heard from me some pathetic complaint, he has repeated it to me while the impression was fresh. In his chapter on Wit and Eloquence, in "Irish Bulls," there is a speech of a poor freeholder to a candidate who asked for his vote: this speech was made to my father when he was canvassing the county of Longford. It was repeated to me a few hours afterwards, and I wrote it down instantly without, I believe, the variation of a word.

TO MISS RUXTON.

EDGEWORTHSTOWN, August 1, 1802.

You are a goose or a gosling, whichever you like best, for I perceive you are in great anxiety lest my poor little imagination should not have been completely set to rights. Now set your heart at ease, for I, putting my left hand upon my heart, because I could not conveniently put my right, which holds the pen, though I acknowledge that would be much more graceful, do hereby declare that I perfectly understood and understand the explanation contained in your last, and am fully satisfied, righted, and delighted therewith.

I have been much interested by the "Letters from Lausanne;" I think them in some parts highly pathetic and eloquent, but as to the moral tendency of the book I cannot find it out, turn it which way I will. I think the author wrote merely with the intention of showing how well he could paint passion, and he has succeeded. The Savage of Aveyron [1] is a thousand times more inter-

____

[1] A little history of a boy found in France, "a wild man of the

esting to me than Caliste. I have not read anything
for years that interested me so much. Mr. Chenevix
will be here in a few days, when we will cross-question
him about this savage, upon whom the eyes of civil-
ized Europe have been fixed. Mr. Chenevix and his
sister, Mrs. Tuite, and with them Mrs. Jephson, spent a
day here last week: she is clever and agreeable. What
did you think of M. Pictet's account of Edgeworthstown ?

Professor Marc-Auguste Pictet, of Geneva, visited the
Edgeworths this summer, coming over from Mr. Tuite's,
of Sonna, where he was staying with Mr. Chenevix.
He afterwards published an interesting account of his
visit to Edgeworthstown in the "Bibliothèque Britan-
nique," as well as in his "Voyage de trois mois en
Angleterre," which was published at Geneva in 1802.
Of Maria Edgeworth he says: —

"I had persuaded myself that the author of the work
on Education, and of other productions, useful as well
as ornamental, would betray herself by a remarkable
exterior. I was mistaken. A small figure, eyes nearly
always lowered, a profoundly modest and reserved air,
with expression in the features when not speaking: such
was the result of my first survey. But when she
spoke, which was too rarely for my taste, nothing could
have been better thought, and nothing better said,
though always timidly expressed, than that which fell
from her mouth."

M. Pictet's account of the society at Paris induced

woods." He was brought to Paris, and the philosophers disputed much
on his mental powers ; but he died before they came to any conclusion.

Mr. Edgeworth to determine on going there. He set out in the middle of September, with Mrs. Edgeworth, Maria, Emmeline, and Charlotte. Emmeline left the rest of the family at Conway, and went to stay with Mrs. Beddoes at Clifton, where she was married to Mr. King (or Konig, a native of Berne), a distinguished surgeon.

In London Mr. Edgeworth purchased a roomy coach, in which his family traveled very comfortably.

TO MISS SOPHY RUXTON.

Loughborough, September 25, 1802.

I calculate, my dear Sophy, that you have accused me at least a hundred times of being lazy and good-for-nothing, because I have not written since we left Dublin; but do not be angry, I was not well during the time we were in Dublin, nor for two or three days after we landed; but three days' rest at Bangor Ferry recovered me completely, and thanks to Dr. Diet, Dr. Quiet, and Dr. Merryman, I am now in perfectly good plight.

To take up things at the beginning. We had a tedious passage, but Charlotte and I sat upon deck, and were well enough to be much amused with all the manœuvring of the sails, etc. The light reflected upon the waters from the lighthouse contracted instead of diverging: I mention this, because there was an argument held upon the subject either at Black Castle or at Collon. As we were all sitting upon deck drinking tea in the morning, a large, very large, woman who was reading opposite to us, fell from her seat with a terrible noise. We all thought she had fallen down dead: the gentlemen gathered round her, and when she was lifted up she was a shocking spectacle, her face covered with blood — she had fallen upon one of the large nails in the deck. She recovered her senses, but when she was carried down to the cabin she fainted again, and remained two hours senseless. "She has a mother, ma'am," said the steward, "who is lying a-dying at Holyhead, and she frets greatly for her." We were told afterwards that this lady has for twenty years crossed the sea annually to visit her mother, though she never could make the passage without swooning. She was a coarse housekeeper-looking woman, without any pretense to sentimentality, but I think she showed more affection and real heroism than many who have been immortalized by the pen or pencil.

Nothing new or entertaining from Holyhead to Bangor. A delightful day at Bangor, pleasant walk: Charlotte drew some Welsh peasants and children; we tried to talk to them, but *Dumsarzna*, or words to that effect, "I don't understand English," was the constant answer, and the few who could speak English seemed to have no wish to enter into conversation with us; the farmers intrenched themselves in their houses and shut their doors as fast as they could when we approached. From Bangor Ferry we took a pleasant excursion to Carnarvon — do not be afraid, I shall not give you a long description of the castle — I know you have seen it, but I wish I knew whether you and I saw it with the same ideas. I could not have conceived that any building or ruin could have appeared to me so sublime. The amazing size! the distinctness of the parts! the simplicity of the design, the thickness of the walls, the air of grandeur even in decay! In the courtyard of

the castle an old horse and three cows were grazing, and
beneath the cornices on the walls two goats, half black,
half white, were browsing. I believe that old castles
interest one by calling up ideas of past times, which are
in such strong contrast with the present. In the courtyard of this castle were brewing vessels in vaults which
had formerly perhaps been durgeons, and pitched sails
stretched upon the walls to dry: the spirit of old
romance and modern manufactures do not agree.

Mr. Waitman, the landlord of the Carnarvon Hotel,
accompanied us to the castle, and he was indeed a glorious contrast to the enthusiastic old man who showed the
ruins. This old man's eyes brightened when he talked
of the Eagle Tower, and he seemed to forget that he
had a terrible asthma whilst he climbed the flights of
stone stairs. Our landlord, a thorough Englishman, in
shrewd, willful independence, entertained my father by
his character and conversation, and pleased him by his
praises of Lovell, of whom he spoke with much gratitude. We returned at night to Bangor Ferry. Early
next morning my father and mother, on two Welsh
ponies, trotted off to see Lord Penrhyn's slate quarries.
We had orders to follow them in a few hours. In the
mean time who do you think arrived? Mr. and Mrs.
Saunderson, with all their children. They seemed as
glad to see me as I was to see them. They had intended to go another road, but went on to Conway on
purpose to spend the day with us. A most pleasant day
we did spend with them. They were going to Bristol
to see their son, and when they found that Emmeline
was going there, they offered in the kindest and most
polite manner to take her with them. We parted with

Emmeline and with them the next morning; they went to Keniogy, which I can't spell, and we went to Holy-well, and saw the copper works, a vast manufactory, in which there seemed to be no one at work. We heard and saw large wheels turning without any visible cause, "instinct with spirit all." At first nothing but the sound of dripping water, then a robin began to sing amongst the rafters of the high and strange roof. The manufactory in which the men were at work was a strong contrast to this desolate place; a stunning noise, Cyclops with bared arms dragging sheets of red-hot cop-per, and thrusting it between the cylinders to flatten it; while it passed between these, the flame issued forth with a sort of screeching noise. When I first heard it I thought somebody was hurt: the flame was occasioned by the burning of the grease put between the rollers. There were a number of children employed drawing straight lines on the sheets of copper, ready for a man with a large pair of shears to cut. The whole process was simple.

Saw the famous well, in which the spring supplies a hundred tuns a minute. Went on to Chester and New-castle, in hopes of finding Jos. Wedgwood at Etru-ria; were told he was not in the country, but just as our chaise whips up, papa espied Wedgwood's partner, who told him Jos. *was* at Etruria — came last night, would stay but one day. Went to Etruria, Jos. re-ceived us as you would expect, and all the time I was with him I had full in my recollection the handsome manner in which you told me he spoke of my father. The mansion-house at Etruria is excellent; but, alas! the Wedgwoods have bought an estate in Dorsetshire, and are going to leave Etruria. I do not mean that they have given up their share in the manufactory. Saw a flint mill worked by a steam-engine just finished, cannot stay to describe it — for two reasons, because I cannot describe it intelligibly, and because I want to get on to the Priory to Mrs. and the Miss Darwins. Poor Dr. Darwin![1] It was melancholy to go to that house to which, in the last lines he ever wrote, he had invited us. The servants in deep mourning; Mrs. Darwin and her beautiful daughters in deep mourning. She was much affected at seeing my father, and seemed to regret her husband as such a husband ought to be regretted. I liked her exceedingly; there was so much heart, and so little constraint or affectation in all she said and did, or looked. There was a charming picture of Dr. Darwin in the room, in which his generous soul appeared and his penetrating benevolent genius. How unlike the wretched misanthropic print we have seen! While I am writing this at Loughborough, my father is a few miles off at Castle Donnington. I forgot to tell you that we spent a delightful day, or remnant of a day, on our return from the Priory, at Mr. Strutt's.

TO MISS SNEYD.

LONDON, NEROT'S HOTEL, September 27, 1802.

We have been here about an hour, and next to the pleasure of washing face and hands, which were all covered with red Woburn sand and Dunstable chalk, and London dust, comes the pleasure of writing to you, my dear good Aunt Mary. How glad I should be to give you any proof of gratitude for the many large and little

[1] Dr. Darwin died 17th April, 1802.

kindnesses you have shown to me.   There is no one in
the world who can deserve to be thought of more at all
times, and in all situations, than you; for there is no
one thinks so much of others.   As long as there is any
one worth your loving upon earth, you cannot be unhappy.   I think you would have been very apt to make
the speech attributed to St. Theresa: "Le pauvre
Diable! comme je le plains! Il ne peut rien aimer.
Ah! qu'il doit être malheureux!"

But whilst I am talking sentiment you may be impatient for news.   The first and best news is, that my
father is extremely well.   Traveling, he says, has done
him a vast deal of good, and whoever looks at him
believes him.   It would be well for all faces if they
had that effect on the spectators, or rather perhaps it
would be ill for the credulous spectators.   Isabella of
Aragon, *or* Lord Chesterfield, or both, call a good countenance the best letter of recommendation.   Whenever
Nature gives false letters of recommendation, she swin-
dles in the most abominable manner.   Where she re-
fuses them where they are best deserved, she only gives
additional motive for exertion (*vide* Socrates or his
bust).[1]   And after all, Nature is forced out of her letters of recommendation sooner or later.   You know that
it is said by Lavater, that the *muscles* of Socrates'
countenance are beautiful, and these became so by the
play given to them by the good passions, etc., etc., etc.

Charlotte tells me she carried you in her last as far
as Loughborough and Castle Donnington; will you be so
good to go on to Leicester with me?   But before we set

---

[1] An alabaster bust of Socrates, which stood on the chimney-piece in
the drawing-room at Black Castle.

out for Leicester, I should like to take you to Castle Donnington, "the magnificent seat of the Earl of Moira." But then how can I do that, when I did not go there myself? Oh! I can describe after a description as well as my betters have done before me in prose and verse, and a description of my father's is better than the reality seen with my own eyes. The first approach to Donnington disappointed him; he looked round and saw neither castle, nor park, nor anything to admire till he came to the top of a hill, when in the valley below suddenly appeared the turrets of a castle, surpassing all he had conceived of light and magnificent in architecture: a real castle! not a modern, bungling imitation. The inside was suitable in grandeur to the outside; hall, staircase, antechambers; the library fitted up entirely with books in plain handsome mahogany bookcases, not a frippery ornament, everything grand, but not gaudy; marble tables, books upon the tables; nothing littered, but sufficient signs of living and occupied beings. At the upper end of the room sat two ladies copying music, a gentleman walking about with a book in his hand; neither Lord Moira nor Lady Charlotte Rawdon in the room. The gentleman, Mr. Sedley, not having an instinct like Mademoiselle Panache for a gentleman, did not, till Lord Moira entered the room and received my father with open arms, feel sure that he was worthy of more than monosyllable civility. Lord Moira took the utmost pains to show my father that he was pleased with his visit, said he must have the pleasure of showing him over the house himself, and finished by giving him a letter to the Princess Joseph de Monaco, who is now at Paris. She was Mrs.

Doyle. He also sent to Mrs. Edgeworth the very finest grapes I ever beheld. I wished the moment I saw them, my dear aunt, that you had a bunch of them.

We proceeded to Leicester. Handsome town, good shops: walked, whilst dinner was getting ready, to a circulating library. My father asked for "Belinda," "Bulls," etc., found they were in good repute — "Castle Rackrent" in better — the others often borrowed, but "Castle Rackrent" often bought. The bookseller, an open-hearted man, begged us to look at a book of poems just published by a Leicester lady, a Miss Watts. I recollected to have seen some years ago a specimen of this lady's proposed translation of Tasso, which my father had highly admired. He told the bookseller that we would pay our respects to Miss Watts, if it would be agreeable to her. When we had dined, we set out with our enthusiastic bookseller. We were shown by the light of a lantern along a very narrow passage between high walls, to the door of a decent-looking house: a maid-servant, candle in hand, received us. "Be pleased, ladies, to walk upstairs." A neatish room, nothing extraordinary in it except the inhabitants. Mrs. Watts, a tall, black-eyed, prim, dragon-looking woman in the background. Miss Watts, a tall young lady in white, fresh color, fair, thin oval face, rather pretty. The moment Mrs. Edgeworth entered, Miss Watts, mistaking her for the authoress, darted forward with arms, long thin arms, outstretched to their utmost swing: "OH, WHAT AN HONOR THIS IS!" each word and syllable rising in tone till the last reached a scream. Instead of embracing my mother, as her first action threatened, she started back to the farthest end of the

room, which was not light enough to show her attitude
distinctly, but it seemed to be intended to express the
receding of awe-struck admiration — stopped by the wall.
Charlotte and I passed by unnoticed, and seated ourselves
by the old lady's desire: she after many twistings of her
wrists, elbows, and neck, all of which appeared to be dis-
located, fixed herself in her armchair, resting her hands on
the black mahogany *splayed* elbows.   Her person was no
sooner at rest than her eyes and all her features began to
move in all directions.   She looked like a nervous and suspicious person electrified.   She seemed to be the acting
partner in this house to watch over her treasure of a daughter, to supply her with worldly wisdom, to look upon her
as a phœnix, and — scold her.   Miss Watts was all ecstasy
and lifting up of hands and eyes, speaking always in
that loud, shrill, theatrical tone with which a puppet-
master supplies his puppets.   I all the time sat like
a mouse.   My father asked, "Which of those ladies,
madam, do you think is your sister authoress?"   "I
am no physiognomist," — in a screech, — "but I do
imagine that to be the lady," bowing as she sat almost
to the ground, and pointing to Mrs. Edgeworth.   "No,
guess again."   "Then that must be *she*," bowing to
Charlotte.   "No."   "Then this lady," looking forward to see what sort of an animal I was, for she had
never seen me till this instant.   To make me some
amends, she now drew her chair close to me, and began
to pour forth praises: "Lady Delacour, O!   Letters for
Literary Ladies, O!"

Now for the pathetic part.   This poor girl sold a
novel in four volumes for ten guineas to Lane.   My
father is afraid, though she has considerable talents, to

recommend her to Johnson, lest she should not *answer*.
Poor girl, what a pity she had no friend to direct her
talents; how much she made me feel the value of mine!

TO MISS SOPHY RUXTON.

BRUSSELS, October 15, 1802.

After admiring on the ramparts of Calais the Pois-
sardes with their picturesque nets, ugly faces, and beautiful legs, we set out for Gravelines, with whips clack-
ing in a manner which you certainly cannot forget.
The stillness and desolation of Gravelines was like the
city in the Arabian Tales, where every one is turned
into stone. Fortifications constructed by the famous
Vauban, lunes, and demilunes, and curtains, all which
did not prevent the French from trotting through it.

We left Gravelines with an equipage at which So-
briety herself could not have forborne to laugh: to our
London coach were fastened by long rope traces six
Flemish horses of different heights, but each large and
clumsy enough to draw an English wagon. The nose
of the foremost horse was thirty-five feet from the body
of the coach, their hoofs all shaggy, their manes all
uncombed, and their tails long enough to please Sir
Charles Grandison himself. These beasts were totally
disencumbered of every sort of harness except one strap
which fastened the saddle on their backs; and high,
high upon their backs, sat perfectly perpendicular, long-
waisted postilions in jack-boots, with pipes in their
mouths. The country appeared one vast flat common,
without hedges, or ditches, or trees, tiled farmhouses of
equal size and similar form at even distances. All that
the power of monotony can do to put a traveler to sleep

is here tried; but the rattling and jolting on the paved roads set Morpheus and monotony both at defiance. To comfort ourselves we had a most entertaining "Voyage dans les Pays Bas par M. Breton" to read, and the charming story of Mademoiselle de Clermont in Madame de Genlis's "Petits Romans." I never read a more pathetic and finely written tale.

Dunkirk is an ugly, bustling town. Strange-looking *charettes*, driven by thin men in cocked hats, — the window-shutters turned out to the streets and painted by way of signs with various commodities. A variety of things, among them little shifts, petticoats, and corsets, were fairly spread upon the ground on the bridges and in the streets. The famous basin, about which there have been such disputes, is little worth. Voltaire wonders at the English and French waging war "for a few acres of snow;" he might with equal propriety have laughed at them for fighting about a *slop-basin*. The *pont-tournant* is well worth seeing, and for those who have strong legs and who have breakfasted, it is worth while to climb the two hundred and sixty-four steps of the tower. Whilst we were climbing the town clock struck, and the whole tower vibrated, and the vibration communicated itself to our ears and heads in a most sublime and disagreeable manner.

At Dunkirk we entered what was formerly called L'ancien Brabant, and all things and all persons began to look like Dutch prints and Dutch toys, especially the women with their drop earrings, and their necklaces like the labels of decanters, their long-waisted, long-flapped jackets of one color, and stiff petticoats of another. Even when moving the people all looked like wooden toys set in motion by strings — the strings in Flanders must be of gold; the Flemings seem to be all a money-making, money-loving people; they are fast recovering their activity after the Revolution.

The road to Bruges, fifty feet broad, solidly paved in the middle, seems, like all French and Flemish roads, to have been laid out by some inflexible mathematician: they are always right lines, the shortest possible between two points. The rows of trees on each side of these never-ending avenues are of the ugliest sort and figure possible: tall poplars stripped almost to the top, as you would strip a pen, and pollarded willows; the giant poplar and the dwarf willow placed side by side alternately, knight and squire. The postilions have badges like the badges of charity schools, strapped round their arms; these are numbered and registered, and if they behave ill, a complaint may be lodged against them by merely writing their names on the register, which excludes them from a pension, to which they would be entitled if they behaved well for a certain number of years. The post-houses are often lone, wretched places, one into which I peeped, a *grenier*, like that described by Smollett, in which the murdered body is concealed. At another post-house we met with a woman calling herself a *servante*, to whom we took not only an aversion, but a horror; Charlotte said that she should be afraid, not of that woman's cutting her throat, but that she would take a mallet and strike her head flat at one blow. Do you remember the woman in "Caleb Williams," when he wakens and sees her standing over him with an uplifted hatchet? Our *servante* might have stood for this picture.

Bruges is a very old, desolate-looking town, which seems to have felt in common with its fellow towns the effects of the Revolution. As we were charged very high at the Hôtel d'Angleterre, at Dunkirk, my father determined to go to the Hotel de Commerce at Bruges, an old strange house which had been a monastery: the man chamber-maid led us through gallery after gallery, upstairs and downstairs, turning all manner of ways, with a bunch of keys in his hand, each key ticketed with a pewter ticket. There were twenty-eight bed-chambers — thank heaven we did not see them all! I never shall forget the feeling I had when the door of the room was thrown open in which we were to sleep. It was so large and so dark, that I could scarcely see the low bed in a recess in the wall, covered with a dark brown quilt. I am sure Mrs. Radcliffe might have kept her heroine wandering about this room for six good pages. When we meet I will tell Margaret of the night Charlotte and I spent in this room, and the footsteps we heard overhead — just a room and just a night to suit her taste.

In the morning we went to see the Central School; it is in what was an old monastery, and the church belonging to it is filled with pictures collected from all the suppressed convents, monasteries, and churches. Buonaparte has lately restored some of their pictures to the churches, but those by Rubens and Raphael are at Paris. In the cabinet of natural history there is the skeleton and the skin of a man who was guillotined, as fine white leather as ever you saw. The preparations for these Écoles Centrales are all too vast and ostentatious; the people are just beginning to send their chil-

dren to them. Government finds them too expensive,
and their number is to be diminished. The librarian
of this École Centrale at Bruges is an Englishman, or
rather a Jamaica man, of the name of Edwards. Brian
Edwards was his great friend, and he was well acquainted with Johnson the bookseller, and Dr. Aikin,
and Mr. and Mrs. Barbauld. Mr. Edwards and his
son had often met Lovell at Johnson's, and spoke of
him quite with affection. The two sons spent the
evening with us, and they and their father accompanied
us next morning part of our way to Ghent. We went
by the canal bark, as elegant as any pleasure-boat I
ever was in. My father entertained the Edwardses with
the history of his physiognomical guesses in a stage-
coach. The eldest son piques himself upon telling
character from handwriting. He was positive that mine
could not be the hand of a woman, and then he came
off by saying it was the writing of a *manly* character!
We had an extremely fine day, and the receding prospect of Bruges, with its mingled spires, shipping, and
windmills, the tops of their giant vanes moving above
the trees, gave a pleasing example of a Flemish landscape, recalling the pictures of Teniers and the prints of
Le Bas. We had good and agreeable company on board
our bark, the Mayor of Bruges and his lady; her friend,
a woman of good family; and an old Baron Triste, of a
sixteen-quartering family. At the name of Mayor of
Bruges, you probably represent to yourself a fat, heavy,
formal, self-sufficient mortal — *tout au contraire:* our
Mayor was a thin gentleman, of easy manners, literature, and amusing conversation; Madame, a beautiful
Provinciale. M. Lerret, the Mayor, found us out to

be the Edgeworths described by M. Pictet in the
"Journal Britannique." Since we came to France we
have found M. Pictet's account very useful, for at every
public library, and in every École Centrale, the "Journal Britannique" is taken, and we have consequently
received many civilities. It was Sunday, and when
we arrived at Ghent all the middling people of the
town, in their holiday clothes, were assembled on the
banks of the canal according to custom to see the bark
arrive; they made the scene very cheerful. The old
Baron de Triste, though he had not dined, and though
he had, as he said of himself, "un faim de diable,"
stayed to battle our coach and trunks through an army
of custom-house officers. We stayed two days at Ghent,
and saw pictures and churches without number. Here
were some fine pictures by that Crayer of whom Rubens
said, "Crayer! personne ne te surpassera!" Do not be
afraid, my dear Sophy, I am not going to overwhelm
you with pictures, nor to talk of what I don't understand; but it is extremely agreeable to me to see paintings with those who have excellent taste and no affectation. At the École Centrale was a smart little librarian,
to whom we were obliged for getting the doors of the
cathedral opened to us *at night:* we went in by moonlight, the appearance was sublime; lights burning on
the altar veiled from sight, and our own monstrous
shadows cast on the pillars, added to the effect. The
verger took one of the tall candles to light us to some
monuments in white marble of exquisite sculpture.
There were no pictures, but the walls were painted in
the manner of the Speaker's room at the Temple, and
by the master who taught De Gray. This kind of

painting seems to suit churches, and to harmonize well with sculpture and statues.

My dear friend, I have not room to say half I intended, but let me make what resolutions I please, I never can get all I want to say to you into a letter.

TO MISS CHARLOTTE SNEYD.

CHANTILLY, October 29, 1802.

I last night sent a folio sheet to Sophy, giving the history of ourselves as far as Brussels, where we spent four days very much to our satisfaction; it is full of fine buildings, charming public walks, the country about it beautiful. In the Place Royale are two excellent hotels, Hôtel d'Angleterre and Hôtel de Flandres, to which we went, and found that Mr. Chenevix and Mr. Knox were in the other.

My father thought it would be advantageous to us to see inferior pictures before seeing those of the best masters, that we might have some points of comparison; and upon the same principle we went to two provincial theatres at Dunkirk and Brussels: but unluckily, I mean unluckily for our *principles*, we saw at Brussels two of the best Paris actors, M. and Madame Talma. The play was Racine's "Andromaque" (imitated in England as the "Distressed Mother"). Madame Talma played Andromaque, and her husband Orestes: both exquisitely well. I had no idea of fine acting till I saw them, and my father, who had seen Garrick, and Mrs. Siddons, and Yates, and Le Kain, says he never saw anything superior to Madame Talma. We read the play in the morning, an excellent precaution, otherwise the novelty of the French mode of declamation would

have set my comprehension at defiance. There was a
ranting Hermione, who had a string too tight round her
waist, which made her bosom heave like the bellows of
a bagpipe whenever she worked with her clasped hands
against her heart to pump out something like passion.
There was also a wretched Pyrrhus, and an old Phœnix,
whose gray wig I expected every moment to fall off.

Next to this beautiful tragedy, the thing that interested and amused me most at Brussels were the dogs;
not lap-dogs, but the dogs that draw carts and heavy
hampers. Every day I beheld numbers of these *traî-
neaux*, often four, harnessed abreast, and driven like
horses. I remember in particular seeing a man standing
upright on one of these little carriages, and behind him
two large hampers full of mussels, the whole drawn by
four dogs. And another day I saw a boy of about ten
years old driving four dogs harnessed to a little carriage;
he crossed our carriage as we were going down a street
called La Montagne de la Cour, without fearing our four
Flemish horses. La Montagne de la Cour is a very
grand name, and you may perhaps imagine that it means
a mountain, but be it known to you, my dear aunt, that
in Le Pays Bas, as well as in the County of Longford,
they make mountains of molehills. The whole road
from Calais to Ghent is as flat and as straight as the
road to Longford. We never knew when we came to
what the innkeeper and postilions call mountains, except by the postilions getting off their horses with great
deliberation and making them go a snail's walk — a
snail's gallop would be much too fast. Now it is no
easy thing for a French postilion to walk himself when
he is in his boots; these boots are each as large and as

stiff as a wooden churn, and when the man in his boots
attempts to walk, he is more helpless than a child in a
go-cart: he waddles on, dragging his boots after him in
a way that would make a pig laugh. As Lord Granard
says, "A pig can whistle, though he has a bad mouth
for it,"[1] I presume that *by a parity of reasoning* a pig
may laugh. But I must not talk any more nonsense.

We left Brussels last Sunday (you are looking in your
pocket-book, dear Aunt Mary, for the day of the month;
I see you looking). The first place of any note we
went to was Valenciennes, where we saw houses and
churches in ruins, the effect of English wars and French
revolutions. Though Valenciennes lace is very pretty
we bought none, recollecting that though Coventry is
famous for ribbons, and Tewkesbury for stockings, yet
only the worst ribbons and the worst stockings are to
be had at Coventry and Tewkesbury. Besides, we are
not expert at counting Flemish money, which is quite
different from French, and puzzling enough to drive the
seven sages of Greece mad. Even the natives cannot
count it without rubbing their foreheads, and counting
in their hands, and repeating *c'a fait, cela fait.* For
my part I fairly gave the point up, and resolved to be
cheated rather than go distracted. But indeed the
Flemish are not cheats, as far as I have seen of them.
They would go to the utmost borders of honesty for a
couronne de Brabant, or a demi-couronne, or a double
escalin, or a single escalin, or a plaquet, or a livre, or a
sous, or a liard, or for any the vilest denomination of

---

[1] A long argument on genius and education, between Lady Moira and
Mr. Edgeworth, had been ended by Lord Granard wittily saying, "A
pig may be made to whistle, but he has a bad mouth for it."

their absurd coin, yet I do not believe they would go beyond the bounds of honesty with any but an English Milor; they are privileged dupes. A maid at the hotel at Dunkirk said to me, "Ah! Madame, nous autres nous aimons bien de voir rouler les Anglais." Yes, because they think the English roll in gold.

Now we will go to Cambray, famous for its cambric and its archbishop. Buonaparte had so much respect for the memory of Fénelon, that he fixed the seat of the present Archbishopric at Cambray instead of at Lille, as had been proposed. We saw Fénelon's head here, preserved in a church. But to return from archbishops to cambrics. Our hostess at Cambray was a dealer in cambrics, and in her bale of *baptistes* she seemed literally to have her being. She was, in spite of cambric and Valenciennes lace, — of which she had a dirty superfluity on her cap lined with pink, — the very ugliest of the female species I had ever beheld. We were made amends for her by a most agreeable family who kept the inn at Roye: their ancestors had kept this inn for a hundred and fifty years; the present landlord and his wife are about sixty-eight and sixty, and their daughter, about twenty, of a slight figure, vast vivacity in her mind and in all her motions; she does almost all the business of the house, and seems to love *papa et maman* better than anything in the world, except talking. My father formed a hundred good wishes for her, — first, when he heard her tell a story, she used such admirable variety of action, that he wished her on the stage; then, when she waited at supper, with all the nimbleness and dexterity of a female harlequin, he wished that she was married to Jack Langan, that she might keep the new inn at Edgeworthstown; but his last and best wish for her was that she should be waiting-maid to you and Aunt Mary. He thought she would please you both particularly; for my part, I thought she would talk a great deal too much for you. However, her father and mother would not part with her for Pitt's diamond.

We saw to-day the residence of the Prince de Condé, and of a long line of princes famous for virtue and talents — the celebrated palace of Chantilly, made still more interesting to us by having just read the beautiful tale by Madame de Genlis, "Mademoiselle de Clermont;" it would delight my dear Aunt Mary, it is to be had in the first volume of the "Petits Romans," and those are to be found by Darcy, if he be not drunk, at Archer's, Dublin.   After going for an hour and a half through thick, dark forest, in which Virginia might have lived secure from sight of mortal man, we came into open day and open country, and from the top of a hill beheld a mass of magnificent building, shaded by wood.   I imagined this was the palace, but I was told that these buildings were only the stables of Chantilly. The palace, alas! is no more! it was pulled down by the Revolutionists.   The stables were saved by a petition from the War Minister, stating that they would make stabling for troops, and to this use they are now applied.   As we drove down the hill we saw the melancholy remains of the palace: only the white arches on which it was built, covered with crumbled stone and mortar.   We walked to look at the riding-house, built by the Prince de Condé, a princely edifice!   Whilst we were looking at it, we heard a flute played near us, and we were told that the young man who played it was one of the poor Prince de Condé's chasseurs. The person who showed the ruins to us was a melancholy-looking man, who had been employed his whole life to show the gardens and palace of Chantilly: he is about sixty, and had saved some hundred pounds in the Prince's service. He now shows their ruins, and tells where the Prince and Princess once slept, and where there *were* fine statues, and charming walks.

We have had but one day's rain since we left you; if we had picked the weather we could not have had finer. The country through which we came from Brussels was for the most part beautiful, planted in side-scenes, after my father's manner, you know. The English who can see nothing worth seeing in this country must certainly pass through it with huge blinkers of prejudice.

Paris, Wednesday.

We arrived about three o'clock, and are lodged for a few days at the Hôtel de Courland. I forgot to tell you that we saw an officer with furred waistcoat, and furred pockets, and monstrous moustache; he looked altogether very like the Little Gibbon in Shaw's "Zoology," only the Little Gibbon does not look as conceited as this man did.

We are now, my dear Aunt Mary, in a magnificent hotel in the fine square, formerly Place Louis Quinze, afterwards Place de la Révolution, and now Place de la Concorde. Here the guillotine was once at work night and day; and here died Louis Seize, and Marie Antoinette, and Madame Roland: opposite to us is the Seine and *La Lanterne*.   On one side of this square are the Champs Elysées.

TO MISS MARY SNEYD.

PARIS, RUE DE LILLE, October 31, 1802.

I left off at the Hôtel de Courlandé.   We were told there was a fine view of Paris from the leads; and so indeed there is, and the first object that struck us was the Telegraph at work! The first *voiture de remise* (job-coach in plain English) into which we got, belonged to — whom do you think? — to the Princess Elizabeth. The Abbé Edgeworth had probably been in this very coach with her. The master of this house was one of the King's guards, a Swiss. Our apartments are all on one floor. The day after our arrival M. Delessert, he whom M. Pictet describes as a French Rumford, invited us to spend the evening with his mother and sister. We went: found an excellent house, a charming family, with whom we felt we were perfectly acquainted after we had been in the room with them for five minutes. Madame Delessert,[1] the mother, an elderly lady of about sixty, has the species of politeness and conversation that my Aunt Ruxton has: I need not say how much I like her. Her daughter, Madame Gautier, has fine large black eyes, very obliging and sensible, well dressed, not at all naked; people need not be naked here unless they choose it. Rousseau's "Letters on Botany" were written for this lady; he was a friend of the family. She has two fine children of eight and ten, to whose education she devotes her time and talents. Her second

---

[1] The benevolence of the generous Madame Delessert is said to be depicted in one of the stories of Berquin's *Ami des Enfans*.

brother, François Delessert, about twenty, was educated chiefly by her, and does her great credit, and what is better for her, is extremely fond of her: he seems the darling of his mother; *François mon fils* she calls him every minute. In his countenance and manners he is something like Henry; he has that sober kind of cheerfulness, that ingenuous openness, and that modest, gentlemanlike ease which pleases without effort, and without bustle. Madame Gautier does not live at Paris, but at a country house at Passy, the Richmond of Paris, about two miles out of town. She invited us to spend a day there, and a most pleasant day we passed. The situation beautiful, the house furnished with elegance and good sense, the society most agreeable. M. Delessert, *père*, an old sensible man, the rest of the family, and Madame de Pastoret,[1] a literary and fashionable lady, with something of Mrs. Saunderson's best style of conversation: M. de Pastoret, her husband, a man of diplomatic knowledge; Lord Henry Petty, son of Lord Lansdowne, with whom my father had much conversation; the Swiss Ambassador, whose name I will not attempt to spell; M. Dumont,[2] a Swiss gentleman, traveling with Lord Henry Petty, very sensible and entertaining, I am sorry that he has since left Paris; M. d'Étaing, of whom I know nothing; and last, but indeed not least, the Abbé Morellet,[3] of whom you have heard

[1] Madame de Pastoret is the "Madame de Fleury" of Miss Edgeworth's story. She first established infant schools in France.

[2] M. Pierre Etienne Louis Dumont, tutor to Lord Henry Petty, had translated Bentham's *Traités sur la législation*, and *Théorie des peines et des récompenses*.

[3] The author of several works on political economy and statistics; born 1727, died 1819.

my father speak. Oh, my dear Aunt Mary, how you would love that man, and we need not be afraid of loving him, for he is near eighty. But it is impossible to believe that he is so old when one either hears him speak, or sees him move. He has all the vivacity, and feeling, and wit of youth, and all the gentleness that youth ought to have. His conversation is delightful, nothing too much or too little; sense, and gayety, and learning, and reason, and that perfect knowledge of the world which mixes so well but so seldom with a knowledge of books. He invited us to breakfast, and this morning we spent with him. My dearest Aunt Mary, I do wish you had been with us; I know that you would have been so much pleased. The house so convenient, so comfortable, so many inventions the same as my father's. He has a sister living with him, Madame de Montigny, an amiable, sensible woman: her daughter was married to Marmontel, who died a few years ago: she, alas! is not at Paris.

My father did not present any of his letters of introduction till yesterday, because he wished that we should be masters and mistresses of our own time to see sights before we saw people. We have been to Versailles — melancholy magnificence — La petite Trianon: the poor Queen! and at the Louvre, or as it is now called, La Musée, to see the celebrated gallery of pictures. I was entertained, but tired with seeing so many pictures, all to be admired, and all in so bad a light, that my little neck was almost broken, and my little eyes almost strained out, trying to see them. We were all extremely interested yesterday seeing what are called Les Monuments Français — all the statues and monuments of the great men of France, arranged according to their dates in the apartments of the ancient Monastery des Augustins.   Here we saw old Hugh Capet, with his nose broken, and King Pepin, with his nose flattened by time, and Catherine de Médicis, in full dress, but not in full beauty, and Francis I., and dear Henry IV.

We have been to the Théâtre Français and to the Théâtre Feydau, both fine houses, decorations, etc., superior to English; acting much superior in comedy; in tragedy they bully, and rant, and throw themselves into Academy attitudes too much.

R. L. EDGEWORTH TO MISS CHARLOTTE SNEYD.

PARIS, November 18, 1802.

Maria told you of M. and Madame de Pastoret; in the same house on another floor — for different families here have entire "apartments," you observe the word, in one house — we met M. and Madame Suard:[1] he is accounted one of the most refined critics of Paris, and has for many years been at the head of newspapers of different denominations; at present he is at the head of "La Publiciste."   He is prudent, highly informed, not only in books, but in the politics of different states and the characters of men in all the different countries of Europe.   Madame Suard has the remains of much beauty, a *belle esprit*, and aims at singularity and independence of sentiment.   Would you believe it, Mr. Day paid his court to her thirty years ago?   She is very civil to us, and we go to their house once a week: literati frequent it, and to each of them she has something to say.

[1] M. Suard was editor of the *Publiciste*.

At Madame de Pastoret's we met M. Degerando[1] and M. Camille Jordan. Not Camille de Jourdan, the assassin, nor Camille Desmoulins, another assassin, nor General Jourdan, another assassin, but a young man of agreeable manners, gentle disposition, and much information; he lives near Paris, with his Pylades Degerando, who is also a man of much information, married to a pretty sprightly domestic woman, who nurses her child in earnest. Camille Jordan has written an admirably eloquent pamphlet on the choice of Buonaparte as first consul for life; it was at first forbidden, but the Government wisely recollected that to forbid is to excite curiosity. We three have had profound metaphysical conferences in which we have avoided contest and have generally ended by being of the same opinion. We went, by appointment, to Madame Campan's — she keeps the greatest boarding-school in France — to meet Madame Récamier, the beautiful lady who had been nearly squeezed to death in London. How we liked the school and its conductress, who professes to follow "Practical Education," I leave to Maria to tell you. How we like Madame Récamier is easily told; she is certainly handsome, but there is nothing noble in her appearance; she was very civil. M. de Prony,[2] who is at the head of the Ingénieurs des Ponts et Chaussées — civil engineers — was introduced to us by Mr. Watt. I forgot to speak of him; he has just left Paris. M. de Prony showed us models and machines which would have delighted William. M. L'Abbé Morellet's niece

1 Marie Joseph Degerando, writer on education and philosophy, 1772-1842.

2 Gaspard Clair François Marie Riche, Baron de Prony, the great mathematician, 1755-1839.

next engaged our attention; she and her husband came
many leagues to see us; and we met also Madame de
Vergennes, Madame Rémusat, and Madame Nansoutit,
all people of knowledge and charming manners. Madame
Lavoisier and the Countess Massulski, General Kos-
ciusko, Prince Jablounsk*i*, and Princess Jablonnsk*a*,
and two other Princesses, I leave to Maria. Mons.
Edelcrantz, private secretary to the King of Sweden;
Mons. Eisenman, a German; Mons. Geofrat, the guar-
dian from Egypt of the Kings of Chaldea and seven
Ibises; Mons. de Montmorenci — that great name; the
Abbé Sicard, who dines here to-morrow; Mons. Pang,
Mons. Bertrant, Mons. Milan, Mons. Dupont, Mons.
Bareuil the illuminati man, and Mr. Bilsbury, I leave
to her and Charlotte.

MRS. EDGEWORTH TO MISS SNEYD.

PARIS, November 21, 1802.

Mr. Edgeworth's summary of events closed, I believe,
last Thursday. Friday we saw beauty, riches, fashion,
luxury, and numbers at Madame Récamier's; she is a
charming woman, surrounded by a group of adorers and
flatterers in a room where are united wealth and taste,
all of modern execution and ancient design that can
contribute to its ornament — a strange *mélange* of mer-
chants and poets, philosophers and parvenus — English,
French, Portuguese, and Brazilian, which formed the
company; we were treated with distinguished politeness
by our hostess, who concluded the evening by taking us
to her box at the Opera, where, besides being in company with the most fashionable women in Paris, *we
were seen* by Buonaparte himself, who sat opposite to us

in a railed box, through which he could see, but not
be seen.

Saturday we saw the magnificent Salle of the Corps
Législatif, and in the evening passed some hours in
the agreeable society of Madame de Vergennes and
her daughters. Sunday we were very happy at home.
Monday morning, just as we were going out, M. Pictet
was announced; we neither heard his name nor distinctly recollected his looks, he is grown so fat and
looks so well — more friendly no man can be. I hope
he perceives we are grateful to him. The remainder of
that day was spent in the gallery of pictures, where we
met Mr. Rogers, the poet, and Mr. Abercrombie. The
evening was spent with M. Pictet at his sister's, an
agreeable, well-informed widow, with three handsome
daughters. Tuesday we went to the National Library,
where we were shown a large number of the finest
cameos, intaglios, and Roman and Greek medals, and
many of the antiquities brought from Egypt; and in
the evening we had again the pleasure of M. Pictet's
company, and of the charming Madame de Pastoret,
who was so obliging as to drink tea with us. Yesterday we had the pleasure of being at home, when several
learned and ingenious men called on us, and consequently heard one of the most lively and instructive
conversations on a variety of topics for three hours; as
I think it is Mr. Edgeworth's plan to knock you down
with names, I will just enumerate those of our visitors:
Edelcrantz, a Swede, Molard, Eisenman, Dupont, and
Pictet the younger. After they went, we paid a short
visit to the pictures and saw the Salle du Tribunat and
the Consul's apartments at the Tuileries: on the dress-

ing-table there were the busts of Fox and Nelson. At our return home we saw the good François Delessert and another man, who was the man who took Robespierre prisoner, and who has since made a clock which is wound up by the action of the air on mercury, like that which Mr. Edgeworth invented for the King of Spain. He told us many things that made us stare, and many that made us shiver, and many more that made us never wish to see him again.

In the evening we went to Madame Suard's. Don't imagine that these ladies are all widows, for they have husbands, and in many instances the husband *vaut mieux que la femme*. At Madame Suard's we met the famous Count Lally Tolendal and the Duc de Crillon. This morning Maria has gone with the Pictets to see the Abbé Sicard's deaf and dumb.

Mr. Edgeworth has not yet seen Buonaparte; he goes to-morrow to wait on Lord Whitworth as a preliminary step. It is a singular circumstance that Lord Whitworth, the new Ambassador, has brought to Paris the same horses, and the same wife, and lives in the same house as the last Ambassador did eleven years ago: he has married the widow of the Duke of Dorset, who was here then.

In England many are the tales of scandal that have been related of the Consul and all his family; I don't believe them. A lady told me it was "vraiment extraordinaire qu'un jeune homme comme lui ait de mœurs si exemplaires — et d'ailleurs on ne s'attend pas qu'un homme soit fidèle à une femme qui est plus agée que lui; mais si agée aussi! Il aime la soumission plus que la beauté: s'il lui dit de se coucher à huit heures, elle se couche; s'il faut se lever à deux heures, elle se lève! Elle est une bonne femme, elle a sauvé bien des vies."

Has Maria told you that she has had her "Belinda" translated into French by the young Count de Ségur, an amiable young man of one of the most ancient families of France, married to a granddaughter of the Chancellor d'Aguesseau? Many people support themselves by writing for journals, and by translating English books, yet the price of literature seems very low, and the price of all the necessaries of life very high. The influx of English has, they say, doubled the price of lodgings and of all luxuries.

MARIA TO MRS. RUXTON.

Paris, December 1, 1802.

I have been treasuring up for some time everything I have seen and heard which I think would interest you; and now my little head is so full that I must empty it, or it would certainly burst. All that I have seen and heard has tended to attach me more firmly to you by the double effect of resemblance and of contrast. Every agreeable person recalls you; every disagreeable, makes me exclaim, how different, etc.

I wish I could paint the different people we have seen in little William's magic-lantern, and show them to you. At Madame Delessert's house there are, and have been for years, meetings of the most agreeable and select society in Paris: she has the courage absolutely to refuse to admit either man or woman of whose conduct she cannot approve; at other houses there is some-times a strange mixture. To recommend Madame

Delessert still more powerfully to you, I must tell you that she was the benefactress of Rousseau; he was, it is said, never good or happy except in her society: to her bounty he owed his retreat in Switzerland. She is nobly charitable, but if it were not for her friends no one would find out half the good she does. One of her acts of beneficence is recorded in Berquin's "Ami des Enfans," but even her own children cannot tell in which story it is. Her daughter, Madame Gautier, gains upon our esteem every day.

Turn the handle of the magic-lantern: who is this graceful figure, with all the elegance of court manners, and all the simplicity of domestic virtue? She is Madame de Pastoret. She was chosen preceptress to the Princess in the *ancien régime* in opposition to the wife of Condorcet, and M. de Pastoret had I forget how many votes more than Condorcet when it was put to the vote who should be preceptor to the Dauphin at the beginning of the Revolution. Both M. and Madame de Pastoret speak remarkably well, each with that species of eloquence which becomes them. He was President of the First Assembly, and at the head of the King's Council; the four other ministers of that council all perished! He escaped by his courage. As for her, the Marquis de Chastelleux's speech describes her: "Elle n'a point d'expression sans grace et point de grace sans expression."

Turn the magic-lantern. Here comes Madame Suard and Monsieur, a member of the Academy: very good company at their house. Among others Lally Tolendal, who is exceedingly like Father Tom, and whose real name of Mullalagh he softened into Lally, said to be more eloquent than any man in France; M. de Mont-morenci, worthy of his great name.

Push on the magic - lantern slide. Here comes Boissy d'Anglas — a fine head! Such a head as you may imagine the man to have who, by his single cour-age, restrained the fury of one of the National Assem-blies when the head of one of the deputies was cut off and set on the table before him.

Next comes Camille Jordan, with great eloquence of pen, not of tongue;[1] and M. de Prony, a great mathe-matician, of whom you don't care to know more, but you would if you heard him.

Who comes next? Madame Campan, mistress of the first boarding-school here, who educated Madame Louis Buonaparte, and who professes to keep her pupils entirely separate from servants, according to "Practical Educa-tion," and who paid us many compliments. Teaches drawing in a manner superior to anything I had any idea of in English schools; she gave me a drawing in a gilt frame, which I shall show to you. At Madame Campan's, as my father told you, we met the beautiful Madame Récamier, and at her dinner we met the most fashionable tragic and comic poet, and the richest man in Paris sat beside Charlotte. We went to the Opera with Madame Récamier, who produces a great sensation whenever she appears in public. She is certainly hand-some, very handsome, but there is much of the magic of fashion in the enthusiasm she creates.

There is a Russian Princess here, who is always car-ried in and out of her carriage by two giant footmen, and a Russian Prince, who is so rich that he is never

1 Orator and statesman, 1771–1821.

able to spend his fortune, and asks advice how he shall do it.   He never thinks, it seems, of *giving* it away.

Who comes next?   Kosciusko,[1] cured of his wounds, simple in his manners, like all truly great men.   We met him at the house of a Polish Countess, whose name I cannot spell.

Who comes next?   M. de Leuze, who translated the "Botanic Garden" as well as it could be translated into Fénelon prose; and M. and Madame de Vindé, who have a superb gallery of paintings, and the best concerts in Paris, and a library of eighteen thousand volumes well counted and well arranged; and what charms me more than either the books or the pictures, a little granddaughter of three years old, very like my sweet Fanny, with stockings exactly the same as those Aunt Mary knitted for her, and listing shoes precisely like what Fanny used to wear; she sat on my knee, and caressed me with her soft, warm little hands, and looked at me with her smiling intelligent eyes.

December 3.

Here I am at the brink of the last page, and I have said nothing of the Apollo, the Invalides, or Les Sourds et Muets.   What shall I do?   I cannot speak of everything at once, and when I speak to you so many things crowd upon my mind.

Here, my dear aunt, I was interrupted in a manner that will surprise you as much as it surprised me, by the coming in of Monsieur Edelcrantz, a Swedish gentleman, whom we have mentioned to you, of superior understanding and mild manners: he came to offer me his hand and heart!!

[1] The Polish patriot and leader, 1756-1817.

My heart, you may suppose, cannot return his attachment, for I have seen but very little of him, and have
not had time to have formed any judgment, except that
I think nothing could tempt me to leave my own dear
friends and my own country to live in Sweden.

My dearest aunt, I write to you the first moment, as
next to my father and mother no person in the world
feels so much interest in all that concerns me. I need
not tell you that my father —

Such in this moment as in all the past, —

is kindness itself; kindness far superior to what I deserve, but I am grateful for it.

TO MISS SOPHY RUXTON.

Paris, Rue de Lille, No. 525, December 8, 1802.

I take it for granted, my dear friend, that you have
by this time seen a letter I wrote a few days ago to my
aunt. To you, as to her, every thought of my mind is
open. I persist in refusing to leave my country and
my friends to live at the Court of Stockholm, and he
tells me (of course) that there is nothing he would not
sacrifice for me except his duty; he has been all his life
in the service of the King of Sweden, has places under
him, and is actually employed in collecting information
for a large political establishment. He thinks himself
bound in honor to finish what he has begun. He says
he should not fear the ridicule or blame that would be
thrown upon him by his countrymen for quitting his
country at his age, but that he should despise himself if
he abandoned his duty for any passion. This is all
very reasonable, but reasonable for him only, not for
me; and I have never felt anything for him but esteem
and gratitude.

Mrs. Edgeworth, however, writes:—

Maria was mistaken as to her own feelings. She refused M. Edelcrantz, but she felt much more for him than esteem and admiration; she was exceedingly in love with him. Mr. Edgeworth left her to decide for herself; but she saw too plainly what it would be to us to lose her, and what she would feel at parting from us. She decided rightly for her own future happiness and for that of her family, but she suffered much at the time and long afterwards. While we were at Paris, I remember that in a shop where Charlotte and I were making some purchases, Maria sat apart absorbed in thought, and so deep in reverie, that when her father came in and stood opposite to her she did not see him till he spoke to her, when she started and burst into tears. She was grieved by his look of tender anxiety, and she afterwards exerted herself to join in society, and to take advantage of all that was agreeable during our stay in France and on our journey home, but it was often a most painful effort to her. And even after her return to Edgeworthstown, it was long before she recovered the elasticity of her mind. She exerted all her powers of self-command, and turned her attention to everything which her father suggested for her to write. But "Leonora," which she began immediately after our return home, was written with the hope of pleasing the Chevalier Edelcrantz; it was written in a style which he liked, and the idea of what he would think of it was, I believe, present to her in every page she wrote. She never heard that he had even read it. From the time they parted at Paris there was no sort of communication between them, and beyond the chance which brought us sometimes into company with travelers who had been in Sweden, or the casual mention of M. Edelcrantz in the newspapers or scientific journals, we never heard more of one who had been of such supreme interest to her, and to us all at Paris, and of whom Maria continued to have all her life the most romantic recollection. I do not think she repented of her refusal, or regretted her decision; she was well aware that she could not have made him happy, that she would not have suited his position at the Court of Stockholm, and that her want of beauty might have diminished his attachment. It was better perhaps that she should think so, as it calmed her mind, but from what I saw of M. Edelcrantz I think he was a man capable of really valuing her. I believe that he was much attached to her, and deeply mortified at her refusal. He continued to reside in Sweden after the abdication of his master, and was always distinguished for his high character and great abilities. He never married. He was, except very fine eyes, remarkably plain. Her father rallied Maria about her preference of so ugly a man; but she liked the expression of his countenance, the spirit and strength of his character, and his very able conversation. The unexpected mention of his name, or even that of Sweden, in a book or a newspaper, always moved her so much that the words and lines in the page became a mass of confusion before her eyes, and her voice lost all power.

I think it right to mention these facts, because I know that the lessons of self-command which she inculcates in her works were really acted upon in her own life, and that the resolution with which she devoted herself to her father and her family, and the industry with which she labored at the writings which she thought were for the advantage of her fellow-creatures, were from the exertion of the highest principle. Her precepts were not the maxims of cold-hearted prudence, but the result of her own experience in strong and romantic feeling. By what accident it happened that she had, long before she ever saw the Chevalier Edel-erantz, chosen Sweden for the scene of "The Knap-sack" I do not know, but I remember his expressing his admiration of that beautiful little piece, and his pleasure in the fine characters of the Swedish gentleman and peasants.

CHARLOTTE EDGEWORTH TO MISS CHARLOTTE
SNEYD.

RUE DE LILLE, CHEZ LE CITOYEN VERBER,
December 8, 1802.

MY DEAR AUNT CHARLOTTE, — One of the great objects of a visit to Paris was, you know, to see Buona-parte; the review is, as you see by the papers, over, and my father has not spoken to the great man — no, he did not wish it. All of our distant friends will be, I am afraid, disappointed, but some here think that my father's refusal to be presented to him shows a proper pride. All the reasons for this mode of conduct will serve perhaps for debate, certainly for conversation when we return.

Madame Suard says that those societies are most agreeable where there are fewest women; if there were not women superior to her I should not hesitate to assent to her proposition, and I should with pleasure read Madame de Staël's book called "Le Malheur d'être Femme." If, on the contrary, all women were Madame de Pastorets, or Madame Delesserts, or Madame Gautiers, I think I should take up the book with the intention not to be convinced.

Some of the most horrible revolutionists were the most skilled in the sciences, and are held in the utmost detestation by numbers of sensible men who admire their ingenuity and talents. We saw one of these, a teacher at one of the chief Academies, and my father, who was standing near him, heard him, after having been talking on several most amusing and interesting subjects, give one of the deepest sighs he ever heard.

The Abbé de Lille reads poetry particularly well, his own verses in a superior manner; we heard him, and were extremely pleased. He is very old, and so blind that his wife, whom he calls "Mon Antigone," is obliged to lead him.

As you may suppose, we go as often as we can to the Gallery. I thank my dear Aunt Mary for thinking of the pleasure I should have in seeing the Venus de Médicis; she has not yet arrived, but I have seen the Apollo, who did surprise me! On our way here we had seen many casts of him, and I have seen with you some prints: I could not have believed that there could have been so much difference between a copy and the original.

10th. You see I am often interrupted. I will introduce you to our company last night at the Delesserts. All soirées here begin at nine o'clock.

"Madame Edgeworth" is announced — room full

without being crowded — enough light and warmth.
M. Delessert, *père*, at a card-table with a gentleman
who is a partner in his bank, and an elderly lady.
There is a warm corner in the room, which is always
large enough to contain Madame Delessert and two or
three ladies and gentlemen. Madame Delessert advances
to receive Madame Edgeworth, and invites her to sit
beside her with many kind words and looks. Madame
Gautier expresses her joy at seeing us. Now we are
seated. M. Benjamin Delessert advances with his bow
to the ladies. Madame Gautier, my father, and Maria
get together. M. Pictet, nephew to our dear Pictet,
makes his bow and adds a few words to each. "Mademoiselle Charlotte," says Madame Delessert to me, "I
was just speaking of you." I forget now what she had
been saying, I have only the agreeable idea. Madame
Grivel enters, a clever, good-natured little woman, wife
to the partner who is at cards. Enter M. François
Delessert and another gentleman. How the company
divides and changes itself I am not at present supposed
to know, for young M. Pictet has seated himself between my mother and me, and has a long conversation
with me, in which Madame Grivel now and then joins:
she is on the other side of me. Mademoiselle Lullin,
our friend Pictet's sister, and his and her virtues are
discussed. Physics and metaphysics ensue; harmony,
astonishing power of chords in music, glass broken by
vibration, dreams, Spain, its manners and government.
Young M. Pictet has been there; people there have
little to do, because their wants are easily supplied.

Here come tea and cakes, sweetmeats, grapes, cream,
and all the goods of life. The lady who was playing at

cards now came and sat beside me, amusing me for a long time with a conversation on — what do you think? — politics and the state of France! M. François repeats some good lines very well. Laughter and merriment. Now we are obliged to go, and with much sorrow we part.

I see I never told you that we saw the review, and we *saw* a man on a white horse ride down the ranks; we *saw* that he was a little man with a pale face, who seemed very attentive to what he was about, and this was all we *saw* of Buonaparte.

MARIA TO MISS SOPHY RUXTON.

PARIS, December, 1802.

I add to the list of remarkables and agreeables the Count and Countess de Ségur, father and mother to our well-bred translator;[1] she a beautiful grandmother, he a nobleman of the old school, who adds to agreeable manners a great deal of elegant literature. Malouet, the amiable and able councillor of the King, must also be added to your list: we met him yesterday, a fine countenance and simple manners; he conversed freely with my father, not at all afraid of *committing* himself. In general I do not see that prodigious fear of committing themselves, which makes the company of some English men of letters and reputation irksome even to their admirers. Mr. Palmer, the great man of taste, who has lived for many years in Italy, is here, and is very much provoked that the French can now see all the pictures and statues he has been admiring, without stirring out of Paris. The Louvre is now so crowded with

---

[1] Of *Belinda*.

pictures, that many of them are seen to disadvantage. The Domenichino, my Aunt Ruxton's favorite, is not at present *visible*. Several of the finest pictures are, as they say, *sick*, and the physicians are busy restoring them to health and beauty. May they not mar instead of mending! A Raphael which has just come out of their hospital has the eyes of a very odd sort of modern blue. The Transfiguration is now in a state of convalescence; it has not yet made its appearance in public, but we were admitted into the sick-room.

Half Paris is now stark mad about a picture by Guérin of Phèdre and Hippolyte, which they actually think equal to Raphael.

Of the public buildings Les Invalides appears to me the finest; here are all the flags and standards used in battle, or won from foreign nations, — a long-drawn aisle of glory that must create ambition in the rising generation of military in France. We saw here a little boy of nine years old with his tutor, looking at Turenne's monument, which has been placed with great taste, alone, with the single word TURENNE upon the sarcophagus. My father spoke to the little boy and his tutor, who told him he had come to look at a picture in which the heroic action of one of the boy's ancestors is portrayed. We went into the hospital library, and found a circle of old soldiers sitting round a stove, all reading most comfortably. It was a very pleasing and touching sight. One who had lost both his hands, and who had iron hooks at the end of his wrists, was sitting at a table reading "Télémaque" with great attention; he turned over the leaves with these hooks.

My aunt asks me what I think of French society?

All I have seen of it I like extremely, but we hear from all sides that we see only the best of Paris, — the men of literature and the *ancienne noblesse*. *Les nouveaux riches* are quite a different set. My father has seen something of them at Madame Tallien's (now Cabarus), and was disgusted. Madame Récamier is of quite an opposite sort, though in the first fashion, a graceful and *decent* beauty of excellent character. Madame de Souza, the Portuguese Ambassadress, is a pretty and pleasing woman, authoress of "Adèle de Senanges," which she wrote in England. Her friends always proclaim her title as author before her other titles, and I thought her a pleasing woman before I was told that she had pronounced at Madame Lavoisier's an eloquent eulogium on "Belinda." I have never heard any person talk of dress or fashions since we came to Paris, and very little scandal. A scandalmonger would be starved here. The conversation frequently turns on the new *petites pièces* and little novels which come out every day, and are talked of for a few days with as much eagerness as a new fashion in other places. They also talk a vast deal about the little essays of criticism. In yesterday's "Journal des Débats," after a flaming panegyric on Buonaparte, "Et après avoir parlé de l'univers de qui peut-on parler? Des plus grandes des Poètes — de Racine;" then follows a criticism on "Phèdre."

We saw the grand review the day before yesterday from a window that looked out on the court of the Louvre and Place du Carrousel. Buonaparte rode down the lines on a fine white Spanish horse. Took off his hat to salute various generals, and gave us a full view of his pale, thin, woebegone countenance. He is very little, but much at ease on horseback: it is said he never appears to so much advantage as on horseback. There were about six thousand troops, a fine show, well appointed, and some, but not all, well mounted. On those who had distinguished themselves in the battle of Marengo all eyes were fixed. While I was looking out of the window a gentleman came in who had passed many years in Spain; he began to talk to me about Madrid, and when he heard my name, he said a Spanish lady is translating "Practical Education" from the French. She understands English, and he gave us her address that we may send a copy of the book to her.

Mr. Knox, who was presented to Buonaparte, and who saw all the wonderful presentations, says that it was a huddled business, all the world received in a very small room. Buonaparte spoke more to officers than to any one else, affected to be gracious to the English. He said, "L'Angleterre est une grande nation, *aussi bien* que la France, il faut que nous soyons amis!" Great men's words, like little men's dreams, are sometimes to be interpreted by the rule of contraries.

TO MISS SNEYD.

Paris, January 10, 1803.
Siècle réparateur, as Monge
has christened this century.

I will give you a journal of yesterday — I know you love journals. Got up and put on our shoes and stockings and cambric muslin gowns, which are in high esteem here, fur-tippets and *fur-clogs*, — God bless Aunt Mary and Aunt Charlotte for them, — and were in coach by nine o'clock; drove to the excellent Abbé

Morellet's, where we were invited to breakfast to meet Madame d'Ouditot, the lady who inspired Rousseau with the idea of Julie. Julie is now seventy-two years of age, a thin woman in a little black bonnet: she appeared to me shockingly ugly; she squints so much that it is impossible to tell which way she is looking; but no sooner did I hear her speak, than I began to like her; and no sooner was I seated beside her, than I began to find in her countenance a most benevolent and agreeable expression. She entered into conversation immediately: her manner invited and could not fail to obtain confidence. She seems as gay and open-hearted as a girl of fifteen. It has been said of her that she not only never did any harm, but never suspected any. She is possessed of that art which Lord Kames said he would prefer to the finest gift from the queen of the fairies, — the art of seizing the best side of every object. She has had great misfortunes, but she has still retained the power of making herself and her friends happy. Even during the horrors of the Revolution, if she met with a flower, a butterfly, an agreeable smell, a pretty color, she would turn her attention to these, and for the moment suspend her sense of misery, not from frivolity, but from real philosophy. No one has exerted themselves with more energy in the service of her friends. I felt in her company the delightful influence of a cheerful temper, and soft, attractive manners, — enthusiasm which age cannot extinguish, and which spends but does not waste itself on small but not trifling objects. I wish I could at seventy-two be such a woman! She told me that Rousseau, whilst he was writing so finely on education, and leaving his own children in the

Foundling Hospital, defended himself with so much eloquence that even those who blamed him in their hearts could not find tongues to answer him. Once at dinner, at Madame d'Ouditot's, there was a fine pyramid of fruit. Rousseau in helping himself took the peach which formed the base of the pyramid, and the rest fell immediately. "Rousseau," said she, "that is what you always do with all our systems; you pull down with a single touch, but who will build up what you pull down?" I asked if he was grateful for all the kindness shown to him. "No, he was ungrateful; he had a thousand bad qualities, but I turned my attention from them to his genius and the good he had done mankind."

After an excellent breakfast, including tea, chocolate, coffee, buttered and unbuttered cakes, good conversation, and good humor, came M. Chéron, husband of the Abbé Morellet's niece, who is translating "Early Lessons," French on one side and English on the other. Didot has undertaken to publish the "Rational Primer," which is much approved of here for teaching the true English pronunciation.

Then we went to a lecture on Shorthand, or *Passigraphy*, and there we met Mr. Chenevix, who came home to dine with us, and stayed till nine, talking of Montgolfier's *belier* for throwing water to a great height. We have seen it and its inventor; something like Mr. Watt in manner, not equal to him in genius. He had received from M. de la Poype a letter my father wrote some years ago about the method of guiding balloons, and as far as he could judge he thought it might succeed.

We went with Madame Récamier and the Russian Princess Dalgourski to La Harpe's house, to hear him repeat some of his own verses.   He lives in a wretched house, and we went up dirty stairs, through dirty passages, where I wondered how fine ladies' trains and noses could go, and were received in a dark small den by the philosopher, or rather dévot, for he spurns the name of philosopher: he was in a dirty reddish nightgown, and very dirty nightcap bound round the forehead with a superlatively dirty chocolate-colored ribbon. Madame Récamier, the beautiful, the elegant, robed in white satin trimmed with white fur, seated herself on the elbow of his armchair, and besought him to repeat his verses.   Charlotte has drawn a picture of this scene. We met at La Harpe's Lady Elizabeth Foster and Lady Besborough — very engaging manners.

We were a few days ago at a Bal d'Enfants; this you would translate a children's ball, and so did we, till we were set right by the learned, — not a single child was at this ball, and only half a dozen unmarried ladies; it is a ball given by mothers to their grown-up children. Charlotte appeared as usual to great advantage, and was much admired for her ease and unaffected manners. She danced one English country dance with M. de Crillon, son of the Gibraltar Duke; when she stood up, a gentleman came to me and exclaimed, "Ah, Mademoiselle votre sœur va danser, nous attendons le moment où elle va *paraître*." She appeared extremely well from not being anxious to appear at all.   To-day we stayed at home to gain time for letters, etc., but thirteen visitors, besides the washerwoman, prevented our accomplishing all our great and good purposes.   The

visitors were all, except the washerwoman, so agreeable,
that even while they interrupted us, we did not know
how to wish them gone.

On the 27th January Mr. Edgeworth received a
peremptory order from the French Government to quit
Paris immediately.   He went with Maria to the village
of Passy.

Our friend, Madame Gautier, generously offered to
him the use of her house there, but he would not com-
promise her.   M. de Pastoret and M. Delessert visited
him the next morning, fearless of Buonaparte and his
orders, and the day after M. Pictet and M. Le Breton
came to say that he could return to Paris.   There had
been some misapprehension from Mr. Edgeworth having been supposed to be brother to the Abbé Edgeworth.
He wrote to Lord Whitworth that he would never deny
or give up the honor of being related to the Abbé.
Lord Whitworth advised him to state the exact degree
of relationship, which he did, and we heard no more of
the matter.[1]

MISS CHARLOTTE EDGEWORTH TO C. S. EDGEWORTH.

PARIS, February 21, 1803.

We went yesterday to see the consecration of a Bishop
at Notre Dame, and here I endured with satisfaction
most intense cold for three hours, and saw a solemn
ridiculous ceremony, and heard music that went through

[1] The Abbé Edgeworth (who called himself M. de Firmont, from the
estate possessed by his branch of the family) was first cousin once removed to Mr. Edgeworth, being the son of Essex, fifth son of Sir John
Edgeworth, and brother to Mr. Edgeworth's grandfather, Colonel Francis Edgeworth of Edgeworthstown.

me; I could not have believed that sounds could have been so fine: the alternate sounds of voices and the organ, or both together, and then the faint, distant murmur of prayers, each peal so much in harmony as to appear like one note beginning softly, rising, rising, rising, — then dying slowly off. There was one man whose voice was so loud, so full and clear, that it was equal to the voices of three men. The church itself is very fine; we were placed so as to see below us the whole ceremony. The solemnity of the manner in which they walked, their all being dressed alike, and differently from the rest of the people, rendered these priests a new set of beings. The ceremony appeared particularly ridiculous, as we could not hear a word that was said, because the church is so large, and we were at too great a distance, and all we could see was a Bishop dressing or undressing, or lying on the ground! The Archbishop of Paris, who performed the chief part of the ceremony, is a man about eighty years of age, yet he had the strength to go through the fatigue which such a ceremony requires for three hours together in very great cold, and every action was performed with as much firmness as a man of fifty could do it, and there was but one part which he left out, — the walking round along with the other bishops with the cross borne before them. We were told that he has often gone through similar fatigue, and in the evening, or an hour after, amused a company at dinner with cheerful, witty conversation: he is not a man of letters, but he has abilities and knowledge of the world. All these men were remarkably tall and fine-looking, some very vener-able; there were about sixty assembled. It appears

extraordinary that there should not be one little or
mean-looking among a set of people who are not, like
soldiers, chosen for their height, and as they must have
come from different parts of France.   I think there is
a greater variety of sizes among the French than among
us; if all the people who stand in the street of Edgeworthstown every Sunday were Frenchmen, you would
see ten remarkably little for one that you see there, and
ten remarkably tall.   I think there are more remarkably tall men in Ireland than in England.

Maria is writing a story,[1] and has a little table by
the fire, at which she sits as she used to do at Edgeworthstown for half an hour together without stirring,
with her pen in her hand; then she scribbles on very
fast.   My father intends to present his lock, with a
paper giving some account of it by way of introduction,
to the society of which he is a member, *La Société
pour encourager les arts et métiers*.   I suppose you
see in the newspapers that the ancient Academy is again
established under the name of the Institute?

MRS. EDGEWORTH TO MISS SNEYD.

PARIS, February 22, 1803.

The cough you mention has been epidemic here.
The thermometer has been as low as 9° on the morning of
the 15th; next day 40°, and the most charming weather
has succeeded; the streets have been so well washed by
the rain and scraped by the snow-cleaners, that they are

---

[1] Miss Edgeworth made a sketch for the story of *Madame de Fleury*
about this time, but did not finish it till long afterwards.   The incident
of the locked-up children was told to her by Madame de Pastoret, to
whom it had happened, and Maria took the name de Fleury from M. de
Pastoret's country house, the Château de Fleury.

actually dry and clean for the first time since October, which is fortunate, as the streets are crowded with people for the carnival, some in masks, some disguised as apothecaries, old women, harlequins, and knight-errants, followed by hundreds and thousands of men, women, and children, to whom they say what they can, generally nonsense devoid of wit.

Last Thursday, *jeudi-gras*, we dined at two, and were at St. Germain at six, at Madame Campan's, where we had been invited to see some plays acted by her pupils. The little theatre appeared already full when we entered. We stood a few seconds near the door, when Madame Campan cried out from above, "Placez Madame Edgeworth, faites monter Madame et sa compagnie." So we went up to the gallery, where we had very good places next to a Polish Princess and half a dozen of her countrywomen, who are all polite and well-bred. The crowd increased, many more than there was room for. The famous Madame Visconti and Lady Yarmouth sat behind us; Lady Elizabeth Foster and Lady Besborough not far from us; and below there were a number of English, the Duchess of Gordon and her beautiful daughter, Lady Georgiana. Madame Louis Buonaparte, who had been one of Madame Campan's *élèves*, was the principal Frenchwoman. The piece, "Esther," was performed admirably; the singing of the choir of young girls charming, and the *petite pièce*, "La Rosière de Salency," was better still; you know it is a charming thing, and was made so touching as to draw tears from every eye.

Mrs. Edgeworth writes: —

At the time this letter was written rumors that war would break out with England began to be prevalent in Paris. Mr. Edgeworth inquired among his friends, who said they feared it was true. He decided to set out immediately, and we began to pack up. Other friends contradicted this fear. We were anxious on another account to leave Paris, from the bad state of Henry Edgeworth's health, his friends at Edinburgh urging us to go there to see him. Better news of him, and the hope that the rumors of war were unfounded, made us suspend our packing. M. Le Breton called, and said he was sure of knowing before that evening the truth as to Buonaparte's warlike intentions, and that if Mr. Edgeworth met him at a friend's that night, he would know by his suddenly putting on his hat that war was imminent. He was unable to visit us again, and afraid if he wrote that his letter might be intercepted, and still more was he afraid of being overheard if he said anything at the party where they were to meet. Mr. Edgeworth went, and saw M. Le Breton, who did suddenly put on his hat, and on Mr. Edgeworth's return to us he said we must go.

The next day was spent in taking leave of our kind friends, from whom we found it so painful to part, and who expressed so much regret at losing us, and so much doubt as to the probability of war, that Mr. Edgeworth promised that if, on his arrival in London, his Paris friends wrote to say Peace, he would return to them, and bring over the rest of his family from Ireland for a year's residence.

MARIA TO MISS SNEYD.

CALAIS, March 4, 1803.

At last, my dear Aunt Mary, we have actually left
Paris. Perhaps we may be detained here for some
days, as the wind is directly against us; but we have
no reason to lament, as we are in Grandsire's excellent
house, and have books and thoughts enough to occupy
us. Thoughts of friends from whom we have parted,
and of friends to whom we are going. How few people
in this world are so rich in friends! When I reflect
upon the kindness which has been shown to us abroad,
and upon the affection that awaits us at home, I feel
afraid that I shall never be able to deserve my share of
all this happiness.

Charlotte is perfectly well; I believe no young woman
was ever more admired at Paris than she has been, and
none was ever less spoiled by admiration.

DOVER, March 6.

All alive and merry: just landed, after a fine passage
of six hours.

Mrs. Edgeworth narrates: —

On our arrival in London, we found the expected
letter from M. Le Breton. It had been agreed that if
there was to be peace, he was to conclude his letter
with "Mes hommages à la charmante Mademoiselle
Charlotte;" if war, the *charmante* was to be omitted.
He ended his letter, which made not the smallest allusion to politics or public events, with "Mes hommages

à Mademoiselle Charlotte," and we set out for Edinburgh.

On the first rumors of war, while we were in France, Mr. Edgeworth wrote to warn his son Lovell, who was on his way from Geneva to Paris, but he never received the letter: he was stopped on his journey, made prisoner, and remained among the *détenus* for eleven years, till the end of the war in 1814.

MARIA TO MISS SNEYD.

EDINBURGH, March 19, 1803.

Just arrived in Edinburgh, all four in perfect health, and I cannot employ myself better than in *bringing up* the history of our last week at Paris. The two most memorable events were Madame Campan's play and the visit to Madame de Genlis. The theatre at Madame Campan's was not much larger than our own; the dresses "magnificent beyond description;" the acting and the dancing infinitely too good for any but young ladies intended for the stage. The play was Racine's "Esther," and it interested me the next day to read Madame de Sévigné's account of its representation by the young ladies of St. Cyr, under the patronage of Madame de Maintenon. Madame de Genlis's beautiful "Rosière de Salency" was acted after "Esther," and the scene where the mother denounces her daughter, and pushes her from her, was so admirably written and so admirably played that it made me forget the stage, the actors, and the spectators, — I could not help thinking it real.

Full of the pleasure I had received from the "Rosière de Salency," I was impatient to pay a visit to Madame de Genlis. A few days afterwards we dined with Mr. and Mrs. Scotto, rather a stupid party of gentlemen. After dinner my father called me out of the room and said, "Now we will go to see Madame de Genlis." She had previously written to say she would be glad to be personally acquainted with Mr. and Miss Edgeworth. She lives — where do you think? — where Sully used to live, at the Arsenal. Buonaparte has given her apartments there. Now I do not know what you imagined in reading Sully's "Memoirs," but I always imagined that the Arsenal was one large building, with a façade to it like a very large hotel or a palace, and I fancied it was somewhere in the middle of Paris. On the contrary, it is quite in the suburbs. We drove on and on, and at last we came to a heavy archway, like what you see at the entrance of a fortified town; we drove under it for the length of three or four yards in total darkness, and then we found ourselves, as well as we could see by the light of some dim lamps, in a large square court, surrounded by buildings: here we thought we were to alight; no such thing; the coachman drove under another thick archway, lighted at the entrance by a single lamp, we found ourselves in another court, and still we went on, archway after archway, court after court, in all which reigned desolate silence. I thought the archways, and the courts, and the desolate silence would never end; at last the coachman stopped, and asked for the tenth time where the lady lived. It is excessively difficult to find people in Paris; we thought the names of Madame de Genlis and the Arsenal would have been sufficient, but the whole of this congregation of courts, and gateways, and houses is called the Arsenal, and

hundreds and hundreds of people inhabit it who are
probably perfect strangers to Madame de Genlis.   At
the doors where our coachman inquired, some answered
that they knew nothing of her, some that she lived in
the Faubourg St. Germain, others believed that she
might be at Passy, others had heard that she had apartments given to her by Government somewhere in the
Arsenal, but could not tell where; while the coachman
thus begged his way, we, anxiously looking out at him
from the middle of the great square where we were left,
listened for the answers that were given, and which
often from the distance escaped our ears.   At last a
door pretty near to us opened, and our coachman's head
and hat were illuminated by the candle held by the
person who opened the door, and as the two figures
parleyed with each other we could distinctly see the
expression of their countenances and their lips move.
The result of this parley was successful; we were directed to the house where Madame de Genlis lived, and
thought all difficulties ended.   No such thing, her
apartments were still to be sought for.   We saw before
us a large, crooked, ruinous stone staircase, lighted by
a single bit of candle hanging in a vile tin lantern in an
angle of the bare wall at the turn of the staircase —
only just light enough to see that the walls were bare
and old, and the stairs immoderately dirty.   There
were no signs of the place being inhabited except this
lamp, which could not have been lighted without hands.
I stood still in melancholy astonishment, while my
father groped his way into a kind of porter's lodge, or
den, at the foot of the stairs, where he found a man
who was porter to various people who inhabited this

house. You know the Parisian houses are inhabited by hordes of different people, and the stairs are in fact streets, and dirty streets, to their dwellings. The porter, who was neither obliging nor intelligent, carelessly said that "Madame de Genlis logeait au second à gauche, qu'il faudrait tirer sa sonnette," he believed she was at home, if she was not gone out. Up we went by ourselves, for this porter, though we were strangers, and pleaded that we were so, never offered to stir a step to guide or to light us. When we got to the second stage, we faintly saw, by the light from the one candle at the first landing-place, two dirty large folding-doors, one set on the right and one on the left, and hanging on each a bell, no larger than what you see in the small parlor of a small English inn. My father pulled one bell and waited some minutes — no answer; pulled the other bell and waited — no answer; thumped at the left door — no answer; pushed and pulled at it — could not open it; pushed open one of the right-hand folding-doors — utter darkness; went in, as well as we could feel, there was no furniture. After we had been there a few seconds we could discern the bare walls and some strange lumber in one corner. The room was a prodigious height, like an old playhouse. We retreated, and in despair went down again to the stupid or surly porter. He came upstairs very unwillingly, and pointed to a deep recess between the stairs and the folding-doors: "Allez, voilà la porte et tirez la sonnette." He and his candle went down, and my father had but just time to seize the handle of the bell, when we were again in darkness. After ringing this feeble bell we presently heard doors open, and little footsteps approaching nigh.

The door was opened by a girl of about Honora's size, holding an ill-set-up, wavering candle in her hand, the light of which fell full upon her face and figure, — her face was remarkably intelligent; dark sparkling eyes, dark hair, curled in the most fashionable long cork-screw ringlets over her eyes and cheeks. She parted the ringlets to take a full view of us, and we were equally impatient to take a full view of her. The dress of her figure by no means suited the head and the elegance of her attitude: what her "nether weeds" might be we could not distinctly see, but they seemed to be a coarse short petticoat, like what Molly Bristow's children would wear, not on Sundays, a woolen gray spencer above, pinned with a single pin by the lapels tight across the neck under the chin, and open all below. After surveying us, and hearing that our name was Edgeworth, she smiled graciously, and bid us follow her, saying, "Maman est chez elle." She led the way with the grace of a young lady who has been taught to dance, across two ante-chambers, miserable looking, but miserable or not, no house in Paris can be without them. The girl, or young lady, for we were still in doubt which to think her, led us into a small room, in which the candles were so well screened by a green tin screen that we could scarcely distinguish the tall form of a lady in black, who rose from her armchair by the fireside as the door opened; a great puff of smoke came from the huge fireplace at the same moment. She came forward, and we made our way towards her as well as we could through a confusion of tables, chairs, and work-baskets, china, writing-desks, and inkstands, and bird-cages, and a harp. She did not speak, and as her back was now turned to both fire and candle, I could not see her face, or anything but the outline of her form, and her attitude; her form was the remains of a fine form, and her attitude that of a woman used to a better drawing-room. I, being foremost, and she silent, was compelled to speak to the figure in darkness: "Madame de Genlis, nous a fait l'honneur de nous mander qu'elle voulait bien nous permettre de lui rendre visite, et de lui offrir nos respects," said I, or words to that effect: to which she replied by taking my hand and saying something in which *charmée* was the most intelligible word. Whilst she spoke she looked over my shoulder at my father, whose bow I presume told her he was a gentleman, for she spoke to him immediately as if she wished to please, and seated us in fauteuils near the fire.

I then had a full view of her face and figure; she looked like the full-length picture of my great-great-grandmother Edgeworth, you may have seen in the garret, very thin and melancholy, but her face not so handsome as my great-grandmother's; dark eyes, long sallow cheeks, compressed thin lips, two or three black ringlets on a high forehead, a cap that Mrs. Grier might wear, — altogether an appearance of fallen fortunes, worn-out health, and excessive, but guarded irritability. To me there was nothing of that engaging, captivating manner which I had been taught to expect by many even of her enemies; she seemed to me to be alive only to literary quarrels and jealousies — the muscles of her face as she spoke, or as my father spoke to her, quickly and too easily expressed hatred and anger whenever any not of her own party were mentioned. She is now, you

know, *dévote acharnément.* When I mentioned with
some enthusiasm the good Abbé Morellet, who has written so courageously in favor of the French exiled
nobility and their children, she answered in a sharp
voice, "Oui, c'est un homme de beaucoup d'esprit, à ce
qu'on dit, à ce que je crois même, mais il faut vous
apprendre q'uil n'est pas des NOTRES." My father
spoke of Pamela, Lady Edward Fitzgerald, and explained how he had defended her in the Irish House
of Commons; instead of being pleased or touched, her
mind instantly diverged into an elaborate and artificial
exculpation of Lady Edward and herself, proving, or
attempting to prove, that she never knew any of her
husband's plans, that she utterly disapproved of them,
at least of all she suspected of them. This defense was
quite lost upon us, who never thought of attacking;
but Madame de Genlis seems to have been so much used
to be attacked, that she has defenses and apologies ready
prepared, suited to all possible occasions. She spoke of
Madame de Staël's "Delphine" with detestation, of
another new and fashionable novel, "Amélie," with ab-
horrence, and kissed my forehead twice because I had
not read it: "Vous autres Anglaises vous êtes modestes!"
Where was Madame de Genlis's sense of delicacy when
she penned and published "Les Chevaliers du Cigne"?
Forgive me, my dear Aunt Mary, you begged me to see
her with favorable eyes, and I went to see her after
seeing her "Rosière de Salency" with the most favorable disposition, but I could not like her; there was
something of malignity in her countenance and conversation that repelled love, and of hypocrisy which anni-
hilated esteem, and from time to time I saw, or thought

I saw through the gloom of her countenance, a gleam of coquetry. But my father judges much more favorably of her than I do; she evidently took pains to please him, and he says he is sure she is a person over whose mind he could gain great ascendency; he thinks her a woman of violent passions, unbridled imagination, and ill-tempered, but *not* malevolent — one who has been so torn to pieces that she now turns upon her enemies, and longs to tear in her turn. He says she has certainly great powers of pleasing, though I neither saw nor felt them. But you know, my dear aunt, that I am not famous for judging sanely of strangers on a first visit, and I might be prejudiced or mortified by Madame de Genlis assuring me that she had never read anything of mine except "Belinda;" had heard of "Practical Education," and heard it much praised, but had never seen it. She has just published an additional volume of her "Petits Romans," in which there are some beautiful stories, but you must not expect another "Mademoiselle de Clermont:" one such story in an age is as much as one can reasonably expect.

I had almost forgotten to tell you that the little girl who showed us in is a girl whom she is educating. "Elle m'appelle maman, mais elle n'est pas ma fille." The manner in which this little girl spoke to Madame de Genlis, and looked at her, appeared to me more in her favor than anything else. She certainly spoke to her with freedom and fondness, and without any affectation. I went to look at what the child was writing; she was translating Darwin's "Zoonomia." I read some of her translation, it was excellent; she was, I think she said, ten years old. It is certain that

Madame de Genlis made the present Duke of Orleans such an excellent mathematician, that when he was during his emigration in distress for bread, he taught mathematics as a professor in one of the German Universities.   If we could see or converse with one of her pupils, and hear what they think of her, we should be able to form a better judgment than from all that her books and enemies say for or against her.   I say her *books*, not her *friends* and enemies, for I fear she has no friends to plead for her, except her books.   I never met any one of any party who was her friend: this strikes me with real melancholy; to see a woman of the first talents in Europe, who had lived and shone in the gay court of the gayest nation in the world, now deserted and forlorn, living in wretched lodgings, with some of the pictures and finery, the wreck of her fortunes, before her eyes, without society, without a single friend, admired — and despised: she lives literally in spite, not in pity.   Her cruelty in drawing a profligate character of the Queen after her execution, in the "Chevaliers du Cigne," her taking her pupils at the beginning of the Revolution to the revolutionary clubs, her connection with the late Duke of Orleans and her hypocrisy about it, her insisting upon being governess to his children when the Duchess did not wish it, and its being supposed that it was she who instigated the Duke in all his horrible conduct; and more than all the rest, her own attacks and *apologies* have brought her into all this isolated state of reprobation.   And now, my dear aunt, I have told you all I know, or have heard, or think about her; and perhaps I have tired you, but I fancied that it was a subject particularly interesting to you, and if I have been mistaken you will with your usual good-nature forgive me and say, "I am sure Maria meant it kindly."

Now to fresh fields. In London you know that we had the pleasure of meeting Mr. and Mrs. Sneyd, and Emma: there is such a general likeness between her and Charlotte, that they might pass for sisters. Mrs. Sneyd bribed us to like her by her extreme kindness. We went to Covent Garden Theatre and saw the new play of "John Bull:" some humor, and some pathos, and one good character of an Irishman, but the contrast between the elegance of the French theatre and the *grossièreté* of the English struck us much. But this is the judgment of a disappointed playwright!

Now, Aunt Mary, scene changes to York, where we stayed a day to see the Minster; and as we had found a parcel of new books for us at Johnson's, from Lindley Murray, we thought ourselves bound to go and see him. We were told that he lived about a mile from York, and in the evening we drove to see him. A very neat-looking house; door opened by a pretty Quaker maid-servant; shown into a well-furnished parlor, cheerful fire, everything bespeaking comfort and happiness. On the sofa at the farther end of the room was seated, quite upright, a Quaker-looking man in a pale brown coat, who never attempted to rise from his seat to receive us, but held out his hand, and with a placid, benevolent smile said, "You are most welcome — I am heartily glad to see you; it is my misfortune that I cannot rise from my seat, but I must be as I am, as I have been these eighteen years." He had lost the use of one arm and side, and cannot walk — not paralytic, but from the

effects of a fever. Such mild, cheerful resignation,
such benevolence of manners and countenance I never
saw in any human being. He writes solely with the
idea of doing good to his fellow-creatures. He wants
nothing in this life, he says, neither fortune nor fame
— he seems to forget that he wants health — he says,
"I have so many blessings." His wife, who seemed to
love and admire "my husband" as the first and best of
human beings, gave us excellent tea and abundance of
good cake.

I have not room here under the seal for the Minster,
nor for the giant figures on Alnwick Castle, nor for the
droll man at the beautiful town of Durham; but I or
somebody better than me will tell of them, and of Mrs.
Green's drawings and painted jessamine in her window,
and Mr. Wellbeloved and his charming children, and
Mr. Horner,[1] at Newcastle, and Dr. Trotter, at ditto.

My father says, "I hope you have done;" and so
perhaps do you.

TO MRS. RUXTON.

EDINBURGH, March 30, 1803.

In a few days I hope we shall see you. I long to
see you again, and to hear your voice, and to receive
from you those kind looks and kind words, which custom cannot stale. I believe that the more variety
people see, the more they become attached to their first
and natural friends. I had taken a large sheet of paper
to tell you some of the wonders we have seen in our
nine days' stay in Edinburgh, but my father has wisely
advised me to content myself with a small sheet, as I

____
[1] Francis Horner.

am to have the joy of talking to you so soon, and may then say volumes in the same time that I could write pages. I cannot express the pleasure we have felt in being introduced to Henry's delightful society of friends here, both those he has chosen for himself and those who have chosen him. Old and young, grave and gay, join in speaking of him with a degree of affection and esteem that is most touching and gratifying. Mr. and Mrs. Stewart[1] surpassed all that I had expected, and I had expected much. Mr. Stewart is said to be naturally or habitually grave and reserved, but towards us he has broken through his habits or his nature, and I never conversed with any one with whom I was more at ease. He has a grave, sensible face, more like the head of Shakespeare than any other head or print that I can remember. I have not heard him lecture; no woman can go to the public lectures here, and I don't choose to go in men's or boy's clothes, or in the pocket of the Irish giant, though he is here and well able to carry me. Mrs. Stewart has been for years wishing in vain for the pleasure of hearing one of her husband's lectures. She is just the sort of woman you would like, that you would love. I do think it is impossible to know her without loving her; indeed, she has been so kind to Henry, that it would be doubly impossible (an Irish impossibility) to us. Yet you know people do not always love because they have received obligations. It is an additional proof of her merit, and of her powers of pleasing, that she makes those who *are*

---

[1] Mr. and Mrs. Dugald Stewart. As Professor at the University of Edinburgh, Mr. Stewart gave those lectures which Sir James Mackintosh said "breathed the love of virtue into whole generations of pupils."

under obligations to her, forget that they are bound to be grateful, and only remember that they think her good and agreeable.

TO MISS HONORA EDGEWORTH.[1]

GLASGOW, April 4, 1803.

I have not forgotten my promise to write to you, and I think I can give you pleasure by telling you that Henry is getting better every day,[2] and that we have all been extremely happy in the company of several of his friends in Edinburgh and Glasgow. He has made these friends by his own good qualities and good conduct, and we hear them speak of him with the greatest esteem and affection. This morning Dr. Birkbeck, one of Henry's friends, took us to see several curious machines, in a house where he gives lectures on mechanical and chemical subjects. He is going to give a lecture on purpose for children, and he says he took the idea for doing so from "Practical Education." He opened a drawer and showed to me a little perspective machine he had made from the print of my father's; and we were also very much surprised to see in one of his rooms a large globe of silk, swelled out and lighted by a lamp withinside, so that when the room was darkened we could plainly see the map of the world painted on it, as suggested in "Practical Education." My father mentioned to this gentleman my Aunt Charlotte's invention of painting the stars on the inside of an umbrella: he was much pleased with it, and I think he

---

[1] The second sister in the family of the name.

[2] Henry was only better for a time; he was never really restored to health, though he lived till 1813.

will make such an umbrella. . . . Tell Sneyd that we saw at Edinburgh his old friend the Irish giant. I suppose he remembers seeing him at Bristol. He is so tall that he can with ease lean his arm on the top of the room door. I stood beside him, and the top of my head did not reach to his hip. My father laid his hand withinside of the giant's hand, and it looked as small as little Harriet's would in John Langan's. This poor giant looks very sallow and unhealthy, and seemed not to like to sit or stand all day for people to look at him.

After the return of the family to Edgeworthstown, Miss Edgeworth at once began to occupy herself with preparing for the press "Popular Tales," which were published this year. She also began "Emilie de Coulanges," "Madame de Fleury," and "Ennui," and wrote "Leonora," with the romantic purpose already mentioned.

In 1804 she found time to write "Griselda," which she amused herself with at odd moments in her own room without telling her father what she was about. When finished, she sent it to Johnson, who had the good-nature, at her request, to print a title-page for a single copy without her name to it: he then sent it over to Mr. Edgeworth as a new novel just come out. Mr. Edgeworth read it with surprise and admiration. He could not believe Maria could have had the actual time to write it, and yet it was so like her style; he at last exclaimed, "It must be Anna's. Anna has written this to please me. It is by some one we are interested in, Mary was so anxious I should read it." Miss Sneyd was in the secret, and had several times put it before him on the table; at last she told him it was Maria's. He was amused at the trick, and delighted at having admired the book without knowing its author.

MARIA TO MISS CHARLOTTE SNEYD.

BLACK CASTLE, December, 1804.

Though Henry will bring you all the news of this enchanted castle, and though you will hear it far better from his lips than from my pen, I cannot let him go without a line. I need not tell you I am perfectly happy here, and only find the day too short. Pray make Henry give you an account of the grand dinner we were at, and the Spanish priest who called Rousseau and Voltaire *vagabones*, and the gentleman who played the "Highland Laddie" on the guitar, and of Mr. Grainger, who was *present* at one of the exhibitions of that German spectre-monger celebrated in Wraxall.

The cottages are improving here, the people have paved their yards, and plant roses against their walls. My aunt likes "Ennui." I had thoughts of finishing it here, but every day I find some excuse for idleness.

TO MISS HONORA EDGEWORTH.

BLACK CASTLE, January, 1805.

I have thought of you often when I heard things that would entertain you, and thought I had collected a great store, but when I rummage in my head, for want of having had or taken time to keep the drawers of my cabinet of memory tidy, I cannot find one single thing that I want, except that it is said that plants raised from cuttings do not bear such fine flowers as those raised from seeds; that a lady, whose parrot had lost

all its feathers, made him a flannel jacket. . . . I will
bring a specimen of the silk spun by the *Processio-
naires*, of whom my aunt gave you the history.   There
is a cock here who is as great a tyrant in his own way
as Buonaparte, and a poor Barbary cock who has no
claws has the misfortune to live in the same yard with
him; he will not suffer this poor defenseless fellow to
touch a morsel or grain of all the good things Margaret
throws to them till he and all his protegées are satisfied.

TO MISS RUXTON.

Edgeworthstown, February 26, 1805.

I have been reading *a power* of good books: "Mon-
tesquieu sur la Grandeur et Décadence des Romains,"
which I recommend to you as a book you will admire,
because it furnishes so much food for thought; it shows
how history may be studied for the advantage of mankind, not for the mere purpose of remembering facts
and repeating them.

Sneyd [1] has come home to spend a week of vacation
with us.   He is now full of logic, and we perpetually
hear the words *syllogisms* and *predicates, majors* and
minors, universals and *particulars, affirmatives* and
negatives, and LAROK and BARBARA, not Barbara
Allen or any of her relations; and we have learnt by
logic that a stone is not an animal, and conversely that
an animal is not a stone.   I really think a man talking
logic on the stage might be made as diverting as the
character of the *Apprentice* who is arithmetically mad;
pray read it: my father read it to us a few nights ago,
and though I had a most violent headache, so that I

---

[1] Second son of Mrs. Elizabeth Edgeworth.

was forced to hold my head on both sides whilst I laughed, yet I could not refrain. Much I attribute to my father's reading, but something must be left to Murphy. I have some idea of writing, in the intervals of my *severer studies* for "Professional Education," a comedy for my father's birthday, but I shall do it up in my own room, and shall not produce it till it is finished. I found the first hint of it in the strangest place that anybody could invent, for it was in Dallas's "History of the Maroons," and you may read the book to find it out, and ten to one you miss it. At all events pray read the book, for it is extremely interesting and entertaining: it presents a new world with new manners to the imagination, and the whole bears the stamp of truth. It is not well written in general, but there are particular parts admirable from truth of description and force of feeling.

Your little goddaughter Sophy is one of the most engaging little creatures I ever saw, and knows almost all the birds and beasts in Bewick, from the tom-tit to the hip-po-pot-a-mus, and names them in a sweet little droll voice.

TO HENRY EDGEWORTH, AT EDINBURGH.

EDGEWORTHSTOWN, March, 1805.

It gives me the most sincere pleasure to see your letters to my father written just as if you were talking to a favorite friend of your own age, and with that manly simplicity characteristic of your mind and manner from the time you were able to speak. There is something in this perfect openness and in the courage of daring to be always yourself, which attaches more than I can express, more than all the Chesterfieldian arts and graces that ever were practiced.

The worked sleeves are for Mrs. Stewart, and you are to offer them to her, — nobody can say I do not know how to choose my ambassadors well! If Mrs. Stewart should begin to say, "Oh! it is a pity Miss Edgeworth should spend her time at such work!" please to interrupt her speech, though that is very rude, and tell her that I like work very much, and that I have only done this at odd times, after breakfast, you know, when my father reads out Pope's Homer, or when there are long sittings, when it is much more agreeable to move one's fingers than to have to sit with hands crossed or clasped immovably. I by no means accede to the doctrine that ladies cannot attend to anything else when they are working: besides, it is contrary, is not it, to all the theories of "Zoonomia"? Does not Dr. Darwin show that certain habitual motions go on without interrupting trains of thought? And do not common sense and experience, whom I respect even above Dr. Darwin, show the same thing?

TO MISS SOPHY RUXTON.

EDGEWORTHSTOWN, March 25, 1805.

To-morrow we all, viz. Mr. Edgeworth, two Miss Sneyds, and Miss Harriet Beaufort, and Miss Fanny Brown, and Miss Maria, and Miss Charlotte, and Miss Honora, and Mr. William Edgeworth, go in one coach and one chaise to Castle Forbes, to see a play acted by the ladies Elizabeth and Adelaide Forbes, Miss Parkins, Lord Rancliffe, Lord Forbes, and I don't know how many grandees with tufts on their heads, for every

grandee man must now, you know, have a tuft or ridge
of hair upon the middle of his pate. Have you read
Kotzebue's "Paris"? Some parts entertaining, mostly
stuff. We have heard from Lovell, still a prisoner, at
Verdun, and in hopes of peace, poor fellow.

TO C. SNEYD EDGEWORTH, AT TRINITY COLLEGE, DUBLIN.

EDGEWORTHSTOWN, May 4, 1805.

We are all very happy and tolerably merry with the
assistance of William and the young tribe, who are
always at his heels and in full chorus with him. Charlotte *cordials* me twice a day with "Cecilia," which she
reads charmingly, and which entertains me as much at
the third reading as it did at the first.

We are a little, but very little afraid of being swallowed up by the French: they have so much to swallow
and digest before they come to us! They did come
once very near, to be sure, but they got nothing by it.

TO MISS SOPHY RUXTON.

EDGEWORTHSTOWN, June 1, 1805.

My father's birthday was kept yesterday, much more
agreeably than last year, for then we had company in
the house. Yesterday Sneyd, now at home for his
vacation, who is ever the promoter of gayety, contrived
a pretty little *fête champêtre*, which surprised us all
most agreeably. After dinner he persuaded me that it
was indispensably necessary for my health that I should
take an airing; accordingly the chaise came to the door,
and Anne Nangle, and my mother, with little Lucy in
her arms, and Maria were rolled off, and after them on

horseback came rosy Charlotte, all smiles, and Henry,
with eyes brilliant with pleasure — riding again with
Charlotte after eight months' absence. It was a delightful evening, and we thought we were pleasing ourselves sufficiently by the airing, so we came home *thinking of nothing at all*, when, as we drove round, our
ears were suddenly struck with the sound of music, and
as if by enchantment, a fairy festival appeared upon the
green. In the midst of an amphitheatre of verdant
festoons suspended from white staffs, on which the scarlet streamers of the yeomen were flying, appeared a
company of youths and maidens in white, their heads
adorned with flowers, dancing; while their mothers and
their little children were seated on benches round the
amphitheatre. John Langan sat on the pier of the
dining-room steps, with Harriet on one knee and Sophy
on the other, and Fanny standing beside him. In the
course of the evening William danced a reel with Fanny
and Harriet, to the great delight of the spectators.
Cakes and syllabubs served in great abundance by good
Kitty, formed no inconsiderable part of the pleasures of
the evening. William, who is at present in the height
of electrical enthusiasm, proposed to the dancers a few
electrical sparks, to complete the joys of the day. All
— men, women, and children — flocked into the study
after him to be *shocked*, and their various gestures and
expressions of surprise and terror mixed with laughter,
were really diverting to my mother, Anne Nangle, and
me, who had judiciously posted ourselves in the gallery.
Charlotte and Sneyd, as soon as it was dark, came to
summon us, and we found the little amphitheatre on the
grass-plat illuminated, the lights mixed with the green

boughs and flowers were beautiful, and boys with flam-
beaux waving about had an excellent effect. I do wish
you could have seen the honest, happy face of George,
as he held his flambeau bolt upright at his station,
looking at his own pretty daughter Mary. Oh, my dear
aunt, how much our pleasure would have been increased
if you had been sitting beside us at the dining-room
window.

TO MISS MARGARET RUXTON.

EDGEWORTHSTOWN, June 21, 1805.

I had a most pleasant long letter from my father
to-day. He has become acquainted with Mrs. Crewe
—"Buff and blue and Mrs. Crewe"—and gives an
account of a *déjeûner* at which he *assisted* at her house
at Hampstead as quite delightful. Miss Crewe charmed
him by praising "To-morrow," and he claimed, he says,
remuneration on the spot—a song, which it is not easy
to obtain; she sang, and he thought her singing worthy
of its celebrity. He was charmed with old Dr. Burney,
who at eighty-two was the most lively, well-bred, agreeable man in the room. Lord Stanhope begged to be
presented to him, and he thought him the most wonderful man he ever met.

Tell my aunt "Leonora" is in the press.

TO MRS. RUXTON.

EDGEWORTHSTOWN, September 6, 1805.

Thank you, thank you. Unless you could jump into
that skin out of which I was ready to jump when your
letter was read, you could not tell how very much I am
obliged by your so kindly consenting to come.

I have been at Pakenham Hall and Castle Forbes; at
Pakenham Hall I was delighted with "that sweetest
music," the praises of a friend, from a person of judgment and taste. I do not know when I have felt so
much pleasure as in hearing sweet Kitty Pakenham
speak of your Sophy; I never saw her look more animated or more pretty than when she was speaking of
her.

Lady Elizabeth Pakenham has sent to me a little
pony, as quiet and almost as small as a dog, on which
I go trit trot, trit trot; but I hope it will never take it
into its head to add

> " When we come to the stile,
>   Skip we go over."

TO MISS SOPHY RUXTON.

EDGEWORTHSTOWN, February 7, 1806.

I am ashamed to tell you I have been so idle that I
have not yet finished "Madame de Fleury." You will
allow that we have gadded about enough lately: Sonna,
Pakenham Hall, Farnham, and Castle Forbes. I don't
think I told you that I grew quite fond of Lady Judith
Maxwell, and I flatter myself she did not dislike me,
because she did not keep me in the ante-chamber of her
mind, but let me into the boudoir at once.

So Lord Henry Petty is Chancellor of the Exchequer
— at twenty-four on the pinnacle of glory!

Sneyd and Charlotte have begun "Sir Charles Grandison;" I almost envy them the pleasure of reading
Clementina's history for the first time. It is one of
those pleasures which is never repeated in life.

TO MRS. EDGEWORTH.

ROSSTREVOR, March 21, 1806.

I have spent a very happy week at Collon;[1] I never saw your mother in such excellent spirits. She and Dr. Beaufort were so good as to bring me to Dundalk, where my aunt had appointed to meet me; but her courage failed her about going over the Mountain road, and she sent Mr. Corry's chaise with hired horses. I foresaw we should have a battle about those horses, and so we had — only a skirmish, in which I came off victorious! Your father, who, next to mine, is, I think, the best and most agreeable traveler in the world, walked us about Dundalk and to the Quay, etc., whilst the horses were resting, and we ate black cherries and were very merry. They pitied me for the ten-mile stage I was to go alone, but I did not pity myself, for I had Sir William Jones's and Sir William Chambers's "Asiatic Miscellany." The metaphysical poetry of India, however, is not to my taste; and though the Indian Cupid, with his bow of sugar-cane and string of bees and five arrows for the five senses, is a very pretty and very ingenious little fellow, I have a preference in favor of our own Cupid, and of the two would rather leave orders with "my porter" to admit the "well-known boy."[2]

Besides the company of Sir William Jones, I had the pleasure of meeting on the road Mr. Parkinson Ruxton

---

[1] Dr. Beaufort, father of the fourth Mrs. Edgeworth, was Vicar of Collon.

[2] From an Address to Cupid, by the Duc de Nivernois, translated by Mr. Edgeworth.

and Sir Chichester Fortescue, who had been commissioned by my aunt to hail me; they accordingly did so, and after a mutual broadside of compliments, they sheered off. The road to Newry is like Wales — Ravensdale, three miles of wood, glen, and mountain.

My aunt and Sophy were on the steps of the inn at Newry to receive me. The road from Newry to Rosstrevor is both sublime and beautiful. The inn at Rosstrevor is like the best sort of English breakfasting inn. But to proceed with my journey, for I must go two miles and a half from Rosstrevor to my aunt's house. Sublime mountains and sea — road, a flat, graveled walk, walled on the precipice side. You see a slated English or Welsh looking farmhouse amongst some stunted trees, apparently in the sea; you turn down a long avenue of firs, only three feet high, but old-looking, six rows deep on each side. The two former proprietors of this mansion had opposite tastes — one all for straight, and the other all for serpentine lines; and there was a war between snug and picturesque, of which the traces appear every step you proceed. You seem driving down into the sea, to which this avenue leads; but you suddenly turn and go back from the shore, through stunted trees of various sorts scattered over a wild common, then a dwarf mixture of shrubbery and orchard, and you are at the end of the house, which is pretty. The front is ugly, but from it you look upon the bay of Carlingford — Carlingford Head opposite to you — vessels under sail, near and distant — little islands, sea-birds, and landmarks standing in the sea. Behind the house the mountains of Morne. I saw all this with admiration, tired as I was, for it was seven o'clock. In the parlor is a surprising chimney-piece, as gigantic as that at Grandsire's at Calais, with wonderful wooden ornaments and a tablet representing Alexander's progress through India, he looking very pert, driving four lions.

After dinner I was so tired, that in spite of all my desire to see and hear, I was obliged to lie down and rest. After resting, but not sleeping, I groped my way down the broad old staircase, *felt* my road, passed *two* clockcases on the landing-place, and arrived in the parlor, where I was glad to see candles and tea, and my dear aunt and Sophy and Margaret's illumined, affectionate faces. Tea. "Come, now," says my aunt, "let us show Maria the wonderful passage; it looks best by candlelight." I followed my guide through a place that looks like Mrs. Radcliffe in lower life — passage after passage, very low-roofed, and full of strange lumber; came to a den of a bedchamber, then another, and a study, all like the hold of a ship, and fusty; but in this study were mahogany bookcases, glass doors, and well-bound, excellent books. All kinds of tables, broken and stowed on top of each other, and parts of looking-glasses, looking as if they had been there a hundred years, and jelly glasses on a glass stand, as if somebody had supped there the night before. Turn from the study and you see a staircase, more like a step-ladder, very narrow, but one could squeeze up at a time, by which we went into a place like that you may remember at the Post House in the Low Countries — two chambers, if chambers they could be called, quite remote from the rest of the house, low ceilings, strange scraps of many-colored paper on the walls, an old camp had a feather bed with half the feathers out, one window, low, but wide.

"Out of that window," said my maid, "as Isabella told us, the corpse was carried."

"Who is Isabella?" cried I; but before my maid could answer I was struck with new wonder at the sight of two French looking-glasses, in gilt frames, side by side, reaching from the ceiling to the floor, and placed exactly opposite the bed.[1]

I was now so tired that I could neither see, hear, or understand, imagine, or wonder any longer. Somebody somehow managed to get my clothes off, and thereby put me into bed. The images of all these people and things flitted before my eyes for a few seconds, and then I was fast asleep.

Mrs. and Miss Fortescue came in the morning, and among other things mentioned the fancy ball in Dublin. Mrs. Sheridan[2] was the handsomest woman there. The Duchess of Rutland was dressed as Mary Queen of Scots, and danced with Lord Darnley. At supper the Duchess motioned to Lady Darnley to come to her table; but Lady Darnley refused, as she had a party of young ladies. The Duchess approached her rather angrily. "Oh," said Lady Darnley, "when the Queen of Scots was talking to Darnley, it would not have done for me to have been so near them."

[1] This mysterious apartment had belonged to a poor crazed lady who died there, and who had, as Isabella, the gardener's wife, related, a passion for fine papers. Different patterns of which were put on the walls to please her, and also the French mirrors, in which she delighted to look from her bed. And when she died her coffin was, to avoid the crooked passages, taken out of the window.

[2] Mrs. Tom Sheridan.

MRS. EDGEWORTH TO MISS SOPHY RUXTON.

EDGEWORTHSTOWN, April 13, 1806.

We were at Gaybrook when your letter came, and when the good news of Miss Pakenham's happiness arrived:[1] it was announced there in a very pleasant, sprightly letter from your friend Miss Fortescue. Your account of the whole affair is really admirable, and is one of those tales of real life in which the romance is far superior to the generality of fictions. I hope the imaginations of this hero and heroine have not been too much exalted, and that they may not find the enjoyment of a happiness so long wished for inferior to what they expected. Pray tell dear good Lady Elizabeth we are so delighted with the news, and so engrossed by it, that, waking or sleeping, the image of Miss Pakenham swims before our eyes. To make the romance perfect we want two material documents — a description of the person of Sir Arthur, and a knowledge of the time when the interview after his return took place.

MARIA TO MRS. EDGEWORTH.

ALLENSTOWN, May Day, 1806.

Dr. Beaufort, tell Charlotte, saw Sir Arthur Wellesley at the Castle — handsome, very brown, quite bald, and a hooked nose. He could not travel with Lady Wellesley; he went by the mail. He had overstayed his leave a day. She traveled under the care of his brother, the clergyman.

---

[1] Catherine, second daughter of the second Lord Longford, married, 10th April, 1806, Sir Arthur Wellesley, afterwards the first and great Duke of Wellington. He had, at this time, just returned from India, after a stay of eleven years.

TO MISS MARGARET RUXTON.

EDGEWORTHSTOWN, May 23, 1806.

I have been laughed at most unmercifully by some of the phlegmatic personages round the library table for my impatience to send you "The Mine." "Do you think Margaret cannot live five minutes longer without it? Saddle the mare, and ride to Dublin, and thence to Black Castle or Chantony with it, my dear!"

I bear all with my accustomed passiveness, and am rewarded by my father's having bought it for me; and it is now at Archer's for you. Observe, I think the poem, as a drama, tiresome in the extreme, and absurd, but I wish you to see that the very letters from the man in the quicksilver mine which you recommended to me have been seized upon by a poet of no inferior genius. Some of the strophes of the fairies are most beautifully poetic.

Lady Elizabeth Pakenham told us that when Lady Wellesley was presented to the Queen, Her Majesty said, "I am happy to see you at my court, so bright an example of constancy. If anybody in this world deserves to be happy, you do." Then Her Majesty inquired, "But did you really never write *one* letter to Sir Arthur Wellesley during his long absence?" "No, never, madam." "And did you never think of him?" "Yes, madam, very often."

I am glad constancy is approved of at courts, and hope "the bright example" may be followed.

TO MISS SOPHY RUXTON.

EDGEWORTHSTOWN, July 12, 1806.

This is the third sheet of paper in the smallest hand I could write I have had the honor within these three days to spoil in your service, stuffed full of geological and chemical facts, which we learned from our two philosophical travelers, Davy and Greenough; but when finished I persuaded myself they were not worth sending. Many of the facts I find you have in Thomson and Nicholson, which, "owing to my ignorance," as pure Sir Hugh Tyrold would say, "I did not rightly know."

Our travelers have just left us, and my head is in great danger of bursting from the multifarious treasures that have been stowed and crammed into it in the course of one week. Mr. Davy is wonderfully improved since you saw him at Bristol: he has an amazing fund of knowledge upon all subjects, and a great deal of genius. Mr. Greenough has not, at first sight, a very intelligent countenance, yet he *is* very intelligent, and has a good deal of literature and anecdote, foreign and domestic, and a taste for wit and humor. He has traveled a great deal, and relates well. Dr. Beddoes is much better, but my father does not think his health safe. I am very well, but shamefully idle, — indeed, I have done nothing but hear; and if I had had a dozen pair extraordinary of ears, and as many heads, I do not think I could have heard or held all that was said.

TO MISS RUXTON.

EDGEWORTHSTOWN, February, 1807.

While Charlotte[1] was pretty well we paid our long promised visit to Coolure, and passed a few very pleasant days there. Admiral Pakenham is very entertaining, and appears very amiable in the midst of his children, who dote on him. He spoke very handsomely of your darling brother, and diverted us by the mode in which he congratulated Richard on his marriage: "I give you joy, my good friend, and I am impatient to see the woman who has made an honest man of you."

Colonel Edward Pakenham burned his instep by falling asleep before the fire, out of which a turf fell on his foot, and so he was, luckily for us, detained a few days longer, and dined and breakfasted at Coolure. He is very agreeable, and unaffected, and modest, after all the flattery he has met with.[2]

TO MRS. RUXTON.

EDGEWORTHSTOWN, September, 1807.

My beloved aunt and friend, — friend to my least fancies as well as to my largest interests, — thank you for the six fine rose-trees, and thank you for the little darling double-flowering almond-tree. Sneyd asked if there was nothing for him, so I very generously gave him the polyanthuses and planted them with my own hands at the corners of his garden pincushions.

Mr. Hammond may satisfy himself as to the union

[1] Charlotte Edgeworth, the idol and beauty of the family, died, after a long illness, 7th April, 1807.

[2] Colonel, afterwards Sir Edward Pakenham, distinguished in the Peninsular War, fell in action at New Orleans, 8th January, 1815.

of commerce and literature by simply reading the history of the Medici, where commerce, literature, and the arts made one of the most splendid, useful, and powerful coalitions that ever were seen in modern times. Here is a fine sentence! Mr. Hammond once, when piqued by my raillery, declared that he never in his life saw, or could have conceived, till he saw me, that a *philosopher* could laugh so much and so heartily.

Inclosed I send a copy of an epitaph written by Louis XVIII., on the Abbé Edgeworth; I am sure the intention does honor to H. M. heart, and the critics here say the Latin does honor to H. M. head. William Beaufort, who sent it to my father, says the epitaph was communicated to him by a physician at Cork, who, being a Roman Catholic of learning and foreign education, maintains a considerable correspondence in foreign countries.

TO HENRY EDGEWORTH, IN LONDON.

PAKENHAM HALL, Christmas Day, 1807.

A Merry Christmas to you, my dear Henry and Sneyd! I wish you were here at this instant, and you would be sure of one; for this is really the most agreeable family and the pleasantest and most comfortable castle I ever was in.

We came here yesterday — the *we* being Mr. and Mrs. Edgeworth, Honora, and M. E. A few minutes after we came, arrived Hercules Pakenham — the first time he had met his family since his return from Copenhagen. My father has scarcely ever quitted his elbow since he came, and has been all ear and no tongue.

Lady Wellesley was prevented by engagements from

joining this party at Pakenham Hall; both the Duke
and Duchess of Richmond are so fond of her as no
tongue can tell.   The Duke must have a real friendship
for Sir Arthur; for while he was at Copenhagen his
Grace did all the business of his office for him.

TO C. SNEYD EDGEWORTH, IN LONDON.

EDGEWORTHSTOWN, January 1, 1808.

A Happy New Year to you, my dear Sneyd.   It is
so dark, I can hardly see to write, and it has been pouring such torrents of rain, hail, and snow, that I began
to think, with John Langan, that the "old prophecies
found in a bog" were all accomplishing, and that Slievegaulry was beginning to set out[1] on its proposed journey.   My mother has told you about these predictions,
and the horror they have spread through the country
entirely.   The old woman who was the cause of the
mischief is, I suppose, no bigger than a midge's wing,
as she has never been found, though diligent search has
been made for her.   Almost all the people in this town
sat up last night to *receive* the earthquake.

We have had the same physiognomical or character-
telling *fishes* that you described to Honora.   Captain
Hercules Pakenham brought them from Denmark, where
a Frenchman was selling them very cheap.   Those we
saw were pale green and bright purple.   They are very
curious: my father was struck with them as much, or
more, than any of the children; for there are some
wonders which strike in proportion to the knowledge,

1 An old woman had, before Christmas, gone about the neighborhood
saying that, on New Year's Day, Slievegaulry, a little hill about five
miles from Edgeworthstown, would come down with an earthquake,
and settle on the village, destroying everything.

instead of the ignorance, of the beholders. Is it a leaf? Is it galvanic? What is it? I wish Henry would talk to Davy about it. The fish lay more quiet in my father's hand than could have been expected; only curled up their tails on my Aunt Mary's; tolerably quiet on my mother's; but they could not lie still one second on William's, and went up his sleeve, which I am told their German interpreters say is the worst sign they can give. My father suggested that the different degrees of dryness or moisture in the hands cause the emotions of these sensitive fish, but after *drying* our best, no change was perceptible. I thought the pulse was the cause of their motion, but this does not hold, because my pulse is slow, and my father's very quick. It was ingenious to make them in the shape of fish, because their motions exactly resemble the breathing, and panting, and floundering, and tail-curling of fish; and I am sure I have tired you with them, and you will be sick of these fish.[1]

TO MISS RUXTON.

EDGEWORTHSTOWN, April, 1808.

We have just had a charming letter from Mrs. Barbauld, in which she asks if we have read "Marmion," Mr. Scott's new poem; we have not. I have read "Corinne" with my father, and I like it better than he

---

[1] It was afterwards ascertained that these conjuring fish had been brought from Japan by the Dutch, and were made of horn cut extremely thin. Their movements were occasioned, as Mr. Edgeworth supposed, from the warm moisture of the hand, but depended upon the manner in which they were placed. If the middle of the fish was made to touch the warmest part of the hand, it contracted, and set the head and tail in motion.

does.   In one word, I am dazzled by the genius, provoked by the absurdities, and in admiration of the taste and critical judgment of Italian literature displayed through the whole work.   But I will not dilate upon it in a letter; I could talk of it for three hours to you and my aunt.   I almost broke my foolish heart over the end of the third volume, and my father acknowledges he never read anything more pathetic.

Pray remember my garden when the Beauforts come to us.   It adds very much to my happiness, especially as Honora and all the children have shares in it, and I assure you it is very cheerful to see the merry, scarlet-coated, busy little workwomen in their territories, sowing, and weeding, and transplanting hour after hour.

June 4.

Lady Elizabeth Pakenham and Mrs. Stewart and her son Henry, a fine intelligent boy, and her daughter Kitty, who promises to be as gentle as her mother, have been here.   I liked Mrs. Stewart's conversation much, and thought her very interesting.

June 9.

My father and mother have gone to the Hills to settle a whole clan of tenants whose leases are out, and who *expect that because* they have all lived under his Honor, they and theirs these hundred years, that his Honor shall and will contrive to divide the land that supported ten people amongst their sons and sons' sons, to the number of a hundred.   And there is Cormac with the reverend locks, and Bryan with the flaxen wig, and Brady with the long brogue, and Paddy with the short, and Terry with the butcher's-blue coat, and

Dennis with no coat at all, and Eneas Hosey's widow, and all the Devines pleading and quarreling about boundaries and bits of bog. I wish Lord Selkirk was in the midst of them, with his hands crossed before him; I should like to know if he could make them understand his "Essay on Emigration."

My father wrote to Sir Joseph Banks to apply through the French Institute for leave for Lovell to travel as a *literate* in Germany, and I have frequently written about him to our French friends; and those passages in my letters were never answered. All their letters are now written, as Sir Joseph Banks observed, under evident constraint and fear.

Mrs. Edgeworth writes: —

This summer of 1808 Mr. and Mrs. Ruxton and their two daughters passed some time with us. My father, mother, and sister came also, and Maria read out "Ennui" in manuscript. We used to assemble in the middle of the day in the library, and everybody enjoyed it. One evening when we were at dinner with this large party, the butler came up to Mr. Edgeworth. "Mrs. Apreece, sir; she is getting out of her carriage." Mr. Edgeworth went to the hall door, but we all sat still laughing, for there had been so many jokes about Mrs. Apreece, who was then traveling in Ireland, that we thought it was only nonsense of Sneyd's, who we supposed had dressed up some one to personate her; and we were astonished when Mr. Edgeworth presented her as the real Mrs. Apreece. She stayed some days, and was very brilliant and agreeable. She continued, as Mrs. Apreece and as Lady Davy, to be a kind friend and correspondent of Maria's.

MARIA TO C. SNEYD EDGEWORTH, AT EDINBURGH.

EDGEWORTHSTOWN, December 30, 1808.

How little we can tell from day to day what will happen to us or our friends. I promised you a merry frankful of nonsense this day, and instead of that we must send you the melancholy account of poor Dr. Beddoes's death.[1] I inclose Emmeline's letter, which will tell you all better than I can. Poor Anna! how it has been possible for her weak body to sustain her through such trials and such exertions, God only knows. My father and mother have written most warm and pressing invitations to her to come here immediately, and bring all her children. How fortunate it was that little Tom[2] came here last summer, and how still more fortunate that the little fellow returned with Henry to see his poor father before he died.

TO MRS. RUXTON.

EDGEWORTHSTOWN, January, 1809.

On Friday we went to Pakenham Hall. We sat down thirty-two to dinner, and in the evening a party of twenty from Pakenham Hall went to a grand ball at Mrs. Pollard's. Mrs. Edgeworth and I went, papa and Aunt Mary stayed with Lady Elizabeth. Lord Long-

---

[1] Dr. Beddoes, who had married Anna Edgeworth, was the author of almost innumerable books. His pupil, Sir Humphry Davy, says: "He had talents which would have exalted him to the pinnacle of philosophical eminence, if they had been applied with discretion."

[2] Thomas Lovell Beddoes, 1803–1849, author of *The Bride's Tragedy*, and of *Death's Jest-Book*.

ford acted his part of Earl Marshal in the great hall, sending off carriage after carriage, in due precedence, and with its proper complement of beaux and belles. I was much entertained: had Mrs. Tuite, and mamma, and Mrs. Pakenham, and the Admiral to talk and laugh with; saw abundance of comedy. There were three Miss ——s, from the County of Tipperary, three degrees of comparison — the positive, the comparative, and the superlative; excellent figures, with white feathers as long as my two arms joined together, stuck in the front of what were meant for Spanish hats. How they towered above their sex, divinely vulgar, with brogues of true Milesian race! Supper so crowded that Caroline Pakenham and I agreed to use one arm by turns, and thus with difficulty found means to reach our mouths. Caroline grows upon me every time I see her; she is as quick as lightning, understands with half a word literary allusions as well as humor, and follows and leads in conversation with that playfulness and good breeding which delight the more because they are so seldom found together. We stayed till between three and four in the morning. Lord Longford had, to save our horses which had come a journey, put a pair of his horses and one of his postilions to our coach: the postilion had, it seems, amused himself at a *club* in Castle Pollard while we were at the ball, and he had amused himself so much that he did not know the ditch from the road; he was ambitious of passing Mr. Dease's carriage — passed it, attempted to pass Mr. Tuite's, ran the wheels on a drift of snow which overhung the ditch, and laid the coach fairly down on its side in the ditch. We were none of us hurt. The *us* were my mother,

Mr. Henry Pakenham, and myself. My mother fell undermost; I never fell at all, for I clung like a bat to the handstring at my side, determined that I would not fall upon my mother and break her arm. None of us were even bruised. Luckily Mrs. Tuite's carriage was within a few yards of us, and stopped, and the gentlemen hauled us out immediately. Admiral Pakenham lifted me up and carried me in his arms, as if I had been a little doll, and set me down actually on the step of Mrs. Tuite's carriage, so I never wet foot or shoe. And now, my dear aunt, I have established a character for courage in overturns for the rest of my life! The postilion was not the least hurt, nor the horses; if they had not been the quietest animals in the world we should have been undone: one was found with his feet level with the other's head. The coach could not be got out of the deep ditch that night, but Lord Longford sent a man to sleep in it, that nobody else might, and that no one might steal the glasses. It came out safe and sound in the morning, not a glass broken. Miss Fortescue, Caroline, and Mr. Henry Pakenham went up just as we left Pakenham Hall to town, or to the Park to Lady Wellesley, who gives a parting ball, and then follows Sir Arthur to England.

EDGEWORTHSTOWN, February 2, 1809.

This minute I hear a carman is going to Navan, and I hasten to send you the "Cottagers of Glenburnie," [1] which I hope you will like as well as we do. I think it will do a vast deal of good, and besides it is extremely

---

[1] By Miss Elizabeth Hamilton, with whom Miss Edgeworth had become intimate at Edinburgh in 1803.

interesting, which all *good* books are not; it has great powers, both comic and tragic. I write in the midst of Fortescues and Pakenhams, with dear Miss Caroline P., whom I like every hour better and better, sitting on the sofa beside me, reading Mademoiselle Clairon's "Memoirs," and talking so entertainingly that I can scarcely tell what I have said, or am going to say.

I like Mrs. Fortescue's conversation, and will, as Sophy desires, converse as much as possible with obliging and ever-cheerful Miss Fortescue. But indeed it is very difficult to mind anything but Caroline.

February 5.

Three of the most agreeable days I ever spent we have enjoyed in the visit of our Pakenham Hall friends to us. How delightful it is to be with those who are sincerely kind and well-bred; I would not give many straws for good breeding without sincerity, and I would give at any time ten times as much for kindness *with* politeness as for kindness without it. There is something quite captivating in Lady Longford's voice and manners, and the extreme vivacity of her countenance, and her quick change of feelings interested me particularly; I never saw a woman so little spoiled by the world. As for Caroline Pakenham, I love her. They were all very polite about the reading out of "Emilie de Coulanges," and took it as a mark of kindness from me, and not as an exhibition. Try to get and read the "Life of Dudley Lord North," of which parts are highly interesting. I am come to the ambition in "Marie de Menzikoff," which I like much, but the love is mere brown sugar and water. The mother's blind-

ness is beautifully described. My father says "Vivian "
will stand next to "Mrs. Beaumont " and "Ennui; " I
have ten days' more work at it, and then huzza! ten
days' more purgatory at other corrections, and then a
heaven upon earth of idleness, and reading, which is my
idleness.   Half of "Professional Education " is printed.

TO MRS. RUXTON.

EDGEWORTHSTOWN, March, 1809.

Indeed you are quite right in thinking that the expressions of affection from my uncle and you are more
delightful to me than all the compliments or admiration
in the world could be.   It is no new thing for me to be
happy at Black Castle, but I think I was particularly
happy there this last time.   You both made me feel
that I added to the pleasures of your fireside, which
after all, old-fashioned or not, are the best of all pleasures.   How I did laugh! and how impossible it is not
to laugh in some company, or to laugh in others.   I
have often wondered how my ideas flow or ebb without
the influence of my will; sometimes, when I am with
those I love, flowing faster than tongue can utter, and
sometimes ebbing, ebbing, till nought but sand and
sludge are left.

We have been much entertained with "Le petit Caril-
loneur."   I would send it to you, only it is a society
book; but I do send by a carman two volumes of Alfieri's "Life " and Kirwan's "Essay on Happiness," and
the Drogheda edition of "Parent's Assistant," which,
with your leave, I present to your servant Richard.

"The Grinding Organ "[1] went off on Friday night

1 Afterwards published in 1827 in a small volume, entitled *Little
Plays*.

better than I could have expected, and seemed to please the spectators. Mrs. Pakenham brought four children, and Mr. and Mrs. Thompson two sons, Mr. and Mrs. Keating two daughters, which, with the Beauforts, Molly, George, and the rest of the servants, formed the whole audience. I am sure you would have enjoyed the pleasure the Bristows showed on seeing and hearing Mary Bristow perform her part, which she did with perfect propriety. Sophy and Fanny excellent, but as they were doomed to be the *good* children, they had not ample room and verge enough to display powers equal to the little termagant heroine of the night. William in his Old Man (to use the newspaper style) correct and natural. Mr. Edgeworth as the English Farmer evinced much knowledge of true English character and humor. Miss Edgeworth as the Widow Ross, "a cursed scold," was quite at home. It is to be regretted that the Widow Ross has no voice, as a song in character was of course expected; the Farmer certainly gave "a fair challenge to a fair lady." His Daniel Cooper was given in an excellent style, and was loudly encored.

April 28.

The Primate [1] was very agreeable during the two days he spent here. My father traveled with him from Dublin to Ardbraccan, and this reputed silent man never ceased talking and telling entertaining anecdotes till the carriage stopped at the steps at Ardbraccan. This I could hardly credit till I myself heard his Grace burst forth in conversation. The truth of his character gives such value to everything he says, even to his

[1] William Stuart, Archbishop of Armagh, fifth son of the third Earl of Bute.

humorous stories.   He has two things in his character which I think seldom meet — a strong taste for humor, and strong feelings of indignation.   In his eye you may often see alternately the secret laughing expression of humor, and the sudden open flash of indignation.   He is a man of the warmest feelings, with the coldest exterior I ever saw — a master mind.   I could not but be charmed with him, because I saw that he thoroughly appreciated my father.

"Tales of Fashionable Life" were published in June, 1809, and greatly added to the celebrity of their authoress.   "Almeria" is the best, and full of admirable pictures of character.   In all, the object is to depict the vapid and useless existence of those who live only for society.   Sometimes the moralizing becomes tiresome.   "Vraiment Miss Edgeworth est digne de l'enthousiasme, mais elle se perd dans votre triste utilité," said Madame de Staël to M. Dumont when she had read them.   In that age of romantic fiction an attempt to depict life as it really was took the reading world by surprise.

"As a writer of tales and novels," wrote Lord Dudley in the "Quarterly Review," "Miss Edgeworth has a very marked peculiarity.   It is that of venturing to dispense common sense to her readers, and to bring them within the precincts of real life and natural feeling.   She presents them with no incredible adventures or inconceivable sentiments, no hyperbolical representations of uncommon characters, or monstrous exhibitions of exaggerated passion.   Without excluding love from her pages, she knows how to assign to it its just limits.

She neither degrades the sentiment from its true dignity, nor lifts it to a burlesque elevation.   It takes its proper place among the passions.   Her heroes and heroines, if such they may be called, are never miraculously good, nor detestably wicked.   They are such men and women as we see and converse with every day of our lives, with the same proportional mixture in them of what is right and what is wrong, of what is great and what is little."

Lord Jeffrey, writing in the "Edinburgh Review," said: "The writings of Miss Edgeworth exhibit so singular an union of sober sense and inexhaustible invention, so minute a knowledge of all that distinguishes manners, or touches on happiness in every condition of human fortune, and so just an estimate both of the real sources of enjoyment, and of the illusions by which they are so often obstructed, that we should separate her from the ordinary manufacturers of novels, and speak of her Tales as works of more serious importance than much of the true history and solemn philosophy that comes daily under our inspection. . . . It is impossible, I think, to read ten pages in any of her writings without feeling, not only that the whole, but that every part of them, was intended to do good."

MARIA TO MISS RUXTON.

EDGEWORTHSTOWN, June, 1809.

A copy of "Tales of Fashionable Life"[1] reached us yesterday in a Foster frank; they looked well enough, — not very good paper, but better than "Popular

---

[1] The first set, containing *Ennui, Madame de Fleury, Almeria, The Dun* and *Manœuvring*, in three volumes. The paper was abominable.

Tales." I am going to write a story called "To-day," [1] as a match for "To-morrow," in which I mean to show that Impatience is as bad as Procrastination, and the desire to do too much to-day, and to enjoy too much at present, is as bad as putting off everything to to-morrow. What do you think of this plan? Write next post, as I am going to write while my father is away a story for his birthday. My other plan was to write a story in which young men of all the different professions should act a part, like the "Contrast" in higher life, [2] or the "Freeman Family," only without princes, and without any possible allusion to our own family. I have another sub-plan of writing "Cœlebina in search of a Husband," without my father's knowing it, and without reading "Cœlebs," that I may neither imitate nor abuse it.

I dare say you can borrow Powell's "Sermons" from Ardbraccan or Dr. Beaufort; the Primate lent them to my father. There is a charge on the connection between merit and preferment, and one discourse on the influence of academical studies and a recluse life, which I particularly admire, and wish it had been quoted in "Professional Education."

Mr. Holland, a grand-nephew of Mr. Wedgwood's and son to a surgeon at Knutsford, Cheshire, and intended for a physician, came here in the course of a pedestrian tour — spent two days — very well informed. Ask my mother when she goes to you to tell you all that Mr. Holland told us about Mr. and Mrs. Barbauld and Mrs. Marcet, who is the author of "Conversations on Chemistry" — a charming woman, by his account.

[1] Never written.   [2] *Patronage.*

TO MISS RUXTON.

EDGEWORTHSTOWN, August 22, 1809.

I have just been reading Carleton's "Memoirs," and am in love with the captain and with his general, Lord Peterborough; and I have also been reading one of the worst-written books in the language, but it has both instructed and entertained me — Sir John Hawkins's "Life of Johnson." He has thrown a heap of rubbish of his own over poor Johnson, which would have smothered any less gigantic genius.

M. Dumont writes from Lord Henry Petty's: "Nous avons lu en société à Bounds, 'Tales of Fashionable Life.' Toute société est un petit théâtre. 'Ennui' et 'Manœuvring' ont eu un succès marqué, il a été très vif. Nous avons trouvé un grand nombre de dialogues du meilleur comique, c'est à dire de ceux où les personnages se developpent sans le vouloir, et sont plaisants sans songer à l'être. Il y a des scènes charmantes dans 'Madame de Fleury.' Ne craignez pas les difficultés, c'est là où vous brillez."

TO MISS HONORA EDGEWORTH.

November 30.

We have had a bevy of wits here — Mr. Chenevix, Mr. Henry Hamilton, Leslie Foster, and his particular friend Mr. Fitzgerald. Somebody asked if Miss White [1] was a bluestocking. "Oh, yes, she is; I can't tell you how blue. What is bluer than blue?" "*Morbleu,*" exclaimed Lord Norbury. Miss White herself comes next week.

[1] The then well-known Miss Lydia White, for many years a central figure in London literary society.

December 11.

Among other things Miss White entertained my father with was a method of drawing the human figure, and putting it into any attitude you please: she had just learned it from Lady Charleville — or rather not learned it. A whole day was spent in drawing circles all over the human figure, and I saw various skeletons in chains, and I was told the intersections of these were to show where the centres of gravity were to be; but my gravity could not stand the sight of these ineffectual conjuring tricks, and my father was out of patience himself. He seized a sheet of paper and wrote to Lady Charleville, and she answered in one of the most polite letters I ever read, inviting him to go to Charleville Forest, and he will go and see these magical incantations performed by the enchantress herself.

TO MISS RUXTON.

December, 1809.

I have spent five delightful days at Sonna and Pakenham Hall. Mrs. Tuite's kindness and Mr. Chenevix's various anecdotes, French and Spanish, delighted us at Sonna; and you know the various charms both for the head and heart at Pakenham Hall.

I have just been reading, for the fourth time, I believe, "The Simple Story," which I intended this time to read as a critic, that I might write to Mrs. Inchbald about it; but I was so carried away by it that I was totally incapable of thinking of Mrs. Inchbald or anything but Miss Milner and Doriforth, who appeared to me real persons whom I saw and heard, and who had such power to interest me, that I cried my eyes almost out before I came to the end of the story: I think it the most pathetic and the most powerfully interesting tale I ever read.   I was obliged to go from it to correct "Belinda" for Mrs. Barbauld, who is going to insert it in her collection of novels, with a preface; and I really was so provoked with the cold tameness of that stick or stone Belinda, that I could have torn the pages to pieces; and really, I have not the heart or the patience to *correct* her.   As the hackney coachman said, "Mend *you!* better make a new one."

TO MRS. RUXTON.

EDGEWORTHSTOWN, January, 1810.

I have had a very flattering and grateful letter from Lydia White; she has sent me a comedy of Kelly's — "A Word to the Wise."   She says the "Heiress" is taken from it.   Just about the same time I had a letter from Mrs. Apreece:[1] she is at Edinburgh, and seems charmed with all the wits there; and, as I hear from Mr. Holland,[2] the young physician who was here last summer, she is much admired by them.   Mrs. Hamilton and she like one another particularly; they can never cross, for no two human beings are, body and mind, form and substance, more unlike.   We thought Mr. Holland, when he was here, a young man of abilities — his letter has fully justified this opinion, it has excited my father's enthusiastic admiration.   He says Walter Scott is going to publish a new poem; I do not augur well of the title, "The Lady of the Lake."   I hope this lady will not disgrace him.   Mr. Stewart has

---

[1] Afterwards Lady Davy.
[2] Afterwards Sir Henry Holland.

not recovered, nor ever will recover, the loss of his son: Mr. Holland says the conclusion of his lectures this season was most pathetic and impressive — "placing before the view of his auditors a series of eight and thirty years, in which he had zealously devoted himself to the duties of his office; and gave the impression that this year would be the period of his public life."

I have had a most agreeable letter from my darling old Mrs. Clifford; she sent me a curiosity — a worked muslin cap, which cost sixpence, in tambour stitch, done by a steam-engine. Mrs. Clifford tells me that Miss Hannah More was lately at Dawlish, and excited more curiosity there, and engrossed more attention, than any of the distinguished personages who were there, not excepting the Prince of Orange. The gentleman from whom she drew "Cœlebs" was there, but most of those who saw him did him the justice to declare that he was a much more agreeable man than Cœlebs. If you have any curiosity to know his name, I can tell you that — young Mr. Harford, of Blaize Castle.

February, 1810.

My father has just had a letter from your good friend Sir Rupert George, who desires to be affectionately remembered to you and my uncle. His letter is in answer to one my father wrote to him about his clear and honorable evidence on this Walcheren business. Sir Rupert says: "I must confess I feel vain in receiving commendations from such a quarter. The situation in which I was placed was perfectly new to me, and I had no rule for the government of my conduct but the one which has, I trust, governed all my actions through life — to speak the truth, and fear not. Allow me on this occasion to repeat to you an expression of the late Mrs. Delaney's to me a few years before she died: ' The Georges, I knew, would always prosper, from their integrity of conduct. Don't call this flattery; I am too old to flatter any one, particularly a grand-nephew; and to convince you of my sincerity, I will add — for which, perhaps, you will not thank me — that there is not an ounce of wit in the whole family.' "

"Oh, how my sister would like to see this letter of Sir Rupert's!" said my father; and straightway he told, very much to Sophy and Lucy's edification, the history of his dividing with sister Peg the first peach he ever had in his life.

March 2.

Have you any commands to Iceland? My young friend Mr. Holland proposes going there from Edinburgh in April. Sir George Mackenzie is the chief mover of the expedition.

This epigram or epitaph was written by Lord I-don't-know-who, upon *Doctor* Addington — Pitt's Addington — in old French: —

> " Cy dessous reposant
>   Le sieur Addington git:
>   Politique soi-disant,
>   Médecin malgré lui."

March 19.

The other day we had a visit from a Mrs. Coffy — no relation, she says, to your Mrs. Coffy. She looked exactly like one of the pictures of the old London Cries.

She came to tell us that she had been at Verdun, and had seen Lovell. From her description of the place and of him, we had no doubt she had actually seen him. She came over to Ireland to prove that some man who is a prisoner at Verdun, and who is a life in a lease, is not dead, but "all alive, ho!" and my father certified for her that he believed she had been there. She knew nothing of Lovell but that he was well, and fat, and a very merry gentleman two years ago. She had been taken by a French privateer as she was going to see her sons in Jersey, and left Verdun at a quarter of an hour's notice, as the women were allowed to come home, and she had not time to tell this to Lovell, or get a letter from him to his friends. She was, as Kitty said, "a comical body," but very entertaining, and acted a woman chopping bread and selling *un liv'* — *deux liv'* — *trois liv'* — *Ah, bon, bon,* as well as Molly Coffy[1] herself acted the elephant. She was children's maid to Mr. Estwick, and Mr. Estwick is, my father says, son to a Mr. Estwick who used to be your partner and admirer at Bath in former times!!

TO C. SNEYD EDGEWORTH, IN LONDON.

EDGEWORTHSTOWN, April, 1810.

I do not like Lord Byron's "English Bards and Scotch Reviewers," though, as my father says, the lines are very strong, and worthy of Pope and "The Dunciad." But I was so much prejudiced against the whole by the first lines I opened upon about the "paralytic muse" of the man who had been his guardian, and is his relation, and to whom he had dedicated his first

---

[1] Mrs. Molly Coffy, for fifty years Mrs. Ruxton's housekeeper.

poems, that I could not relish his wit.   He may have
great talents, but I am sure he has neither a great nor
good mind; and I feel dislike and disgust for his Lord-
ship.

TO MISS RUXTON.

EDGEWORTHSTOWN, May, 1810.

Now I have to announce the safe arrival of my aunts
and Honora in good looks and good spirits.   My father
went to Dublin to meet them.   I am sorry he did not
see the Count de Salis,[1] but he was much pleased with
Harriet Foster, which I am glad of; for I love her.

TO MRS. RUXTON.

EDGEWORTHSTOWN, June 21, 1810.

When shall we two meet again?   This is a question
which occurs to me much oftener than even you think,
and it always comes into my mind when I am in any
society I peculiarly like, or when I am reading any
book particularly suited to my taste and feelings; and
now it comes apropos to the Bishop of Meath and Mrs.
O'Beirne and "The Lady of the Lake."   By great good
fortune, and by the good-nature of Lady Charlotte Rawdon, we had "The Lady of the Lake" to read just
when the O'Beirnes were with us.   A most delightful
reading we had; my father, the Bishop, and Mr. Jephson reading it aloud alternately.   It is a charming
poem: a most interesting story, generous, finely-drawn
characters, and in many parts the finest poetry.   But

---

[1] The Count de Salis, just then going to be married to Miss Foster,
daughter of Mr. Edgeworth's old friend and schoolfellow, the Bishop of
Clogher.

for an old prepossession — an unconquerable prepossession — in favor of the old minstrel, I think I should prefer this to either the "Lay" or "Marmion." Our pleasure in reading it was increased by the sympathy and enthusiasm of the guests.

Have you read, or tried to read, Mademoiselle de l'Espinasse's three volumes of Letters? and have you read Madame du Deffand?[1] Some of the letters in her collection are very entertaining: those of the Duchesse de Choiseul, the Count de Broglie, Sir James Macdonald, and a few of Madame du Deffand's; the others are full of *fade* compliments and tiresome trifling, but altogether curious as a picture of that profligate, heartless, brilliant, and *ennuyed* society. There is in these letters, I think, a stronger picture of *ennui* than in Alfieri's "Life." Was his passion for the Countess of Albany, or for horses, or for pure Tuscan, the strongest? or did not he love notoriety better than all three?

September, 1810.

Sir Thomas and Lady Ackland spent a day here; he is nephew to my friend Mrs. Charles Hoare. He says he is twenty-three, but he looks like eighteen.

TO MISS RUXTON.

October, 1810.

We have had a visit from Captain Pakenham, the Admiral's son, this week; I like him. I was particularly pleased with his respectful manner to my father. He has some of his father's quickness of repartee, but with his *own* manner — no affectation of his father's

---

[1] The blind friend and correspondent of Horace Walpole.

style. We were talking of a Mrs. ——. "What," said I, "is she alive still? The last time I saw her she seemed as if she had lived that one day longer by particular desire." "I am sure, then," said Captain Pakenham, in a slow, gentle voice, — "I am sure, then, I cannot tell at *whose desire.*"

I have been hard at work at Mrs. Leadbeater: I fear my notes are rubbish.

Mrs. Edgeworth writes: —

Mrs. Leadbeater, the Quaker lady who lived at Ballitore, whose father had been tutor to Edmund Burke, and whose Letters have been published, wrote to Maria this year, asking her advice about a book she had written, "Cottage Dialogues," and sent the MS. to her. Mr. Edgeworth was so much pleased with it, that Maria offered, at Mr. Edgeworth's suggestion, to add a few notes to give her name to the book; and it was published by Johnson's successor with great success.

Mr. Edgeworth, Maria, and I went this autumn to Kilkenny to see the amateur theatricals, with which we were much delighted. Mr. Edgeworth, who remembered Garrick, said he never saw such tragic acting as Mr. Rothe, in Othello; how true to nature it was, appeared from the observation of our servant, Pat Newman, who had never seen a play before, when Mr. Edgeworth asked him if he did not pity the poor woman smothered in bed: "It was a pity of her, but I declare I pitied the man the most." The town was full to overflowing, but we were most hospitably received, though our friends the O'Beirnes were their guests, by

Doctor and Mrs. Butler. He had been a friend of Mr. Edgeworth's when he lived in the County of Longford, and she had been, when Miss Rothwell, a Dublin acquaintance of mine. This visit to Kilkenny was rich in recollections for Maria; the incomparable acting, the number of celebrated people there assembled, the supper in the great gallery of old grand Kilkenny Castle, the superb hospitality, the number of beautiful women and witty men, the gayety, the spirit, and the brilliancy of the whole, could have been seen nowhere else.

MARIA TO MISS RUXTON.

EDGEWORTHSTOWN, November, 1810.

MY DEAR SOPHY, — We are to set out for Dublin on the 13th, to hear Davy's lectures. Lord Fingal was so kind as to come here yesterday with Lady Teresa Dease, and he told me that my uncle is gone to Dublin. Tell me everything about it clearly. Honora, Fanny, and William go with us.

Mrs. Edgeworth interpolates: —

We spent a few weeks in Dublin. Davy's lectures not only opened a new world of knowledge to ourselves and to our young people, but were especially gratifying to Mr. Edgeworth and Maria, confirming, by the eloquence, ingenuity, and philosophy which they displayed, the high idea they had so early formed of Mr. Davy's powers.

MARIA TO MISS RUXTON.

EDGEWORTHSTOWN, April, 1811.

I think Hardy's "Life of Lord Charlemont" interesting, and many parts written in a beautiful style; but I don't think he gives a clear, well-proportioned history of the times. There is a want of *keeping* and perspective in it. The pipe of the man smoking out of the window is as high as the house. Mr. Hardy is more a portrait than a history painter.

If you have any curiosity to know the names of the writers of some of the articles in the "Edinburgh Review," I can tell you, having had to-day, from my literary intelligencer, Mr. Holland, two huge sheets, very entertaining and sensible. Jeffrey wrote the article on Parliamentary Reform, and that on the Curse of Kehama, Sydney Smith that on Toleration, and Malthus that on Bullion; and if you have any curiosity, I can also tell you those in the "Quarterly," among whom Canning is one. Thank my aunt for her information about Walter Scott; my father will write immediately to ask him here. I wish we lived in an old castle, and had millions of old legends for him. Have you seen Campbell's poem of "O'Connor's Child"? It is beautiful. In many parts I think it is superior to Scott.

May Day.

This being May Day, one of the wettest I have ever seen, I have been regaled, not with garlands of May flowers, but with the *legal* pleasures of the season; I have heard of nothing but *giving notices to quit, taking possession, ejectments, flittings*, etc. What do

you think of a tenant who took one of the nice new
houses in this town, and left it with every lock torn off
the doors, and with a large stone, such as John Langan
could not lift, driven actually through the boarded floor
of the parlor? The brute, however, is rich, and if he
does not die of whiskey before the law can get its hand
into his pocket, he will pay for this waste.

I have had another odd letter [1] signed by three young
ladies, — Clarissa Craven, Rachel Biddle, and Eliza
Finch, — who, after sundry compliments in very pretty
language, and with all the appearance of seriousness,
beg that I will do them the favor to satisfy the curiosity
they feel about the wedding dresses of the Frankland
family in the "Contrast." I have answered in a way
that will stand for either jest or earnest; I have said
that, at a sale of Admiral Tipsey's smuggled goods,
Mrs. Hungerford bought French cambric muslin wedding gowns for the brides, the collars trimmed in the
most becoming manner, as a Monmouth milliner assured
me, with Valenciennes lace, from Admiral Tipsey's
spoils. I have given all the particulars of the bride-
grooms' accoutrements, and signed myself the young
ladies' "obedient servant and perhaps *dupe.*"

I am going on with "Patronage," and wish I could
show it to you. *Do* get "O'Connor's Child," Campbell's beautiful poem.

Last Saturday there was the most violent storm of
thunder and lightning I ever saw in Ireland, and once
I thought I felt the ground shake under me, for which

---

[1] No less than five letters were received by Miss Edgeworth at different times, from different young people, asking for a description of the
dresses in the *Contrast.*

thought I was at the time laughed to scorn; but I find that at the same time the shock of an earthquake was felt *in the country, which shook Lissard House to its foundations.* I tell it to you in the very words in which it was told to me by Sneyd, who had it from Counsellor Cummin. A man was certainly killed by the lightning near Finae, *for* the said counsellor was knocked up at six o'clock in the morning, *to know* if there was to be a coroner's inquest.

TO MRS. RUXTON.

EDGEWORTHSTOWN, August 30, 1811.

I have written a little play for our present large juvenile audience,[1] not for them to act, but to hear; I read it out last night, and it was liked. The scene is in Ireland, and the title "The Absentee." When will you let me read it to you? I would rather read it to you up in a garret than to the most brilliant audience in Christendom.

Anna's children are very affectionate. Henry is beautiful, and the most graceful creature I ever saw. The eight children are as happy together as the day is long, and give no sort of trouble.

What book do you think Buonaparte was reading at the siege of Acre?—"Madame de Staël sur l'Influence des Passions!" His opinion of her and of her works has wonderfully changed since then. He does not follow Mazarin's wise maxim, "Let them *talk*, provided they let me *act*." He may yet find the recoil of that press, with which he meddles so incautiously, more

---

[1] Mrs. Beddoes and her three children were now at Edgeworthstown.

dangerous than those cannon of which he well knows the management.

Note Physical and Economical. — I am informed from high authority, that if you give Glauber's salts to hens, they will lay eggs as fast as you please!

TO MISS RUXTON.

EDGEWORTHSTOWN, October, 1811.

Davy spent a day here last week, and was as usual full of entertainment and information of various kinds. He is gone to Connemara, I believe, to fish, for he is a little mad about fishing; and very ungrateful it is of me to say so, for he sent to us from Boyle the finest trout! and a trout of Davy's catching is, I presume, worth ten trouts caught by vulgar mortals. Sneyd went with him to Boyle, saw Lord Lorton's fine place, and spent a pleasant day. Two of Mr. Davy's fishing friends have since called upon us — Mr. Solly, a great mineralogist, and Mr. Children, a man of Kent.

I am working away at "Patronage," but cannot at all come up to my idea of what it should be.

TO MISS SNEYD.

ARDBRACCAN HOUSE, November, 1811.

Nothing worthy of note occurred on our journey to Pakenham Hall, where we found to our surprise dear Lady Longford and Lord Longford, who had come an hour before on one of his flying visits, and a whole tribe of merry laughing children, Stewarts and Hamiltons. Lady Longford showed us a picture of Lady Wellington and her children; they are beautiful, and

she says very like — Lady Wellington is not like; it is
absurd to attempt to draw Lady Wellington's face; she
has no *face*, it is all countenance.   My father and Lady
Elizabeth played at cribbage, and I was looking on;
they counted so quickly fifteen two, fifteen four, that I
was never able to keep up with them, and made a sorry
figure.   Worse again at some genealogies and inter-
marriages, which Lady Elizabeth undertook to explain
to me, till at last she threw her arms flat down on each
side in indignant despair, and exclaimed, "Well! you
are the stupidest creature alive!"

When Lord Longford came in I escaped from cribbage and heard many entertaining things; one was of
his meeting a man in the mail coach, who looked as if
he was gouty, and seemed as if he could not stir without great difficulty, and never without the assistance of
a companion, who never moved an inch from him.   At
last Lord Longford discovered that this *gentleman's*
gouty overalls covered *fetters ;* that he was a malefactor
in irons, and his companion a Bow Street officer, who
treated his prisoner with the greatest politeness.   "Give
me leave, sir — excuse me — one on your arm and one
on mine, and then we are sure we can't leave one another."

A worse traveling companion this than the bear,
whom Lord Longford found one morning in the coach
when day dawned, opposite to him — the gentleman in
the fur cloak, as he had all night supposed him to be!

A second series of "Tales of Fashionable Life" appeared in 1812.   Of these "The Absentee" was a mas-
terpiece, and contains one scene which Macaulay declared

to be the best thing written of its kind since the opening of the twenty-second book of the Odyssey. Yet
Mrs. Edgeworth tells that the greater part of "The
Absentee" was written under the torture of the toothache; it was only by keeping her mouth full of some
strong lotion that Maria could allay the pain, and yet,
though in this state of suffering, she never wrote with
more spirit and rapidity. Mr. Edgeworth advised the
conclusion to be a Letter from Larry, the postilion; he
wrote one, and she wrote another; he much preferred
hers, which is the admirable finale to "The Absentee."

MARIA TO MISS MARGARET RUXTON.

EDGEWORTHSTOWN, July 20, 1812.

I am heartily obliged to my dear Sophy — never
mind, you need not turn to the direction, it *is* to Margaret, my dear, though it begins with thanks to Sophy
— for being in such haste to relieve my mind from the
agony it was in that "Fashionable Tales" should reach
my aunt. I cannot by any form of words express how
delighted I am that you are none of you angry with me,
and that my uncle and aunt are pleased with what they
have read of "The Absentee." I long to hear whether
their favor continues to the end and extends to the
catastrophe, that dangerous rock upon which poor authors, even after a prosperous voyage, are wrecked,
sometimes while their friends are actually hailing them
from the shore. I have the *Rosamond* vase[1] madness
so strong upon me, that I am out of my dear bed regu-
larly at half-past seven in the morning, and never find

---

[1] A glass vase which Miss Edgeworth painted for Mrs. Ruxton, in
brown, from Flaxman's designs for the Odyssey.

it more than half an hour till breakfast time, so happy am I daubing. On one side I have Ulysses longing to taste Circe's cakes, but saying, "No, thank you," like a very good boy; and on the other side I have him just come home, and the old nurse washing his feet, and his queen fast asleep in her chair by a lamp, which I hope will not set her on fire, though it is, in spite of my best endeavors, so much out of the perpendicular that nothing but a miracle can keep it from falling on Penelope's crown.

Little Pakenham is going on bravely (not two months old), and I am just *beginning* to write again, and am *in* "Patronage," and have corrected all the faults you pointed out to me; and Susan, who was a fool, is now Rosamond and a wit.

I suppose you have heard various *jeux d'esprit* on the marriage of Sir Humphry Davy and Mrs. Apreece. I scarcely think any of them worth copying; the best *idea* is stolen from the *bon mot* on Sir John Carr, "The Traveler be*k*nighted."

"When Mr. Davy concluded his last lecture by saying that we were but in the *Dawn* of Science, he probably did not expect to be so soon be*k*nighted."

I forget the lines; the following I recollect better: —

> " To the famed widow vainly bow
>   Church, Army, Bar, and Navy;
> Says she, I dare not take a vow,
>   But I will take my Davy."

Another my father thinks is better: —

> " Too many men have often seen
>   Their talents underrated ;
> But Davy owns that his have been
>   Duly *Appreeciated*."

August 22.

I inclose a copy of Lovell's letter, which will give my dear aunt exquisite pleasure. His request to my father to pass him over, a prisoner and of precarious health, and make his next brother his heir, shows that if he has suffered he has at least had an opportunity of showing what he is. We shall do all we can to get at Talleyrand or some friend for his exchange. How happy Lady Wellington must be at this glorious victory. Had you in your paper an account of her *running* as fast as she could to Lord Bury at Lord Bathurst's when he alighted, to learn the first news of her husband! *Vive l'enthousiasme!* Without it characters may be very snug and comfortable in the world, but there is a degree of happiness which they will never taste, and of which they have no more idea than an oyster can have.

TO MRS. EDGEWORTH.

BLACK CASTLE, October, 1812.

After a most delightful journey with Mr. and Mrs. Henry Hamilton, laughing, singing, and talking, we dined with them.[1] Dear old Mr. Sackville Hamilton dined with us, fresh from London; intellectual and corporeal dainties in abundance. The first morning was spent in cursing Mr. Sadler for not going up, and in seeing the Dublin Society House. A charming picture

---

[1] Mr. and Mrs. Hamilton were paying us a visit, when the papers announced Mr. Sadler's intention of crossing the Channel in a balloon from Dublin. Mr. Edgeworth proposed to Mr. Hamilton that they should go to Dublin together to see the ascent, and he and Mr. and Mrs. Hamilton, Maria, Sneyd, William, and two little sisters formed the party.

of Mr. Foster, by Beachy, with plans in his hand, looking full of thought and starting into life and action. Spent an hour looking over the books of prints in the library. Fanny particularly pleased with a Houbracken; Harriet with Daniel's Indian Antiquities; my father with Sir Christopher Wren's and Inigo Jones's designs. After dinner Richard Ruxton came in, and said my aunt and uncle had thoughts of coming up to see the balloon. In the evening at Astley's. The second day to see the elephant; how I pitied this noble animal, cooped up under the command of a scarcely human creature, who had not half as much reason as himself. Went on to see the Panorama of Edinburgh; I never saw a sight that pleased me more; Edinburgh was before me — Princes Street and George Street — the Castle — the bridge over dry land where the woman met us and said, "Poor little things they be." At first a mistiness, like what there is in nature over a city before the sun breaks out; then the sun shining on the buildings, trees, and mountains.

Thursday morning, to our inexpressible joy, was fine, and the flag, the signal that Sadler would ascend, was, to the joy of thousands, flying from the top of Nelson's Pillar. Dressed quickly — breakfasted I don't know how — job coach punctual; crowds in motion even at nine o'clock in the streets; tide flowing all one way to Belvidere Gardens, lent by the proprietor for the occasion; called at Sneyd's lodgings in Anne Street; he and William gone; drove on; when we came near Belvidere such strings of carriages, such crowds of people on the road and on the raised footpath, there was no stirring; troops lined the road at each side, guard with officers at each entrance to prevent mischief; but unfortunately there were only two entrances, not nearly enough for such a confluence of people. Most imprudently we and several others got out of our carriages upon the raised footpath, in hopes of getting immediately at the garden door, which was within two yards of us, but nothing I ever felt was equal to the pressure of the crowd; they closed over our little heads, I thought we must have been flattened, and the breath squeezed out of our bodies. My father held Harriet fast, I behind him held Fanny with such a grasp! and dragged her on with a force I did not know I possessed. I really thought your children would never see you again with all their bones whole, and I cannot tell you what I suffered for ten minutes, — my father, quite pale, calling with a stentor voice to the sentinels. A fat woman nearly separated me from Fanny. My father fairly kicked off the terrace a man who was intent upon nothing but an odious bag of cakes which he held close to his breast, swearing and pushing. Before us Mrs. Smyley and Mr. Smyley, with a lady he was protecting, and unable to protect anybody, looked more frightened than if he had lost a hundred causes; the lady continually saying, "Let me back! let me back! if I could once get to my carriage!"

The tide carried us on to the door. An admirable Scotch officer, who was mounting guard with a drawn sword, his face dropping perspiration, exclaimed at the sight of Harriet, "Oh, the child! take care of that child! she will be crushed to death!" He made a soldier put his musket across the doorway, so as to force a place for her to creep under; quick as lightning in she darted, and Fanny and I and my father after her. All serene, uncrowded, and fresh within the park.

Instantly met Sneyd and William, and the two Mr. Foxes. Music and the most festive scene in the gardens; the balloon, the beautiful many-colored balloon, chiefly maroon color, with painted eagles, and garlands, and arms of Ireland, hung under the trees, and filling fast from pipes and an apparatus which I leave for William's scientific description; terrace before Belvidere House — well-dressed groups parading on it; groups all over the gardens, mantles, scarves, and feathers floating; all the commonalty outside in fields at half-price. We soon espied Mr. and Mrs. Hamilton, and joined company, and were extremely happy, and wished for you and dear Honora. Sun shining, no wind. Presently we met the Solicitor-General; he started back, and made me such a bow as made me feel my own littleness; then shook my hands most cordially, and in a few moments told me more than most men could tell in an hour; just returned from Edinburgh — Mrs. Bushe and daughters too much fatigued to come and see the balloon.

The Duke and Duchess of Richmond, and Sir Charles Vernon, and Sir Charles Saxton. The Miss Gunns seated themselves in a happily conspicuous place, with some gentlemen, on the roof of Belvidere House, where, with veils flying and telescopes and opera-glasses continually veering about, they attracted sufficient attention.

Walking on, Sneyd exclaimed, "My Uncle Ruxton!" I darted to him; "Is my aunt here?" "Yes, and Sophy, and Margaret, but I have lost them; I'm looking for them." "Oh, come with me and we'll find them." Soon we made our way behind the heels of the troopers' horses, who guarded a sacred circle round the balloon; found my aunt, and Sophy, and Mag — surprise and joy on both sides; got seats on the pedestal of some old statue, and talked and enjoyed ourselves; the balloon filling gradually. Now it was that my uncle proposed our returning by Black Castle.

The drum beats! the flag flies! balloon full! It is moved from under the trees over the heads of the crowd; the car very light and slight — Mr. Sadler's son, a young lad, in the car. How the horses stood the motion of this vast body close to them I can't imagine, but they did. The boy got out. Mr. Sadler, quite composed, this being his twenty-sixth aerial ascent, got into his car; a lady, the Duchess of Richmond, I believe, presented to him a pretty flag; the balloon gave two majestic nods from side to side as the cords were cut. Whether the music continued at this moment to play or not, nobody can tell. No one spoke while the balloon successfully rose, rapidly cleared the trees, and floated above our heads; loud shouts and huzzas, one man close to us exclaiming, as he clasped his hands, "Ah, musha, musha, God bless you! God be wid you!" Mr. Sadler, waving his flag and his hat, and bowing to the world below, soon pierced a white cloud, and disappeared; then emerging, the balloon looked like a moon, black on one side, silver on the other; then like a dark bubble; then less and less, and now only a speck is seen; and now the fleeting rack obscures it. Never did I feel the full merit of Darwin's description till then.

Next day, at eight in the morning, my father and William (who proceed to the Bishop of Derry's) and Fanny went to Collon. Sneyd, Harriet, and I came here.

TO MRS. RUXTON.

EDGEWORTHSTOWN, October 26, 1812.

Elections have been the order of the day with us as well as with you. I am glad to tell you that Lord Longford's troubles are over; he is now here, and has just been telling us that his victory for Colonel Hercules was as complete as his heart could wish. There would have been a duel but for Admiral Pakenham. One gentleman in his speech said that another had made the drummer of his corps play "Protestant Boys." The other said, "That's a lie;" and both were proceeding to high words, when the Admiral stepped between them, and said, very gravely, "Gentlemen, I did not know this meeting was a music meeting, but since you appeal to us electors to decide your cause by your musical merits, let the past be past; and now for the present give us each of you a song, and here's the sheriff" — who has no more ear than a post — "shall be judge between you." Everybody laughed, and the two angry gentlemen had to laugh off their quarrel.

Another gentleman said to the Admiral, after the election was over, "Do you know, I had a mind to have stood myself; if I had, what would you have said?" "That it was all a game of brag, and that, as you had the shuffling of the pack, there was no knowing what knave might turn up."

Lord Longford told us of Colonel Hercules Pakenham, at the siege of Badajos, walking with an engineer;

a bomb whizzed over their heads and fell among the
soldiers; and as they were carrying off the wounded,
when the Colonel expressed some regret, the engineer
said, "I wonder you have not steeled your mind to
these things. These men are carried to the hospital,
and others come in their place. Let us go to the
dépôt."

Here the engineer had his wheelbarrows all laid out
in nice order, and his pickaxes arranged in stars and
various shapes; but, just as they were leaving the
dépôt, a bomb burst in the midst of them. "Oh, heav-
enly powers, my picks!" cried the engineer, with
clasped hands, in despair.

TO C. SNEYD EDGEWORTH, IN DUBLIN.

EDGEWORTHSTOWN, February 10, 1813.

"Rokeby" is, in my opinion, — and let every soul
speak for themselves, — most beautiful poetry; the four
first cantos and half the fifth are all I have yet read.
I think it a higher and better, because less Scotch, more
universal style of poetry than any he has yet produced,
though not altogether perfect of its kind; more discrimi-
nation of character, more knowledge of human nature,
more generalized reflection, much more moral aim.

In March, Miss Edgeworth accompanied her father
and stepmother to England.

MARIA TO MISS SNEYD.

BANGOR FERRY, March 31, 1813.

"I will go and write a few lines of a letter to my
dear Aunt Mary."

"Oh! why should you write now, my dear? You have nothing new to tell her."

"Nothing new, but I love her, and wish to write to her; if I did not love her, I should be worse than Caliban."

"Well, write only a few lines."

"That is just what I mean to do, and go on with my letter at any odd place where we *stop the night.*"

You have heard of all we saw at Howth, so I go on from Holyhead. Breakfasted in company with Mr. Grainger; he has lived in very good company abroad, and told us a variety of entertaining anecdotes; Caulincourt, now Duc de Vincennes, was brought up in the family of the Prince de Condé, *l'enfant de la Maison,* the playfellow of the Duc d'Enghien. Buonaparte employed Caulincourt to seize the Duc d'Enghien; the wretch did so, and has been repaid by a dukedom.

We asked how the present Empress was liked in France. "Not at all by the Parisians; she is too haughty, has the Austrian scornful lip, and sits back in her carriage when she goes through the streets." The same complaint was made against Marie Antoinette. On what small things the popularity of the high and mighty depends!

Josephine is living very happily, amusing herself with her gardens and her shrubberies. This *ci-devant* Empress and Kennedy and Co., the seedsmen, are, as Mr. Grainger says, in partnership; she has a license to send to him what shrubs and seeds she chooses from France, and he has license to send cargoes in return to her. Mr. Grainger will carry over my box to Madame Récamier.

At the inn door at Bangor Ferry we saw a most curiously packed curricle, with all manner of portmanteaus and hat-boxes slung in various ingenious ways, and behind the springs two baskets, the size and shape of Lady Elizabeth Pakenham's basket. A huge bunch of white feathers was sticking out from one end of one of these baskets; and as we approached to examine it, out came the live head of a white peacock — a Japan peacock and peahen. The gentleman to whom the carriage belonged appeared next, carrying on a perch a fine large macaw. This perch was made to fasten behind the carriage. The servant who was harnessing the horses would not tell to whom the carriage belonged. He replied to all inquiries, "It belongs to that there gentleman."

We have enjoyed this fine day; had a delightful walk before dinner in a hanging wood by the waterside — pretty sheep-paths, wood anemones in abundance, with their white flowers in full blow. Two ploughs going in the field below the wood; very cheerful the sound of the Welshmen's voices talking to their horses. The ploughing, giving the idea of culture and civilization, contrasted agreeably with the wildness of the wood and mountains. Good-night.

Thursday.

This morning we set out for the slate-quarries; we took our time, and full time to see everything at leisure. The railways are above six miles long; they are very narrow. I had formed an idea of their being much more magnificent, but in this country canals and railways are made as useful and as little splendid as possible. I was surprised to see these railways winding round the rocks, and going over heaps of rubbish where you would think no wheelbarrow even could go.

From the slate-cutting we went to the slate-quarries. We had been admiring the beauty of the landscape. My father did not say anything to raise my expectations, but when we arrived near the place, he took me by the hand, and led me over a heap of rubbish, on the top of which there was a railway. We walked on until we came between two slate mountains, and found ourselves in the midst of the quarries. It was the most sublime sight of all the works of man I ever beheld. The men looked like pygmies. There is a curious cone of grayish-colored slate standing alone, which the workmen say is good for nothing; but it is good for its picturesque appearance. A heavy shower of hail came on, which, falling between the rifts of the rocks, and blown by the high wind, added to the sublimity of the scene; we were comfortably sheltered in one of the sheds.

Finding that Mr. Worthington was at Liverpool, my father determined to go there, and we have come on to Conway. During a storm of wind, thunder, and lightning last night it snowed just enough to cover the tops of the mountains with white, to increase the beauty of the prospect for us; they appeared more majestic from the strong contrast of bright lights and broad shades; the leaves of the honeysuckles all green in the hedges, fine hollies, primroses in abundance; it was literally spring in the lap of winter. Penmanmawr has, my father says, considerably altered its appearance, since he knew it first, from the falling of masses of rock, and the crumbling away of the mighty substance. Cultiva-

tion has crept up its sides to a prodigious height. A
little cottage nestled just under the mountain's huge
stone cap. The fragments of rock that have rolled
down, some of them across the road, are ten times the
size of the rock in Mr. Keating's lawn,[1] and in contrast
with this idea of danger are sheep and lambs feeding
quietly; the lambs looking not larger than little Francis's deceased kittens, Muff and Tippet.

We reached Conway at six o'clock. The landlady
of the Harp Inn knew my father, and recollected Lovell
and my Aunt Ruxton. The boy to whom Lovell used
to be so good, and who stopped my father on Penmanmawr to tell him that Lovell had given him Lazy Lawrence, was drowned with many others crossing the ferry
in a storm. The old harper who used to be the delight
of travelers is now in a state of dotage. There was no
harper at Bangor; the waiter told us "they were no
profit to master, and was always in the way in the passage; so master never lets them come now."

In the midst of all the sublime and beautiful I had
a happy mixture of the comic, for we had a Welsh
postilion who entertained us much by his contracted
vocabulary, and still more contracted sphere of ideas.
He and my father could never understand one another,
because my father said "qu*a*rry," and the Welshman
said "qu*e*rry;" and the burden of all he said was continually asking if we would not like to be "driven to
Caernarvon."

Friday morning, seven o'clock, dressed, and ready

---

[1] A curious isolated stone, about ten feet by four, which stood in the
Vicarage lawn at Edgeworthstown, said to have been aimed at the
church by a Pagan giant from the Hill of Ardagh. It is now destroyed.

to go on with my scribbling. I assure you, my dear
kind Aunt Mary, it is a great pleasure to me to write
this letter at odd minutes while the horses are changing,
or after breakfast or dinner for a quarter of an hour at
a time, so that it is impossible that it should tire me.
I owe all my present conveniences for writing to various Sneyds; I use Emma Sneyd's pocket-inkstand; my
ivory-cutter penknife was the gift of my Aunt Charlotte,
and my little Sappho seal a present of Aunt Mary's.

For miles we have had beautiful hollies in the
hedges; I wish my Aunt Charlotte would be so kind as
to have a few small hollies out of Wilkinson's garden
planted in the new ditch between Wood's and Duffy's;
also some cuttings of honeysuckles and pyracanthus —
enough can be had from my garden. I must finish
abruptly.

TO MRS. RUXTON.

LIVERPOOL, April 6, 1813.

Many times — a hundred times within this week —
have I wished, my dearest aunt, to talk over with you
the things and people I have seen. I am very well,
very happy, and much entertained and interested.

Liverpool is very fine and very grand, and my father
soon found out Mr. Roscoe; he was so good as to come
to see us, and invited us to his house, Allerton Hall,
about seven miles from Liverpool. He is a benevolent,
cheerful, gentlemanlike old man; tall, neither thin nor
fat, thick gray hair. He is very like the prints you
have seen of him; his bow courteous, not courtly; his
manner frank and prepossessing, without pretension of
any kind. He enters into conversation readily, and

immediately tells something entertaining or interesting, seeming to follow the natural course of his own thoughts, or of yours, without effort. Mrs. Roscoe seems to adore her husband, and to be so fond of her children, and has such a good understanding and such a warm heart, it is impossible not to like her. Mr. Roscoe gave himself up to us the whole day. Allerton Hall is a spacious house, in a beautiful situation; fine library, every room filled with pictures, many of them presents from persons in Italy who admired his Leo the Tenth. One of Tasso has a sort of mad vigilance in the eyes, as if he that instant saw the genius that haunted him. Mr. Roscoe has arranged his collection admirably, so as to show, in chronological order in edifying gradation, the progress of painting. The picture which he prized the most was by one of Raphael's masters, not in the least valuable in itself, but for a frieze below it by Michael Angelo, representing the destruction of the Oracles; it is of a gray color. Mr. Roscoe thinks it one of Michael Angelo's earliest performances, and says it is *conceded* to be the only original Michael Angelo in England. Of this I know nothing, but I know that it struck me as full of genius, and I longed for you and Margaret when we looked at a portfolio full of Michael Angelo's sketches, drawings, and studies. It is admirable to see the pains that a really great man takes to improve a first idea. Turning from these drawings to a room full of Fuseli's horribly distorted figures, I could not help feeling astonishment, not only at the bad taste, but at the infinite conceit and presumption of Fuseli. How could this man make himself a name! I believe he gave these pictures to Mr. Roscoe, else I suppose they would not be here sprawling their fantastic lengths, like misshapen dreams. Instead of *le beau*, they exhibit *le laid* ideal.

At dinner Darwin's poetry was mentioned, and Mr. Roscoe neither ran him down nor cried him up. He said exactly the truth, that he was misled by a false theory of poetry — that everything should be picture — and that therefore he has not taken the means to touch the feelings; and Mr. Roscoe made what seemed to me a new and just observation, that writers of secondary powers, when they are to represent either objects of nature or feelings of the human mind, always begin by a simile; they tell you what it is like, not what it is.

April 9.

I finish this at Mr. Holland's, at Knutsford. We spent a delightful day at Manchester, where we owed our chief pleasure to Dr. Ferrier and his daughter.

TO MISS HONORA EDGEWORTH.

DERBY, April 25, 1813.

We have been now five days at Mr. Strutt's. We have been treated with so much hospitality and kindness by him, and he showed such a high esteem, and I may say affection for my father, that even if he had not the superior understanding he possesses, it would be impossible for me not to like him. From the moment we entered his house he gave up his whole time to us, his servants, his carriage; everything and everybody in his family were devoted to us, and all was done with such simplicity of generosity, that we felt at ease even while we were loaded with favors. This house is in-

deed, as Sneyd and William described it, a palace; and
it is plain that the convenience of the inhabitants has
everywhere been consulted; the ostentation of wealth
nowhere appears.

Seven hours of one day Mr. Strutt and his nephew
Jedediah gave up to showing us the cotton-mills, and
another whole morning he gave up to showing to us the
infirmary; he built it — a noble building; hot air from
below conveyed by a *cockle* all over the house.   The
whole institution a most noble and touching sight; such
a *great* thing, planned and carried into successful execution in so few years by one man!

We dined at Mr. Joseph Strutt's, and were in the
evening at Mr. George Strutt's; and I will name some
of the people we met, for Sneyd and William will like
to know whom we saw: Dr. Forrester, Mr. French,
Miss French, who has good taste, as she proved by her
various compliments to Sneyd; Miss Broadhurst, not
my heiress, though she says that, after the publication
of "The Absentee," people used to turn their heads
when she was announced, and ask if that was Miss
Edgeworth's Miss Broadhurst!   She met Sneyd in
Dublin; has been lately at Kilkenny, and admired
Mr. Rothe's acting of Othello.   We saw a good deal of
Mr. Sylvester,[1] who is, I think, a man of surprising
abilities, of a calm and fearless mind; an original and
interesting character.   Edward Strutt is indeed all that
Sneyd and William described — a boy of great abilities,
affectionate, and with a frank countenance and manner
which win at once.   One of our greatest pleasures has
been the hearing everybody, from Edward upwards,

[1] The inventor of the cockle or Sylvester stove.

speak of Sneyd and William with such affection, and with such knowledge of their characters. We all like Miss Lawrence.

We have been at the Priory; Mrs. Darwin at first much out of spirits. Besides the death of her son, she had lost a grandchild, and her daughter Harriet, Mrs. Maling, had just sailed with her husband for the Mediterranean. The Priory is a beautiful place, and Emma Darwin very beautiful.

We breakfasted at Markeaton with Mr. Mundy; he is a charming old gentleman, lively, polite, and playful as if he was twenty. He was delighted to see my father, and they talked over their school-days with great zest. My father was, you know, at school, Mr. Mundy's horse, "Little Driver."

CAMBRIDGE, Wednesday.

My mother will tell you the history of our night-travels over the bad road between Leicester and Kettering; my father holding the lantern stuck up against one window, and my mother against the other the bit of wax-candle Kitty gave me. I don't think we could have got on without it. Pray tell her, for she laughed when I put it in my box, and said it might be of vast use to us at some odd place.

Mr. Smedley has just called; tell Sneyd we think him very pleasing. I inclose the "Butterfly's Ball" for Sophy, and a letter to the King written by Dr. Holland when six years old; his father found him going with it to the post. Give it to Aunt Mary.

This letter was an offer from Master Holland to raise

a regiment.   He and some of his little comrades had
got a drum and a flag, and used to go through the
manual exercise.   It was a pity the letter did not reach
the King; he would have been delighted at it.

TO C. SNEYD EDGEWORTH.

LONDON, May 1, 1813.

Please to take this in small doses, but not fasting.

Let us go back, if you please, to Cambridge.   Thursday morning we went to breakfast with Mr. Smedley.
It had been a dreadful rainy night, but luckily the rain
ceased in the morning, and the streets were dried by
the wind on purpose for us.   In Sidney College we
found your friend in neat, cheerful rooms, with orange-
fringed curtains, pretty drawings, and prints; breakfast-
table as plentifully prepared as you could have had it —
tea, coffee, tongue, cold beef, exquisite bread, and many
inches of butter.   I suppose you know, but no one else
at home can guess, why I say *inches* of butter.   All
the butter in Cambridge must be stretched into rolls a
yard in length and an inch in diameter, and these are
sold by inches, and measured out by compasses, in a
truly mathematical manner, worthy of a university.

Mr. Smedley made us feel at home at once; my
mother made tea, I coffee; he called you "Sneyd," and
my father seemed quite pleased.   After having admired
the drawings and pictures, and Fanny's kettle-holder,
we sallied forth with our friendly guide.   It was quite
fine and sunshiny, and the gardens and academic shades
really beautiful.   We went to the University Hall —
the election of a new Professor to the Chemical Professorship was going on.   Farish was one of the candi-

dates: the man of whom Leslie Foster used to talk in such raptures when he first came from Cambridge; the man who lectured on arches, and whose paradox of the one-toothed wheel William will recollect. My father was introduced to him, and invited him to dine with us; Mr. Farish accepted the invitation. We sat on a bench with a few ladies. A number of Fellows, with black tiles on their heads, walked up and down the hall, whispering to one another; and in five minutes Mr. Smedley said, "The election is over; I must go and congratulate Mr. Professor Farish."

We next proceeded to the University Library, not nearly so fine as the Dublin College Library. Saw Edward the Sixth's famous little MS. exercise-book; hand good, and ink admirable; shame to the modern chemists, who cannot make half as good ink now! Saw Faustus's first printed book and a Persian letter to Lord Wellesley, and an Indian idol, said to be made of rice, looking like, and when I lifted it feeling as heavy as, marble. Mr. Smedley smiled at my being so taken with an idol, and I told him that I was curious about this *rice-marble*, because we had lately seen at Derby a vase of similar substance, about which there had been great debates. Mr. Smedley then explained to me that the same word in Persian expresses rice and the composition of which these idols are made.

We saw the MS. written on papyrus leaves; I had seen the papyrus at the Liverpool Botanic Garden, and had wondered how the stiff bark could be rolled up; and here I saw that it is not rolled up, but cut in strips and fastened with strings at each end.

In this library were three casts, taken after death —

how or why they came there I don't know, but they were very striking — one of Charles XII., with the hole in the forehead where the bullet entered at the siege of Frederieshall; that of Pitt, very like his statue from the life, and all the prints of him; and that of Fox, shocking! no character of greatness or ability — nothing but pain, weakness, and imbecility. It is said to be so unlike what he was in health, that none would know it. One looks at casts taken after death with curiosity and interest, and yet it is not probable that they should show the real natural or habitual character of the person; they can often only mark the degree of bodily pain or ease felt in the moment of death. I think these casts made me pause to reflect more than anything else I saw this day.

Went next to Trinity College Library; beautiful! I liked the glass doors opening to the gardens at the end, and trees in full leaf. The proportions of this room are excellent, and everything but the ceiling, which is too plain. The busts of Bacon and Newton excellent; but that of Bacon looks more like a courtier than a philosopher; his ruff is elegantly plaited in white marble. By Cipriani's painted window, with its glorious anachronisms, we were much amused; and I regret that it is not recorded in "Irish Bulls." It represents the presentation of Sir Isaac Newton to His Majesty George the *Third*, seated on his throne, and *Bacon* seated on the steps of the said throne writing! Cipriani had made the King Henry VIII., but the Fellows of the College thought it would be pretty to pay a compliment to His Gracious Majesty George III., so they made Cipriani cut off Henry VIII.'s head, and stick King George in his place; the junction is still to be seen in the first design of the picture, covered with a pasted paper cravat! like the figure that changes heads in the "Little Henry" book.

Saw Milton's MSS. of his lesser poems, and his letters and his plan of a tragedy on the subject of "Paradise Lost," which tragedy I rejoice he did not write. I have not such delight in seeing the handwriting of great authors and great folk as some people have; besides, by this time I had become very hungry, and was right glad to accept Mr. Smedley's proposal that we should repair to his rooms and take some sandwiches.

Rested, ate, talked, looked at the engravings of Clarke's marbles, and read the account of how these ponderous marbles had been transported to England. We saw the marbles themselves. The famous enormous head of Ceres must have belonged to a gigantic statue, and perhaps at a great height may have had a fine effect. It is in a sadly mutilated condition; there is no face; the appearance of the head in front is exactly like that of Sophy's doll, whose face has peeled off, yet Clarke strokes it and talks of its beautiful *contour*. The hair is fine, and the figure, from its vast size, may be sublime.

After having recruited our strength, we set out again to the Vice-Chancellor Davis's, to see a famous picture of Cromwell. As we knocked at his Vice-Chancellorship's door, Mr. Smedley said to me, "Now, Miss Edgeworth, if you would but settle in Cambridge! here is our Vice-Chancellor a bachelor . . . *do* consider about it."

We went upstairs; found the Vice-Chancellor's room

empty; had leisure before he appeared to examine the fine picture of Cromwell, in which there is more the expression of greatness of mind and determination than his usual character of hypocrisy. This portrait seems to say, "Take away that bauble," not "We are looking for the corkscrew."

The Vice-Chancellor entered, and such a wretched, pale, unhealthy object I have seldom beheld! He seemed crippled and writhing with rheumatic pains, hardly able to walk. After a few minutes had passed, Mr. Smedley came round to me and whispered, "Have you made up your mind?" "Yes, quite, thank you."

Now for the beauty of Cambridge — the beauty of beauties — King's College Chapel! On the first entrance I felt silenced by admiration. I never saw anything at once so beautiful and so sublime. The prints give a good idea of the beauty of the spandreled ceiling, with its rich and light ornaments; but no engraved representation can give an idea of the effect of size, height, and *continuity* of grandeur in the whole building. Besides, the idea of DURATION, the sublime idea of having lasted for ages, is more fully suggested by the sight of the real building than it can be by any representation or description, for which reason I only tell you the effect it had upon my mind.

The organ began to play an anthem of Handel's while we were in the chapel; I wished for you, my dear Sneyd, particularly at that moment! Your friend took us up the hundred stairs to the roof, where he was delighted with the sound of the organ and the chanting voices rising from the choir below. My father was absorbed in the mechanical wonders of the roof; that stone roof, of which Sir Christopher Wren said, "Show me how the first stone was laid, and I will show you how the second is laid."

Mr. Smedley exclaimed, "Is not the sound of the organ fine?" To which my father, at cross-purposes, answered, "Yes, the iron was certainly added afterwards."

Mr. Smedley at once confessed that he had no knowledge or taste for mechanics, but he had the patience and good nature to walk up and down this stone platform for three quarters of an hour. He stood observing my mother's very eager examination with my father of the defects in the wooden roof, and pointing out where it had been cut away to admit the stone, as a proof that the stone roof had been an afterthought; and at last turned to me with a look of astonishment. "Mrs. Edgeworth seems to have this taste for mechanics *too*." He spoke of it as a kind of mania. So I nodded at him very gravely, and answered, "Yes, you will find us all tinctured with it, more or less."

At last, to Mr. Smedley's great joy, he got my father alive off this roof, and on his way to Downing, the new college of which Leslie Foster talked so much, and said was to be like the Parthenon. Shockingly windy walk; thought my brains would have been blown out. Passed Peter House, and saw the rooms in which Gray lived, and the irons of his fire-escape at the window. Warned Mr. Smedley of the danger of my father being caught by a coachmaker's yard which we were to pass. My father overheard me, laughed, and contented himself with a side glance at the springs of gigs, and escaped that danger. I nearly disgraced myself, as the company were admiring the front of Emmanuel College, by looking at a tall man stooping to kiss a little child. Got at last, in spite of the wind and coachmakers' yards, within view of Downing College, and was sadly disappointed. It will never bear comparison with King's College Chapel.

Home to dinner; Mr. Farish and Mr. Smedley were very agreeable and entertaining, and *did* very well together, though such different persons.   Mr. Farish is the most primitive, simple-hearted man I ever saw.

The bells were ringing in honor of Professor Farish's election, or, as Mr. Smedley said, at the Professor's expense.

Farish insisted upon it very coolly that they were not ringing for him, but for a shoulder of mutton.

"A shoulder of mutton! what do you mean?"

"Why, a man left to the University a shoulder of mutton for every Thursday, on condition that the bells should always ring for him on that day; so this is for the shoulder of mutton."

Mr. Farish paid us no compliments in words, but his coming to spend the evening with us the day of his election, when I suppose he might have been feasted by all the grand and learned in the University, was, I think, the greatest honor my father has received since he came to England; and so he felt it.

I suppose you know that Mr. Smedley has published minutes of the trial of that Mr. Kendal who was accused of having set fire to Sidney College, and who, though brought off by the talents of Garrow, was so generally thought to be guilty, and to have only escaped by a quirk of the law, that he has been expelled the University.   What a strange thing that this trial at Cambridge and that in Dublin, of incendiaries,[1] should take place within so short a time of each other! It seems as if the fashion of certain crimes prevailed at certain times.

"Good-by, Mr. Smedley! I hope you like us half as well as we liked you." We thought it well worth our while to have come thirty miles out of our way to see him and Cambridge, and you, Sneyd, have the thanks of the whole party for your advice.

In passing through the village of Trumpington, and just as we came within sight of Dr. Clarke's house,[2] I urged my father to call upon him.

"Without an introduction, and two ladies with me! No, with all my impudence, my dear Maria, I cannot do that."

"Oh, do! you will repent afterwards if you do not; we shall never have another opportunity of seeing him."

"Well, at your peril, then, be it."

He let down the glass, and ordered the postilion to drive up to Dr. Clarke's house. I quailed in the corner the moment I heard the order given, but said nought. Out jumped my father, and during two or three minutes whilst he was in the house, and my mother and I waiting in the carriage at the door, I was in an agony. But it was soon over; for out came little Dr. Clarke flying to us, all civility, and joy, and gratitude, and honor, and pleasure, "ashamed and obliged," as he handed us up the steps and into a very elegant drawing-room.

I do not know whether you have seen him, but from

1 The trial in Dublin was that of "Moscow Cavendish."

2 Edward Daniel Clarke, 1769–1822, one of the most distinguished travelers of the eighteenth century, was Professor of Mineralogy at Cambridge.

the print I had imagined he was a large man, with dark
eyes and hair, and a penetrating countenance. No such
thing; he is a little, square, pale, flat-faced, good-
natured-looking, fussy man, with very intelligent eyes,
yet great credulity of countenance, and still greater
benevolence. In a moment he whisked about the different rooms upstairs and down, to get together books,
sketches, everything that could please us; and Angelica's
drawings — she draws beautifully.

Angelica herself, Mrs. Clarke, is a timid, dark, soft-
eyed woman, with a good figure. I am told it is rude
to say a person is very clean, but I may praise Angelica
for looking elegantly clean, brilliantly white, with a
lace Mary-Queen-of-Scots cap, like that which I am
sure you remember on Lady Adelaide Forbes. She
received us with timid courtesy, but her timidity soon
wore off, and the half hour we spent here made us wish
to have spent an hour. Dr. Clarke seemed highly
gratified that his travels in Greece had interested us so
much; showed us the original drawings of Moscow, and
a book of views of the ruins at Athens by the draughts-
man who went out with the Duc de Choiseul Gouffier
— beautifully done; mere outlines, perfectly distinct,
and giving, I think, better architectural ideas than we
have from more finished and flattered drawings.

We were sorry not to see more, and glad we had seen
so much, of Dr. Clarke and his Angelica, and his fine
little boy about five years old. A tall, dark-eyed, fine,
fashionable-looking man, Dr. Clarke introduced to us as
Mr. Walpole. My father entered into conversation
with him, and found he had known Captain Beaufort
in the Mediterranean.

When we were going away, Dr. Clarke, between my mother and me, seemed puzzled how to get us both into the carriage at once; but he called to Mr. Walpole.

"Walpole, put this lady into the carriage."

And with a "Meadows" air he obeyed.

Now we are again on the London road, and nothing interrupted our perusal of "Pride and Prejudice" for the rest of the morning.   I am desired not to give you my opinion of "Pride and Prejudice," but desire you to get it directly, and tell us yours.

TO MISS RUXTON.

LONDON, May, 1813.

I fear Madame de Staël's arrival may be put off till after we leave town.   The Edinburgh review of her book has well prepared all the world for her.   The first persons who came to see us were Sir Humphry and Lady Davy, who have been uniformly and zealously kind and attentive to us.   We have been frequently at their dinners and parties, and I should fill a roll as long as that genealogy Foote unrolled across the stage, if I were to give you a list of the names of all the people we have met at their house.   Of Lord Byron I can tell you only that his appearance is nothing that you would remark.   The Miss Berrys are all that you have heard of them from people of various tastes; consequently you know that they are well bred, and have nice tact in conversation.   Miss Catharine Fanshawe I particularly like; she has delightful talents.   Her drawings have charmed my mother, full of invention as well as taste; her Village School and Village Children at Play are beautiful compositions, and her drawings for the Bath Guide are full of humor and character.

Lady Crewe has still the remains of much beauty. Except her dress, which happened to be blue, there appeared to be nothing else *blue* about her. The contrast between her really fashionable air and manners and that of the *strugglers* and imitators struck me much; Lady Elizabeth Whitbread is, in one word, delightful. Miss Fox very agreeable — converses at once, without preface or commonplace; Lady Charlotte Lindsay ditto; Lady Darnley has been very polite in her attentions; both Lord and Lady Hardwick peculiarly gracious. Lord Somerville I cannot help being charmed with, for he says he is charmed with Lady Delacour and Lady Geraldine, whom he pronounces to be perfect women of fashion, and says they are in high repute in the equerry's room at court. He was quite indignant against certain pretenders to fashion. I told him the remark of a friend of ours, that a gentleman or gentlewoman cannot be made under two generations. "In less than *five*, madam, I think it scarcely possible," said he.

Lady Lansdowne, taking in beauty, character, conversation, talents, and manners, I think superior to any woman I have seen; perfectly natural, daring to be herself, gentle, sprightly, amiable, and engaging. Lydia White has been very kind to us, and eager to bring together people who would suit and please us; very agreeable dinner at her house; she conducts these *bel esprit* parties well; her vivacity breaks through the constraint of those who stand upon great reputations, and are afraid of committing themselves.

Charming amiable Lady Wellington! as she truly said of herself, she is always "Kitty Pakenham to her friends;" after comparison with crowds of others, *beaux*

esprits, fine ladies and fashionable *scramblers* for notoriety, her dignified graceful simplicity rises in one's
opinion, and we feel it with more conviction of its
superiority.   She showed us her delightful children.
Lord Longford just come to town; met us yesterday
at the Exhibition of Sir Joshua Reynolds's pictures.
Some of these are excellent; his children, from the
sublime Samuel to the arch Gipsy, are admirable.

We hope to see Mrs. Siddons act on the 25th; it was
thought impossible to get a box, but the moment my
father pronounced the name Edgeworth, Mr. Brandon,
the box-keeper, said he should have one.   Lady Charleville, who is a very clever woman, goes with us with
her daughter and Lord Tullamore.   We have been to a
grand night at Mrs. Hope's — the rooms really deserve
the French epithet of *superbe* — all of beauty, rank,
and fashion that London can assemble, I may say in the
newspaper style, were there.   The Prince Regent stood
one third of the night, holding converse with Lady
Elizabeth Monk, she leaning gracefully on a bronze
ornament in the centre of the room, in the midst of the
sacred but very small circle etiquette could keep round
them.   About 900 people were at this assembly; the
crowd of carriages was so great, that after sitting waiting in ours for an hour, the coachman told us there was
no chance of our getting in unless we got out and
walked.   Another good-natured coachman backed his
horses, and we bravely crossed the line and got into the
house and up the staircase, but no power of ours could
have got on, but for the gloriously large body and the
good-natured politeness of the Archbishop of Tuam,
who fortunately met us at the door, recognized us just

as he would have done at Mrs. Bourke's, in the County of Longford, and made way for us through the crowd, and in the wake of his greatness we sailed on prosperously, and never stopped till he presented us to his beautiful daughter, who received us with a winning smile. I asked Mr. Hope who some one was. "I really don't know; I don't know half the people here, nor do they know me or Mrs. Hope even by sight. Just now I was behind a lady who was making her *speech*, as she thought, to Mrs. Hope, but she was addressing a stranger." Among the old beauties the Duchess of Rutland held her preëminence and looked the youngest.

A few days after we came to town we were told by Mr. Wakefield that there was to be at the Freemasons' tavern a meeting on the Lancasterian schools, at which the reports of the Irish Education Committee were to be alluded to, and that the Dukes of Kent and Sussex, Lord Lansdowne, Sir James Mackintosh, and Mr. Whitbread were all to speak. We went; fine large hall, ranged with green benches like a lecture room; raised platform at one end for the *performers;* armchairs for the Royal Dukes, and common chairs for common men. Waited an hour, and were introduced to various people, among others, to Mr. Allen, who is famous for his generous benevolence, who lives most economically and gives thousands as easily as others would give pence. Dumont came and seated himself between my mother and me, and the hour's waiting was so filled with conversation that it seemed but five minutes.

Enter on the platform the royal Dukes preceded by stewards with white staves; gentlemen of the Commit-

tee ranged at the back of the theatre, one row in front
on each side of the Dukes, Lord Lansdowne, Mr. Whitbread, Mr. Lancaster, two or three others, and Mr.
Edgeworth.　The object of the meeting was to effect a
junction between the Bell and Lancasterian parties.　It
had been previously agreed that Lancaster should have
his debts paid, and should retire and give up his schools.
Lord Lansdowne spoke extremely well, matter and
manner; when he adverted to the Board of Education
he turned to my father and called upon him to support
his assertion, that the dignified clergy in Ireland among
those commissioners had acted with liberality.　It had
been previously arranged that my father was to move
the vote of thanks to the ladies, but of this we knew
nothing; and when he rose and when I heard the Duke
of Kent in his sonorous voice say "Mr. Edgeworth," I
was so frightened I dared not look up, but I was soon
reassured.　My father's speaking was, next to Lord
Lansdowne's, the best I heard, and loud plaudits convinced me that I was not singular in this opinion.　The
Duke of Kent speaks well and makes an excellent chairman.

Yesterday my father was invited to a Lancasterian
dinner; for an account of it I refer you to Lord Fingal,
next to whom my father sat, but as you may not see
him immediately I must tell you that my father's
health was drank, and that when his name was mentioned, loud applause ensued, and the Duke of Bedford,
after speaking of the fourteenth report of the Irish
Board of Education, pronounced a eulogium on "the
excellent letter which is appended to that report, full
of liberality and good sense, on which indeed the best

part of the report seems founded. I mean the letter by Mr. Edgeworth, to whom this country as well as Ireland is so much indebted."

Yesterday I had a good hour in comfort to write to you before breakfast, which was scarcely ended when Mr. Wakefield came in with a letter from the Duke of Bedford, who is anxious to see my father's experiments on the draft of wheel-carriages tried. Then came Lord Somerville, who sat and talked and invited us to his country-house, but all this did not forward my letter. Then came Lady Darnley; and then my father walked off with Lord Somerville, and we gave orders no one should be let in; so we only heard vain thunders at the door, and I got on half a page, but then came poor Peggy Langan,[1] and her we admitted; she is in an excellent place, with Mrs. Haldimand, Mrs. Marcet's sister-in-law, and she, Peggy, sat and talked and told of how happy she was, and how good her mistress was, and we liked her simplicity and goodness of heart, but as I said before, all this did not forward my letter. Coach at the door. "Put on your hat, Maria, and come out and pay visits."

To save myself trouble, I send a list of the visits we made just as my mother marked them on the card by which we steered. God knows how I should steer without her. The crosses mark the three places where we were let in. Lady Milbanke is very agreeable, and has a charming well-informed daughter. Mrs. Weddell is a perfectly well-bred, most agreeable old lady, sister to Lady Rockingham, who lived in the Sir Joshua

---

[1] Granddaughter to the original of Thady, in *Castle Rackrent*. Her sister was the origin of Simple Susan.

Reynolds set; tells anecdotes of Burke, Fox, and Windham — magnificent house — fine pictures. We spoke of having just seen the exhibition of Sir Joshua Reynolds's pictures. "Perhaps if you are fond of paintings you would take the trouble of walking into the next room, and I will show you what gives me a particular interest in Sir Joshua Reynolds's pictures." Large folding-doors opened — large room full of admirable copies from Sir Joshua Reynolds in crayons, done by Mrs. Weddell herself. My mother says they are quite astonishing. Her conversation, as good as her painting, passed through many books lightly with touch-and-go ease. I mentioned a curious anecdote of Madame d'Arblay; that when she landed at Portsmouth a few months ago, and saw on a plate at Admiral Foley's a head of Lord Nelson, and the word Trafalgar, she asked what Trafalgar meant. She actually, as Lady Spencer told me, who had the anecdote from Doctor Charles Burney, did not know that the English had been victorious, or that Lord Nelson was dead! This is the mixed effect of the recluse life she led, and of the care taken in France to keep the people ignorant of certain events. I mentioned a similar instance in Thiebault's "Memoirs," of the Chevalier Mason, living at Potsdam, and not knowing anything of the Seven Years' War. Then Mrs. Weddell went through Thiebault and Madame de Bareith's "Memoirs," and asked if I had ever happened to meet with an odd entertaining book, Madame de Baviere's "Memoirs." How little I thought, my dear Aunt Ruxton, when you gave me that book, that it would stand me *in stead* at Mrs. Weddell's — we talked it over and had a great deal of laughing and diversion.

Came home; found my father dressing to go to Sir Samuel Romilly's — we two were to dine at Lady Levinge's; while we were dressing a long note from Miss Berry, sent by her own maid, to apologize for a mistake of her servants who had said "not at home," and to entreat we would look in on her this evening — much hurried. Lady Levinge's dinner, which was not on the table till eight o'clock, was very entertaining, because quite a new set of people. Called in the evening at Miss Berry's — quite like French society, most agreeable — had a great deal of conversation with Lady Charlotte Lindsay. Mr. Ward was there, but I did not hear him. Went, shamefully late, to Mrs. Sneyd's — then home; found my father in bed — stood at the foot of it, and heard his account of his dinner. Dr. Parr, Dumont, Malthus, etc., but I have not time to say more. I have been standing in my dressing-gown writing on the top of a chest of drawers, and now I must dress for a breakfast at Lady Davy's, where we are to meet Lord Byron; but I must say, that at the third place where we were let in yesterday, Lady Wellington's, we spent by far the most agreeable half-hour of the day.

Mrs. Edgeworth continues: —

One day, coming late to dinner at Mr. Horner's, we found Doctor Parr very angry at our having delayed, and then interrupted, dinner, but he ended by giving Maria his blessing. One of our pleasantest days was a breakfast at Mr. and Mrs. Carr's, at Hampstead, where we met General and Mrs. Bentham, just come from Russia, full of interesting information. Maria also spent a day in the country with Sir Samuel and Lady Romilly, who was so beautiful and so engaging; and to this day's happiness Maria often recurred. We met one evening at Lady Charleville's Mrs. Abington, with whom Maria was much entertained; she recited two epilogues for us with exquisite wit and grace — she spoke with frankness and feeling of her career, when often after the triumph of success in some brilliant character, splendidly dressed, in the blaze of light, with thunders of applause, she quitted the theatre for her poor little lonely lodging — and admirably described her disenchanted, dispirited sensations.

One morning Maria and I went to Westminster Abbey with some friends, among whom was Sir James Mackintosh — only one morning: days might have been spent without exhausting the information he so easily, and with such enjoyment to himself, as well as to his hearers, poured forth with quotations, appropriate anecdotes, and allusions historical, poetical, and biographical, as we went along.

We unfortunately missed seeing Madame d'Arblay, and we left London before the arrival of Madame de Staël. We went on the 16th of June to Clifton, where we spent some days with Mr. and Mrs. King.[1]

From Clifton we went to Gloucester, where Maria took up a link of her former life, paying a visit to Mrs. Chandler, from whom she had received much kindness at Mr. Day's when her eyes were inflamed. We then went on to Malvern, where Mrs. Beddoes[2] was then living.

---

1 Mr. Edgeworth's second daughter, Emmeline.
2 The third daughter — Anna Edgeworth.

MARIA TO MRS. RUXTON.

MALVERN LINKS, June, 1813.

How good you have been, my dear aunt, in sparing Sophy to Edgeworthstown, and since you have been so good it is in encroaching human nature to expect that you will be still better, and that you and my uncle and Mag will come to Edgeworthstown for her; we shall be home in a fortnight. What joy, what delight to meet you among the dear faces who will welcome us there. The brilliant panorama of London is over, and I have enjoyed more pleasure and have had more amusement, infinitely more than I expected, and received more attention, more kindness than I could have thought it possible would be shown to me; I have enjoyed the delight of seeing my father esteemed and honored by the best judges in England; I have felt the pleasure of seeing my true friend and mother, for she has been a mother to me, appreciated in the best society, and now with the fullness of content I return home, loving my own friends and my own mode of life preferably to all others, after comparison with all that is fine and gay, and rich and rare.

We spent four days at Clifton with Emmeline, and if our journey to England had been productive of no other good, I should heartily rejoice at our having accomplished this purpose. My father was pleased and happy, and liked all his three grandchildren very much. You may imagine how much pleasure this gave me.

We came here the day before yesterday, and have spent our time delightfully with Anna and her children, and now the carriage is at the door to take us to Mrs.

Clifford's.   Yesterday we went to see Samuel Essington,[1] at the Essington hotel.   He thought it was a carriage full of strangers and was letting down the steps when he beheld my father; his whole face glowed with delight, and the tears stood in his projecting eyes. "Master! Master, I declare! Oh, sir, ma'am, miss, Mrs. Beddoes, Miss Edgeworth; how glad I am!"

He showed us his excellent house, and walked us round his beautiful little lawn and shrubberies, all his own making; and cut moss roses and blush roses for us with such eagerness and delight.   "And all, all owing to you, sir, that first taught me."

At Mrs. Clifford's we stayed some days — a beautiful country, not far from Ross, which we visited, and Maria was delighted to see all the scenes of the Man of Ross. At Mrs. Clifford's we had one day of most brilliant conversation between Maria, her father, and Sir James Mackintosh, who had just come into that neighborhood. He joined us, unexpectedly, one morning as we were walking out, and touching a shawl Mrs. Clifford wore, "A thousand looms," he said, "are at work in Cashmere at this instant providing these for you."

TO MISS SNEYD AT EDGEWORTHSTOWN.

MRS. CLIFFORD'S, June, 1813. Saturday Evening.

Received Sneyd's letter.[2]   Astonishment!   Dear Sneyd, I hope he will be as happy as love and fortune

---

[1] The servant who was so faithful and so frightened at the time of the rebellion.   He had saved some money and quitted the service of the Edgeworths in 1800.

[2] Announcing his engagement to Miss Broadhurst.   It was singular that this was the name of the heroine in Miss Edgeworth's *Absentee*,

can make him. All my ideas are thrown into such confusion by this letter that I *can* no more. We go to Derby on Tuesday.

TO MRS. RUXTON.

EDGEWORTHSTOWN, July 26, 1813.

I have delayed a few days writing to you in the expectation of the arrival of two frankers to send an extract from Dr. Holland's last letter, which will, I hope, entertain you as much as it entertained us. I shall long to hear of our good friend Mrs. Elizabeth Hamilton's visit to Black Castle.

We have every reason to be in great anxiety at this moment about a certain trunk containing all our worldly *duds*, and "Patronage" to boot, but still I have not been able to work myself into any fears about it, though it is a month since we ought to have seen it, nor have we heard any news of it. In the mean time, as I cannot set about revising "Patronage," I have begun a new series of "Early Lessons,"[1] for which many mothers told me they wished. I feel that I return with fresh pleasure to literary work from having been so long idle, and I have a famishing appetite for reading. All that we saw in London, I am sure I enjoyed while it was passing as much as possible, but I should be very sorry to live in that whirling vortex, and I find my taste and conviction confirmed on my return to my natural friends and my dear home.

I am glad that some of those who showed us hospi-

who selected from her lovers the one who united *worth* and wit, in reminiscence of an epigram of Mr. Edgeworth on himself, concluding : —

"There 's an edge to his wit and there 's worth in his heart."

[1] The second parts of *Frank*, *Rosamond*, and *Harry and Lucy*.

tality and kindness in England should have come so
soon to Ireland, that we may have some little opportunity of showing our sense of their attentions. Lord
Carrington, who franks this, is most amiable and benevolent, without any species of pretension, thinking the
best that can be thought of everything and everybody.
Mr. Smith, his son, whom we had not seen in London,
accompanies him, and his tutor, Mr. Kaye, a Cambridge man, and Lord Gardner, Lord Carrington's son-in-
law, suffering from the gouty rheumatism, or rheumatic
gout — he does not know or care which; between the
twitches of his suffering he is entertaining and agreeable.

We have just seen a journal by a little boy of eight
years old, of a voyage from England to Sicily; the boy
is Lord Mahon's son, Lord Carrington's grandson.[1]   It
is one of the best journals I ever read, full of facts;
exactly the writing of a child, but a very clever child.
It is peculiarly interesting to us from having seen Dr.
Holland's letters from Palermo.   Lord Mahon says that
the alarm about the plague at Malta is much greater
than it need be — its progress has been stopped; it was
introduced by a shoemaker having, contrary to law and
reason, surreptitiously brought some handkerchiefs from
a vessel that had not performed quarantine.   You will
nevertheless rejoice that Dr. Holland did not go to
Malta.   How you will regret the loss of the portman-
teau of which that vile Ali Pasha robbed him.

Mr. Fox dined with us to-day, and was very agreeable.   Lord Carrington and his traveling companions
were at Farnham, where they were most hospitably
received.   They had no letters of introduction or inten-

1 Philip Henry, afterwards fifth Earl Stanhope, the historian.

tion of going there; but, finding a horrid inn at Cavan, they applied for charity to a gentleman for lodging. The gentleman took them to walk in Lord Farnham's grounds. Lord and Lady Farnham saw and invited them to the house, and they are full of admiration and almost affection, I think, for Lord and Lady Farnham: they are so charmed by their hospitality, their goodness to the poor, their care of the young Foxes, their magnificent establishment, their neat cottages for their tenants, and, as Lord Gardner sensibly said, "their judicious economy in the midst of magnificence."

August 9.

I like Miss Elizabeth Hamilton better than ever upon further acquaintance. She is what the French would call *bonne à vivre*; so good-humoured, so cheerful, so little disposed to exact attention or to take an authoritative tone in conversation, so ready to give everybody their merits, so indulgent for the follies and frailties, and so hopeful of the reformation of even the faults and vices of the world, that it is impossible not to respect and love her. She dines upon us daily, and mixes so well with this family, that I always forget she is a stranger.

Lady Davy is in high glory at this moment, introducing Madame de Staël everywhere, enjoying the triumph and partaking the gale. They went down, a delightful party, to Cobham — Madame de Staël, Lady Davy, Lord Erskine, Rogers, etc.

Have you heard that Jeffrey, the reviewer, is gone to America in pursuit of a lady, or, as some say, to take possession of an estate left to him by an uncle! He is to be back in time for the "Edinburgh Review" in September!

August 19.

Lord and Lady Lansdowne came to us on Tuesday. Mr. Greenough comes on Saturday, and after that I think we shall get to Black Castle. Lord Longford came yesterday, and though he is not, you know, exuberant in praise, truly says Lord and Lady Lansdowne are people who must be esteemed and liked the more they are known.

Mr. Forbes, just returned from Russia, has this moment come, and is giving a most interesting account of Petersburgh and Moscow; give me credit for retiring to finish this letter. My father is calling, calling, calling.

November 19.

Last night a letter came from Lady Farnham, announcing Francis Fox's marriage, and naming next Monday for us to go to Farnham. We went last Monday to a play at Castle Forbes, or rather to three farces — "Bombastes Furioso," "Of Age To-morrow," and "The Village Lawyer," taken from the famous "Avocat Patelin;" the cunning servant-boy shamming simplicity was admirably acted by Lord Rancliffe.

Tell me whether you have seen Madame de Staël's "Essai sur la Fiction," prefixed to Zulma, Adelaide, and Pauline — the essay is excellent; I shall be curious to know whether you think as I do of Pauline. Madame de Staël calls Blenheim "a magnificent tomb; splendor without, and the deathlike silence of ennui within." She says she is very proud of having made the Duke of Marlborough speak four words. At the moment she was announced he was distinctly heard to utter these words; "Let me go away." We have just got her "Allemagne." We have had great delight in Mrs. Graham's "India," — a charming woman, writing, speaking, thinking, or feeling.

November 25.

A letter from Lady Romilly — so easy, so like her conversation. All agree that Madame de Staël is frankness itself, and has an excellent heart. During her brilliant fortnight at Bowood, where, besides Madame de Staël, her Albertine, M. de Staël, and Count Palmella, there were the Romillys, the Mackintoshes, Mr. Ward, Mr. Rogers, and M. Dumont — if it had not been for chess-playing, music, and dancing between times, poor human nature never could have borne the strain of attention and admiration.

January 1, 1814.

Hunter has sent a whole cargo of French translations — "Popular Tales," with a title under which I should never have known them, "Conseils à mon Fils! Manœuvring; La Mère Intrigante; Ennui" — what can they make of it in French? "Leonora" will translate better than a better thing. "Emilie de Coulanges," I fear, will never stand alone. "L'Absent, The Absentee," — it is impossible that a Parisian can make any sense of it from beginning to end. But these things teach authors what is merely local and temporary. "Les deux Griseldis de Chaucer et Edgeworth;" and, to crown all, two works surreptitiously printed in England under our name, and which are *no better than they should be.*

Pray read "Letters to Sir James Mackintosh on Madame de Staël's 'Allemagne.'" My mother says it is exactly what you would have written; we do not know who is the author.

January 25.

To-day it began to thaw, and thawed so rapidly that we were in danger of being flooded, wet pouring in at all parts, and tubs, and jugs, and pails, and mops running about in all directions, and voices calling, and avalanches of snow thrown by arms of men from gutters and roofs on all sides, darkening windows, and falling with thundering noise.

We have been charmed with a little French play, "Les deux Gendres." I wish you could get it, and get Mr. Knox to read it to you; he is still blocked up by the snow at Pakenham Hall.

We have had an entertaining letter, giving an account of a gentleman who is now in England, a native of Delhi; practiced as an advocate in the native courts of Calcutta, from Calcutta to Prince of Wales Island, and thence to London, and is now Professor of Oriental Languages at Addiscombe. He was at Dr. Malkin's; Mrs. Malkin offered him coffee; he refused, and backed. "Not coffee in the house of Madam-Doctor. I take coffee to keep awake; no danger of being drowsy in the house of Madam-Doctor." He was at a great ball where Lord Cornwallis was expected, and he said he would go to him and "bless his father's memory for his conduct in India."

Poor old Robin Woods is very ill, and he has a tame robin that sits on his foot, and hops up for crumbs.

One day that I went in, when they were at dinner with a bowl of potatoes between them, I said, "How happy you two look!" "Yes, miss, we were that every day since we married."

TO MRS. RUXTON.

15 BAGGOT STREET,[1] DUBLIN,
March, 1814.

Here we are; arrived at three o'clock; found Henrica looking very well. Such a nice, pretty, elegant house! and they have furnished it so comfortably. It is delightful to see my father here; he enjoys himself so much in his son's house, and Sneyd and Henrica are so happy seeing him pleased with everything. Lady Longford has been here this morning; told us Sir Edward Pakenham was so fatigued by riding an uneasy horse at the battle of Vittoria, he was not able to join for four days. A buckle of Lord Wellington's sword-belt saved him; he wrote four times in one week to Lady Wellington, without ever mentioning his wound. I long for you to see Henrica; she is so kind, and so well-bred and easy in her manners.

In April Mr. Edgeworth had a dangerous illness. He was just out of danger, when, late at night on the 10th of May, his son Lovell arrived from Paris, liberated by the peace after eleven years' detention.

[1] Mr. and Mrs. Sneyd Edgeworth's house in Dublin.

TO MRS. RUXTON.

EDGEWORTHSTOWN, May 16, 1814.

My father's contentment at Lovell's[1] return has done him more good than all the advice of all the surgeons, I do believe, now that the danger is over. If you have suffered from suspense in absence, yet, my dear aunt, you have been spared the torturing terrors we have felt at the sight of the daily, hourly changes, so rapid, so unaccountable; one day, one hour all hope, the next all despair! The lamp of life, now bright, starting up high and brilliant, then sinking suddenly almost to extinction; the flame flitting, flickering, starting, *leaping*, as it were, on and off by fits. Some day we shall talk it over in security; now I can hardly bear to look back to it.

All that has passed in France in the last few weeks! a revolution without bloodshed! Paris taken without being pillaged! the Bourbons, after all hope and season for hope had passed, restored to their capital and their palaces! With what mixed sensations they must enter those palaces! I dare say it has not escaped my aunt that the Venus de Médicis and Apollo Belvidere are both missing together; I make no remarks. I hate scandal — at least I am not so fond of it as the lady of whom it was said she could not see the poker and tongs standing together without suspecting something wrong! I wonder where our ideas, especially those of a playful sort, go at some times; and how it is that they all come junketing back faster than there is room for them at

[1] The only son of Mr. Edgeworth's second marriage, with Miss Honora Sneyd.

other times.   How is it that hope so powerfully excites, and fear so absolutely depresses all our faculties?

August 24.

Sneyd has received a very polite letter from the Marquis de Bonay, who is now ambassador at the Court of Denmark.   Mrs. O'Beirne and the Bishop, who like Mons. de Bonay so much, and who have not heard of him for such a length of time, will be delighted to hear of his emerging into light and life.   What is more to our purpose is, that he says he can furnish Sneyd with some notes for the Abbé Edgeworth's life, which he had once intended to write himself; he did put a short notice of his life into the foreign papers at Mittau.   He says he never knew so perfect a human creature as the Abbé.

I had a letter from Dr. Holland this morning saying at the beginning I should be surprised at its contents; and so I was.   The Princess of Wales has invited him to accompany her abroad as her physician!   After consulting with his friends he accepted the invitation.

TO MRS. RUXTON.

EDGEWORTHSTOWN, October 13, 1814.

I had a letter from the Duchess of Wellington the day before yesterday, dated from Deal, just when she was going to embark for France.   The whole of the letter was full of her children and of sorrow for quitting them.

Two days ago came a young gentleman, Mr. James Gordon, a nephew of Lady Elizabeth Whitbread's, with a very polite introductory note from Lady Elizabeth.

He has a great deal of anecdote and information.   He has just come from Paris, and he has given me a better account of Paris, and more characteristic, well-authenticated anecdotes than I have heard from anybody else. He mentioned some instances of the gratitude which Louis XVIII. has shown to people of inferior note in England from whom he had received kindness, especially to the innkeeper's wife at Berkhampstead.   I am glad for the honor of human nature that this is so.

What do you think Walter Scott says is the most poetical performance he has read for years?   That account of the battle of Leipsic which Richard lent to us.

We went to Coolure and had a pleasant day.   "Waverley" was in everybody's hands.   The Admiral does not like it; the hero, he says, is such a shuffling fellow. While he was saying this I had in my pocket a letter from Miss Fanshawe, received that morning, saying it was delightful.   Lady Crewe tells me that Madame d'Arblay cannot settle in England because the King of France has lately appointed M. d'Arblay to some high situation in consequence of his distinguished services.

Shall I tell you what they, my father and all of them are doing at this moment?   Sprawling on the floor, looking at a new rat-trap.   Two pounds of butter vanished the other night out of the dairy; they had been put in a shallow pan with water in it, and it is averred the rats ate it, and Peggy Tuite, the dairymaid, to make the thing more credible, gives the following reason for the rats' conduct.   "Troth, ma'am, they were affronted at the new rat-trap, they only licked the milk off it, and that occasioned them to run off with the butter!"

Mr. and Mrs. Pollard have spent a day here, and brought with them Miss Napier. My father is charmed with her beauty, her voice, and her manners. We talked over "Waverley" with her. I am more delighted with it than I can tell you; it is a work of first-rate genius.

TO THE AUTHOR OF "WAVERLEY."

EDGEWORTHSTOWN, October 23, 1814.

Aut Scotus, aut Diabolus.

We have this moment finished "Waverley." It was read aloud to this large family, and I wish the author could have witnessed the impression it made — the strong hold it seized of the feelings both of young and old — the admiration raised by the beautiful descriptions of nature — by the new and bold delineations of character — the perfect manner in which every character is sustained in every change of situation from first to last, without effort, without the affectation of making the persons speak in character — the ingenuity with which each person introduced in the drama is made useful and necessary to the end — the admirable art with which the story is constructed and with which the author keeps his own secrets till the proper moment when they should be revealed, whilst in the mean time, with the skill of Shakespeare, the mind is prepared by unseen degrees for all the changes of feeling and fortune, so that nothing, however extraordinary, shocks us as improbable; and the interest is kept up to the last moment. We were so possessed with the belief that the whole story and every character in it was real, that we could not endure the occasional addresses from the author to the reader. They are like Fielding; but for that reason we cannot bear them, we cannot bear that an author of such high powers, of such original genius, should for a moment stoop to imitation. This is the only thing we dislike, these are the only passages we wish omitted in the whole work; and let the unqualified manner in which I say this, and the very vehemence of my expression of this disapprobation, be a sure pledge to the author of the sincerity of all the admiration I feel for his genius.

I have not yet said half we felt in reading the work. The characters are not only finely drawn as separate figures, but they are grouped with great skill, and contrasted so artfully, and yet so naturally, as to produce the happiest dramatic effect, and at the same time to relieve the feelings and attention in the most agreeable manner. The novelty of the Highland world which is discovered to our view excites curiosity and interest powerfully; but though it is all new to us it does not embarrass or perplex, or strain the attention. We never are harassed by doubts of the probability of any of these modes of life; though we did not know them, we are quite certain they did exist exactly as they are represented. We are sensible that there is a peculiar merit in the work which is in a measure lost upon us, the *dialects* of the Highlanders and the Lowlanders, etc. But there is another and a higher merit with which we are as much struck and as much delighted as any true born Scotchman could be; the various gradations of Scotch feudal character, from the high-born chieftain and the military baron, to the noble-minded lieutenant Evan Dhu, the robber Beau Lean, and the

savage Callum Beg.   The *Pre*— the Chevalier is beautifully drawn —

> "A prince : aye, every inch a prince!"

His polished manners, his exquisite address, politeness
and generosity, interest the reader irresistibly, and he
pleases the more from the contrast between him and
those who surround him.   I think he is my favorite
character; the Baron Bradwardine is my father's.   He
thinks it required more genius to invent, and more
ability uniformly to sustain this character than any one
of the masterly characters with which the book abounds.
There is indeed uncommon art in the manner in which
his dignity is preserved by his courage and magnanimity, in spite of all his pedantry and his *ridicules*, and
his bear and bootjack, and all the raillery of MacIvor.
MacIvor's unexpected "bear and bootjack" made us
laugh heartily.

But to return to the dear good baron; though I acknowledge that I am not as good a judge as my father
and brothers are of his recondite learning and his law
Latin, yet I feel the humor, and was touched to the
quick by the strokes of generosity, gentleness, and
pathos in this old man, who is, by the bye, all in good
time worked up into a very dignified father-in-law for
the hero.   His exclamation of "Oh! my son! my
son!" and the yielding of the fictitious character of the
baron to the natural feelings of the father is beautiful.
(Evan Dhu's fear that his father-in-law should die
quietly in his bed, made us laugh almost as much as
the bear and bootjack.)

Jinker, in the battle, pleading the cause of the mare
he had sold to Balmawhapple, and which had thrown

him for want of the proper bit, is truly comic; my father says that this and some other passages respecting horsemanship could not have been written by any one who was not master both of the great and little horse.

I tell you without order the great and little strokes of humor and pathos just as I recollect, or am reminded of them at this moment by my companions. The fact is that we have had the volumes only during the time we could read them, and as fast as we could read, lent to us as a great favor by one who was happy enough to have secured a copy before the first and second editions were sold in Dublin. When we applied, not a copy could be had; we expect one in the course of next week, but we resolved to write to the author without waiting for a second perusal. Judging by our own feeling as authors, we guess that he would rather know our genuine first thoughts, than wait for cool second thoughts, or have a regular eulogium or criticism put in the most lucid manner, and given in the finest sentences that ever were rounded.

Is it possible that I have got thus far without having named Flora or Vich Ian Vohr — the *last Vich Ian Vohr!* Yet our minds were full of them the moment before I began this letter; and could you have seen the tears forced from us by their fate, you would have been satisfied that the pathos went to our hearts. Ian Vohr from the first moment he appears, till the last, is an admirably drawn and finely sustained character — new, perfectly new to the English reader — often entertaining — always heroic — sometimes sublime. The gray spirit, the Bodach Glas, thrills *us* with horror. *Us!* What effect must it have upon those under the influence of the superstitions of the Highlands? This circumstance is admirably introduced; this superstition is a weakness quite consistent with the strength of the character, perfectly natural after the disappointment of all his hopes, in the dejection of his mind, and the exhaustion of his bodily strength.

Flora we could wish was never called *Miss MacIvor*, because in this country there are tribes of vulgar Miss *Macs*, and this association is unfavorable to the sublime and beautiful of *your* Flora — she is a true heroine. Her first appearance seized upon the mind and enchanted us so completely, that we were certain she was to be your heroine, and the wife of your hero — but with what inimitable art you gradually convince the reader that she was not, as she said of herself, *capable of making Waverley happy;* leaving her in full possession of our admiration, you first make us pity, then love, and at last give our undivided affection to Rose Bradwardine — sweet Scotch Rose! The last scene between Flora and Waverley is highly pathetic — my brother wishes that *bridal garment* were *shroud;* because when the heart is touched we seldom use metaphor, or quaint alliteration; bride-favor, bridal garment.

There is one thing more we could wish changed or omitted in Flora's character. I have not the volume, and therefore cannot refer to the page; but I recollect in the first visit to Flora, when she is to sing certain verses, there is a walk, in which the description of the place is beautiful, but *too long*, and we did not like the preparation for *a scene* — the appearance of Flora and her harp was too like a common heroine, she should be far above all stage effect or novelist's trick.

These are, without reserve, the only faults we found or *can* find in this work of genius.   We should scarcely have thought them worth mentioning, except to give you proof positive that we are not flatterers.   Believe me, I have not, nor can I convey to you the full idea of the pleasure, the delight we have had in reading "Waverley," nor of the feeling of sorrow with which we came to the end of the history of persons whose real presence had so filled our minds — we felt that we must return to the *flat realities* of life, that our stimulus was gone, and we were little disposed to read the "Postscript, which should have been a Preface."

"Well, let us hear it," said my father, and Mrs. Edgeworth read on.

Oh! my dear sir, how much pleasure would my father, my mother, my whole family, as well as myself have lost, if we had not read to the last page!   And the pleasure came upon us so unexpectedly — we had been so completely absorbed that every thought of ourselves, of our own authorship, was far, far away.

Thank you for the honor you have done us, and for the pleasure you have given us, great in proportion to the opinion we had formed of the work we had just perused — and believe me, every opinion I have in this letter expressed was formed before any individual in the family had peeped to the end of the book, or knew how much we owed you.

Your obliged and grateful

MARIA EDGEWORTH.

TO MISS RUXTON.

EDGEWORTHSTOWN, December 26, 1814.

"A Merry Christmas and a Happy New Year" to you, my dear Sophy, and to my aunt, and uncle, and Margaret. I have just risen from my bed, where I had been a day and a half with a violent headache and pains, or, as John Langan calls them, *pins* in my bones. We have been much entertained with "Mansfield Park." Pray read "Eugène et Guillaume," a modern "Gil Blas;" too much of opera intrigues, but on the whole it is a work of admirable ability. Guillaume's character beautiful, and the gradual deterioration of Eugène's character finely drawn; but the following it out becomes at last as disgusting and horrible as it would be to see the corruption of the body after the spirit had fled.

January, 1815.

I send you some beautiful lines to Lord Byron, by Miss Macpherson, daughter of Sir James Macpherson. As soon as my father hears from the Dublin Society we shall go to Dublin.

TO THE SAME.

15 BAGGOT STREET, DUBLIN,
February, 1815.

Our time here has been much more agreeably spent than I had any hopes it would be. My father has been pleased at some dinners at Mr. Knox's, Mr. Leslie Foster's, and at the Solicitor-General's. Mrs. Stewart is admirable, and Caroline Hamilton the most entertaining and agreeable *good* person I ever saw; she is as good as any saint, and as gay, and much gayer, than any sinner I ever happened to see, male or female.

The Beauforts are at Mrs. Waller's; they came up in a hurry, summoned by a Mrs. Codd, an American, or from America, who has come over to claim a considerable property, and wants to be identified. She went a journey when she was thirteen, with Doctor and Mrs. Beaufort and my mother, and they are the only people in this country who can and will swear *to* her and *for* her. I will tell you when we meet of her entrée with Sir Simon Bradstreet, — and I will tell you of Honora's treading on the parrot at Mrs. Westby's party, — and I will tell you of Fenaigle and his A B C. I think him very stupid. Heaven grant me the power of forgetting his Art of Memory.

TO C. S. EDGEWORTH.

BLACK CASTLE, May 10, 1815.

We, that is, my father, mother, little Harriet, and I, went on Sunday last to Castletown — the two days we spent there, delightful. Lady Louisa Connolly is one of the most respectable, amiable, and even at seventy, I may say, charming persons I ever saw or heard. Having known all the most worthy, as well as the most celebrated people who have lived for the last fifty years, she is full of characteristic anecdote, and fuller of that indulgence for human creatures which is consistent with a thorough knowledge of the world, and a quick perception of all the foibles of human nature — with a high sense of religion, without the slightest tincture of ostentation, asperity, or bigotry. She is all that I could have wished to represent in Mrs. Hungerford,

and her figure and countenance gave me back the image
in my mind.

Her niece, Miss Emily Napier, is graceful, amiable,
and very engaging.

My father went home with Harriet direct from Castletown, but begged my mother and me to return to
Dublin for a fancy ball. We did not go to the Ro-
tunda, but saw enough of it at Mrs. Power's. Lady
Clarke (Lady Morgan's sister), as "Mrs. Flannigan, a
half gentlewoman, from Tipperary," speaking an admirable brogue, was by far the best character, and she had
presence of mind and a great deal of real humor — her
husband attending her with kitten and macaw.

Next to her Mr. Robert Langrishe, as a Frenchwoman, admirably dressed. Mrs. Airey was a Turkish
lady, in a superb dress, given to her by Ali Pasha.
There were *thatched* "Wild Men from the North,"
dancing and stamping with whips and clumping of the
feet, from which Mrs. Bushe and I fled whenever they
came near us. Having named Mrs. Bushe, I must
mention that whenever I have met her, she has been
my delight and admiration from her wit, humor, and
variety of conversation.

TO MISS RUXTON.

Edgeworthstown, August, 1815.

I send a note from Lady Romilly, and one from Mr.
Whishaw; the four travelers mentioned in that note
called upon us yesterday, — Mr. and Mrs. Smith, of
Easton Grey, Miss Bayley, and Mr. Fuller. Mrs.
Smith is stepdaughter to a certain Mrs. Chandler, who
was very kind to me at Mrs. Day's, and I was heartily

glad to see her daughter, even stepdaughter, at Edge-worthstown, and *my* kind, dear, best of stepmothers, seconded my intentions to my very heart's wish; I am sure they went away satisfied. I gave them a note to Lady Farnham, which will, I think, produce a note of admiration! While these visitors were with us Mrs. Moutray came over from Lissard, and we rejoiced in pride of soul to show them our Irish Madame de Sévigné. *Her* Madame de Grignan is more agreeable than ever. Mrs. Moutray told me of a curious debate she heard between Lady C. Campbell, Lady Glenbervie, and others, on the Modern Griselda, with another lady, and a wager laid that she would not read it out to her husband. Wager lost by skipping.

TO MRS. RUXTON.

October 16.

I send you a letter of Joanna Baillie's; her simple style is so different from the *fine* or the *gossip* style.

Did you ever hear this epigram, a translation from Martial?

> "Their utmost power the gods have shown,
>   In turning Niobe to stone :
>   But man's superior power you see,
>   Who turns a stone to Niobe."

Here is an epigram quite to my taste, elegant and witty, without ill-nature or satire.

Barry Fox has come home with his regiment, and is very gentleman-like.

Captain Fox had been serving in Canada, when on Buonaparte's return from Elba his regiment, the 97th, was summoned home, but when the transport entered

Plymouth harbor, and the officers were told that Buonaparte was in the vessel they had just sailed past, they thought it an absurd jest.

January 10, 1816.

The authoress of "Pride and Prejudice" has been so good as to send to me a new novel just published, "Emma." We are reading "France in 1814 and 1815," by young Alison and Mr. Tytler; the first volume good. We are also reading a book which delights us all, though it is on a subject which you will think very little likely to be interesting to us, and on which we had little or no previous knowledge. I bought it on Mr. Brinkley's recommendation, and have not repented — Cuvier's "Theory of the Earth." It is admirably written, with such perfect clearness as to be intelligible to the meanest, and satisfactory to the highest capacity.

I have enlarged my plan of plays, which are not now to be for young people merely, but rather "Popular Plays,"[1] for the same class as "Popular Tales." Excuse huddling things together. Mrs. O'Beirne, of Newry, who has been here, told us a curious story. A man near Granard robbed a farmer of thirty guineas, and hid them in a hole in the church wall. He was hurried out of the country by some accident before he could take off his treasure, and wrote to the man he had robbed and told him where he had hid the money: "Since it can be of no use to me you may as well have it." The owner of the money set to work *grouting* under the church wall, and many of the good people of Granard were seized with Mr. Hill's fear there was a

---

[1] Published in 1817, in one volume, containing *Love and Law*.

plot to undermine the church, and a great piece of work
about it.

March 21.

I send a letter of Mrs. O'Beirne's, telling of Archdeacon de Lacy's [1] marrying Madame de Staël's daughter to the Duc de Broglie! My father is pretty well
to-day, and has been looking at a fine bed of crocuses
in full blow in my garden, and is now gone out in the
carriage, and I must have a *scene* ready for him on his
return.

I have been ever since you were here mending up
the little plays; cobbling work, which takes a great
deal of time, and makes no show.

It was in January, 1816, that Maria Edgeworth received a letter from Miss Rachel Mordecai, of Richmond, Virginia, gently reproaching her with having so
often made Jews ridiculous in her writings, and asking
her to give a story with a good Jew. This was the
origin of "Harrington," and the commencement of a
correspondence with Miss Mordecai, and of a friendship
with her family.

July 24.

Mr. Strutt and his son have within these few minutes
arrived here. He wrote only yesterday to say that
being at Liverpool, he would not be so near Ireland
without going to Edgeworthstown; I hope my father
may be able to enjoy their company, but he was very
ill all last night and this morning.

---

[1] It happened that when Albertine de Staël was to be married to M.
de Broglie, at Florence, the only Protestant clergyman to be had was
our fellow-countryman, Archdeacon de Lacy, son-in-law to Mrs. Moutray, the friend of Nelson and Collingwood.

August 25.

I lose not a moment, my dearest aunt, in communicating to you a piece of intelligence which I am sure will give you pleasure; Lord Longford is going to be married — to Lady Georgiana Lygon, daughter of Lord Beauchamp. You will be glad to see the letter Lord Longford wrote upon the occasion.

Everybody is writing and talking about Lord Byron, but I am tired of the subject. *The all for murder, all for crime* system of poetry will now go out of fashion; as long as he appeared an outrageous mad villain he might have ridden triumphant on the storm, but he has now shown himself too base, too mean, too contemptible for anything like an heroic devil. Pray, if you have an opportunity, read Haygarth's poem of "Greece." I like it much; I like the mind that produced it, — the poetry is not always good, but there is a *spirit* through the whole that sustains it and that elevates and invigorates the mind of the reader.

September 18.

You know, my dear aunt, it is a favorite opinion of my father's that *things come in bundles;* that *people* come in bundles is, I think, true, as, after having lived without seeing a creature but our own family for months, a press of company comes all at once. The very day after the Brinkleys had come to us, and filled every nook in the house, the inclosed letter was brought to me. I was in my own little den, just beginning to write for an hour, as my father had requested I would, "let who would be in the house." On opening the letter and seeing the signature of Ward, I was in hopes it was the Mr. Ward who made the fine speech and wrote the review of "Patronage" in the "Quarterly," and of whom Madame de Staël said that he was the only man in England who really understood the art of conversation. However, upon reëxamining the signature, I found that our gentleman who was waiting at the gate for an answer was another Ward, who is called "the great R. Ward," — a very gentleman-like, agreeable man, full of anecdotes, bon mots, and compliments. I wish you had been here, for I think you would have been entertained much, not only by his conversation, but by his character; I never saw a man who had lived in the world so anxious about the opinions which are formed of him by those with whom he is conversing, so quick at discovering, by the countenance and by *implication*, what is thought of him, or so incessantly alert in guarding all the suspected places in your opinion. He disclaimed memory, though he has certainly the very best of memories for wit and bon mots that man was ever blessed with. Mr. Ward was Under-Secretary of State during a great part of Pitt's administration, and has been one of the Lords of the Admiralty, and is now Clerk of the Ordnance, and has been sent to Ireland to reform abuses in the Ordnance. He speaks well, and in agreeable voice. He told me that he had heard in London that I had a sort of Memoria Technica, by which I could remember everything that was said in conversation, and by certain motions of my fingers could, while people were talking to me, note down all the ridiculous points!! He happened to have passed some time

in his early life at Lichfield, and knew Miss Seward
and Dr. Darwin, and various people my father and aunts
knew; so this added to his power of making himself
agreeable.   Of all the multitude of good things he told
us, I can only at this moment recollect the lines which
he repeated, by Dr. Mansel, the Bishop of Bristol, on
Miss Seward and Mr. Hayley's flattery of each other: —

> "Prince of poets, England's glory,
>   Mr. Hayley, *that is* you!"
> "Ma'am, you carry all before you,
>   Lichfield Swan, indeed you do!"
> "In epic, elegy, or sonnet,
>   Mr. Hayley, you 're divine!"
> "Madam, take my word upon it,
>   You yourself are all the Nine."

Some of his stories at dinner were so entertaining,
that even old George's face cut in wood could not stand
it; and John Bristow and the others were so bewil-
dered, I thought the second course would never be on
the table.

November 18.

We are reading one of the most entertaining and
interesting and NEW books I ever read in my life —
Tully's "Residence in Tripoli," written by the sister
of the consul, who resided there for ten years, spoke
the language, and was admitted to a constant intercourse
with the ladies of the seraglio, who are very different
from any seraglio ladies we ever before heard of.   No
Arabian tale is equal in magnificence and entertainment;
no tragedy superior in strength of interest to the tragedy
recorded in the last ten pages of this incomparable book.
Some people affect to disbelieve, and say it is manufac-

tured; but it would be a miracle that it was invented
with such consistency.

January, 1817.

Mr. Knox has come and gone; two of the plays were
read to him. My father gave him a sketch of each,
and desired him to choose; he chose the genteel comedy,
"The Two Guardians," and I read it; and those who
sat by told me afterwards that Mr. Knox's countenance
showed he was much amused, and that he had great
sympathy. For my part, I had a *glaze* before my eyes,
and never once saw him while I was reading. He made
some good criticisms, and in consequence I altered one
scene, and dragged out Arthur Onslow by the head and
heels — the good boy of the piece; and we found he
was never missed, but the whole much lightened by
throwing this heavy character overboard. Next night
"The Rose, Thistle, and Shamrock;" Mr. Knox
laughed, and seemed to enjoy it much.

Mr. Edgeworth was now failing rapidly, though as
much interested as ever in all that was going on around.
"How I do enjoy my existence!" he often exclaimed.
His daughter, however, says that "he did not for his
own sake desire length of life; he only prayed that his
mind might not decay before his body," and it did not;
his mental powers were as bright and vigorous as ever
to the last.

On the 16th of February Maria Edgeworth read out
to her father the first chapter of "Ormond" in the carriage, going to Pakenham Hall to see Lord Longford's
bride. It was the last visit that Mr. Edgeworth paid

anywhere. He had expressed a wish to his daughter
that she should write a story as a companion to "Harrington," and in all her anguish of mind at his state of
health, she, by a remarkable effort of affection and
genius, produced those gay and brilliant pages — some
of the gayest and most brilliant she ever composed.
The interest and delight which her father, ill as he was,
took in this beginning, encouraged her to go on, and
she completed the story. "Harrington," written as an
apology for the Jews, had dragged with her as she
wrote it, and it dragged with the public. But in
"Ormond" she was on Irish ground, where she was
always at her very best. Yet the characters of King
Corny and Sir Ulick O'Shane, and the many scenes full
of wit, humor, and feeling, were written in agony of
anxiety, with trembling hand and tearful eyes. As she
finished chapter after chapter, she read them out — the
whole family assembling in her father's room to listen
to them. Her father enjoyed these readings so exceedingly, that she was amply rewarded for the efforts she
made.

MARIA TO MISS RUXTON.

EDGEWORTHSTOWN, May 31, 1817.

This day, so anxiously expected, has arrived — the
only birthday of my father's for many, many years
which has not brought unmixed feelings of pleasure.
He had had a terrible night, but when I went into his
room and stood at the foot of his bed, his voice was
strong and cheerful, as usual. I put into his hand the
hundred and sixty printed pages of "Ormond" which
kind-hearted Hunter had successfully managed to get

ready for this day. How my dear father can, in the
midst of such sufferings, and in such an exhausted state
of body, take so much pleasure in such things, is astonishing. Oh, my dear Sophy, what must be the fund
of warm affection from which this springs! and what
infinite, exquisite pleasure to me! "Call Sneyd directly," he said, and swallowed some stirabout, and
said he felt renovated. Sneyd was seated at the foot
of his bed. "Now, Maria, dip anywhere, read on." I
began; "King Corny recovered." Then he said, "I
must tell Sneyd the story up to this."

And most eloquently, most beautifully did he tell the
story. No mortal could ever have guessed that he was
an invalid if they had only *heard* him *speak*.

Just as I had here stopped writing my father came
out of his room, looking wretchedly, but ordered the
carriage, and said he would go to Longford to see Mr.
Fallon about materials for William's bridge. He took
with him his three sons, and "Maria to read ' Ormond,' "
— great delight to me. He was much pleased, and this
wonderful father of mine drove all the way to Longford;
forced our way through the tumult of the most crowded
market I ever saw — his voice heard clear all the way
down the street — stayed half an hour in the carriage
on the bridge talking to Mr. Fallon; and we were not
home till half-past six. He could not dine with us,
but after dinner he sent for us all into the library. He
sat in the armchair by the fire; my mother in the
opposite armchair, Pakenham in the chair behind her,
Francis on a stool at her feet, Maria beside them;
William next, Lucy, Sneyd; on the sofa opposite the
fire, as when you were here, Honora, Fanny, Harriet,

and Sophy; my aunts next to my father, and Lovell
between them and the sofa.   He was much pleased at
Lovell and Sneyd's coming down for this day.

Mr. Edgeworth died on the 13th of June, in his
seventy-second year.   He had been — by his different
wives — the father of twenty-one children, of whom
thirteen survived him.   The only son of his second
marriage, Lovell Edgeworth, succeeded to Edgeworthstown, but persuaded his stepmother and his numerous
brothers and sisters still to regard it as a home.

To enable the reader to understand the relationships
of the large family circle, it may be well to give the
children of Mr. Edgeworth.

1st marriage, with Anna Maria Elers.

- Richard, *b.* 1765; *d. s. p.* 1796.
- *Maria*, *b.* 1767; *d.* unmarried, 1849.
- Emmeline, married, 1802, John King, Esq.
- Anna, married, 1794, Dr. Beddoes.

2d marriage, with Honora Sneyd.

- Lovell, *b.* 1776; *d.* unmarried, 1841.
- Honora, *d.* unmarried, 1790.

3d marriage, with Elizabeth Sneyd.

- Henry, *b.* 1782; *d.* unmarried, 1813.
- Charles Sneyd, *b.* 1786; *d. s. p.* 1864.
- William, *b.* 1788; *d.* 1792.
- Thomas Day, *b.* 1789; *d.* 1792.
- William, *b.* 1794; *d. s. p.* 1829.
- Elizabeth, *d.* 1800.
- Charlotte, *d.* 1807.
- Sophia, *d.* 1785.
- Honora, married, 1831, Admiral Sir J. Beaufort, and *d.*, his widow, 1858.

4th marriage, with
Frances Anna
Beaufort.

- Francis Beaufort, *b.* 1809; married, 1831, Rosa Florentina Erolas, and had four sons and a daughter. The second son, Antonio Erolas, eventually succeeded his uncle Sneyd at Edgeworthstown.
- Michael Pakenham, *b.* 1812; married, 1846, Christina Macpherson, and had issue.
- Francis Maria (Fanny), married, 1829, Lestock P. Wilson, Esq., and *d.* 1848.
- Harriet, married, 1826, Rev. Richard Butler, afterwards Dean of Clonmacnoise.
- Sophia, married, 1824, Barry Fox, Esq., and *d.* 1837.
- Lucy Jane, married, 1843, Rev. T. R. Robinson, D. D.

During the months which succeeded her father's death, Maria wrote scarcely any letters; her sight caused great anxiety. The tears, she said, felt in her eyes like the cutting of a knife. She had overworked them all the previous winter, sitting up at night and struggling with her grief as she wrote "Ormond;" and she was now unable to use them without pain.

In October she went to Black Castle, and remained there till January, 1818, having the strength of mind to abstain almost entirely from reading and writing.

It required all Maria Edgeworth's inherited activity of mind, and all her acquired command over herself, to keep up the spirits of her family on their return to Edgeworthstown; from which the Master-mind was gone, and where the light was quenched. But notwithstanding all the depression she felt, she set to work

immediately at what she now felt to be her first duty —
the fulfillment of her father's wish that she should complete the Memoirs of his life, which he had himself
begun. Yet her eyes were still so weak that she seldom allowed herself what had been her greatest relaxa-
tion — writing letters to her friends.

MARIA TO MRS. RUXTON.

EDGEWORTHSTOWN, January 24, 1818.

My dearest aunt and friend — friend of my youth
and age, and beloved sister of my father, how many
titles you have to my affection and gratitude, and how
delightful it is to me to feel them all! Since I have
parted from you, I have felt still more than when I was
with you the peculiar value to me of your sympathy
and kindness. I find my spirits sink beyond my utmost effort to support them when I leave you, and they
rise involuntarily when I am near you, and recall the
dear trains of old associations, and the multitude of
ideas I used to have with him who is gone forever.
Thank you, my dear aunt, for your most kind and
touching letter. You have been for three months daily
and hourly soothing, and indulging, and nursing me
body and mind, and making me forget the sense of pain
which I could not have felt suspended in any society
but yours. My uncle's opinion and hints about the
Life I have been working at this whole week. Nothing
can be kinder than Lovell is to all of us.

I have read two thirds of Bishop Watson's life. I
think he *bristles* his independence too much upon every
occasion, and praises himself too much for it, and above
all complains too much of the want of preferment and

neglect of him by the Court. I have Madame de Staël's Memoirs of her father's private life; I have only read fifty pages of it — too much of a French éloge — too little of his private life. There is a *Notice*, by Benjamin Constant, of Madame de Staël's life prefixed to this work, which appears to me more interesting and pathetic than anything Madame de Staël has yet said of her father.

February 21.

I must and will write to my Aunt Ruxton to-day, if the whole College of Physicians, and the whole conclave of cardinal virtues, with Prudence primming up her mouth at the head of them, stood before me. I entirely agree with you, my dearest aunt, on one subject, as indeed I generally do on most subjects, but particularly about "Northanger Abbey" and "Persuasion." The behavior of the General in "Northanger Abbey," packing off the young lady without a servant or the common civilities which any bear of a man, not to say gentleman, would have shown, is quite outrageously out of drawing and out of nature. "Persuasion" — excepting the tangled, useless histories of the family in the first fifty pages — appears to me, especially in all that relates to poor Anne and her lover, to be exceedingly interesting and natural. The love and the lover admirably well drawn; don't you see Captain Wentworth, or rather don't you in her place feel him, taking the boisterous child off her back as she kneels by the sick boy on the sofa? And is not the first meeting after their long separation admirably well done? And the overheard conversation about the nut? But I must stop; we have got no farther than the disaster of Miss Musgrave's jumping off the steps.

I am going on, but very slowly, and not to my satisfaction with my work.

TO MRS. SNEYD EDGEWORTH.

EDGEWORTHSTOWN, March 27.

I agree with you in thinking the MS. de St. Hélène a magnificent performance.   My father was strongly of opinion that it was not written by Buonaparte himself, and he grounded this opinion chiefly upon the passages relative to the Duc d'Enghien: *c'était plus qu'un crime, c'était une faute;* no man, he thought, not even Nero, would, in writing for posterity, say that he had committed a crime instead of a fault.   But it may be observed that in the Buonaparte system of morality which runs through the book, nothing is considered what we call a crime, unless it be what he allows to be a fault.   His proof that he did not murder Pichegru is, that it would have been useless.   *Le cachet de* Buonaparte is as difficult to imitate as *le cachet de Voltaire.* I know of but three people in Europe who could have written it: Madame de Staël, Talleyrand, or M. Dumont. Madame de Staël, though she has the ability, could not have got so plainly and shortly through it.   Talleyrand has *l'esprit comme un démon,* but he could not for the soul of him have refused himself a little more wit and wickedness.   Dumont has not enough audacity of mind.

TO MRS. STARK.[1]

Spring Farm, N. T., Mount Kennedy,
June, 1818.

I am, and have been ever since I could any way command my attention, intent upon finishing those Memoirs of himself which my father left me to finish and charged me to publish. Yet I have accepted an invitation to Bowood, from Lady Lansdowne, whom I love, and as soon as I have finished I shall go there. As to Scotland, I have no chance of getting there at present, but if ever I go there, depend upon it, I shall go to see you. Never, never can I forget those happy days we spent with you, and the warm-hearted kindness we received from you and yours; those were "sunny spots" in my life.

TO MRS. EDGEWORTH.

Bowood, September, 1818.

I will tell you how we pass our day. At seven I get up — this morning at half-past six, to have the pleasure of writing to you, my dearest mother; be satisfied I never write a word at night; breakfast is at half after nine, very pleasant; afterwards we all *stray* into the library for a few minutes, and settle when we shall meet again for walking, etc.; then Lady Lansdowne goes to her dear dressing-room and dear children, Dumont to his attic, Lord Lansdowne to his out-of-door works, and we to our elegant dressing-room, and Miss Carnegy to hers. Between one and two is luncheon; happy time! Lady Lansdowne is so cheerful, polite,

---

[1] Daughter of Mr. Bannatyne, of Glasgow.

and easy, just as she was in her walks at Edgeworthstown; but very different walks are the walks we take
here, most various and delightful, from dressed shrubbery and park walks to fields with inviting paths, wide
downs, shady winding lanes, and happy cottages — not
dressed, but naturally well placed, and with evidence in
every part of their being suited to the inhabitants.

After our walk we dress and make haste for dinner.
Dinner is always pleasant, because Lord and Lady Lansdowne converse so agreeably — Dumont also — towards
the dessert. After dinner, we find the children in the
drawing-room; I like them better and better the more I
see of them. When there is company there is a whist
table for the gentlemen. Dumont read out one evening
one of Corneille's plays, "Le Florentin," which is beautiful, and was beautifully read. We asked for one of
Molière, but he said to Lord Lansdowne that it was
impossible to read Molière aloud without a quicker eye
than he had *pour de certains propos* — however, they
went to the library and brought out at last as odd a
choice as could well be made, with Mr. Thomas Grenville as auditor, "Le vieux Célibataire," an excellent
play, interesting and lively throughout, and the old
bachelor himself a charming character. Dumont read
it as well as Tessier could have read it; but there were
things which seemed as if they were written on purpose
for the Célibataire who was listening, and the Célibataire who was reading.

Lord Lansdowne, when I asked him to describe
Rocca[1] to me, said he heard him give an answer to
Lord Byron which marked the indignant frankness of

____
[1] Second husband of Madame de Staël.

his mind.   Lord Byron at Coppet had been going on abusing the stupidity of the good people of Geneva; Rocca at last turned short upon him — "Eh! milord, pourquoi donc venez-vous vous *fourrer* parmi ces honnêtes gens?"

Madame de Staël — I jumble anecdotes together as I recollect them — Madame de Staël had a great wish to see Mr. Bowles, the poet, or as Lord Byron calls him the sonneteer; she admired his sonnets, and his "Spirit of Maritime Discovery," and ranked him high as an English genius.   In riding to Bowood he fell, and sprained his shoulder, but still came on.   Lord Lansdowne alluded to this in presenting him to Madame de Staël before dinner in the midst of the listening circle.   She began to compliment him and herself upon the exertion he had made to come and see her: "Oh, ma'am, say no more, for I would have done a great deal more to see so great a *curiosity!*"

Lord Lansdowne says it is impossible to describe the *shock* in Madame de Staël's face — the breathless astonishment and the total change produced in her opinion of the man.   She afterwards said to Lord Lansdowne, who had told her he was a simple country clergyman, "Je vois bien que ce n'est qu'un simple curé qui n'a pas le sens commun, quoique grand poète."

Lady Lansdowne, just as I was writing this, came to my room and paid me half an hour's visit.   She brought back my father's MS., which I had lent to her to read; she was exceedingly interested in it; she says, "It is not only entertaining but interesting, as showing how such a character was formed."

· TO MISS RUXTON.

Bowood, September 19, 1818.

You know our history up to Saturday last, when Lord and Lady Grenville left Bowood; there remained Mr. Thomas Grenville, Le vieux Célibataire, two Horts, Sir William, and his brother, Mr. Gally Knight, and Lord and Lady Bathurst, and their two daughters. Mr. Grenville left us yesterday, and the rest go to-day. Mr. Grenville was very agreeable; dry, quiet humor; grave face, dark, thin, and gentleman-like; a lie-by manner, entertained, or entertaining by turns. It is curious that we have seen within the course of a week one of the heads of the ministerial, and one of the ex-ministerial party. In point of ability, Lord Grenville is, I think, far superior to any one I have seen here. Lord Lansdowne, with whom I had a delightful *tête-à-tête* walk yesterday, told me that Lord Grenville can be fully known only when people come to do political business with him; there he excels. You know his preface to Lord Chatham's "Letters." His manner of speaking in the House is not pleasing, Lord Lansdowne says: from being very near-sighted he has a look of austerity and haughtiness, and as he cannot see all he wants to see, he throws himself back with his chin up, determined to look at none. Lord Lansdowne gave me an instance — I may say a warning — of the folly of judging hastily of character at first sight from small circumstances. In one of Cowper's letters there is an absurd character of Lord Grenville, in which he is represented as a *petit maître*. This arose from Lord Grenville taking up his near-sighted glass several times during his visit. There cannot, in nature or art, be a man further from a *petit maître.*

Lady Bathurst is remarkably obliging to me; we have many subjects in common, — her brother, the Duke of Richmond, and all Ireland; her aunt, Lady Louisa Connolly, and Miss Emily Napier, and all the Pakenhams and the Duchess of Wellington. The Duke lately said to Mrs. Pole, "After all, home is what we must look to at last."

Lady Georgiana is a very pretty, and I need scarcely say, fashionable-looking young lady, easy, agreeable, and quite unaffected.

This visit to Bowood has surpassed my expectation in every respect. I much enjoy the sight of Lady Lansdowne's happiness with her husband and her children; beauty, fortune, cultivated society, in short, everything that the most reasonable or unreasonable could wish. She is so amiable and so desirous to make others happy, that it is impossible not to love her; and the most envious of mortals, I think, would have the heart opened to sympathy with her. Then Lord and Lady Lansdowne are so fond of each other, and show it, and *don't show it,* in the most agreeable manner. His conversation is very various and natural, full of information, given for the sake of those to whom he speaks, never for display. What he says always lets us into his feelings and character, and therefore is interesting.

TO MRS. EDGEWORTH.

THE GROVE, EPPING, October 4, 1818.

I mentioned one day at dinner at Bowood that children have very early a desire to produce an effect, a sensation in company. "Yes," said Lord Lansdowne, "I remember distinctly having that feeling, and acting upon it once in a large and august company, when I was a young boy, at the time of the French Revolution, when the Duke and Duchess de Polignac came to Bowood, and my father was anxious to receive these illustrious guests with all due honor. One Sunday evening, when they were all sitting in state in the drawing-room, my father introduced me, and I was asked to give the company a sermon. The text I chose was, quite undesignedly, 'Put not your trust in princes.' The moment I had pronounced the words, I saw my father's countenance change, and I saw changes in the countenances of the Duke and Duchess, and of every face in the circle. I saw I was the cause of this; and though I knew my father wanted to stop me, I would go on, to see what would be the effect. I repeated my text, and preached upon it, and as I went on, made out what it was that affected the congregation."

Afterwards Lord Shelburne desired the boy to go round the circle and wish the company good-night; but when he came to the Duchess de Polignac, he could not resolve to kiss her; he so detested the patch of rouge on her cheek, he started back. Lord Shelburne whispered a bribe in his ear — no, he would not; and they were obliged to laugh it off. But his father was very much vexed.

HAMPSTEAD, October 13.

We had a delightful drive here yesterday from Epping. Joanna Baillie and her sister, most kind, cordial, and warm-hearted, came running down their

little flagged walk to welcome us.   Mrs. Hunter, widow
of John Hunter, dined here yesterday; she wrote "The
son of Alnomac shall never complain," and she entertained me exceedingly; and both Joanna and her sister
have most agreeable and new conversation, not old, trum-
pery literature over again, and reviews, but new circumstances worth telling, apropos to every subject that is
touched upon; frank observations on character, without
either ill-nature or the fear of committing themselves;
no blue-stocking tittle - tattle, or habits of worshiping
or being worshiped; domestic, affectionate, good to
live with, and, without fussing continually, doing what
is most obliging, and whatever makes us feel most at
home.   Breakfast is very pleasant in this house, and
the two good sisters look so neat and cheerful.

October 15.

We went to see Mrs. Barbauld at Stoke Newington.
She was gratified by our visit, and very kind and agreeable.

Bowood, November 3, 1818.

We have just returned to dear Bowood.   We went
to Wimbledon, where Lady Spencer was very attentive
and courteous; she is, I may say, the cleverest person
I have seen since I came to England.   At parting she
"God blessed" me.   We met there Lady Jones, widow
of Sir William — thin, dried, tall old lady, nut-cracker
chin, penetrating, benevolent, often-smiling, black eyes;
and her nephew, young Mr. Hare;[1] and, the last day,
Mr. Brunel.[2]

[1] Augustus William Hare, one of the authors of *Guesses at Truth*.

[2] Afterwards Sir Mark Isamband Brunel, engineer of the Thames
tunnel, Woolwich Arsenal, etc., 1769–1849.

This moment Mrs. Dugald Stewart, who was out walking, has come in — the same dear woman! I have seen Mr. Stewart — very, very weak — he cannot walk without an arm to lean on.

Bowood, November 4, 1818.

The newspapers have told you the dreadful catastrophe — the death, and the manner of the death, of that great and good man, Sir Samuel Romilly. My dearest mother, there seems no end of horrible calamities. There is no telling how it has been felt in this house. I did not know till now that Mr. Dugald Stewart had been so very intimate with Sir Samuel, and so very much attached to him — forty years his friend; he has been dreadfully shocked. He was just getting better, enjoyed seeing us, conversed quite happily with me the first evening, and I felt reassured about him; but what may be the consequence of this stroke none can tell. I rejoice that we came to meet him here: they say that I am of use conversing with him. Lord Lansdowne looks wretchedly, and can hardly speak on the subject without tears, notwithstanding all his efforts.

TO MISS WALLER.[1]

BYRKELY LODGE, November 24, 1818.

In the gloom which the terrible and most unexpected loss of Sir Samuel Romilly cast over the whole society at Bowood during the last few days we spent there, I recollect some minutes of pleasure. When I was consulting Mrs. Dugald Stewart about my father's MS., I

---

[1] Miss Waller was aunt of Captain Beaufort and the fourth Mrs. Edgeworth.

mentioned Captain Beaufort's opinion on some point; the moment his name had passed my lips, Mr. Stewart's grave countenance lighted up, and he exclaimed, "Captain Beaufort! I have the very highest opinion of Captain Beaufort ever since I saw a letter of his, which I consider to be one of the best letters I ever read. It was to the father of a young gentleman who died at Malta, to whom Captain Beaufort had been the best of friends. The young man had excellent qualities, but some frailties. Captain Beaufort's letter to the father threw a veil over the son's frailties, and without departing from the truth, placed all his good qualities in the most amiable light. The old man told me," continued Mr. Stewart, "that this letter was the only earthly consolation he ever felt for the loss of his son; he spoke of it with tears streaming from his eyes, and pointed in particular to the passage that recorded the warm affection with which his son used to speak of him."

It is delightful to find the effect of a friend's goodness thus coming round to us at a great distance of time, and to see that it has raised him in the esteem of those we most admire.

Mr. Stewart has not yet recovered his health; he is more alarmed, I think, than he need to be by the difficulty he finds in recollecting names and circumstances that passed immediately before and after his fever. This hesitation of memory, I believe, everybody has felt more or less after any painful event. In every other respect Mr. Stewart's mind appears to me to be exactly what it ever was, and his kindness of heart even greater than we have for so many years known it to be.

We are now happy in the quiet of Byrkely Lodge. We have not had any visitors since we came, and have paid only one visit, to the Miss Jacksons. Miss Fanny is, you know, the author of "Rhoda;" Miss Maria, the author of a little book of advice about "A Gay Garden." I like the Gay Garden lady best at first sight, but I will suspend my judgment prudently till I see more.

I have just heard a true story worthy of a postscript even in the greatest haste. Two stout foxhunters in this neighborhood, who happened each to have as great a dread of a spider as ever fine lady had or pretended to have, chanced to be left together in a room where a spider appeared, crawling from under a table, at which they were sitting. Neither durst approach within arm's length of it, or touch it even with a pair of tongs; at last one of the gentlemen proposed to the other, who was in thick boots, to get on the table and jump down upon his enemy, which was effected to their infinite satisfaction.

TO MRS. RUXTON.

BYRKELY LODGE, January 20, 1819.

I see my little dog on your lap, and feel your hand patting his head, and hear your voice telling him that it is for Maria's sake he is there. I wish I was in his place, or at least on the sofa beside you at this moment, that I might in five minutes tell you more than my letters could tell you in five hours.

I have scarcely yet recovered from the joy of having Fanny actually with me, and with me just in time to go to Trentham, on which I had set my foolish heart. We met her at Lichfield. We spent that evening there

— the children of four different marriages all united and happy together. Lovell took Francis [1] on with him to Byrkely Lodge, and we went to Trentham.

When Honora and I had Fanny in the chaise to ourselves, ye gods! how we did talk! We arrived at Trentham by moonlight, and could only just see outlines of wood and hills; silver light upon the broad water, and cheerful lights in the front of a large house, with wide open hall door. Nothing could be more polite and cordial than the reception given to us by Lady Stafford, and by her good-natured, noblemanlike lord. During our whole visit, what particularly pleased me was the manner in which they treated my sisters; not as appendages to an authoress, not as young ladies merely *permitted*, or to fill up as *personnages muets* in society; on the contrary, Lady Stafford conversed with them a great deal, and repeatedly took opportunities of expressing to me how much she liked and valued them for their own sake. "That sister Fanny of yours has a most intelligent countenance; she is much more than pretty; and what I so like is her manner of answering when she is asked any question — so unlike the Missy style. They have both been admirably well educated." Then she spoke in the handsomest manner of my father — "a master-mind; even in the short time I saw him that was apparent to me."

Lady Elizabeth Gower is a most engaging, sensible, unaffected, sweet pretty creature. While Lady Stafford in the morning was in the library doing a drawing in

---

[1] Son of the fourth Mrs. Edgeworth, who was going to the Charter-house, and who had accompanied his sister Fanny, with Lovell, from Edgeworthstown.

water colors to show Honora her manner of finishing
quickly, Fanny and I sat up in Lady Elizabeth's darling little room at the top of the house, where she has
all her drawings, and writing, and books, and harp.
She and her brother, Lord Francis, have always been
friends and companions; and on her table were bits of
paper on which he had scribbled droll heads, and verses
of his, very good, on the "Expulsion of the Moors from
Spain;" Lady Elizabeth knew every line of these, and
had all that quick feeling, and *coloring* apprehension,
and *slurring* dexterity, which those who read out what
is written by a dear friend so well understand.

Large rooms filled with pictures, most of them modern
— Reynolds, Moreland, Glover, Wilkie; but there are
a few ancient; one of Titian's, that struck me as beautiful — "Hermes teaching Cupid to read." The chief
part of the collection is in the house in town. After a
happy week at Trentham we returned here.

Mercy on my poor memory! I forgot to tell you
that Lady Harrowby and her daughter were at Trentham, and an *exquisite*, or tiptop dandy, Mr. Standish,
and young Mr. Sneyd, of Keil — very fashionable.
Lady Harrowby deserves Madame de Staël's good word,
she calls her "*compagne spirituelle*" — a charming
woman, and very quick in conversation.

The morning after Mr. Standish's arrival, Lady Stafford's maid told her that she and all the ladies' maids
had been taken by his *gentleman* to see his toilette —
"which, I assure you, my lady, is the thing best worth
seeing in this house, all of gilt plate, and I wish, my
lady, you had such a dressing box." Though an exquisite, Mr. Standish is clever, entertaining, and agreeable.

One day that he sat beside me at dinner, we had a delightful battledore and shuttlecock conversation from grave to gay as quick as your heart could wish; from "L'Almanac des Gourmandes" and *le respectable porc*, to "Dorriforth and the Simple Story."

January 22.

My letter has been detained two days for a frank. My aunts[1] are pretty well, and we feel that we add to their cheerfulness. Honora plays cribbage with Aunt Mary, and I read Florence Macarthy; I like the Irish characters, and the Commodore, and Lord Adelm — that is Lord Byron; but Ireland is traduced in some of her representations. "Marriage" is delightful.

TO MRS. EDGEWORTH.

BYRKELY LODGE, February 8, 1819.

Mrs. Sneyd took me with her to-day to Lord Bagot's to return Lady Dartmouth's visit; she is a charming woman, and appears most amiable, taking care of all those grandchildren. Lord Bagot very melancholy, gentlemanlike, and interesting. Fine old cloistered house, galleries, painted glass, coats of arms, and family pictures everywhere. It was the first time Lord Bagot had seen Mrs. Sneyd since his wife's death; he took both her hands and was as near bursting into tears as ever man was. He was very obliging to me, and showed me all over his house, and gave me a most sweet bunch of Daphne Indica.

TETSWORTH INN, March 4.

On Tuesday morning we left dear, happy, luxurious, warm Byrkely Lodge. At taking leave of me, Mr.

---

[1] The Miss Sneyds were now living for a time at Byrkely Lodge.

Sneyd began thanking me as if I had been the person obliging instead of obliged, and when I got up from the breakfast table and went round to stop his thanks by mine, he took me in his arms and gave me a squeeze 'hat left me as flat as a pancake, and then ran out of the room absolutely crying.

We arrived at tea-time at Mrs. Moilliet's,[1] Smethwick, near Birmingham, much pleased with our reception, and with Mr. Moilliet and their five children. He has purchased a delightful house on the banks of the Lake of Geneva, where they go next summer, and most earnestly pressed us to visit them there.

Mr. Moilliet told us an anecdote of Madame la Comtesse de Rumford and her charming Count; he one day, in a fit of ill-humor, went to the porter and forbade him to let into his house any of the friends of Madame la Comtesse or of M. Lavoisier — all the society which you and I saw at her house; they had been invited to supper; the old porter, all disconsolate, went to tell the Countess the order he had received. "Well, you must obey your master, you must not let them into the house, but I will go down to your lodge, and as each carriage comes, you will let them know what has happened, and that I am there to receive them."

They all came; and by two or three at a time went into the porter's lodge and spent the evening with her; their carriages lining the street all night, to the Count's infinite mortification.

Mr. Moilliet also told Fanny of a Yorkshire farmer who went to the Bank of England, and, producing a Bank of England note for £30,000, asked to have it

[1] Daughter of Mr. Keir, Mrs. Edgeworth's old friend.

changed. The clerk was surprised and hesitated, said that a note for so large a sum was very uncommon, and that he knew there never had been more than two £30,000 bank notes issued. "Oh, yes!" said the farmer, "I have the other at home."

We went to see dear old Mr. Watt: eighty-four, and in perfect possession of eyes, ears, and all his comprehensive understanding and warm heart. Poor Mrs. Watt is almost crippled with rheumatism, but as good-natured and hospitable as ever, and both were heartily glad to see us. So many recollections, painful and pleasurable, crowded and pressed upon my heart during this half-hour. I had much ado to talk, but I did,[1] and so did he, — of forgeries on bank notes, no way he can invent of avoiding such but by having an inspecting clerk in every country town. Talked over the committee report — paper-marks, vain — Tilloch — "I have no great opinion of his abilities — Bramah — yes, he is a clever man, but set down this for truth: no man is so ingenious, but what another may be found equally ingenious. What one invents, another can detect and imitate."

Watt is at this moment himself the best encyclopædia extant; I dare not attempt to tell you half he said; it would be a volume. Chantrey has made a beautiful, I mean an admirable, bust of him. Chantrey and Canova are now making rival busts of Washington.

I must hop, skip, and jump as I can from subject to subject. Mr. and Mrs. Moilliet took us in the evening to a lecture on poetry, by Campbell, who has been invited by a Philosophical Society of Birmingham gen-

---

[1] Mr. Watt had been one of Mr. Edgeworth's most intimate friends.

tlemen to give lectures; they give tickets to their friends. Mr. Corrie, one of the heads of this society, was *proud* to introduce us. Excellent room, with gas spouting from tubes below the gallery. Lecture good enough. Mr. Campbell introduced to me after lecture; asked very kindly for Sneyd; many compliments. Mr. Corrie drank tea, after the lecture, at Mr. Moilliet's — very agreeable benevolent countenance, most agreeable voice. We liked particularly his enthusiasm for Mr. Watt; he gave a history of his inventions, and instances of Watt's superiority both in invention and magnanimity when in competition with others.

Mr. and Mrs. Moilliet have pressed us to come again. Mr. and Mrs. Watt, ditto, ditto. Mr. Watt almost with tears in his eyes; and I was ashamed to see that venerable man standing bareheaded at his door to do us the last [1] honor, till the carriage drove away.

I beg your pardon for going backward and forward in this way in my hurry-skurry. I leave the Stratford-upon-Avon, and Blenheim, and Woodstock adventures, and Oxford to Honora and Fanny, whose pens have been going *à l'envie l'une de l'autre;* we are writing so comfortably. I at my desk with a table to myself, and the most comfortable little black stuffed arm-chair. Fanny and Ho. at their desks and table near the fire.

"We must have two pairs of snuffers."

"Yes, my lady, directly."

So now, my lady, good-night; for I am tired, a little, just enough to pity the civilest and prettiest of Swiss-looking housemaids, who says in answer to my "we shall come to bed very soon," "Oh, dear, my lady, we

---

[1] It was the last. Mr. Watt died a few months afterwards.

bees no ways particular in this house about times o' going to bed."

TO MRS. RUXTON.

GROVE HOUSE, KENSINGTON GORE, March, 1819.

We arrived here on Saturday last; found Lady Elizabeth Whitbread more kind and more agreeable than ever. Her kindness to us is indeed unbounded, and would quite overwhelm me but for the delicate and polite manner in which she confers favors, more as if she received than conferred them. Her house, her servants, her carriage, her horses, are not only entirely at my disposal, but she had the good-natured politeness to go down to the door to desire the coachman to have George Bristow always on the box with him, as the shaking would be too much for him behind.

Yesterday we spent two hours at Lady Stafford's. I had most agreeable conversation with her and Lord Stafford, while Lady Elizabeth Gower showed the pictures to Honora and Fanny.

Mr. Talbot [1] is often here, *l'ami de la maison* and very much ours. Lady Grey, Lady Elizabeth's mother, is a fine amiable old lady. Mr. Ellice, the brother-in-law, very good-humored and agreeable. Mr. and Mrs. Lefevre, the son-in-law and daughter, very agreeable, good, and happy. I am more and more convinced that happiness depends upon what is in the head and heart more than on what is in the purse or the bank, or on the back or in the stomach. There must be enough in the stomach, but the sauce is of little consequence. By the bye, Lady Elizabeth's cook is said to be the best in

---

[1] Son of Lady Talbot de Malahide, a lawyer.

England; lived with her in the days of her prosperity, as she says, and has followed her here.

TO THE SAME.

KENSINGTON GORE, March 24, 1819.

I have a moment to write to you, and I will use it. We are going on just as when I last wrote to you. We began by steadily settling that we would not go out to any dinner or evening parties, because we could not do so without giving up Lady Elizabeth's society; she never goes out but to her relations. The mornings she spends in her own apartments, and when we had refused all invitations to dinner our friends were so kind as to contrive to see us at our own hours; to breakfast or luncheon.

Twice with Lady Lansdowne — luncheon; found her with her children just the same as at Bowood.

Miss Fanshawe's — breakfast; Lord Glenbervie there, very agreeable; much French and Italian literature — beautiful drawings, full of genius — if there be such a thing allowed by practical education.

Three breakfasts at dear Mrs. Marcet's; the first quite private; the second literary, very agreeable; Doctor Holland, Mr. Wishaw, Captain Beaufort, Mr. Mallet, Lady Yonge; third, Mr. Mill — British India — was the chief *figurante;* not the least of a *figurante* though, excellent in sense and benevolence.

Twice at Mr. Wilberforce's; he lives next door to Lady Elizabeth Whitbread; there we met Mr. Buxton — admirable facts from him about Newgate and Spitalfields weavers. One fact I was very sorry to learn, that Mrs. Fry, that angel woman, was very ill.

Breakfast with Mr. and Mrs. Hope — quite alone — he showed the house to Honora and Fanny while I sat with Mrs. Hope.

On St. Patrick's Day, by appointment to the Duchess of Wellington, nothing could be more like Kitty Pakenham: a plate of shamrocks on the table, and as she came forward to meet me, she gave a bunch to me, pressing my hand and saying in a low voice with her sweet smile, "Vous en êtes digne." She asked individually for all her Irish friends. I showed to her what was said in my father's life, and by me, of Lord Longford, and the drawing of his likeness, and asked if his family would be pleased; she spoke very kindly, — "would do her father's memory honor; could not but please every Pakenham." She was obliging in directing her conversation easily to my sisters as well as to myself. She said she had purposely avoided being acquainted with Madame de Staël in England, not knowing how she might be received by the Bourbons, to whom the Duchess was to be Ambassadress. She found that Madame de Staël was well received at the Bourbon Court, and consequently she must be received at the Duke of Wellington's. She arrived, and walking up in full assembly to the Duchess, with the fire of indignation flashing in her eyes: —

"Eh! Madame la Duchesse, vous ne voulez pas donc faire ma connaissance en Angleterre?"

"Non, Madame, je ne le voulais pas."

"Eh! comment, Madame? Pourquoi donc?"

"C'est que je vous *craigniais*, Madame."

"Vous me *craignez*, Madame la Duchesse?"

"Non, Madame, je ne vous crains plus."

Madame de Staël threw her arms round her: "Ah! je vous adore!"

I must end abruptly. No; I have one minute more. While we were at the Duchess of Wellington's a jeweller's man came in with some bracelets; one was a shell like your Roman shell cameo, of the Duke's head, of which she was correcting the profile. She showed us pictures of her sons, and Fanny sketched from them while we sat with her. We saw in the hall, or rather in the corner of the staircase, Canova's gigantic "Apollo-Buonaparte," which was sent from France to the Regent, who gave it to the Duke. It is ten feet high, but I could not judge of it where it is cooped up — shockingly ill-placed.

Sunday — Lady Harrowby's by invitation, as it is Lord Harrowby's only holiday. Mr. Ellis, a young man, just entered Parliament, from whom great things are expected. Mr. Wilmot, and Mr. Frere — Lady Ebrington and Lady Mary Ryder — Lord Harrowby, most agreeable conversation. Folding doors thrown open. The Duke of ——. Post — letter must go.

TO MISS RUXTON.

Duchess Street, Mrs. Hope's,
April 2, 1819.

I left off abruptly just as the folding doors were thrown open, and the Duke of Wellington was announced in such an unintelligible manner that I did not know what Duke it was, nor did I know till we got into the carriage who it was — he looks so old and wrinkled. I never should have known him from likeness to bust or picture. His manner is very agreeable, perfectly simple and dignified. He said only a few words, but listened to some literary conversation that was going on, as if he was amused, laughing once very heartily. Remind me to tell you some circumstances about Adèle de Senange which Lord Harrowby told me, and two expressions of Madame de Staël's — "On dépose fleur à fleur la couronne de la vie," [1] and "Le silence est l'antichambre de la mort."

Mr. Hope is altered, and he has in his whole appearance the marks of having suffered much. The contrast between his and Mrs. Hope's depression of spirits, and the magnificence of everything about them, speaks volumes of moral philosophy.

They were even more kind than I expected in their manner of receiving us. One large drawing-room Mr. Hope gave us for the reception of our friends. Mrs. Hope had not since her coming to town had a dinner party, but she assembled all the people she thought we might like to see. One day Miss Fanshawe; another day the Duke and Duchess of Bedford, Lord Palmerston, Lord and Lady Darnley, and Mr. Ellis; Lady Darnley was very kind, just what she was when I saw her before. Lady Jersey is particularly agreeable, and was particularly obliging to us, and gave us tickets for the French play, now one of the London objects of curiosity. The Duchess of Bedford talked much to me, and very agreeably, of her travels.

---

[1] Maria had quoted this expression with admiration to Lord Harrowby, objecting to a criticism of it by M. Dumont, "d'abord la vie n'a pas de couronne." To which Lord Harrowby replied by quoting Johnson's

> " Year follows year, decay pursues decay,
>   Still drops from life some withering joy away."

It was to this conversation that the Duke of Wellington listened with smiling attention.

Mrs. Hope was so exhausted by the effort of seeing all these people that she could not sleep, and looked wretchedly the next day, when nobody was at dinner but her own sister and Captain Beaufort. Next day, Lady Tankerville and her daughter, Lady Mary Bennet, came and sat half an hour.

TO MRS. RUXTON.

KENSINGTON GORE, April 28, 1819.

We spent ten days delightfully with the kind Hopes at Deepdene, and a most beautiful place it is. The valley of Dorking is so beautiful that even Rasselas would not have desired to escape from that happy valley. Fanny was well enough to enjoy everything, especially some rides on a stumbling pony with Henry Hope, a fine boy of eleven, well informed, and very good-natured. We went to see Norbury Park, Mr. Locke's place, and Wotton, Mr. Evelyn's, and a beautiful cottage of Mrs. Hibbert's, of all which I shall have much to say to you on my own little stool at your feet.

We were received on our return here with affectionate kindness by Lady Elizabeth Whitbread.

Remember that I don't forget to tell you of Lady Bredalbane's having been left in her carriage fast asleep, and rolled into the coach-house of an hotel at Florence and nobody missing her for some time, and how they went to look for her, and how ever so many carriages had been rolled in after hers, and how she wakened, and — I must sign and seal.

EDGEWORTHSTOWN, July 7, 1819.

At Longford last Sunday we heard an excellent sermon by a Mr. McLelland, the first he ever preached; a terrible brogue, but full of sense and spirit. Some odd faults — quoting the "Quarterly Review" — citing Hogarth's "Idle Apprentice" — "the Roman poet tells us," etc.; but it was altogether new and striking, and contained such a fine address to the soldiers present on the virtues of peace, after the triumphs of war, as touched every heart. The soldiers all with one accord looked up to the preacher at the best passages.

TO MRS. SNEYD EDGEWORTH, AT PARIS.

EDGEWORTHSTOWN, September 15, 1819.

I rejoice that you and Sneyd are well enough to enjoy the pleasures of Paris. I do not know what Sneyd can have done to make Madame Récamier laugh; in my time she never went beyond the smile prescribed by Lord Chesterfield as graceful in beauty.

This last week we have had the pleasure of having our kind friends Mrs. and Miss Carr. Except the first day, which was Irish rainy, every day has been sunshiny, and my mother has taken advantage of the shrievalty four horses and two yellow jackets to drive about. They went to Baronston, where there is a link of connection with the Carrs through an English friend, Mrs. Benyon. Lady Sunderlin and Miss Catherine Malone did the joint honors of their house most amiably, and gave as fine a collation of grapes, nectarines, and peaches as France could supply.

Another morning we took a tour of the tenants. Hugh Kelly's house and parlor and gates and garden, and all that should accompany a farmhouse, as nice as any England could afford. James Allen, though grown very old, and in a forlorn black shag wig, looked like a respectable yeoman, "the country's pride," and at my instance brought out as fine a group of grandchildren as ever graced a cottage lawn.

In driving home at the cross-roads by Corbey we had the good fortune to come in for an Irish dance, the audience or spectators seated on each side of the road on opposite benches; all picturesque in the sunshine of youth and age, with every variety of attitude and expression of enjoyment. The dancers, in all the vivacity and graces of an Irish jig, delighted our English friends; and we stood up in the landau for nearly twenty minutes looking at them.

TO MISS RUXTON.

October 14.

We have been much interested in the life and letters of that most excellent, amiable, and unpretending Lady Russell.[1] There are touches in these letters which paint domestic happiness, and the character of a mother and a wife, with beautiful simplicity. I even like Miss Berry much the better for the manner in which she has edited this book.

November 5.

Have you the fourth number of "Modern Voyages and Travels," which contains Chateauvieux's travels in Italy? I have been so much delighted with it, and feel

---

[1] Lady Rachel Wriothesley, second daughter of Thomas Earl of Southampton, who married (1) Francis Lord Vaughan; (2) William Lord Russell, the patriot, beheaded July 21, 1683.

so sure of its *transporting* my aunt, that I had hardly
read the last words before I was going to pack it off
post-haste to Black Castle, but Prudence, in the shape
of Honora, in a lilac tabinet gown, whispered, "Better
wait till you hear whether they have read it."

Have I mentioned to you Bassompiere's "Memoirs"?
a new edition, with notes by Croker, which make the
pegs on which they hang gay and valuable. What an
extraordinary collection of strange facts and strange
thoughts are dragged together in the "Quarterly Review," of the Cemeteries and Catacombs of Paris; the
Jewish "House of the Living;" the excommunicated
skeletons coming into the church to parley with the
Bishop; and the Parisian sentimentalist in the country
who sent for barrels of ink from Paris to put his trees
in mourning for the death of his mother; and the foun-
tain, called the *weeping eye*, for the death of his wife,
by the Dane. I hope, my dear friends, that you have
been reading these things, and that they have struck you
as they did me; there are few things pleasanter than
these "jumping thoughts."

Now that I have a little time, and eyes to read again,
I find it delightful, and I have a voracious appetite, and
a relish for food, good, bad, and indifferent, I am afraid,
like a half-famished, shipwrecked wretch.

28th.

Such a scene of lying and counter-lying as we have
had with the cook and her accuser, the kitchen maid!
The cook was dismissed on the spot. One expression
of Peggy Tuite's I must tell you — with her indignant
figure of truth defending herself against falsehood —

when Rose, the vile public accuser, said, in part of her
speech, recollecting from Peggy Tuite's dress, who came
clean from chapel, that it was Sunday, "And it's two
masses I have lost by you already!" to which Peggy
replied, "Oh, Rose, the mass is in the heart, not in the
chapel! Only speak the truth."

Maria's steadiness in resting her eyes, neither reading
nor writing for nearly two years, was rewarded by their
complete recovery; and she was able to read, write, and
work with ease and comfort all the rest of her life.

This autumn of 1819 she was made happy by the
return of the two Miss Sneyds[1] from England to Edgeworthstown, where with short intervals they continued
to reside as long as they lived.

TO MISS RUXTON.

EDGEWORTHSTOWN, January 1, 1820.

Have you seen a life of Madame de Staël by that
Madame Necker de Saussure, of whom Madame de
Staël said, when some one asked, "What sort of woman
is she?" "Elle a tous les talents qu'on me suppose, et
toutes les vertus qui me manquent." Is not that touching and beautiful?

January 14.

Poor Kitty Billamore breathed her last this morning
at one o'clock. A more faithful, warm-hearted, excellent creature never existed. How many successions of
children of this family she has nursed, and how many

[1] Sisters of her two former stepmothers, the second and third wives of
R. L. Edgeworth.

she has attended in illness and death, regardless of her own health! I am glad that sweet, dear little feeling Francis, her darling, was spared being here at her death. Harriet, who, next to him,[1] had always been a great favorite, was with her to the last. All the poor people loved her, and will long feel her loss. Lovell[2] intends that she should be buried in the family vault, as she deserves, for she was more a friend than a servant, and he will attend her funeral himself.

Having finished the memoirs of her father's life, and settled that it should be published at Easter, Maria determined to indulge herself in what she had long projected — a visit to Paris with two of her young sisters, Fanny and Harriet. They set out on the 3d of April.

TO MISS LUCY EDGEWORTH.

DUBLIN, April 10, 1820.

In my letter to my mother of the 8th I forgot — no, I had not time to say that we had a restive mare at Dunshaughlin, who paid me for all I ever wrote about Irish posting, and put me in the most horrible and reasonable apprehension that she would have broken my aunt's carriage to pieces against the corner of a wall. The crowd of people that assembled, the shouts, the "never fears," the scolding of the landlord and postilions, and the group surveying the scene, was beyond anything I could or can paint. The stage coach drove

---

[1] Francis and Harriet, children of the fourth Mrs. Edgeworth.

[2] Lovell, only son of the second Mrs. Edgeworth (Honora Sneyd), who had succeeded to the property.

to the door in the midst of it, and ladies and bandboxes stopped, and all stood to gaze.

There was also a professional fool in his ass cart with two dogs, one a white little curly dog, who sat upon the ass's head behind his ears, and another a black, shaggy mongrel, with longish ears, who sat up in a begging attitude on the hinder part of the ass, and whom the fool-knave had been tutoring with a broken crutch, as he sat in his covered cart. Fanny made a drawing of him, and he and his dogs *sat* for a fivepenny, which I honestly gave him for his and his dog's tricks.

Steamboats had only begun to ply between Dublin and Holyhead in 1819, and Maria Edgeworth's first experience of a steamboat was in crossing now to Holyhead. She disliked the *jigging* motion, which she said was like the shake felt in a carriage when a pig is scratching himself against the hind wheel while waiting at an Irish inn door.

TO MISS HONORA EDGEWORTH.

Mrs. Watt's, Heathfield, April, 1820.

I was much surprised at finding that the postilion who drove us from Wolverhampton could neither tell himself, nor learn from any one up the road, along the heath, at the turnpike, or even in the very suburbs of Birmingham, the way to Mr. Watt's! I was as much surprised as we were at Paris in searching for Madame de Genlis; so we went to Mr. Moilliet's, and stowed ourselves next day into their traveling landau, as large as our own old, old delightful coach, and came here.

Oh, my dear Honora, how melancholy to see places

the same — persons, and such persons, gone! Mrs. Watt, in deep mourning, coming forward to meet us alone in that gay trellis, the same books on his table, his picture, his bust, his image everywhere, *himself* nowhere upon this earth. Mrs. Watt has, in that poor little shattered frame, a prodigiously strong mind; indeed she could not have been so loved by such a man for such a length of time if she had not superior qualities. She was more kind than I can express, receiving Fanny and Harriet as if they had been of her own family.

In the morning I fell to penning this letter, as we were engaged to breakfast at Mr. James Watt's, at Aston Hall. You remember the fine old brick palace? Mr. Watt has fitted up half of it so as to make it superbly comfortable; fine hall, breakfast-room, Flemish pictures, Bolton and Watt at either end. After breakfast, at which was Mr. Priestley, an American, son of Dr. Priestley, we went over all the habitable and uninhabitable parts of the house; the banqueting-room, with a most costly, frightful ceiling, and a chimney-piece carved up to the cornice with monsters, one with a nose covered with scales, one with human face on a tarantula's body. Varieties of little staircases, and a garret gallery called Dick's haunted gallery; a blocked-up room called the King's room; then a modern dressing-room, with fine tables of Bullock's making, one of wood from Brazil — Zebra wood — and no more to be had of it for love or money.

But come on to the great gallery, longer than that at Sudbury, — about one hundred and thirty-six feet long, — and at the furthest end we came to a sort of oriel, separated from the gallery only by an arch, and there

the white marble bust of the great Mr. Watt struck me
almost breathless.   What everybody went on saying I
do not know, but my own thoughts, as I looked down
the closing lines of this superb gallery, now in a half-
ruined state, were very melancholy, on life and death,
family pride, and the pride of wealth, and the pride of
genius, all so perishable.

TO MRS. EDGEWORTH.

CANTERBURY, April 21.

I wrote to your dear father the history of our visit to
Mr. Wren's at Wroxall Abbey, and Kenilworth, and
Warwick, and Stratford-upon-Avon, and our pleasant
three hours at Oxford.   When we were looking at the
theatre, Mr. Biddulph told us, that when all the Em-
perors and Kings came with the Regent, the theatre
was filled in every part; but such was the hush you
could have heard a pin drop till the Prince put his foot
upon the threshold, when the whole assembly rose with
a tremendous shout of applause.   The Prince was su-
premely gratified, and said to the Emperor of Russia,
" You heard the London mob hoot me, but you see how
I am received by the young gentlemen of England! "

When Lord Grenville was installed as chancellor, he
was, the instant he took his seat, assailed with loud
hisses and groans.   Mr. Biddulph said he admired the
dignity with which Lord Grenville behaved, and the
presence of mind of the Bishop of Peterborough (Par-
sons), who said in Latin, "Either this disturbance must
instantly cease, or I dismiss you from this assembly! "
Dead silence ensued.

PARIS, PLACE DU PALAIS BOURBON, April 29.

One moment of reward for two days of indescribable hurry I have at this quiet interval after breakfast, and I seize it to tell you that Fanny is quite well; so far for health. For beauty, I have only to say that I am told by everybody that my sisters are *lovely* in English, and *charmante* in French. Last night was their *début* at Lady Granard's — a large assembly of all manner of lords, ladies, counts, countesses, princes, and princesses, French, Polish, and Italian; Marmont and Humboldt were there. I was told by several persons of rank and taste — Lady Rancliffe, the Countess de Salis, Lady Granard, Mrs. Sneyd Edgeworth, *and* a Polish Countess, that my sister's dress, the grand affair at Paris, was *perfection*, and I believed it! Humboldt is excessively agreeable, but I was twice taken from him to be introduced to grandeurs just as we had reached the most interesting point of conversation.

May 3.

On Sunday we went with the Countess de Salis and the Baronne de Salis, who is also Chanoinesse, but goes into the world in roses and pink ribbons nevertheless, and is very agreeable, moreover, and M. le Baron, an officer in the Swiss Guards, an old bachelor, to St. Sulpice, to hear M. Fressenus; he preached in the Kirwan style, but with intolerable monotony of thumping eloquence, against *les Libérales*, Rousseau, etc.; it seemed to me old stuff, ill embroidered, but it was much applauded. *Mem. :* the *audience* were not half so attentive or silent at St. Sulpice as they were at the Théâtre Français the night before.

After Church a visit to Madame de Pastoret. Oh,

my dear mother, think of my finding her in that very boudoir, everything the same! Fanny and Harriet were delighted with the beauty of the house till they saw her, and then nothing could be thought of but her manner and conversation. They are even more charmed with her than I expected; she is little changed.

After a ball at the Polish Countess Orlowski's (the woman who is charmed with "Early Lessons," etc.), where Fanny and Harriet were delighted with the children's dancing — they waltzed like angels, if angels waltz — after this ball I went with the Count and Countess de Salis and La Baronne — I was told that the first time it must be without my sisters — to the Duchesse d'Escars, who *receives* for the King at the Tuileries; mounted a staircase of one hundred and forty steps — I thought the Count's knees would have failed while I leaned on his arm; my own ached. A long gallery, well lighted, opened into a suite of *little* low apartments, most beautifully hung, some with silk and some with cashmere, some with tent drapery, with end ottomans, and lamps in profusion. These rooms, with busts and pictures of kings, swarmed with old nobility, with historic names, stars, red ribbons, and silver bells at their button-holes; ladies in little white satin hats and *toques*, with a profusion of ostrich or, still better, *marabout* powder-puff feathers; and the roofs were too low for such lofty heads.

After a most fatiguing morning at all the impertinent and pertinent dressmakers and milliners, we finished by the dear delight of dining with Madame Gautier at Passy. The drive there was delicious; we found her with her Sophie, now a matron mother with her Caroline, like what Madame Gautier and her Sophie were in that very room eighteen years ago. All the Delessert family that remain were assembled except Benjamin, who was detained by business in Paris. Madame Benjamin is very handsome, nearer the style of Mrs. Admiral Pakenham than anybody I know; François the same as you saw him, only with the additional crow's-feet of eighteen years, sobered into a husband and father, the happiest I ever saw in France. They have three houses, and the whole three terraces form one long pleasure-ground. Judas-tree, like a Brobdingnag almond-tree, was in full flower; lilacs and laburnums in abundance. Alexandre Delessert takes after the father — good, sensible, commercial conversation. He made a panegyric on the Jews of Hamburg, who received him at their houses with the utmost politeness and liberality. This was apropos of Walter Scott's Jewess, and, vanity must add, my own Jew and Jewess, who came in for more than their due share.

Bank-notes were talked of; François tells me that the forging of bank-notes is almost unknown at Paris; the very best artists — my father's plan — are employed.

Tuesday we were at the Louvre; many fine pictures left. Dined at home; in the evening to Madame de Pastoret's, to meet the Duchesse de Broglie; very handsome — little, with large, soft, dark eyes; simple dress, winning manner, soft Pastoret conversation; speaks English better than any foreigner I ever heard; not only gracious, but quite *tender* to me.

After Madame de Pastoret's we went to the Ambassador's and were received in the most distinguished manner. Crowds of fine people; we saw and conversed with Talleyrand, but he said nought worth hearing.

May 20.

Paris is wonderfully embellished since we were here in 1803. Fanny and Harriet are quite enchanted with the beauty of the Champs Élysées and the Tuileries gardens; the trees are out in full leaf, and the deep shade under them is delightful. I had never seen Paris in summer, so I enjoy the novelty. Some of our happiest time is spent in driving about in the morning, or returning at night by lamp or moonlight.

Lady Elizabeth Stuart has been most peculiarly civil to "Madame Maria Edgeworth et Mesdemoiselles ses sœurs," which is the form on our visiting tickets, as I was advised it should be. The Ambassador's Hotel is the same which Lord Whitworth had, which afterwards belonged to the Princess Borghese. It is delightful! opening into a lawn-garden, with terraces and conservatories, and a profusion of flowers and shrubs. The dinner was splendid, but not formal; and nobody can *represent* better than Lady Elizabeth. She asked us to go with her and Mrs. Canning to the opera, but we were engaged to Madame Récamier; and as she is no longer rich and prosperous, I could not break the engagement.

We went to Madame Récamier's, in her convent, L'Abbaye aux Bois, up seventy-eight steps; all came in with the asthma; elegant room, and she as elegant as ever. Matthieu de Montmorenci, the ex-Queen of Sweden, Madame de Boigne — a charming woman, and Madame la Maréchale de Moreau — a battered beauty, smelling of garlic, and screeching in vain to pass for a wit.

Yesterday we had intended to have killed off a great

many visits, but the fates willed it otherwise. Mr.
Hummelaur, attached to the Austrian Embassy, came;
and then Mr. Chenevix, who converses delightfully,
but all the time holding a distorting magnifying glass
over French character, and showing horrible things
where we thought everything was delightful. While
he was here came Madame de Villeneuve and Madame
de Kergolay. Scarcely were they all gone, when I
desired Rodolphe to let no other person in, as the
carriage had been ordered at eleven, and it was now
near two. "*Miladi!*" cried Rodolphe, running in
with a card, "voilà une dame qui me dit de vous faire
voire son nom."

It was "Madame de Roquefeuille," with her bright,
benevolent eyes; and much agreeable conversation.
There is a great deal of difference between the manners,
tone, pronunciation, and quietness of demeanor of
Madame de Pastoret, Madame de Roquefeuille, and the
little old Princess de Broglie Revel, old nobility, and
the striving, struggling of the new, with all their riches
and titles, who can never attain this indescribable, in-
communicable charm. But to go on with Saturday;
Madame de Roquefeuille took leave, and we caparisoned
ourselves, and went to Lady de Ros. She was at her
easel, copying very well a portrait of Madame de Grignan, and it was a very agreeable half-hour. Lady de
Ros and her daughter are very agreeable people. She
has asked Fanny to meet her at the Riding-House three
times a week, where she goes to take exercise.

We were engaged to Cuvier's in the evening, and
went first to M. Jullien's, in the Rue de *l'Enfer*, not
far from the Jardin des Plantes, and there we saw one

of the most extraordinary of all the extraordinary persons we have seen — a Spaniard, squat, black-haired, black-browed, and black-eyed, with an infernal countenance, who has written the history of the Inquisition, and who related to us how he had been sent to a monastery *en pénitence* by the Inquisition, and escaped by presenting a certain number of kilogrammes of good chocolate to the monks, who represented him as very penitent.   But I dare not say more of this man, lest we should never get to Cuvier's, which, in truth, I thought we never should accomplish alive.   Such streets! such turns! in the old, old parts of the city; lamps strung at great distances; a candle or two from high houses, making darkness visible; then bawling of coach or cart men, "Ouais! ouais!" backing and scolding, for no two carriages could by any possibility pass in these narrow alleys.   I was in a very bad way, as you may guess, but I let down the glasses, and sat as still as a frightened mouse; once I diverted Harriet by crying out, "Ah, mon *cher* cocher, arrêtez;" like Madame de Barri's, "Un moment, *Monsieur* le Bourreau."   It never was so bad with us that we could not laugh.   At last we turned into a *porte-cochère*, under which the coachman bent literally double; total darkness; then suddenly trees, lamps, and buildings, and one, brighter than the rest by an open portal, illuminating large printed letters, "Collége de France."

Cuvier came down to the very carriage door to receive us, and handed us up narrow, difficult stairs into a smallish room, where were assembled many ladies and gentlemen of most distinguished names and talents. Prony, as like an honest water-dog as ever; Biot ("et

moi aussi je suis père de famille ") a fat, double volume
of himself — I could not see a trace of the young *père
de famille* we knew — round-faced, with a bald head
and black ringlets, a fine-boned skull, on which the
tortoise might fall without cracking it.   When he began to converse, his superior ability was immediately
apparent.   Then Cuvier presented Prince Czartorinski,
a Pole, and many compliments passed; and then we
went to a table to look at Prince Maximilian de Neuf-
chatel's "Journey to Brazil," magnificently printed in
Germany, and all tongues began to clatter, and it became
wondrously agreeable; and behind me I heard English
well spoken, and this was Mr. Trelawny, and I heard
from him a panegyric on the Abbé Edgeworth, whom
he knew well, and he was the person who took the first
letter and news to the Duchesse d'Angoulême at Mittau,
after she quitted France.   She came out in the dead of
the night in her nightgown to receive the letter.

Tea and supper together; only two thirds of the
company could sit down, but the rest stood or sat
behind, and were very happy, loud, and talkative;
science, politics, literature, and nonsense in happy proportions.   Biot sat behind Fanny's chair, and talked of
the parallax and Dr. Brinkley.   Prony, with his hair
nearly in my plate, was telling me most entertaining
anecdotes of Buonaparte; and Cuvier, with his head
nearly meeting him, talking as hard as he could; not
striving to show learning or wit — quite the contrary;
frank, open-hearted genius, delighted to be together at
home, and at ease.   This was the most flattering and
agreeable thing to me that could possibly be.   Harriet
was on the off-side, and every now and then he turned

to her in the midst of his anecdotes, and made her completely one of us; and there was such a prodigious noise
nobody could hear but ourselves. Both Cuvier and
Prony agreed that Buonaparte never could bear to have
any answer but a *decided* answer. "One day," said
Cuvier, "I nearly ruined myself by considering before
I answered. He asked me, ' Faut-il introduire le sucre
de betterave en France?' ' D'abord, Sire, il faut songer
si vos colonies — ' ' Faut-il avoir le sucre de betterave
en France?' 'Mais, Sire, il faut examiner — ' ' Bah!
je le demanderai à Berthollet.' "

This despotic, laconic mode of insisting on learning
everything in two words had its inconveniences. One
day he asked the master of the woods at Fontainebleau,
"How many acres of wood here?" The master, an
honest man, stopped to recollect. "Bah!" and the
under-master came forward and said any number that
came into his head. Buonaparte immediately took the
mastership from the first, and gave it to the second.
"Qu'arrivait-il?" continued Prony; "the rogue who
gave the guess answer was soon found cutting down and
selling quantities of the trees, and Buonaparte had to
take the rangership from him, and reinstate the honest
hesitater."

Prony is, you know, one of the most absent men
alive. "Once," he told me, "I was in a carriage with
Buonaparte and General Caffarelli; it was at the time
he was going to Egypt. He asked me to go. I said
I could not; that is, I would not; and when I had said
those words I fell into a reverie, collecting in my own
head all the reasons I could for not going to Egypt.
All this time Buonaparte was going on with some confi-

dential communication to me of his secret intentions and views; and when it was ended, le seul mot, Arabie, m'avait frappé l'oreille. Alors, je voudrais m'avoir arraché les cheveux," making the motion so to do, "pour pouvoir me rapeller ce qui'l venait de me dire. But I never could recall one single word or idea."

"Why did you not ask Caffarelli afterwards?"

"I dared not, because I should have betrayed myself to him."

Prony says that Buonaparte was not obstinate in his own opinion with men of science about those things of which he was ignorant; but he would bear no contradiction in tactics or politics.

May 29.

Madame Récamier has no more taken the veil than I have, and is as little likely to do it. She is still beautiful, still dresses herself and her little room with elegant simplicity, and lives in a convent[1] only because it is cheap and respectable. M. Récamier is living; they have not been separated by anything but misfortune.

We have at last seen a comedy perfectly well acted — the first representation of a new piece, "Les Folliculaires;" it was received with thunders of applause, admirably acted in every character to the life. It was in ridicule of journalists and literary young men.

La Celle, M. de Vindé's Country House,
June 4.

Is it not curious that, just when you wrote to us, all full of Mrs. Strickland at Edgeworthstown, we should have been going about everywhere with Mr. Strickland at Paris? I read to him what you said about his little

---

[1] The Abbaye aux Bois.

girl and Foster, as he was going with us to a breakfast at Cuvier's, and he was delighted even to tears.

We breakfasted at Passy on our way here; beautiful views of Paris and its environs from all the balconied rooms; and Madame François showed us all their delightful comfortable rooms — the bed in which Madame Gautier and Madame François had slept when children, and where now her little Caroline sleeps. There is something in the duration of these family attachments which pleases and touches one, especially in days of revolution and change.

We arrived here in good time. La Celle [1] is as old as Clotwold, the son of Clovis, who came here to make a hermitage for himself — La Cellule. Wonderfully changed and enlarged, it became the residence of Madame de Pompadour. The rooms are wainscoted; very large *croisées* open upon shrubberies, with rose acacias and rhododendrons in profuse flower; the garden is surrounded by lime-trees thick and high, and cut, like the beech-walk at Collon, at the end into arches through the foliage, and the stems left so as to form rows of pillars, through which you see, on one side, fine views of lawn and distant country, while on the other the lime-grove is continued in arcades, eight or nine trees deep.

To each bedroom and dressing-room there are little dens of closets and ante-chambers, which must have seen many strange exits and entrances in their day. In one of these, ten feet by six, the white wainscot — now

---

[1] La Celle St. Cloud, built by Bachelier, first valet de chambre of Louis XIV., afterwards sold to Madame de Pompadour, who sold it again in two years.

very yellow — is painted in gray, with monkeys in men and women's clothes in groups in compartments, the most grotesque figures you can imagine. I have an idea of having read of this cabinet of monkeys, and having heard that the principal monkey who figures in it was some real personage.

The situation of La Celle is beautiful, and the country about it. The grounds, terraces, orchards, farmyard, dairy, etc., would lead me too far, so I shall only note that, to preserve the hayrick from the incursion of rats, the feet of the stand, which is higher than that in our back yard, are not only slated, but at the part next the hay covered with panes of glass; this defies climbing reptiles.

M. and Madame de Vindé are exactly what you remember them; and her granddaughter, Beatrice, the little girl you may remember, is as kind to Fanny and Harriet as M. and Madame de Vindé were to their sister.

Mr. Hutton wrote to me about a certain Count Brennar, a German or Hungarian — talents, youth, fortune — assuring me that this transcendental Count had a great desire to be acquainted with us. I fell to work with Madame Cuvier, with whom I knew he was acquainted, and he met us at breakfast at Cuvier's; and I asked Prony if M. and Madame de Vindé would allow me to ask the Count to come here; and so yesterday Prony came to dinner, and the Count at dessert, and he ate cold cutlets and good salad, and all was right; and whenever any of our family go to Vienna, he gave me and mine, or yours, a most pressing invitation thither — which will never be any trouble to him.

I have corrected before breakfast here all of the second volume of "Rosamond,"[1] which accompanies this letter. We have coffee brought to us in our rooms about eight o'clock, and the family assemble at breakfast in the dining-room about ten; this breakfast has consisted of mackerel stewed in oil; cutlets; eggs, boiled and poached, *au jus ;* peas stewed; lettuce stewed, and rolled up like sausages; radishes; salad; stewed prunes; preserved gooseberries; chocolate biscuits; apricot biscuits — that is to say, a kind of flat tartlet, sweetmeat between paste; finishing with coffee. There are sugar-tongs in this house, which I have seen nowhere else except at Madame Gautier's. Salt-spoons never to be seen, so do not be surprised at seeing me take salt and sugar in the natural way when I come back.

Carriages come round about twelve, and we drive about seeing places in the neighborhood — afterwards go to our own rooms or to the *salon*, or play billiards or chess. Dinner is at half-past five; no luncheon and no dressing for dinner. I will describe one dinner — Bouilli de bœuf — large piece in the middle, and all the other dishes round it — rôtie de mouton — ris de veau piqué — maquereaux — pâtes de cervelle — salad. 2d service; œufs aux jus — petits pois — lettuce stewed — gâteaux de confitures — prunes. Dessert; gâteaux, cerises, confiture d'abricot et de groseille.

Hands are washed at the side-table; coffee is in the saloon; men and women all gathering round the table as of yore. But I should observe that a great change has taken place; the men huddle together now in France as

----

[1] The sequel, or last part of *Rosamond.*

they used to do in England, talking politics with their backs to the women in a corner, or even in the middle of the room, without minding them in the least, and the ladies complain and look very disconsolate, and many ask if this be Paris, and others scream *ultra* nonsense or *liberal* nonsense, to make themselves of consequence and to attract the attention of the gentlemen.

But to go on with the history of our day. After coffee, Madame de Vindé sits down at a round table in the middle of the room, and out of a work-basket, which is just the shape of an antediluvian work-basket of mine, made of orange-paper and pasteboard, which lived long in the garret, she takes her tapestry work: a chair cover of which she works the little blue flowers, and M. Morel de Vindé, pair de France, ancien Conseiller de Parlement, etc., does the ground! He has had a cold, and wears a black silk handkerchief on his head and a hat over it in the house; three waistcoats, two coats, and a spencer over all. Madame de Vindé and I talk, and the young people play billiards.

When it grows duskish we all migrate at a signal from Madame de Vindé, "Allons, nous passerons chez M. de Vindé;" so we all cross the billiard-room and dining-room, and strike off by an odd passage into M. de Vindé's study, where, almost in the fire, we sit round a small table playing a game called loto, with different colored pegs and collars for these pegs, and whoever knows the game of loto will understand what it is, and those who have never heard of it must wait till I come home to make them understand it. At half-past ten to bed; a dozen small round silver-handled candlesticks, bougeoirs, with wax candles ready for us.

Who dares to say French country houses have no comforts? Let all such henceforward except La Celle.

The three first days we were here M. de Prony and Count Brennar were the only guests, the Count only for one day. M. de Prony is enough without any other person to keep the most active mind in conversation of all sorts, scientific, literary, humorous. He is less changed than any of our friends. His humor and good-humor are really delightful; he is, as Madame de Vindé says, the most harmless good creature that ever existed; and he has had sense enough to stick to science and keep clear of politics, always pleading "qu'il n'était bon qu'à cela." He accompanied us in our morning excursions to Malmaison and St. Germain.

Malmaison was Josephine's, and is still Beauharnais's property, but is now occupied only by his steward. The place is very pretty — profusion of rhododendrons, as underwood in the groves, on the grass, beside the rivers, everywhere, and in the most luxuriant flower. Poor Josephine! Do you remember Dr. Marcet telling us that when he breakfasted with her, she said, pointing to her flowers, "These are my subjects; I try to make them happy."

The grounds are admirably well taken care of, but the solitude and silence and the continual reference to the dead were strikingly melancholy, even in the midst of sunshine and flowers, and the song of nightingales. In one pond we saw swimming in graceful desolate dignity two black swans, which, as rare birds, were once great favorites. Now they curve their necks of ebony in vain.

The grounds are altogether very small, and so is the

house, but fitted up with exquisite taste. In the saloon
is the most elegant white marble chimney-piece my eyes
ever did or ever will behold, a present from the Pope
to Beauharnais. The finest pictures have been taken
from the gallery; the most striking that remains is one
of General Dessain, reading a letter, with a calm and
absorbed countenance — two mamclukes eagerly examining his countenance. In the finely parqueted floor
great holes appear; the places from which fine statues
of Canova's were, as the steward told us, dragged up
for the Emperor of Russia. This the man told under
his breath, speaking of his master and of the armies
without distinctly naming any person, as John Langan
used to talk of the robbles (rebels). You may imagine
the feelings which made us walk in absolute silence
through the library, which was formerly Napoleon's;
the gilt N.'s and J.'s still in the arches of the ceiling,
busts and portraits all round — that of Josephine admirable.

At St. Germain, that vast palace which has been of
late a barrack for the English army, our female guide
was exceedingly well informed; indeed, Francis I.,
Henry IV., Mary de Médicis, Louis XIV., and Madame
de la Vallière seem to have been her very intimate
acquaintances. She was in all their secrets; showed us
Madame de la Vallière's room, poor soul! all gilt — the
gilding of her woe. This gilding, by accident, escaped
the revolutionary destruction. In the high, gilt dome
of this room, the guide showed us the trap-door through
which Louis XIV. used to come down. How they
managed it I don't well know; it must have been a
perilous operation, the room is so high. But my guide,

who I am clear saw him do it, assured me His Majesty came down very easily in his armchair; and as she had great keys in her hand, and is as large nearly as Mrs. Liddy, I did not hazard a contradiction or doubt.

Did you know that it was Prony who built the Pont Louis XVI.? Perronet was then eighty-four, and Prony worked under him. One night, when he had supped at Madame de Vindé's, he went to look at his bridge, when he saw — but I have not time to tell you that story.

During Buonaparte's Spanish War he employed Prony to make logarithm, astronomical, and nautical tables on a magnificent scale. Prony found that to execute what was required would take him and all the philosophers of France a hundred and fifty years. He was very unhappy, having to do with a despot who *would* have his will executed, when the first volume of Smith's "Wealth of Nations" fell into his hands. He opened on the division of labor, our favorite pinmaking: "Ha, ha! voilà mon affaire; je ferai mes calcules comme on fait les épingles!" And he divided the labor among two hundred men, who knew no more than the simple rules of arithmetic, whom he assembled in one large building, and there these men-machines worked on, and the tables are now complete.

Paris, June 9.

All is quiet here now, but while we were in the country there have been disturbances. Be assured that, if there is any danger, we shall decamp for Geneva.

June 22.

We have spent a day and a half delightfully with M. and Madame Molé at Champlatreux, their beautiful country place. He is very sensible, and she very obliging. Madame de Ventimille there, and very agreeable and kind; Madame de Nansouti and Madame de Bezancourt, granddaughter of Madame d'Houtitot: all remember you most kindly.

June 24.

You ask for Dupont de Fougères — alas! he has been dead some years. I went to see Camille Jordan, who is ill, and unable to leave his sofa; but he is fatter and better-looking than when we knew him — no alteration but for the better. He has got rid of all that might be thought a little affected — his vivacity elevated into energy, and his politeness into benevolence; his pretty little good wife sitting beside him.

Everybody, of every degree of rank or talent, who has read the "Memoirs," speaks of them in the most gratifying and delightful manner. Those who have fixed on individual circumstances have always fixed on those which we should have considered as most curious. Mr. Malthus this morning spoke most highly of it, and of its useful tendency both in a public and private light. Much as I dreaded hearing it spoken of, all I have yet heard has been what best compensates for all the anxiety I have felt.

TO MISSES MARY AND CHARLOTTE SNEYD.

PARIS, July 7, 1820.

It is a greater refreshment to me, my dearest Aunt Mary and Charlotte, to have a quiet half-hour in which to write to you, while Fanny and Harriet are practicing with M. Deschamp, their dancing-master, in the next room.

We had a delightful breakfast at Degerando's, in a room hung round with some very valuable pictures; one in particular, which was sent to Degerando by the town of Pescia, as a proof of gratitude for his conduct at the time when he was in Italy under Buonaparte — sent to him after he was no longer in power. There was an Italian gentleman, Marchese Ridolfi, of large fortune and benevolent mind, intent on improving his people. We also met Madame de Villette, Voltaire's *belle et bonne;* she has still some remains of beauty, and great appearance of good-humor. It was delightful to hear her speak of Voltaire with the enthusiasm of affection, and with tears in her eyes beseeching us not to believe the hundred misrepresentations we may have heard, but to trust her, the person who had lived with him long, and who knew him best and last. After breakfast she took us to her house, where Voltaire had lived, and where we saw his chair and writing-desk turning on a pivot on the arm of the chair; his statue smiling, keen-eyed, and emaciated, said to be a perfect resemblance; in one of the hands hung the brown and withered crown of bays, placed on his head when he appeared the last time at the Théâtre Français. She showed us some of his letters — one to his steward, about sheep, etc., ending with, "Let there be no drinking, no rioting, no beating of your wife." The most precious relic in this room of Voltaire's is a little piece carved in wood by an untaught genius, and sent to Voltaire by some peasants, as a proof of gratitude. It represents him sitting, listening to a family of poor peasants, who are pleading their cause; it is excellent.

Two of the Miss Lawrences are at Paris. They are very sensible, excellent women. They brought a letter from Miss Carr, begging me to see them; and I hope I have had some little opportunity of obliging them, for which they are a thousand times more grateful than I deserve. Indeed, next to the delight of seeing my sisters so justly appreciated and so happy at Paris, my greatest pleasure has been in the power of introducing people to each other, who longed to meet, but could not contrive it before. We took Miss Lawrence to one of the great schools here established on the Lancastrian principles, and we also took her to hear a man lecture upon the mode of teaching arithmetic and geometry which my father has recommended in "Practical Education;" the sight of the little cubes was at once gratifying and painful.

I have just heard from Hunter that he is printing "Rosamond," and that my friends at home will correct the proofs for me — God bless them! We spent a very pleasant day at dear Madame de Roquefcuille's, at Versailles; and, returning, we paid a *latish* visit to the Princess Potemkin. What a contrast the tone of conversation and the whole of the society from that at Versailles!

Certainly, no people can have seen more of the world than we have done in the last three months. By seeing the world I mean seeing varieties of characters and manners, and being behind the scenes of life in many different societies and families. The constant chorus of our moral as we drive home together at night is, "How happy we are to be so fond of each other! How happy we are to be independent of all we see here! How happy that we have our dear home to return to at last!"

But to return to the Princess Potemkin: she is Russian, but she has all the grace, softness, and winning manners of the Polish ladies, and an oval face, pale, with the finest, softest, most expressive *chestnut* dark eyes. She has a sort of politeness which pleases peculiarly — a mixture of the ease of high rank and early habit with something that is sentimental without affectation. Madame Le Brun is painting her picture; Madame Le Brun is sixty-six, with great vivacity as well as genius, and better worth seeing than her pictures; for though they are speaking, she speaks, and speaks uncommonly well.

Madame de Noisville, *dame d'honneur* to the Princess Potemkin, educated her and her sisters; the friendship of the pupil and the preceptress does honor to both. Madame de Noisville is a very well-bred woman, of superior understanding and decided character, very entertaining and agreeable. She told us that Rostopchin, speaking of the Russians, said he would represent their civilization by a naked man looking at himself in a gilt-framed mirror.

The Governor of Siberia lived at Petersburg, and never went near his government. One day the Emperor, in presence of this governor and Rostopchin, was boasting of his far-sightedness. "Commend me," said Rostopchin, "to M. le Gouverneur, who sees so well from Petersburg to Siberia." Good-by.

An evening which Miss Edgeworth spent at Neuilly

en famille impressed her with the unaffected happiness of the Orléans family. The Duke showed her the picture of himself teaching a school in America; Mademoiselle d'Orléans pointed to her harp, and said she superintended the lessons of her nieces; both she and her brother acknowledging how admirably Madame de Genlis had instructed them. The Duchess sat at a round table working, and in the course of the evening the two eldest little boys ran in from an École d'Enseignement *mutuel* which they attended in the neighborhood, with their school-books in their hands, and some prizes they had gained, eager to display them to their mother. A happy simple family party.

TO MRS. RUXTON.

PARIS, July, 1820.

From what I have seen of the Parisians, I am convinced that they require, if not a despot, at least an absolute monarch to reign over them; but, leaving national character to shift for itself, I will go on with what will interest you more — our own history. We have been much pleased, interested, and instructed at Paris by all that we have seen of the arts, have heard of science, and have enjoyed of society. The most beautiful work of art I have seen at Paris, next to the façade of the Louvre, is Canova's "Magdalene." The *prettiest* things I have seen are Madame Jacotot's miniatures, enameled on porcelain — La Vallière, Madame de Maintenon, Molière, all the celebrated people of that time; and next to these, which are exquisite, I should name a porcelain table, with medallions all round of the marshals of France, by Isabey, surrounding a full-length of Napoleon in the centre. This table is generally supposed to have been broken to pieces, but by the favor of a friend we saw it in its place of concealment.

We have twice dined at the Duchesse Douairière d'Orleans'[1] little court at Ivry, and we shall bring Mr. William Everard there, as you may recollect he knew her at Port Mahon. She has a benevolent countenance, and good-natured, dignified manners, and moves with the air of a princess. Her striking likeness to Louis XIV. *favors* this impression. One of her *dames d'honneur*, la Marquise de Castoras, a Spaniard, is one of the most interesting persons I have conversed with.

Yesterday William Everard went with us to the Chapelle Royale, where we saw Monsieur, the Duchesse d'Angoulême, and all the court. In the evening we were at a *fête de village* at La Celle, to which Madame de Vindé had invited us, as like an Irish *pattern* as possible, allowing for the difference of dress and manner. The scene was in a beautiful grove on each side of a romantic road leading through a valley. High wooded banks; groups of gayly dressed village belles and beaux seen through the trees, in a quarry, in the sand-holes, everywhere where there was space enough to form a quadrille. This grove was planted by Gabrielle d'Etrées, for whom Henry IV. built a lodge near it. Fanny and Harriet danced with two gentlemen who were of our party, and they all danced on till dewfall, when the lamps — little glasses full of oil and a wick suspended to the branches of the trees — were lighted,

---

1 Louise Marie Adelaide de Bourbon Condé, widow of Louis Philippe Joseph, Duc d'Orléans, daughter of the Duc de Penthièvre. Born March 13, 1783. Died June 23, 1821.

and we returned to La Celle, where we ate ice and sat in a circle, playing "trouvez mon ami"—mighty like "why, when, and where"—and then played loto till twelve. Rose at six, had coffee, and drove back to Paris in the cool of the delicious morning. To-day we are going to dine again at Neuilly with the other Duchess of Orléans, daughter-in-law of the good old Duchess, who by the bye spoke of Madame de Genlis in a true Christian spirit of forgiveness, but in a whisper, and with a shake of her head, allowed, "qu'elle m'avait causée bien des chagrins."

Among some of the most agreeable people we have met are some Russians and Poles. Madame Swetchine, a Russian, is one of the cleverest women I ever heard converse. At a dinner at the young and pretty Princess Potemkin's, on entering the dining-room we saw only a round table covered with fruit and sweetmeats, as if we had come in at the dessert; and so it remained while, first, soup, then cutlets, then fish, one dish at a time, ten or twelve one after another, were handed round, ending with game, sweet things, and ice.

A few days ago I saw, at the Duchesse d'Escar's, Prince Rostopchin, the man who burned Moscow, first setting fire to his own house. I never saw a more striking Calmuck countenance. From his conversation as well as from his actions, I should think him a man of great strength of character. This *soirée* at Madame d'Escar's was not on a public night, when she *receives* for the King, but one of those *petits comités*, as they call their private parties, which I am told the English seldom see. The conversation turned, of course, first on the Queen of England, then on Lady Hester Stan-

hope, then on English *dandies*. It was excessively
entertaining to hear half a dozen Parisians all speaking
at once, giving their opinions of the English *dandies*
who have appeared at Paris, describing their manners
and imitating their gestures, and sometimes by a single
gesture giving an idea of the whole man; then discuss-
ing the difference between the *petit marquis* of the old
French comedy and the present dandy. After many
attempts at definition, and calling in Madame d'Arblay's
Meadows, with whom they are perfectly acquainted,
they came to "d'ailleurs c'est inconcevable ça." And
Madame d'Escar, herself the cleverest person in the
room, summed it up: "L'essentiel c'est que notre
dandy il veut plaire aux femmes s'il le peut; mais votre
dandy Anglais ne le voudrait, même s'il le pourrait!"

Pray tell Mrs. General Dillon I thank her for making
us acquainted with the amiable family of the Creeds,
who have been exceedingly kind, and who, I hope, like
us as much as we like them. The Princess de Craon,
too, I like in another way, and Mademoiselle d'Alpy;
they have introduced us to the Mortemars — Madame
de Sévigné's "Esprit de Mortemar."

TO MISS RUXTON.

Passy, July 19.

Most comfortably, most happily seated at a little table
in dear Madame Gautier's cabinet, with a view of soft
acacias seen through half-open Venetian blinds, with a
cool breeze waving the trees of this hanging garden, and
the song of birds and the cheerful voices of little Caroline Delessert and her brother playing with bricks in
the next room to me, I write to you, my beloved friend.

I must give you a history of one of our last days at Paris —

Here entered Madame Gautier with a sweet rose and a sprig of verbena and mignonette — so like one of the nosegays I have so often received from dear Aunt Ruxton, and bringing gales of Black Castle to my heart. But to go on with my last days at Paris.

Friday, July 14. — Dancing-master nine to ten; and while Fanny and Harriet were dancing, I paid bills, saw tradespeople, and cleared away some of that necessary business of life which must be done behind the scenes. Breakfasted at Camille Jordan's; it was half-past twelve before the company assembled, and we had an hour's delightful conversation with Camille Jordan and his wife in her spotless white muslin and little cap, sitting at her husband's feet as he lay on the sofa, as clean, as nice, as fresh, and as thoughtless of herself as my mother. At this breakfast we saw three of the most distinguished of that party who call themselves "Les Doctrinaires" — and say they are more attached to measures than to men. Camille Jordan himself has just been deprived of his place of Conseiller d'État and one thousand five hundred francs per annum, because he opposed government in the law of elections. These three Doctrinaires were Casimir Perrier, Royer Collard, and Benjamin Constant, who is, I believe, of a more violent party. I do not like him at all; his countenance, voice, manner, and conversation are all disagreeable to me. He is a fair, *whithky*-looking man, very near-sighted, with spectacles which seem to pinch his nose. He pokes out his chin to keep the spectacles on, and yet looks over the top of his spectacles, *squinching* up his eyes so that you cannot see your way into his mind. Then he speaks through his nose, and with a lisp, strangely contrasting with the vehemence of his emphasis. He does not give me any confidence in the sincerity of his patriotism, nor any high idea of his talents, though he seems to have a mighty high idea of them himself. He has been well called *Le* hero *des Brochures.* We sat beside one another, and I think felt a mutual antipathy. On the other side of me was Royer Collard, suffering with toothache and swelled face; but, notwithstanding the distortion of the swelling, the natural expression of his countenance, and the strength and sincerity of his soul made their way, and the frankness of his character and plain superiority of his talents were manifest in five minutes' conversation.

Excellent Degerando [1] gave me an account of all he had done in one district in Spain, where he succeeded in employing the poor and inspiring them with a desire to receive the wages of industry, instead of alms from hospitals, etc. At Rome he employed the poor in clearing away many feet of earth withinside the Colosseum, and discovered beneath a beautiful pavement; but when the Pope returned the superstition of the people took a sudden turn, and conceiving that this earth had been consecrated, and ought not to have been removed, they set to work and filled in all the rubbish again over the pavement!

After this breakfast we went to the Duchesse d'Uze's — little, shriveled, thin, high-born, high-bred old lady, who knew and admired the Abbé Edgeworth, and re-

---

[1] A friend whom the Edgeworths had constantly met in Madame de Pastoret's salon in 1802.

ceived us with distinction as his relations. Her great-grandfather was the Duc de Chatillon, and she is great-granddaughter, or something that way, of Madame de Montespan, and her husband grand-nephew straight to Madame de la Vallière : their superb hotel is filled with pictures of all sizes, from miniatures by Petitôt to full lengths by Mignard, of illustrious and interesting family pictures — in particular, Mignard's " La Vallière en Madeleine; " we returned to it again and again, as though we could never see it enough : a full-length of Madame de Montespan, prettier than I wished.   After a view of these pictures and of the garden, in which there was a catalpa in splendid flower, we departed.

This day we dined with Lord Carrington and his daughter, Lady Stanhope :[1] the Count de Noé, beside whom I sat, was an agreeable talker.   In the evening we received a note from Madame Lavoisier — Madame de Rumford, I mean — telling us that she had just arrived at Paris, and warmly begging to see us.   Rejoiced was I that my sisters should have this glimpse of her, and off we drove to her ; but I must own that we were disappointed in this visit, for there was a sort of *chuffiness*, and a sawdust kind of unconnected cutshortness in her manner, which we could not like.   She was almost in the dark, with one ballooned lamp and semicircle of black men round her sofa, on which she sat cushioned up, giving the word for conversation — and a very odd course she gave to it — on some wife's separation from her husband ; and she took the wife's part, and went on for a long time in a shrill voice, proving that, where a husband and wife detested each other, they should separate,

<hr>

[1] Catherine Lucy, wife of the fourth Earl Stanhope.

and asserting that it must always be the man's fault
when it comes to this pass! She ordered another lamp,
that the gentlemen might, as she said, see my sisters'
pretty faces; and the light came in time to see the
smiles of the gentlemen at her matrimonial maxims.
Several of the gentlemen were unknown to me. Old
Gallois sat next to her, dried, and in good preservation,
tell my mother; M. Garnier ("Richesses des Nations")
and Cuvier, with whom I had a comfortable dose of good
conversation. Just as we left the room Humboldt and
the Prince de Beauveau arrived, but we were engaged to
Madame Récamier.

15th. — We breakfasted with Madame de l'Aigle, sister
to the Duc de Broglie. (Now Madame Gautier is putting on her bonnet, to take us to La Bagatelle.) I forgot to tell you that Prince Potemkin is nephew to *the*
famous Potemkin. He has just returned from England,
particularly pleased with Mr. Coke, of Norfolk, and
struck by the noble and useful manner in which he
spends his large fortune. This young Russian appears
very desirous to apply all he has seen in foreign countries to the advantage of his own.

After our breakfast at Madame de l'Aigle's, we went
home, and met Prince Edmond de Beauveau by appointment, and went with him to the Invalides; saw the
library, and plans and models of fortifications, for which
the Duc de Coigny, unasked, sent us tickets, and there
we met his secretary, a warm Buonapartist, whom we
honored for his gratitude and attachment to his old
master.

Dined at Passy and met Mrs. Malthus, M. Garnier,
and M. Chaptal — the great Chaptal — very interesting

man.   In the evening at the Princesse de Beauveau's and Lady Granard's.

Sunday with the Miss Byrnes to Notre Dame, and went with them to introduce them to Lady (Sydney) Smith ; charming house, gardens, and pictures.   To Madame de Rumford's, and she was very agreeable this morning.   Dined at Mr. Creed's under the trees in their garden, with Mr. and Mrs. Malthus, and Mrs. and Miss Eyre, fresh from Italy — very agreeable.

Now we have returned from a very pleasant visit to La Bagatelle.   What struck me most there was the bust of the Duc d'Angoulême, with an inscription from his own letter during the Cent Jours, when he was detained by the enemy : *J'espère — j'exige même que le Roi ne fera point de sacrifice pour me ravoir ; je crains ni la prison ni la mort.*

Yesterday we went to Sèvres — beautiful manufacture of china, especially a table, with views of all the royal palaces, and a vase six feet and a half high, painted with natural flowers.

Louis XV. was told that there was a man who had never been out of Paris ; he gave him a pension, provided he never went out of town ; he quitted Paris the year after !   I have not time to make either prefaces or moral. We breakfast at Mr. Chenevix's on Monday, and propose to be at Geneva on Saturday.

TO MISS LUCY EDGEWORTH.

Passy, July 23, 1820.

I hope this will find you under the tree in my garden, with Sophy Ruxton near you, and my mother and Sophy and Pakenham, who will run and call my aunts, for whom Honora will set chairs; and Lovell will, I hope, be at home too; so I picture you to myself all happily assembled, and you have had a good night, and all is right, and Honora has placed my Aunt Mary with her back to the light — AND Maria is very like Mr. Fitzherbert, who always tells his friends at home what *they* are doing, instead of what he is doing, which is what they want to know.

Yesterday we dined — for the last time, alas! this season — with excellent Benjamin Delessert. The red book which you will receive with this letter was among the many other pretty books lying on the table before dinner, and I was so much delighted with it, and wished so much that Pakenham was looking at it with me, that dear François Delessert procured a copy of "Les Animaux savants" for me the next morning. We never saw Les Cerfs at Trivoli, but we saw a woman walk down a rope in the midst of the fireworks, and I could not help shutting my eyes. As I was looking at the picture of the stag rope-dancer in this book, and talking of the wonderful intelligence and feeling of animals, an old lady who was beside me told me that some Spanish horses she had seen were uncommonly proud-spirited, resenting always an insult more than an injury. One of these, who had been used to be much caressed by his master, saw him in a field one day talking to a friend, and came up, according to his custom, to be caressed. The horse put his head in between the master and his friend, to whom he was talking; the master, eager in conversation, gave him a box on the ear; the horse withdrew his head instantly, took it for an affront, and never more would permit his master to caress or mount him again.

The little *dessert* directed for Pakenham [1] was picked out for him from a dish of bonbons at the last dessert at Benjamin's. It is impossible to tell you all the little exquisite instances of kindness and attention we have received from this excellent family. The respect, affection, and admiration with which, apropos to everything great and small, they remember my father and mother, is most touching and gratifying.

Yesterday morning we had been talking of Mrs. Hofland's "Son of a Genius," which is very well translated under the name of "Ludovico." I told Madame Gautier the history of Mrs. Hofland, and then went to look for the lines which she wrote on my father's birthday. Madame Gautier followed me into this cabinet to read them. I then showed to her Sophy's lines, which I love so much.

Sophy! I see your color rising; but trust to me! I will never do you any harm.

Madame Gautier was exceedingly touched with them. She pointed to the line,

"Those days are past which never can return,"

and said in English, "This is the day on which we all used to celebrate my dear mother's birthday, but I never *keep* days now, except that, according to our Swiss custom, we carry flowers early in the morning to the grave. She and my father are buried in this garden, in a place you have not seen; I have been there at six o'clock this morning. You will not wonder, then, my dear friend, at my being touched by your sister Sophy's verses. I wish to know her; I am sure I shall love

[1] Her youngest brother.

her.   Is she most like Fanny or Harriet ? "   This led to a conversation on the difference between our different sisters and brothers; and Madame Gautier, in a most eloquent manner, described the character of each of her brothers, ending with speaking of Benjamin. " Men have often two kinds of consideration in society; one derived from their public conduct, the other enjoyed in their private capacity. My brother Benjamin has equal influence in both. We all look up to him ; we all apply to him as to our guardian friend. Besides the advantage of having such a friend, it gives us a pleasure which no money can purchase — the pleasure of feeling the mind elevated by looking up to a character we perfectly esteem, and that repose which results from perfect confidence."

I find always, when I come to the end of my paper, that I have not told you several entertaining things I had treasured up for you. I had a history of a man and woman from Cochin China, which must now be squeezed almost to death. Just before the French Revolution a French military man went out to India, was wrecked, and with two or three companions made his way, Lord knows how, to Cochin China. It happened that the King of Cochin China was at war, and was glad of some hints from the French officer, who was encouraged to settle in Cochin China, married a Cochin Chinese lady, rose to power and credit, became a mandarin of the first class, and within the last month has arrived in France with his daughter. When his relations offered to embrace her, she drew back with horror. She is completely Chinese, and her idea of happiness is to sit still and do nothing, not even to blow her nose. I hope she will not half change her views and opinions while she is in

France, or she would become wholly unhappy on her return to China. Her father is on his word of honor to return in two years.

I send by Lord Carrington a cutting of cactus, for my mother, from this garden : it is carefully packed, and will, I think, grow in the greenhouse.

TO MRS. RUXTON.

At Mr. Moilliet's, Pregny, Geneva,
August 5, 1820.

Whenever I feel any strong emotion, especially of pleasure, you, friend of my youth and age, — you, dear resemblance of my father, — are always present to my mind ; and I always wish and want immediately to communicate to you my feelings.

I did not conceive it possible that I should feel so much pleasure from the beauties of nature as I have done since I came to this country. The first moment when I saw Mont Blanc will remain an era in my life — a new idea, a new feeling, standing alone in the mind.

We are most comfortably settled here : Dumont, Pictet, Dr. and Mrs. Marcet, and various others, dined and spent two most agreeable evenings here ; and the fourth day after our arrival we set out on our expedition to Chamouni with M. Pictet, as kind, as active, and as warm-hearted as ever. Mrs. Moilliet was prevented, by the indisposition of Susan, from accompanying us ; but Mr. Moilliet and Emily came with us at five o'clock in the morning in Mr. Moilliet's landau ; raining desperately — great doubts — but on we went : rain ceased — the sun came out, the landau was opened, and all was delightful.

My first impression of the country was that it was like Wales; but snow-capped Mont Blanc, visible everywhere from different points of view, distinguished the landscape from all I had ever seen before. Then the sides of the mountains, quite different from Wales indeed — cultivated with garden care, green vineyards, patches of *blé de Turquie*, hemp, and potatoes, all without inclosure of any kind, mixed with trees and shrubs: then the garden-cultivation abruptly ceasing — bare white rocks and fir above, fir measuring straight to the eye the prodigious height. Between the foot of the mountain and the road a border-plain of verdure, about the breadth of the lawn at Black Castle between the trellis and Suzy Clarke's, rich with chestnut and walnut trees, and scarlet barberries painting the green.

The inns on the Chamouni roads are much better than those on the road from Paris; we grew quite fond of the honest family of the hotel at Chamouni. Pictet knows all the people, and wherever we stopped they all flocked round him with such cordial gratitude in their faces, from the little children to the gray-headed men and women; all seemed to love "Monsieur le Professeur." The guides, especially Pierre Balmat and his son, are some of the best-informed and most agreeable men I ever conversed with. Indeed for six months of the year they keep company with the most distinguished travelers of Europe. With these guides, each of us armed with a long pole with an iron spike, such as my uncle described to me ages ago, and which I never expected to wield, we came down La Flegère, which we mounted on mules. In talking to an old woman who brought us strawberries, I was surprised to hear her pronounce the Italian proverb, "Poco a poco fa lontano nel giorno." I thought she must have been beyond the Alps — no, she had never been out of her own mountains. The patois of these people is very agreeable — a mixture of the Italian fond diminutives and accents on the last syllable, — Septembré, Octobré.

Our evening walk was to the arch of ice at the source of the Arveiron, and we went in the dusk to see a manufactory of cloth, made by a single individual peasant — the machinery for spinning, carding, weaving, and all made, woodwork and ironwork, by his own hands. He had in his youth worked in some manufactory in Dauphiny. The workmanship was astonishing, and the modesty and philosophy of the man still more astonishing. When I said, " I hope all this succeeds in making money for you and your family," he answered, " Money was not my object; I make just enough for myself and my family to live by, and that is all I want; I made it for employment for ourselves in the long winter evenings. And if it lasts after me, it may be of service to some of them; but I do not much look to that. It often happens that sons are of a different way of thinking from their fathers; mine may think little of these things, and if so, no harm."

The table-d'hôte at Chamouni — thirty people — was very entertaining. We had a most agreeable addition to our party in M. and Madame Arago; he was very civil to us at Paris, and very glad to meet us again. As we were walking to a cascade, he told me most romantic adventures of his in Spain and Algiers, which I will tell you hereafter: but I must tell you now a curious anecdote of Buonaparte. When he had abdicated after the battle of Waterloo, he sent for Arago, and offered him a considerable sum of money if he would accompany him to America. He had formed the project of establishing himself in America, and of carrying there in his train several men of science! Madame Bertrand was the person who persuaded him to go to England. Arago was so disgusted at his deserting his troops, he would have nothing more to do with him.

We returned by the beautiful valley of Sallenches and St. Gervais to Geneva. I forgot to mention about a dozen cascades, one more beautiful than the other, and I thought of Ondine, which you hate, and " mon Oncle Friedelhausen." We had left our carriage at St. Martin, and traveled in *char-à-bancs*, with which you and Sophy made me long ago acquainted — cousin-german to an Irish jaunting-car. We were well drenched by the rain ; and as we had imprudently lined our great straw hats with green, we arrived at St. Gervais with chins and shoulders dyed green. The hotel at St. Gervais is the most singular-looking house I ever saw. You drive through a valley, between high pine-covered mountains that seem remote from human habitation — when suddenly in a scoop-out in the valley you see a large, low, strange wooden building round three sides of a square, half Chinese, half American-looking, with galleries and domes and sheds — the whole unpainted wood. Under the projecting roof of the gallery stood a lady in a purple silk dress, plaiting straw, and various other figures in shawls, and caps, and flowered bonnets, some looking very fine, others deadly sick — all curious to see the new-comers. M. Goutar, the master, reminded me of Samuel Essington :[1] full of gratitude to M. Pictet, who

[1] An old servant.

had discovered these baths for him, he whisked about
with his round, perspiring face, eager to say a hundred
things at once, with a tongue too large for his mouth,
and a goitre which impeded his utterance, and showed us
his douches and contrivances, and spits turned by water
— very ingenious.   Dinner in a long, low, narrow room
— about fifty people; and after dinner we were ushered
into a room with calico curtains, very smart — a select
party let in.   Many unexpected compliments on "Patronage" from a Dijon Marquise, who was at the baths to
get rid of a redness in her nose.   Enter a sick but very
gentlewoman-like Prussian Countess, "Patronage" again:
Walter Scott's novels, as well known as in England,
admirably criticised.   She promised me a letter to Madame de Montolieu.

At Chamouni there is a little museum of stones and
crystals, etc., where MM. Moilliet and Pictet contrived
to treat their geological souls to seven napoleons' worth
of specimens.   An English lady was buying some bau-
bles, when her husband entered: "God bless my soul
and body, *another* napoleon gone!"

At the inn at Bonneville — *shackamarack* gilt dirt,
Irish-French.   Pictet bought a sparrow some boys in the
street threw up at the window, and said he would bring
it home for his little grandson.   It was ornamented with
a topping made of scarlet cloth.   He put it in his hat,
and tied a handkerchief over it; and hatless in the burning sun he brought it to Geneva.

August 6.

The day after our return we dined at Mrs. Marcet's
with M. Dumont, M. and Madame Prevost, M. de la
Rive, M. Bonstettin, and M. de Candolle, the botanist,

a particularly agreeable man. He told us of many experiments on the cure of goitres. In proportion as the land has been cultivated in some districts the goitres have disappeared. M. Bonstettin told us of some cretins, the lowest in the scale of human intellect, who used to assemble before a barber's shop and laugh immoderately at their own imitations of all those who came to the shop, ridiculing them in a language of their own.

TO MRS. EDGEWORTH.

Pregny, August 10, 1820.

I wrote to my Aunt Ruxton a long — much too long an account of our Chamouni excursion, since which we have dined at Pictet's with his daughters, Madame Prevost Pictet and Madame Vernet, agreeable, sensible, and the remains of great beauty; but the grandest of all his married daughters is Madame Enard. M. Enard is building a magnificent house, the admiration, envy, and *scandal* of Geneva; we have called it the Palais de la République.

Dumont, tell Honora, is very kind and cordial; he seems to enjoy universal consideration here, and he loves Mont Blanc next to Bentham, above all created things; I had no idea till I saw him here how much he enjoyed the beauties of nature. He gave us a charming anecdote of Madame de Staël when she was very young. One day M. Suard, as he entered the saloon of the Hôtel Necker, saw Madame Necker going out of the room, and Mademoiselle Necker standing in a melancholy attitude with tears in her eyes. Guessing that Madame Necker had been lecturing her, Suard went towards her to comfort her, and whispered, " Une caresse du papa vous dedommagera bien de tout ça." She immediately, wiping the tears from her eyes, answered, " Eh! oui, Monsieur, mon père songe à mon bonheur présent, maman songe à mon avenir." There was more than presence of mind, there was heart and soul and greatness of mind, in this answer.

Dumont speaks to me in the kindest, most tender, and affectionate manner of our " Memoirs ; " he says he hears from England, and from all who have read them, that they have produced the effect we wished and hoped ; the MS. had interested him, he said, so deeply, that with all his efforts, he could not then put himself in the place of the indifferent public.

M. Vernet, Pictet's son-in-law, mentioned a compliment of a Protestant curé at Geneva to the new Catholic Bishop which French politeness might envy, and which I wish that party spirit in Ireland and all over the world could imitate. " Monseigneur, vous êtes dans un pays où la moitié du peuple vous ouvre leurs cœurs, et l'autre moitié vous tendent les bras."

We have taken a pretty and comfortable calèche for our three weeks' tour with the Moilliets. But I must tell you of our visit to M. and Madame de Candolle ; we went there to see some volumes of drawings of flowers which had been made for him. I will begin from the beginning : Joseph Buonaparte, who has been represented by some as a mere drunkard, did, nevertheless, some good things ; he encouraged a Spaniard of botanical skill to go over to Mexico and make a Mexican flora ; he employed Mexican artists, and expended considerable sums of money upon it ; the work was completed, but the engraving had not been commenced when the revolution drove Joseph from his throne. The Spaniard withdrew from Spain, bringing with him his botanical treasure, and took refuge at Marseilles, where he met De Candolle, who, on looking over his Mexican flora, said it was admirably well done for Mexicans, who had no access to European books, and he pointed out its deficiencies; they worked at it for eighteen months, when De Candolle was to return to Geneva, and the Spaniard said to him, "Take the book — as far as I am concerned, I give it to you, but if my government should reclaim it, you will let me have it." De Candolle took it, and returned to Geneva, where he became not only famous, but beloved by all the inhabitants. This summer he gave a course of lectures on botany, which has been the theme of universal admiration. Just as the lectures finished, a letter came from the Spaniard, saying he had been unexpectedly recalled to Spain, that the King had offered to him the professorship he formerly held, that he could not appear before the King without his book; and that, however unwilling, he must request him to return it in eight days. One of De Candolle's young lady-pupils was present when he received the letter, and expressed his regret at losing the drawings: she exclaimed, "We will copy them for you." De Candolle said it was impossible — 1500 drawings in eight days! He had some duplicates, however, and some which were not peculiar to Mexico he threw aside; this reduced the number to a thousand, which were distributed among the volunteer artists. The talents and the industry shown, he says, were astonishing; all joined in this benevolent undertaking without vanity and without rivalship; those who could not paint, drew the outlines ; those who could not draw, traced ; those who could not trace made themselves useful by carrying the drawings backwards and forwards.   One was by an old lady of eighty.   We saw thirteen folio volumes of these drawings done in the eight days !   Of course some were much worse than others, but even this I liked : it showed that individuals were ready to sacrifice their own *amour propre* in a benevolent undertaking.

De Candolle went himself with the original Flora to the frontier; he was to send it by Lyons.   Now the custom-house officers between the territory of Geneva and France are some of the most strict and troublesome in the universe, and when they saw the book they said, "You must pay 1500 francs for this."   But when the chief of the Douane heard the story, he caught the enthusiasm, and with something like a tear in the corner of his eye, exclaimed, "We must let this book pass.   I hazard my place ; but let it pass."

TO MISS LUCY EDGEWORTH.

Pregny, August 13, 1820.

Ask to see "Lettres Physiques et Morales sur l'Histoire de la Terre et de l'Homme, adressées à la Reine d'Angleterre.   Par M. de Luc.   1778."

Ask your mother to send a messenger forthwith to Pakenham Hall to borrow this book ; and if the gossoon does not bring it from Pakenham Hall, next morning at flight of night send off another or the same to Castle Forbes, and to Mr. Cobbe, who, if he has not the book, ought to be hanged, and if he has, drawn and quartered if he does not send it to you.   But if, nevertheless, he

should not send it, do not rest satisfied under three fruit-
less attempts ; let another — not the same boy, as I presume his feet are weary — gossoon be off at the flight of
night for Baronstown, and in case of a fourth failure
there, neither to stint nor stay till he reaches Sonna,
where I hope he will at last find it.   Now if, after all,
it should not amuse you, I shall be much mistaken, that's
all.   Skip over the tiresome parts, of which there are
many, and you will find an account of the journey we
are going to make, and of many of the feelings we have
had in seeing glaciers, seas of ice and mountains.

I believe I mentioned in some former letter that we
had become acquainted with M. Arago, who, in his
height and size, reminded us of our own dear Dr. Brinkley, but I am sure I did not tell what I kept for you,
my dear Lucy, that you might have the pleasure of telling it to your mother and all the friends around you.

When M. Arago was with us in our excursion to
Chamouni, he was speaking of the voyage of Captain
Scoresby to the Arctic regions, which he had with him
and was reading with great delight.   As I found he was
fond of voyages and travels, and from what he said of
this book perceived that he was an excellent judge of
their merits, I asked if he had ever happened to meet
with a book called "Karamania," by a Captain Beaufort.
He knew nothing of our connection with him, and I
spoke with a perfect indifference from which he could
not guess that I felt any interest about the book or the
person, but the sort of lighting up of pleasure which you
have seen in Dr. Brinkley's face when he hears of a
thing he much approves, immediately appeared in Monsieur Arago's face, and he said "Karamania" was, of all

the books of travel he had seen, that which he admired the most: that he had admired it for its clearness, its truth, its perfect freedom from ostentation. He said it contained more knowledge in fewer words than any book of travels he knew, and must remain a book of reference — a standard book. Then he mentioned several passages that he recollected having liked, which proved the impression they had made; the Greek fire, the amphitheatre at Sidé, etc. He knew the book as well as we do, and alluded to the parts we all liked with great rapidity and delight in perceiving our sympathy. He pointed out the places where an ordinary writer would have given pages of amplification. He was particularly pleased with the manner in which the affair of the sixty Turks is told, and said, "That marked the character of the man and does honor to his country."

I then told him that Captain Beaufort was uncle to the two young ladies with me!

He told me he had read an article in the "Journal des Savants" in which "Karamania" is mentioned and parts translated. I have recommended it to many at Paris who wanted English books to translate, but I am sorry to say that little is read there besides politics and novels. Science has, however, a better chance than literature.

Whenever any one in your Book Society wants to bespeak a book, perhaps you could order "Recueil des Éloges," par M. Cuvier. They contain the *Lives*, not merely the *Éloges*, of all the men of science since 1780, beautifully written, and with an excellent introduction. The lives of Priestley and Cavendish are written with so much candor towards the English philosophers that even Mr. Chenevix cannot have anything to complain of.

TO MISS HONORA EDGEWORTH.

BERNE, August 19, 1820.

The day we set out from Pregny we breakfasted at Coppet; from some misunderstanding M. de Staël had not expected us and had breakfasted, but as he is remarkably well-bred, easy, and obliging in his manners he was not *put out*, and while our breakfast was preparing he showed us the house. All the rooms once inhabited by Madame de Staël we could not think of as common rooms — they have a classical power over the mind, and this was much heightened by the strong attachment and respect for her memory shown in every word and look, and *silence* by her son and by her friend, Miss Randall. He is correcting for the press the "Dix Années d'Exil." M. de Staël after breakfast took us a delightful walk through the grounds, which he is improving with good taste and judgment. He told me that his mother never gave any work to the public in the form in which she originally composed it; she changed the arrangement and expression of her thoughts with such facility, and was so little attached to her own first views of the subject, that often a work was completely remodeled by her while passing through the press. Her father disliked to see her make any formal preparation for writing when she was young, so that she used to write often on the corner of the chimney-piece, or on a pasteboard held in her hand, and always in the room with others, for her father could not bear her to be out of the room — and this habit of writing without preparation she preserved ever afterwards.

M. de Staël told me of a curious interview he had

with Buonaparte when he was enraged with his mother, who had published remarks on his government — concluding with " Eh, bien ! vous avez raison aussi. Je conçois qu'un fils doit toujours faire la defense de sa mère, mais enfin, si Monsieur veut écrire des libelles, il faut aller en Angleterre. Ou bien s'il cherche la gloire c'est en Angleterre qu'il faut aller. C'est Angleterre, ou la France — il n'y a que ces deux pays en Europe — dans le monde."

Before any one else at Paris, Miss Randall told me, had the MS. of " S. Hélène," a copy had been sent to the Duke of Wellington, who lent it to Madame de Staël; she began to read it eagerly, and when she had read about half, she stopped and exclaimed, " Where is Benjamin Constant ? we will wait for him." When he came she began to give him an account of what they had been reading; he listened with the indifference of a person who had already seen the book, and when she urged him to read up to them, he said he would go on where they were. When it was criticised, he defended it, or writhed under it as if the attack was personal. When accused of being the author, he denied it with vehemence, and Miss Randall said to him, " If you had simply denied it I might have believed you, but when you come to swearing, I am sure that you are the author."

M. de Staël called his little brother Alphonse Rocca, to introduce him to us; he is a pleasing, gentle-looking, ivory-pale boy with dark-blue eyes, not the least like Madame de Staël. M. de Staël speaks English perfectly, and with the air of an Englishman of fashion. After our walk he proposed our going on the lake — and we rowed for about an hour. The deep, deep blue of the water, and the varying colors as the sun shone and the shadows of the clouds appeared on it were beautiful. When we returned and went to rest in M. de Staël's cabinet, Dumont, who had quoted from Voltaire's "Ode on the Lake of Geneva," read it to us. Read it and tell me where you think it ought to begin.

We slept at Morges on Tuesday, and arrived late and tired at Yverdun. Next morning we went to see Pestalozzi's establishment; he recognized me and I him; he is, tell my mother, the same wild-looking man he was, with the addition of seventeen years. The whole superintendence of the school is now in the hands of his masters; he just shows a visitor into the room, and reappears as you are going away with a look that pleads irresistibly for an obole of praise.

While we were in the school, and while I was stretching my poor little comprehension to the utmost to follow the master of mathematics, I saw enter a benevolent-looking man with an open forehead and a clear, kind eye. He was obviously an Englishman, and from his manner of standing I thought he was a captain in the navy. My attention was called away, and I was intent upon an account of a school for deaf and dumb, which I was interested in, on account of William Beaufort, when a lady desired to be introduced to me; she said she had been talking to Mrs. Moilliet, taking her for Miss Edgeworth — she was "the wife of Captain Hillyar, Captain Beaufort's friend." What a revolution in all our ideas! We almost ran to Captain Hillyar, my benevolent-looking Englishman, and most cordially did he receive us, and insisted upon our all coming to dine with him.

When I presented Fanny and Harriet to him as Captain
Beaufort's nieces, he did look so pleased, and all the way
home he was praising Captain Beaufort with such delight to himself. "But I never write to the fellow,
faith! I 'll tell you the truth; I can't bring myself
to sit down and write to him, he is such a superior
being; I can't do it; what can I have to say worth
his reading? Why, look at his letters, one page of them
contains more sense than I could write in a volume."

At dinner, turning to Fanny and Harriet, he drank
"Uncle Francis's health; " and when we took leave he
shook us by the hand at the carriage door. "You
know we sailors can never take leave without a hearty
shake of the hand. It comes from the heart, and I
hope will go to it."

From Yverdun our evening drive by the lake of Neuf-
chatel was beautiful, and mounting gradually we came
late at night to Paienne, and next day to Fribourg,
at the dirtiest of inns, as if kept by chance, and such a
mixture of smells of onions, grease, dirt, and dunghill!
But, never mind! I would bear all that, and more,
to see and hear Père Gérard. But this I keep for
Lovell, as I shall tell him all about Pestalozzi, Fel-
lencurg, and Père Gérard's schools. You shall not even
know who Père Gérard is.

So we go on to Berne. The moment we entered this
canton we perceived the superior cultivation of the land,
the comfort of the cottagers, and their fresh-colored,
honest, jolly, independent, hard-working appearance.
Trees of superb growth, beech and fir, beautifully
mixed, on the sides of the mountains. On the road
here we had the finest lightning I ever saw flashing

from the horizon.   Berne is chiefly built of a whitish
stone, like Bath stone, and flagged walks arched over,
like Chester.   A clear rivulet runs through the middle
of each street; delightful public walks.   On Sunday
we saw the peasants in their holiday costume, very
pretty, etc.

I have kept to the last that M. de Staël and Miss
Randall spoke in the most gratifying terms of praise
of my father's Life.